W9-BVP-453

THE CALLING

Ken Altabef

This is a work of fiction. Names, characters, places, and incidents are the product of the author's imagination or are used fictitiously, and any resemblance to actual persons, living or dead, business establishments, events or locales is entirely coincidental.

Cat's Cradle
Press

Copyright © 2014 Ken Altabef

All rights reserved. This book, or parts thereof, may not be reproduced in any form without permission.

ISBN: 1502845296
ISBN-13: 978-1502845290

CHAPTER 1

A DEMON AMONG US

The sight of her sister's body lying so pale and motionless on the sleeping platform made Alaana's heart twist slowly in her chest. Her father stepped back, his expression frightful, and the world suddenly turned colder than ever before.

Alaana had never seen her father afraid. Kigiuna was a strong man, a successful hunter and a good provider for the family. Even during winter's long unbroken darkness when a sense of helplessness settled over them all, when there was little to do but sleep and tell stories in the dim glow of the soapstone lamp awaiting spring's dawn, he was never afraid. Framed by shoulder-length hair, wavy and black, and the sparse, curly beard that hung from his chin, Kigiuna's face was usually quick with a smile. But now his voice sounded strangely high-pitched and his eyes were wild in their sockets.

"The snow has already melted," whispered Amauraq, indicating a little puddle pooling on the ledge where the melt had trickled down from Avalaaqiaq's forehead. In contrast to her husband, Mother's fears were well known to the entire family. She feared that her children wouldn't have enough to eat, and she feared that her husband might die out on the hunt, victim to a treacherous stretch of ice floe or the mauling attack of an enraged bull walrus or the inexorable pull of the ever-present, numbing cold. She was afraid when the storms blew against their tents, and she was afraid when the blubber in the lamps ran low.

"Melted already?" asked Kigiuna. He placed a hand along Avalaaqiaq's cheek. Despite a thick layer of sleeping furs, a violent shiver wracked the child's body as she slept on the driftwood platform. "She's burning from the inside. Look at her skin."

Alaana squeezed in for a closer look. Her father's words had not been meant for her. She and her brothers were quickly shoved away. Alaana had only a fleeting glimpse of the oozing blisters that riddled Ava's face.

"We need the shaman," said Amauraq in a tone so heavy with desperation it broke Alaana's heart.

Kigiuna turned to Alaana's eldest brother. "Maguan," he said, "The house of the *angatkok* is not far. Bring him quickly."

"Alaana, you go with him," added Amauraq.

Relieved at finally having something to do, Alaana raced out the tent flap, close behind her brother.

"Maguan!" she called out, but her brother neither hesitated nor turned back. Alaana wanted to ask if Maguan thought Ava was going to die, but was glad the opportunity passed. To give voice to such a fear would surely bring an ill omen to the family. The idea was too painful to even think about. Not Avalaaqiaq. At eleven, Alaana was only two winters younger than Ava, and being so close in age the two were nearly inseparable. They were forever running races along the beach and wrestling in the snow, and Ava had promised to teach Alaana to use the slingshot just as soon as Maguan had finished teaching her.

Alaana was not swift enough to keep pace with her eldest brother, who was already a man, but it felt good to push herself. The exertion left her less time to worry about Ava. Weaving a path through the Anatatook encampment, she darted between sod houses and tents of stretched caribou skin. The chill of spring's evening had hardened the day's melt into an uneven surface that stabbed against the soles of her mukluks, threatening to turn an ankle at any careless step.

Of the three shamans who served the Anatatook, Civiliaq was closest at hand. He sat perched atop a large rock at the bend of the river, giving himself a tattoo with a slender ivory needle and a pot of ash. His clean-shaven face betrayed no pain as he dragged the needle, dipped in the black soot, under the skin of his forearm. Thin streams of blood trickled from the many punctures he had already made. Despite the cold Civiliaq always went bare-chested and barefoot. He enjoyed showing off both his natural ability to generate heat and the impressive tattoos that covered his upper body and arms.

"*Angatkok! Angatkok!*" shouted Maguan.

Civiliaq acted as if he could not hear them, taking up his clay pipe. As he put the long stem to his mouth the bowl sparked to life. The shaman drew a short puff of thick black smoke.

"Does one hear some little bird calling one's name?" he said as if to himself.

"Please," shouted Maguan, "My little sister is sick. I think she's going to—" Maguan stopped short, but although he had not said it, his words confirmed Alaana's dread. He too thought Ava might die. "She's on fire!"

As Civiliaq stood up, the many charms strung about his neck tinkled to life. He gazed down at his two worried visitors. "On fire?"

"Father said she's burning up. Snow placed on her forehead melts faster than in the pot. Please come."

Civiliaq took one last puff of the pipe and wound it around his forehead just below the ornate black-feathered headpiece he

3

wore. The rigid stem somehow went around his head without breaking. This was one of Civiliaq's favorite tricks for impressing the children but Alaana had no time for it now.

Civiliaq pointed a long, black crow feather at Maguan. "It's good you came to me," he said. "Was that your idea, boy?"

"My father's," replied Maguan. He held back from adding that the choice was based on the fact that of the three shamans who served the Anatatook, Civiliaq had simply been the closest at hand.

"Ah, Kigiuna," said Civiliaq, nodding thoughtfully. "Let's go then." He gathered up his medicine bundle and the things he had been using for the tattoo, moving much too slowly for Alaana's liking.

"Hurry, please," Alaana whispered.

With his gangly, long-legged stride the shaman followed them back to their tent, stopping only for a moment at his house to pick up a small round drum.

"We've done nothing wrong," said Kigiuna.

"Someone must have," returned Civiliaq. He bent over Ava with an intent look on his face.

Kigiuna flushed at the shaman's rebuke. His anger slowly dissolved into a look of sincere reflection as he pondered the awful question as to whether he might have broken one of the taboos after all.

Civiliaq gently stroked Ava's cheek, then pulled his fingers quickly away as if they'd been burned by the blisters. He cocked his head and sniffed, drawing attention to an odd smell in the tent, sickly sweet, much like the cloying scent of the red poppy.

The shaman shook out the contents of his medicine pouch, emptying a small clutter of objects onto the packed snow floor beside the sleeping platform. The soapstone lamp had been turned out by Amauraq, Alaana's mother, as she thought to help cool Ava.

Civiliaq reached for the lamp. As he tapped the end of the wick it immediately sparked to life. He sprinkled some dried herb into the simmering pool of seal oil and a mellow woody scent began to overwhelm the sickly odor in the tent.

Sitting cross-legged before the shelf, Civiliaq began to sing. He beat a tiny drum in rhythm to his chant, gently at first, then more forcefully as the cryptic words of the song came faster and faster. His eyes closed, his face set in deep concentration, his breath came quick and strident between the lyrics. His slender neck and shoulders trembled wildly, setting the many necklaces and amulets to a jangling accompaniment of his healing song.

His eyes popped open and Alaana noted a deep look passing from the shaman to the unconscious girl on the slab. This was the look, she knew, which shamans used to see into the spirit world.

Suddenly Civiliaq leapt straight up and began dancing around the little room, jumping and thrusting his legs out to the sides, knocking Mother's cooking things from their places and tumbling the lamp onto its side. Whooping, he spun around three times and launched himself at Ava. With the tiny drum held tightly to the child's forehead, the shaman pressed his lips against the drumhead. He came up with a mouthful of black ichor. He spewed the ghastly liquid at Kigiuna's feet.

He also spat out a small stone, sending it rolling across the floor. It came to rest close to where Alaana was standing.

"The evil is drawn out," announced Civiliaq. "I can't yet say whether she will live. We must still discover the cause of this malady. But that is for later."

Alaana stared down at the little stone. Where it was not splotched with the black ooze she saw a distinctive shade of brown lined with reddish streaks. She remembered playing with that very stone the day before. She had seen Civiliaq pick it up just as he was entering the tent.

5

"You took that from outside," Alaana said, pointing to the stone.

"Don't be ridiculous, girl," said Civiliaq with a congenial smile. "Everyone saw me draw it from your sister's body." He began gathering up the feathers and dried herbs that went into his medicine bag.

"Alaana!" shouted her mother.

"But I saw him pick it up outside! I saw him!"

Civiliaq whirled around. This time his face was anything but congenial. "Does a little bird question her shaman's methods?"

"She certainly does not," said Amauraq. She grabbed her daughter's arm, but Alaana twisted away.

Alaana was caught in a terrifying situation. She knew what she had seen, but everyone wanted her to be quiet. And yet she didn't want her sister to die because of the shaman's faulty healing magic. This was too important. For the first time in her life she didn't care if she angered her parents.

"You lie!" she said. Then her father was coming toward her, the angriest look in the world on his face. Alaana cast a final glance at poor Ava, still lying asleep on the ledge, before she darted out of the tent. She ran through the snow until she could go no farther. By the time her father had finished apologizing to the shaman, she was long gone.

Crouched among the ice and rocks at the river's elbow, Alaana fought back the tears. Except for Ipalook, who was seated atop an upright *umiak* at the bend of the river keeping watch for the salmon run, there was no one else in sight.

The rocks in the stream glistened with a stunning mosaic of spring color. Patches of moss speckled the gray surfaces with delicate circles of orange, green and black. The water sparkled in the sunlight, a joyous dance of spring, as it sent frothy bubbles in

6

eddies and whirls about the stones. A pair of old-squaw ducks called softly from the opposite bank. The running water answered with a soothing whisper, a muffled conversation which dangled just beyond her realm of perception, telling of age-old mysteries trickling down from the north. To Alaana, the river was both fascinating and profoundly beautiful.

She thought also that her sister Avalaaqiaq was beautiful. Her face was perfectly round when she smiled, her teeth perfectly crooked when she grinned, and her laugh an irresistible tickle that ran up and down the spine of anyone who heard it. And now she lay dying.

Alaana leaned forward so that her tears would plop down into the eddy pool between the toes of her mukluks. She didn't want Ava to cross into the distant land, to leave and never come back. But there was nothing she could do about it, and attacking the shaman hadn't helped. Alaana knew her father must be furious with her; she cast a nervous glance over her shoulder. She wasn't afraid of her father's anger; she was more upset that she had caused Kigiuna pain and embarrassment. She had never meant to do that.

"We all make mistakes," said an unnaturally deep rumble of a voice.

Alaana turned to see Old Manatook standing behind her. The fact that she had observed no one approaching when she'd looked over her shoulder just a moment ago did not seem strange. That was the way with Old Manatook.

From his imposing height, Old Manatook's gaze washed sternly down on Alaana like cold water running down from an iceberg. The old shaman had an impressive beard as perfectly white and curly as his luxurious hair, a broad sloping nose, and dark sympathetic eyes. He wore a hoary old parka whose caribou hide had faded almost completely white and a luxurious set of trousers made from polar bear fur.

7

"But then again," said Old Manatook. "No one likes a disrespectful child."

"I don't care," spat Alaana.

"Sun and Moon, this one's going to be trouble," the shaman said, turning his head. He had a strange habit of talking to his left shoulder.

"I saw him pick up that stone," said Alaana. "I only told what I saw."

"You shouldn't question things you don't understand."

"Then how am I to learn anything?"

"Trouble," said Old Manatook to his left shoulder. He turned back to the girl. "In matters of faith," he said, "skepticism will get you nowhere. There's good reason a shaman uses such a stone."

"To fool people?"

Old Manatook cast a self-righteous glance at his left shoulder. His mouth gaped open then closed again as if he had decided not to speak at it this time. He returned his stern gaze to Alaana. "Certainly not."

"Then why?"

"It's not something I can explain."

"You could if you wanted to," said Alaana.

Old Manatook huffed. "It's not something for girls to know."

"Well, now," said the storyteller, "What shall it be today?"

Higilak ran her withered hands down the front of her parka as she always did when about to begin a tale, smoothing the folds in the blue fox trim. She was the oldest woman Alaana had ever seen. Her hair, absolutely white and a perfect match to that of her husband Old Manatook, was carefully arranged in a bun atop her head. Her face was a gentle nest of wrinkles, permanently tanned over the years by the sharp arctic winds.

8

The old woman ran an expectant gaze across the circle of children gathered in the close confines of her tent. It was her job keeping watch over the young ones while the adults were busy with their important spirit-calling at the *karigi*.

Alaana had no interest in the story, not with her sister lying so ill at home. She sat beside a handsome boy named Mikisork. She held his hand as she almost always did whenever they sat together. The comforting touch of his warm hand was the only thing keeping her from bolting out of the tent.

Higilak adjusted the two fussy infants balanced on her lap. "The Beforetime?" she said, in response to one child's suggestion. "And why not? It's my favorite too."

She smiled broadly, showing a tiny row of teeth, all worn down from a lifetime of chewing the skins. With a deep breath she made sure all eyes were still fixed on her, then began.

"In the time before time, all was beauty and light. In the Beforetime, no one knew cold or hunger or darkness. People and animals both lived on the world, but there was no difference between them. They were free and interchangeable. A person could become an animal, and an animal could become a human being. Wolf, fox, owl, bear — it did not matter. They were all the same. They may have had different habits, but all spoke the same tongue, lived in the same kind of house, and lived and hunted in the same way.

"Life here on earth in the very earliest times, the Beforetime, was such that no one can understand it now. That was the time when magic words were made. A word spoken by chance would suddenly become powerful, and what people wanted to happen could happen, and nobody could explain how it was. They could travel effortlessly in the sky, taking whatever form they wished. Anyone could wander between the worlds. For in those days heaven, earth and the underworld formed a whole. Death was unknown; people lived in freedom from sickness and suffering."

Higilak glanced at Alaana, no doubt thinking of her sister's plight. She looked at a few of the other children whose family members had also fallen prey to the same sickness. In the past few days the fever had so spread among the Anatatook that there was not a family among them who did not see some person suffer.

"Today the unity is broken. All things live separate from each other, their bonds severed, the connections shattered. Now we have spirits and men, animals and human beings. And such is the world that must be bargained with, by the few among us who can still walk between the worlds. The shamans."

"But how did it happen?" asked Aquppak. "What caused the Great Scattering in the first place?"

"Ah, well, no one really knows," said Higilak. "It was during the Beforetime that one of the spirits rose up, the one which we now call The Thing That Was Cast Into The Outer Darkness, and caused some great trouble. Another came up to battle it, and that one we call the Long-ago Shaman. The battle was long and furious, surely one to rock the heavens themselves, and the end of it saw the Great Rift, the scattering, the *Aviktuqaluk*."

One of the babes in her lap took to squealing. When Higilak bent to soothe the child Alaana found the opportunity she'd been waiting for. She grabbed Mikisork's hand and pulled him toward the back flap of the tent.

"What are you doing?" he asked.

"Going to the *karigi*."

"Alaana, we shouldn't!"

"Don't you want to know what they're doing in there? I do."

"I'm not going," he said.

"We're almost old enough," Alaana returned, "Besides, they'll never even notice us." She let go his hand and ran for the *karigi*. "Stay if you want. I don't need your help anyway."

10

"My help?" he asked, but she was already too far ahead. "Wait for me," Miki hissed, running to keep up.

They approached the *karigi*, a gigantic tent in the center of camp which the shamans used for ceremonial purposes and community meetings. Alaana shifted one of the round stones weighing down the bottom of the tent and stuck her head under the joint. It was intensely warm inside with all the people packed closely together, and almost everyone was stripped bare to the waist. Many of the women were crying, taking turns telling of their misfortunes. Every family had someone who had fallen ill to the fever and the blisters on the face. It looked as if her own mother might have just finished speaking, for she was weeping the loudest and a few of the others had stopped to offer her comfort.

Sitting before the people were the three shamans of the Anatatook. Bare-chested Civiliaq sat tapping softly at a round flat-headed drum. Next to him kneeled Old Manatook with his curly white beard, as grim and intense as ever. Then came Kuanak — sour-faced, dour, with a thin mustache and beard and one droopy eye looking sideways out of his creased face. The hood of his parka sported bristly frills of gray wolf hair, and for this reason he was often called Wolf Head. He clapped a small red rattle against the armored chest plate he wore to protect against the bad spirits. His other arm, held raised to the heavens, shook with a palsy he had acquired during some previous encounter with a revengeful ghost.

Old Manatook and Kuanak began a soothing chant meant to quiet the sobbing women and the moaning men. Civiliaq rattled a withered old sealskin in front of the people in order to blow away their troubles. The rotten old leather made a peculiar crackling sound as he waved it around.

Alaana felt awfully warm with her head tucked into the sweltering *karigi*, but didn't dare pull away. She had to see what would happen next.

11

"We shouldn't be doing this," whispered Mikisork. "What if we anger the spirits?"

"You sound like my mother."

"Then maybe you should listen to your mother more often. It's dangerous to spy on the shamans."

"You're probably right," she admitted, but what she'd seen at Ava's bedside still troubled her. "But I don't care. I have to find out what they're planning to do about Ava."

Civiliaq stood up and the three *angatkuit* broke off their chant.

"This trouble came here," Civiliaq said solemnly. "Someone has brought this trouble here."

The people said nothing. They looked warily about, exchanging suspicious glances.

"We must find the cause," said Civiliaq. He held a solitary black feather which he twirled three times in a tiny circle. He pointed the feather at Kanak, one of the most successful hunters among the Anatatook.

"Is it you, Kanak?" Civiliaq asked.

Kanak, looking both surprised and offended, shook his head. "It's not me."

The accusatory raven feather did not waver. "Did you do something?"

Kanak's eyes roved around the room although his head remained absolutely still. "Nothing."

"You did do something. You did something and we will have it out!" insisted Civiliaq. "Did you look at your brother's wife?"

Kanak's eyes sought out the ventilation hole at the top of the *karigi*. His head moved from one side to the other as he made up his mind what to do. "Yes," he said unconvincingly. "Yes, I did look at my brother's wife."

The black raven feather tapped Kanak atop his head. "It is only a small offense," Civiliaq said. "A minor trespass, and now that

12

it is come out, it is meaningless." His feather jutted out towards Kanak's brother, whose name was Mequsaq. "Is it not meaningless, Mequsaq?"

"It doesn't matter," said the brother.

"That's good. And now we move on." Civiliaq sent the point of the black feather questing out around the great expanse of the tent, carefully examining the faces of the people who sat all in a tangled mass on the floor. "The spirits are angry and this sickness is their sign. What about you, Amauraq? What did you do?"

Alaana gasped. Civiliaq had indicated her mother. Her face flushed; suddenly it felt difficult to breathe. It was so hot in the tent, especially with the rest of her body still outside in the evening cool.

Amauraq put her hand to her face, covering her eyes. "I may have scraped some skins while the caribou hunt was on."

"I thought as much," said Civiliaq. "It's no wonder these troubles have come." He addressed this comment to the roof of the *karigi*, and perhaps to the spirits beyond. "When we have so many among us who are careless and stupid."

"Enough," cried Wolf Head. "The spirits are angry, but we must give them what they need. And what they need is the truth."

Civiliaq turned to face him.

"You know as well as I what caused this," said Kuanak. There was no mistaking his angry tone. He stood up. "What brought the evil here? Somebody did something. We shamans did it. A lapse of friendship, a rivalry, a jealousy. Civiliaq and I distrusted each other."

All fell silent in the wake of Kuanak's confession, but Alaana had begun to hear a buzzing in her ears which blurred the shaman's words. Her head felt like it had somehow blown up to twice its normal size. She reached for Mikisork's hand where their bodies lay still outside the tent.

He pulled away. "Alaana," he whispered. "Your hand feels hot."

"Distrust between shamans is an ugly thing, and certain to anger the spirits," said Wolf Head. "Civiliaq considered himself a superior shaman to me. He challenged me. Foolishly we took our quarrel onto the spiritual plane to test our prowess. In one such contest, he blew himself up to the size of a mountain ridge and dared me to push him aside if I were strong enough. Of course the real mountain became offended."

Wolf Head's typically grave countenance was particularly evident as he detailed these disgraceful breaches. His thorny eyebrows drooped further still; the corners of his mouth down-turned into a grimace of guilt. "Another time we burrowed under the glacier to see who could get the farthest through, but the glacier took offense and tried to swallow us up. We argued, and I left him there to die."

"But I forced my way out anyway," Civiliaq was quick to point out.

"Indeed," Wolf Head barked at him. "We were distracted from our duties, we should have been protecting the people, not bickering over who was perceived to be the greater. The fault is our own."

The villagers erupted into a wild clamor. The noise filled Alaana's ears with a roar that set her head to pounding. That was the last thing she heard before the entire scene faded to white.

CHAPTER 2

THE THREE SHAMANS

The familiar contours of her father's face loomed over her, mist-shrouded and uncertain. Alaana couldn't hear anything but a wild rushing in her ears as if she was under water. But water would feel blessedly cool and she was intolerably hot. So weak and tired she could hardly move, she was lost, swimming in a doughy heat that smelled like the slop they used to feed the dogs.

She tried to call out to Kigiuna but her tongue stuck in her mouth. She wanted to say she was sorry for all the wrong she had done. She had questioned the shaman. She had embarrassed her father. She had violated the *karigi*. She'd been so worried about her sister's life, she had ruined everything.

With eyelids half crusted shut, she could not raise her hand to clear them. Alaana tried to make out the expression on her father's face, but it wasn't her father's face anymore. The features had dissolved away into the stern expression, the bristly beard and eyebrows, the long sloping nose of Old Manatook.

Would the old shaman be willing to help? Could he help? The shaman hadn't done much good for her poor sister, but that had been Civiliaq. Old Manatook had always seemed bigger and stronger than his brash younger counterpart. Still, Alaana didn't want to see Old Manatook's pale face looking disdainfully down at her. She pleaded with the swirling mists to bring her father back, smiling and happy.

The mist surged forward, blending with Old Manatook's white hair and beard. A pair of savage eyes appeared dead center as the mist resolved itself into the wickedly leering face of a pale old woman. If eyes could be said to speak, these uttered one word with deadly force. Hunger.

The hag reached a withered claw toward her face. Alaana wriggled away. She wanted to scream at the top of her lungs but only a small cry emerged from her throat.

The horrible old woman smiled, showing rotten pegs in blackened gums. Alaana had never seen anything so loathsome as the inside of her mouth, which was alive with a mass of writhing worms embedded in rotting flesh.

Panic seized Alaana. She was alone. Where were the shamans? Where was her father? Most of all she wanted her father.

As the demon leaned down, the tip of a slimy gray tongue emerged from dry, cracked lips. Its touch was like fire, burning a track along Alaana's cheek and jaw. The wicked old hag laughed again, bringing a withered breast toward Alaana's face. It pushed the greasy flesh at her as if to suckle her at the vile teat. Alaana turned her head away in desperate revulsion. The demon shoved the nipple at her mouth, smothering her, but she refused it. Undaunted, it gave the breast a squeeze, releasing a spurt of putrid black slime which splashed thickly against her face. Alaana choked and gagged as that rotten mother's milk dribbled into her mouth. Her heart raced at the horror of it, but she was helpless to do anything to stop it.

Looking down at Alaana, Old Manatook saw the demon leering over her shoulder. Alaana tossed fitfully in sleep, her short black hair plastered across her damp forehead. She was a slightly odd-looking girl with a quirky fullness to her lips and a squat, round button-nose, but to the old shaman all children were equally beautiful. The cloying scent of red poppy stung his nostrils. He recognized that smell. This particular fever demon was old and virulent, having burned long and consumed many. This disease, sometimes called the Red Ke'le, had recently raged in the south, where the fever and the blisters had wiped out several bands completely. It traveled hidden among the white traders the Anatatook so fervently avoided, passed along freely with their tobacco and sugar. If allowed to run unchecked it would devastate the entire settlement.

The withered old hag didn't return his gaze, reserving its attentions solely for the girl asleep on the platform. The depraved ministrations it was heaping upon the child kindled a furious anger in Manatook. Although tempted to recklessly engage the demon, wisdom and experience held him back.

Kigiuna perceived none of this. He saw only his youngest daughter in grave danger, burning with the fever. Pushing a sweat-soaked clump of black hair from Alaana's forehead, his fingers gently skimmed the tiny blisters that had begun to form across her brow. It pained him to witness his daughter's formerly carefree, gap-toothed smile transformed into a grimace of fear and suffering. He gazed contemptuously at the old shaman. "Can't you help?" he demanded.

"Not directly," said Old Manatook. "This fever demon is a strong one. It has killed many in the southlands."

"There must be something…"

"We are all of a piece here. This family, your brother's family, all the others. What happens to one happens to us all."

Anger blazed from Kigiuna's cold blue eyes. He grabbed the front of the shaman's parka. "Listen to me. I've lost one child

17

already. I won't lose another!"

Old Manatook brought his gaze slowly down to the hand gripping the front of his parka. "This does not help," he said in a surprisingly even tone.

Kigiuna released his hold and turned away.

Old Manatook glanced over at where Avalaaqiaq lay bundled up at the far corner of the tent. Amauraq knelt weeping beside her daughter's lifeless body.

"We shamans shall make things right," he said. "Trust in us."

The three shamans, dressed in blood red parkas, sat in front of the *karigi*. A protective circle had been set up to safeguard the spectators, an invisible net in which the demon would become hopelessly entangled should it try to escape the conflict. The circle was represented in this reality by a thin line of black soot poured out along the snow. Kuanak's idea, Old Manatook considered the gesture a useless waste of time. As revealed by his spirit-vision, the fever demon already had its hooks and tendrils into at least half the people gathered around them. If the *angatkuit* should fail this day, the entire village would be consumed before winter's night once again darkened the arctic wastes.

Most of the able-bodied Anatatook men and women had come to the *karigi*, forming a rough semicircle of nearly fifty adults and their children. Old Manatook reached his consciousness out to them, drinking in their feelings of good will and support. Their confidence was still not as high as he would have liked. Fear and desperation posed major distractions. Another day of chanting and drumming might bring them better into line, but the need was pressing and time was short. Too many had already fallen ill. The situation was spinning out of control and, as the shaman well knew, loss of control presaged the end of all things.

As he met their eyes Old Manatook felt their strength flow

into him — the devotion of the hunters, the courage of the mothers, the innocent faith of the young. These sentiments lent a welcome boost to his own weary soul. He smiled confidently back at them, showing big white teeth. The task ahead was a daunting one, the enemy formidable. And yet there was no place for doubt. He must believe in their ultimate success.

He did believe it. Despite the foolish rivalry that had developed between the other two, and he would have much to say on that matter after this ordeal was done, the three shamans each possessed unique talents and abilities which complemented each other. Working together they would meet this challenge.

Old Manatook continued to bind Kuanak, wrapping his torso in tight coils of harpoon line. Kuanak wore his hair drawn up into a knot and his sleeves rolled back. He preferred to be bound in order to attain the proper trance state. Old Manatook yanked the sealskin cord tight as it wound around again. The pain would help Kuanak focus on his journey to the Underworld.

"It was our transgression," whispered Kuanak. "This is our responsibility. You don't need to go with us."

Old Manatook answered, "If we three don't destroy it, we will all die." He motioned with his chin toward the assembled Anatatook so that his meaning would be clear. "All of us."

Seeing that his knots were good, Old Manatook took a square of walrus leather and placed it into Kuanak's mouth. The surly shaman bit down on the scrap, cutting off the conversation in favor of ritual words mumbled under his breath.

Since Kuanak's arms were tied tightly behind his back, Old Manatook laid Wolf Head's weapon across his knees. This was a long staff fashioned from a single narwhal horn, ornately carved with the signs and sigils of Kuanak's spirit guardian Quammaixiqsuq, the master of lightning.

Old Manatook took his place between the other two, kneeling

19

on a prayer mat woven from long strands of dark musk ox mane.

Civiliaq, for all his arrogance, possessed the ability to enter the trance state on demand. Already his face had gone blank, his clean-shaven chin slumped against his bare chest.

Old Manatook huffed. Headstrong fool. He should have waited.

Closing his eyes, he took up his own power chant. He quickened his heartbeat, blunted his breathing — these alterations of the body helped prepare his mind for journeying and seeing in the realms beyond. It was a familiar trip, a breach he had leapt in spirit many times before.

As his own spirit guardian Tornarssuk, who was the avatar of the polar bears, spent much time in the depths of the earth, the way was quickly opened before him. Old Manatook envisioned the entrance as a swirling vortex just below his knees where they rested on the woven mat. To match his accelerated heartbeat, the vortex spun faster and faster. The pack snow became soft and immaterial as it whirled, and the impenetrable ever-frost dissolved away, as did the solid rock of the world itself.

Old Manatook's *inuseq* stepped out of his body and left it behind, an empty shell of flesh and blood and bone. He went traveling down the tube created by the spinning vortex of his imagination, passing through concentric rings of rock and ice circling an endless void.

A barrage of new and unpleasant sensations, sensed with neither ears nor eyes but by his outflung mind itself, assaulted the shaman's soul as he entered the Underworld.

The scene was cast entirely in odd shades of gray that alternately shimmered, glowed, or shone with absolute darkness. He entered a series of caves below the earth. Some were dimly lit and others lay swathed in darkness; some had water running through them and others did not. Seen up close the surfaces of the rock walls held weird textures that did not exist in ordinary reality; they were not smooth and glistening, but made of innumerable tiny spikes in agitated motion. The water that trickled down was not water at all, but grainy particles of dust each with a will of its own, marking a chaotic pattern of movement, flowing down and up and in a sideways crawl along the rock.

Caught between the unfamiliar and the unknown, the mood of this place was as dangerous and dark as any he had ever experienced. In this world without scent, his imagination supplied the pungent smell of scorched stone as lord over all.

Kuanak awaited him in a large dark cavern that rang with the howling of demons and the melancholy songs of dead men. Wolf Head's spirit-form possessed a distinctly more feral character than his ordinary appearance. His hair flew long and free, the gray folds of fur that lined his parka in the normal reality merged inseparably with the lines of his face. His eyes shone with a strange golden tint. In his unfettered hands he held the power staff.

"Civiliaq?" asked Old Manatook.

"He's gone ahead," said Kuanak. "I can sense him. He's not far, but we have to hurry."

Old Manatook called out in the way the shamans spoke through the air over distance. *"Civiliaq, wait!"*

Civiliaq's answer drifted back. *"Nonsense, I'll have done with this long before either of you old men catch up."*

"Fool!" roared Old Manatook.

A swarm of ragged, bat-like creatures cut across the cavern. Old Manatook recognized them as the corrupted souls of women who had died in childbirth. Their acid guano spattered down at the two shamans, threatening to eat away at the skin of their soul-men with its unrelenting taint of remorse and bitter regret.

"Away!" shouted Old Manatook. The fickle tatterdemalions proved more afraid of the shamans than intent on mischief. They darted quickly away to their desolate caves and lonely roosts.

"Hurry," said Kuanak. He sidestepped a crumbling altar whose face depicted one of the foul, monstrous creatures who made their home in the Underworld.

The walls of the next chamber were composed of fleshy skin covered with shimmering gray scales. Old Manatook balked at the delay as he and Kuanak fought their way through vast congeries of psychic webs and tendrils that rang of guilt and shame and the sting of missed opportunities. The going was slow, and Old Manatook kept a sharp eye along the shadows for the weaver of such a web, though no such monster presented itself. It was too easy to fall into a trap here. Too many evil and perverted things lay in wait in this wretched place.

As he batted the dusty obstructions from their path, Old Manatook's deepest worries were realized. He sensed Civiliaq had reached the enemy's lair and had engaged the fever demon on his own.

According to his distant perceptions the monster was large and formidable, consisting of a vast and indistinct smoky haze, ragged sooty breathing, and a pervasive stench of rotting meat and piss and blood.

Civiliaq perhaps envisioned something else, for Old Manatook heard him think, cryptically, "*Only a woman.*"

"*Don't be a fool!*" Old Manatook projected the warning across the distance. "*Appearances may mislead.*"

Civiliaq fearlessly stood his ground. The younger shaman's confidence was as much an asset as his overbearing arrogance was weakness. The lone black feather with which he was so fond of pointing out the transgressions of others existed on this plane as an obsidian dagger. He held the blade upright before him, in a steady hand. The spirit helper within the dagger purred, showing itself hungry for demon blood. Its name was Tuqutkaa, a fierce and loyal servant, having aided its master in slaying many a demon in days past.

With an arrogant chuckle Civiliaq unleashed a group of his spirit helpers at the monster. These were airborne barbs made of parts of wild auks — each an odd mixture of clumped feathers and beak and claw — that squawked savagely as they darted forward. The demon made short work of them, sending beaks and streamers of bloodied entrails buzzing about the cavern.

Tuqutkaa growled. Civiliaq stepped forward with the dagger, but when the demon-woman turned and smiled at him, his face ripened with doubt and wilted with fear. Old Manatook and Kuanak, still rushing to the scene of the battle, both sensed Civiliaq's fatal flaw. His was an underlying fear that he wasn't good enough. A weakness he covered with flash and bravado, but never completely laid to rest. Doubt and fear.

Old Manatook's impressions of the scene were interrupted as, in the next cavern, a pack of *itgitlit* rushed to meet them. These creatures, wild dogs with human heads and hands, were eager to attack Manatook, sensing an instinctual enemy. But they hesitated in their charge, leery of the wolf-like Kuanak. Hesitation most often proved fatal in the Underworld, and the same held true for the *itgitlit*. In a fit of snarling rage, Kuanak kicked them out of the way.

They found Civiliaq's *inuseq* where it lay on the floor of the next chamber. Old Manatook bent to him, sensing immediately that his spirit was crushed, with little spark left to cling to life. He turned to Kuanak for aid, thinking perhaps between the two of them they might be able to heal their friend.

"No use," said Kuanak, "the strain would be too great. To try and save him we must pull back, and then all will be lost."

Civiliaq's spirit-man offered his familiar dry chuckle. "Too late. I've made the same mistake yet again."

"You should know by now, you needn't prove yourself to us,"

said Old Manatook.

Civiliaq let out a heart-rending groan. "Miserable pride. And in the end, it proved me false. I wasn't good enough."

Old Manatook felt a rising and dangerous panic. "We must strike together, we three before it is too late."

Civiliaq shook his head sadly.

"We must stand together," repeated Old Manatook.

"Too late," said Kuanak.

Civiliaq was dead. His spirit-man shriveled up before their very eyes, shrinking away to the thin, dry consistency of a rind of shedded tree bark. Trapped here forever, his soul would never know peace.

Old Manatook growled with rage.

Kuanak picked up the obsidian blade.

CHAPTER 3

ON SILA'S WINGS

To Kigiuna and the others watching in front of the *karigi*, the fate of Civiliaq became immediately known. His head lolled lifelessly on his chest. His face rapidly darkened, taking on a deep black color that engulfed his spiritual tattoos. In an accelerated form of disease, his cheeks and forehead erupted into flocks of blisters so numerous they ran and flowed into each other like melting tallow as the skin burned itself away. A gigantically swollen tongue, wracked with pustules, slid out between his lips.

His wife shrieked.

The shaman's belly opened in a wide slit and his guts poured forth, spilling out in a bloody rush onto the crust of snow.

Alaana writhed uneasily on the sleeping platform in her family's tent, her head rocked by a dull throbbing as if it were a wheel being rolled back and forth along a patch of rough ice. Sweat stung as it dripped into her eyes, propelled by an uncontrollable shivering that left her breath ragged and desperate between the spasms. Was that her mother's voice calling softly to her, there and then gone, lost beneath the ever louder thumping of her own heartbeat? Alaana could not be sure. Her pulse was quick and growing quicker, like the pounding of a crazy man beating at the drum.

I'm going to die, she thought. This is the end. No more Mother or Father. Gone her brothers Maguan and Itoriksak, and her beloved Avalaaqiaq. All gone.

She was breathing hard and fast, but like a ladle dipping only shallowly at the pot there was not enough air. Helplessness and despair lay heavily upon her, a pair of sleeping furs so hot and smothering, so inexorable in their downward pull, she had no means to resist. And above all the pounding, pounding of that drum.

With a tremendous gust of wind the roof panel of their house, a double layer of brown and tan caribou hide, blew skyward.

Alaana felt herself lifted up, naked out of bed, nudged suddenly this way and that, pushed higher and higher by a multitude of unseen hands that seemed to be made of air. Up and up she went. As the cool evening draft rushed past her face a moment of inescapable panic took hold. From this new height she could see her body where it lay on the platform. Her mother, sobbing, bent over it.

That startling vision receded in a jerky fashion as she continued to be buffeted on the insistent wind; she could feel it tugging at her soul from a hundred directions at once, pushing, nudging, carrying her higher.

As Alaana kept on rising up, the breath caught in her lungs. She realized she was not breathing at all, did not need to breathe as the thump, thump of her rapid heartbeat grew fainter and fainter and she rose higher and higher, leaving her body behind, leaving it all behind.

The thought of death terrified her, but there was nothing she could do about it. Resignation began to slowly quell the fear. In fact, she realized, it felt not so bad at all. All the discomforts had been left behind — the pains in the head, the labored breathing, her aching limbs would trouble her no more.

Alaana marveled at the full expanse of the Anatatook spring settlement as it lay sprawled out below. A crowd of people had gathered in front of the *karigi*. She could see with incredible clarity every detail of the entire village, nestled in the curl of the river as it stretched out to the north. From such a height the arrangement of tents and enclosures, the kennels and meat racks, formed an oddly organic shape like a baby asleep and nestled comfortably in the folds of the tundra. It all seemed so small. And suddenly the great fear of dying left her completely. For who could be afraid of dying when they were flying through the air?

She had often gazed upward, imagining herself a bird, a ruddy plover or ptarmigan or perhaps one of the great gray gulls sailing over the sea. She had wondered what it would feel like to soar through the sky weightless and totally free. And in this wondrous moment she came to know that exaltation.

"Sila." It was a warm and calming sound, a voice which was in fact a multitude of voices, a great buzzing chorus comprised of every voice she had ever heard. In that voice was the trill and coo of every bird, from longspur to whimbrel and snow sparrow. The grunting, groaning, moaning sounds of the walrus, the gentle calls of the caribou, the lonely whine of a fox.

Alaana's mind was filled with a perfect inner calm as she relaxed within the manifold embrace of the warm voice. Sila, the Dweller In The Wind, had drawn her up out of her shivering body and taken her into gentle, windswept arms.

The voice had a face, but the face was impossible to see clearly, at once forming and unforming, it was there and yet it wasn't, laughing or crying, coming and going. A face that was many faces, without discernible eyes or mouth. But somehow she basked in the glow of its kindly gaze and felt the grandfatherly warmth of its gentle smile.

Sila spoke again. "Come, little one. Let me show you the

world as it truly is."

The wind spirit bore her aloft, carrying her higher still.

Floating far above the village, Alaana beheld not only the summer settlement and its collection of familiar people below, but also the vast expanse of tundra from glacier to open sea that made up Nunatsiaq, the beautiful land the Anatatook and the other bands called home. She witnessed the crystalline majesty of the ice mountains to the north as they calved icebergs and cast them into the sea, the lonely roosts of the seabirds atop cliffs high above, the walrus and bearded seal deftly dodging the crashing floes far below. Her gaze extended farther than any human eye could possibly see.

More than that, it was a panorama both seen and experienced down to the smallest sensation.

A merging of mind and matter took place. She was light — the sun's blazing fire, the lamp's soothing glow, the moon's mysterious shimmer. She was air — the wind whipping along the tundra, the salt across the sea, the breath of life. She was one with the land — rocks, sand and glacier, all snow and ice. She was the heaving tides and crashing waves, the seals and the whales, the life-sustaining bounty of the ocean. This mind-bending moment of clarity, this intense joy of communion with the elements — this was the *allaruk,* the vision trance. It was a song of incredible beauty.

"That is the beginning of knowledge," announced Sila. "An understanding of the nature of being. This, now, is my gift to you."

The world reshaped itself again.

Throughout the incredible landscape below a vast number of golden sparkles flared up abruptly, their radiance as deeply felt as seen. Suddenly it was clear to Alaana how the souls of all things were connected, like innumerable glittering embers in a giant smoldering hearth. She was fire — the spark of life in every living thing, miniscule in an infinite universe. From the lowliest creature scrabbling beneath the snows to the loftiest falcon, even the great frosted mountain peaks and the giant floes of implacable ice, every stone and plant and drift possessed an individual and unique spirit. And she came to know them all. It was a kaleidoscopic world where everything was alive. As her soul blew apart into countless fragments scattered on the wind, a process as indescribably thrilling as it was terrifying, each part forged a connection to some dauntless or struggling spirit, to each and every soul-light twinkling below.

"This is the spirit-vision," said Sila, the Walker In The Wind. "The world is ever-changing. The wind blows one way, and then the other. Those shimmering souls you see before you strive for order, for that is what they need to survive. You are a part of that struggle as are all people, a crust of lichen clinging to the surface of a pebble cast into a raging sea. Such is your nature. It is not given to you to decide.

"And while I revel in the chaos, yet there must be balance. The wind can not too long follow the same course. It must reverse direction, it must also flow back. You are that balance."

"Why me?" said Alaana. The enormity of all she'd just witnessed left her feeling bewildered and small.

The many-faceted voice of Sila laughed. "Ha! Not many would stand before me and ask such a question. I knew you would be different from the others! You see beauty where they see only dust and air, you question what others blindly accept. There is no limit to what you can imagine. You will do magnificent things. You will make things right."

"I don't understand."

Sila sighed, a sound as deep and momentous as a rumble of distant thunder. "You don't need to understand. Perhaps you never will. Two shamans fall this day, and destiny requires someone replace them. Though you had not the calling before, you will rise to it, Alaana."

Alaana was stunned by the sound of her own name as

pronounced by the unfettered wind. She nearly lost herself in its endless echo.

Then Sila sent her back.

The plunge was drastic and breathtaking, yet came to a surprisingly gentle end when her soul settled once again into her trembling body. She fell into a restful slumber.

A fragment of the ecstasy that was the *allaruk* lingered within her mind. She had touched the spirits in all things. She had achieved a union with every living thing at once. That bond would not soon be broken.

The demon purred its contentment. Gazing at what was left of Civiliaq it said, "That young one was a tasty snack, but I prefer my meat a bit more seasoned."

A thin greasy drool slavered from between blackened and cracked lips. Standing revealed to his spirit-vision at last, Old Manatook saw the demon had indeed taken the form of a woman, hairless and naked. Twice the height of a man, it looked as one who had been dragged through the flames. Its body was steaming, dripping melted fat and strings of gristle. Skin, boiled and blackened as it seethed with thick gray smoke, sizzled with its every move.

Seeing that Manatook carried no weapons, the demon went straight for Kuanak. Wolf Head hurled the obsidian dagger. But with the death of Civiliaq, the valiant spirit helper within the blade had already departed the Underworld. The weapon crumbled to dust as it flew through the air.

The dagger was mere distraction. Kuanak had readied an attack of his own. He held the power staff extended, and in his gruff voice invoked his guardian spirit Quammaixiqsuq, lord of the lightning. The tip of the narwhal horn crackled to life and a white-hot blast of energy burst forth; tiny sparks shot out from the tips of Kuanak's long hair. But Brother Lightning is weak below the surface of the earth and, absent his thunder sister Kallularuq, the blast had little effect on the fever demon.

Laughing, it closed with Kuanak, the bony staff knocked away, blackened and burned at her slightest touch. The demon enveloped Wolf Head in a fiery embrace. He disappeared beneath the folds of its charred, simmering spirit-flesh.

Kuanak's final agonizing scream shook Manatook's very soul.

He felt the beast stir within him. The deaths of his companions fueled his rage and battle-hunger. Imbued by the power of Tornarssuk, master of the polar bears, he transformed into the spirit-form of a great white bear.

The demon released Kuanak, who fell to the cave floor still writhing in agony. She paused to offer a playful smile. "It will do you no good to take another form."

"A beast knows not the sins of man," said Old Manatook coyly. "The sickness that affects human beings does no harm to animals."

The demon took a tentative step toward him. "As a man pretending to be a bear, this tactic is useless."

Old Manatook's voice was unnaturally deep in reply. "Things are not always what they seem. Perhaps I am really a bear who has been pretending he is a man."

The demon's brow creased, and Old Manatook knew he had her. Although she faltered only for a moment, doubt was most often fatal in the Underworld. Before she could completely reject the idea, Manatook attacked with the full savagery of the beast. A massive paw swung at the demon's head while the other followed a lower course, striking gobbets of steaming flesh from her body. Old Manatook kept on rending and tearing with an inhuman fury.

His claws flensed away the rotting meat and gristle, stripping her bare. For a moment her essential nature lay revealed. Her name had been Aneenaq. Her favorite thing in the entire world had been

31

to watch the hatchling murres as they took their first flight from the cliffs by the sea. Hunger. Rage. Her mother's tear-streaked face, having already strangled her two little sisters with the thong about the neck. They had suffered a deep hunger period with nothing at all to soothe their aching stomachs except scraps of rawhide and boot laces. Without a man to provide for them, Mother decided she must kill the girls so that one of her children, Aneenaq's brother, might have a chance to live. Unlike her younger sisters, Aneenaq did not agree. She refused the thong around the neck. It did not matter. Her mother turned away. She was left abandoned in the snow, to die starving and alone, burning with anger.

Old Manatook was shocked at this glimpse of the innocent young girl, the songs of the baby murres still in her head, before tragedy had twisted her soul.

And yet he could brook no hesitation. His vast experience of the spirit world would allow no such mistake. No pity. No doubt. He pressed forward, pounding huge hairy paws at what was left of the demon until she was driven down into the floor of the cave.

This would not kill the demon, for such a corrupted spirit could never be killed, but he left her trapped deep in the ice. She would bother the Anatatook no more.

Old Manatook's *inuseq* once again clothed itself in his physical body. When he stood up, a collective gasp rose from the crowd gathered at the *karigi*.

Civiliaq lay to his right, a crumpled form strewn among blood-soaked snow. The sight of his mutilated friend threatened to rip away Old Manatook's composure; he would not allow his gaze to linger on it.

To his left, Kuanak kneeled atop his prayer mat. Wolf Head was still strapped tightly in his sealskin lines, sweating profusely, a vacant look in his eyes. His arms, still bound at his back, were bloody to the elbows and a crimson smear bubbled at his lips. His mouth popped open and the pad of walrus hide fell out on a trickle of foamy pink saliva.

Kuanak's wife rushed toward him.

"Don't put your hands on him," cautioned Old Manatook. "The fire of the Underworld still burns within his soul." He cut Kuanak's bonds and the poor man slumped forward with a groan. Remaining on his knees, the gruff old shaman seemed no longer to recognize his surroundings.

"He lives," said the wife, her eyes wide with hope.

"Do not rejoice," said Old Manatook sadly. "He won't live much longer. The demon has built around his heart a wall of stone which draws ever tighter, a cage of thorns to make his world smaller and smaller. Nothing can be done."

The wife looked around in frantic horror. No one dared offer any aid; the people were shocked into immobility. She stepped forward as if the urge to embrace her husband compelled her even unto death. Taking her firmly by the shoulder, Old Manatook held her back.

"He gave his life for us," he said softly. Then turning to address the people in a strong voice, he announced definitively, "The evil has passed!"

Alaana crouched at the bend of the river.

She looked upon the landscape with new eyes. A fragment of the *allaruk* persisted within her as the spirit-vision, revealing the sparkle of life within each and every element of the scene. The soft shimmer inside the rocks, the patient acceptance of the receding snow and ice, the hopeful glow of the moss and the eider ducks across the way, even the water itself showed her its pleasant, flowing spirit. The indistinct babble of the stream was babble no longer. In her ears rang out the voice of the soul of the river, promising many tales to tell.

And as she watched, a huge grouping of tiny soul-lights, glimmering orange and yellow, approached through the water like dancing firelights fighting their way upstream.

Alaana stood up and waved eagerly at the young man waiting atop the *umiak*.

"Ipalook! They come! The salmon are coming!"

Ipalook gazed intently at where she pointed at the water but couldn't yet see any fish bobbing above the surface. He smiled and waved back but did not yell out the call.

Alaana watched the salmon come on.

Again Old Manatook appeared at her shoulder.

"Something happened to me..." she said.

"I know. I can see the difference in you." Old Manatook sat beside her on the rocks. The old shaman had always intimidated her and this new closeness made Alaana even more nervous. And yet Old Manatook's coal-black eyes were aglow with kindness. "I can tell who has the light and who doesn't."

"Sila said it was a gift, but it's too bright. It hurts."

"It will fade. You will learn to control it. I will teach you. It's not going to be easy, especially for you. But this is important. You must not turn away."

Alaana saw the old shaman now in a completely different way. Old Manatook's *inua* was unlike anyone else's. It shone very bright, so vivid and overwhelming as to be almost painful. The shaman's soul-light was most visible around his luminous eyes which seemed to overflow with that pure white light. Indeed when his gaze shifted, the brilliant rim surrounding the sockets moved like a ripple in an ocean of light. For the first time Alaana glimpsed the oddly shaped creature perched on Old Manatook's left shoulder, clinging with a spindly claw to his bushy white beard. Seething and insubstantial, its outline was difficult to see directly, as if on the verge of boiling away at any moment. It flapped its wings gamely at Alaana.

"Sila has given you the ability to light up what others can only perceive as darkness," continued Old Manatook.

At that moment a cry went out from the upturned *umiak*. Ipalook had spotted the oncoming salmon. He jumped down from the boat, waving both hands above his head, and shouted the news toward the camp.

The old shaman held out his hand, an orange-brown stone in his palm. It was the same one Civiliaq had used in the healing of Avalaaqiaq.

"I still don't understand," said Alaana. "I saw Civiliaq pick up that little stone outside my tent."

Old Manatook sighed contentedly. "For a shaman it is easy to dismiss the trappings; the world is wondrous enough to our sight without them. But the others…"

The shaman gazed down at his hands. They were large, with bulging knuckles and laced with thick veins. "The health of the people depends largely on their faith in our powers. It is easy enough for a shaman to believe what he can see with his own eyes, but what of them? What do they require?"

The old shaman shrugged. "Sometimes a little song, a little dance is a good thing."

Old Manatook brought the stone close to Alaana's face. She could see the life essence of the rock, a dull silvery glow. Trapped within its center was another spirit — a spark of reddish light writhing as flame. The stone held a bit of the demon which had been drawn out of her sister Ava.

"What if the spirit within the stone agrees to help?" mused Old Manatook. "What if the shaman, having sucked the evil out of the patient, deposits it within the stone for safe keeping? What would it matter where the shaman obtained the stone?"

35

CHAPTER 4

NO CHOICE

The little snipe, having just begun to turn brown, was nearly invisible from the ground. Alaana saw it first, but then again she had a distinct advantage. The tiny bird's *inua* cut a sharp orange outline against the ashy gray sky of early spring. Alaana could clearly see the coruscating flashes of color, fiery red and golden yellow, that marked the bird's soul-light. The soul screamed of great joy and freedom, laced with just a sprinkling of panic at being all alone in the sky. Usually these birds traveled in groups as they came down along the shoreline to take advantage of the warmer weather, but here was one little *kuukukiaq* drifting playfully in fancy circles high up above.

It was an important moment, the first bird of spring, and someone should sing a song of welcome to the brave little scout. Alaana wanted to tell the other children but she wasn't allowed to speak to them. And with her friends playing so noisily along the river bank, she would have had to shout.

A hard wind had blown up from the south, leaving large piles of newly broken ice against the banks of the river. One such pile was ideal for the children's purpose, positioned perfectly alongside a shallow frozen pool. The warming sun melted a thin layer of slush atop the snow and ice, creating an opportunity too good to ignore.

Mikisork climbed up the snow pack and launched himself, but he didn't get very far out on the pool of ice. He laughed anyway and offered a wave to Alaana where she sat atop a high rock at the bend of the river.

Iggianguaq went next. He was the adopted son of Kanak, one of the most important hunters in the village. During an inland hunt some few winters earlier, Kanak had found the boy and his mother nearly starved to death in a cave. Since his rescue Iggy never stopped eating; he seemed always in a mad dash to make up for the terrific hunger he'd experienced. At Kanak's house there was always plenty of food and Iggy had a certain advantage over the others in this game. He was built like a block and heavier than most anyone else his age. When he went sailing down the pile, whooping with glee, he slid far and long, getting about halfway across the pool. Iggy raised his head at the end of his slide, panting like a puppy, tongue jutting playfully from below his cheerfully ugly features. Miserable as she was, Alaana laughed a little too. Iggy was always good fun.

The last to take a run was Aquppak. Tall and slender, he seemed to have no chance of besting Iggy's slide. But Aquppak was the craftiest of the Anatatook children. Alaana noticed how he climbed up at a different angle on the pile, stomping the drift flat as he went. He began his slide from the absolute highest point. Kicking off with his legs, Aquppak came shooting down the slope faster than any of the others and made a good showing on the ice. Still not as far as Iggy, but that couldn't be helped. There was something to be said for size after all.

Again the children burst out laughing and Alaana watched their auras shimmer and glow. She was delighted, seeing them in this new way. How beautiful they were.

Since she had a death in her house, Alaana could only watch them. For the five days of mourning a child was not allowed to play or speak with any of the other children, for fear the dead would become angry. It didn't matter; she didn't feel like playing with them now anyway. With Ava gone she wouldn't have felt right laughing and splashing in the snow.

Because they had lost so many, the entire village had restrictions. Tugtutsiak, the headman, had decided not to move the camp until the five days were spent. During that time the spirits of the newly dead still hovered around their corpses. In order to give their spirits peace in the next world, all kayaks and tools were positioned facing away from water and no unnecessary work or activity was allowed. Villagers were prohibited from combing their hair, feeding the dogs, or cleaning the cooking lamps.

Worst of all, at least from Alaana's point of view, the mourners were not allowed to change their clothes or undress inside the tent for the full five days. And the lice had gotten altogether too comfortable inside her parka. The itch was unbearable.

Aquppak was not satisfied with losing at the slide. He challenged the others to another run. This time they decided that Iggy should go first. Clearly Aquppak did not want the others to see that he'd chosen an even better place from which to launch. With his famous war whoop, Iggy sailed down the pile and again made a good showing across the ice.

But the game was interrupted by Mikisork's mother, Aolajut.

"Aiyah! Stop that, children!" she called. "Sweet children, you mustn't do that. In a short while you won't have any seats left in your pants at all."

She motioned for Iggianguaq to stand up. "Get up, you overgrown bear cub. Get up! Now you, Miki, you come down from there this instant."

Chuckling, Miki launched himself down the slope.

"Ai! Miki! You know that's not what I meant," said Aolajut but her admonitions were cut short by the lone snipe who chose just that moment to dive groundward. Practicing for courtship, its fluttering wings made a distinctive sound, a shrill whoop of hello as it plummeted toward the camp. The snipe righted itself before hitting the tundra, then up it soared again for another run.

"Oh, look there," cried Aolajut. "That's the first one, isn't it?"

Everyone watched the snipe dive again, as Aolajut recited her song:

"First little bird of spring, we welcome you,
Pretty little bird of spring, bringing us the new year,
Blameless as the blue sky,
Good tidings you bring this year to us all.
Thank you, thank you."

She waved at the little *kuukukiaq* as it spun and whirled away.

"Now you children remember what I said. No more sliding on the ice."

She hurried back toward the tents, eager to tell the others the good tidings the bird had brought them.

Aquppak marked off the spot Iggy had reached on the ice and then went right on up the pile. His next attempt brought him close, but again he fell a little short of the mark.

Aolajut appeared again, seemingly out of nowhere. "Now children! Consider your hard-working fathers. How they have to travel far in the dark and the cold to hunt those caribou for your clothes. And your sorry mothers, working their fingers down to nothing, sewing these skins all the time, chewing them to make them soft for you. You mustn't be so disrespectful. Miki you come down here right now, and I don't mean on the seat of your pants this time."

Miki was slow to comply, so his mother undertook the climb up the pile to get him. She hadn't accounted for the layer of slush atop the hard packed snow. The children had made it look easy, but

39

in no time Aolajut slipped. With a startled screech she slid down the pile and out across the ice. Her face reddened as she came to rest. Aquppak danced a slippery dance about her, noting that she had beaten Iggy's mark by several paces and loudly declared her the winner. Her anger melted away and Aolajut laughed and laughed, just as if she were a young girl again.

Their game officially ended, the children each set out for home.

Alaana stood and brushed the snow from her leggings. The day was nearly done. The sun dipped low on the horizon, casting the ice and snow in startling shades of amber. She walked toward her family's tent.

She passed Kuanak, who was still kneeling in front of the *karigi*. Wolf Head had stood out all night even as the fierce wind blew in from the south. Although his bonds had been cut, his hands were still pressed behind his back. His widow stood before him, brushing the frost away from his forehead.

Old Manatook had removed Civiliaq's body, which had looked to Alaana like a burned-out shell. His soul had never returned from its journey.

Kuanak's aura was still visible as a tiny spark, glowing faintly around his forehead. His face was a frozen mask of pain and suffering. With each labored breath he grunted softly, his mouth frothing with spittle.

His widow burst into a new fit of wailing and her two sons, both grown men, did their best to comfort her. Alaana knew their vigil was almost ended. Old Manatook had had the final word. Nothing could be done.

Alaana didn't want to linger at this scene. It was getting late and the cold, which had followed the wind up from the south, was deepening by the minute. She was miserable and hungry. She hadn't eaten anything all day, she'd been worrying herself so much over Avalaaqiaq. Time for home.

Outside her family's tent, she caught Old Manatook and her father arguing. Kigiuna was hauling a carcass to the meat rack. His sleeves were rolled up, his hands covered in fat and blood from having just flensed the last seal of the day.

"You must reconsider," Old Manatook was saying, his voice barely a growl.

"The answer is no," barked Kigiuna. "Alaana stays with us. I think perhaps it is because you have no children of your own, that you wish to take one of mine."

Alaana crouched down at the side of the tent, out of sight of the men. She pretended to be resting there, her face cradled in the arm of her parka in case anyone else should see. She knew she probably shouldn't be listening in on the conversation but they were talking about her after all. Was Old Manatook saying she should leave her family?

"I must be mistaken," said the shaman. "The sound I got in my head made it seem as though you were accusing me of being dishonest."

Having hoisted the seal up onto the rack out of the reach of the dogs, Kigiuna gave the carcass a solid slap. "Your ears are sharp as ever, old man."

"Don't you dare bare your teeth at me, Kigiuna," roared Old Manatook. The shaman stood a full head taller than Alaana's father. "Alaana must come to my household to learn. It's not for you to decide."

Kigiuna stood his ground. "My house, my family."

"Your words are senseless things. This community lives and dies by its shamans." Manatook's tone was as sharp as a blade, driving home the notion that in a world of spirits and forces dangerous beyond mortal comprehension, the shamans were all that stood in the way of disaster. "There is more at stake than just your own family, or a father's pride."

"Pride?" Kigiuna shook a bloodied fist up at Old Manatook. "I've lost one child already because of your folly. And for what? My poor Avalaaqiaq. An innocent girl. You shamans caused this."

Alaana saw the old shaman flinch. Was that a flash of guilt across his wizened face? Visible for just a moment, then gone.

Old Manatook tilted his tangled beard down at Kigiuna. "Your daughter has received the call. Alaana is changed now. Surely her own father can tell. The entire world is different for her. And the world expects much of her."

"Now who's not making sense?" asked Kigiuna. "You know as well as I do that girls can't be shamans. There's no such thing."

"Until now," said Old Manatook.

"No." Kigiuna waved a pejorative finger at the old shaman. "That's a man's job. I won't allow it."

"And yet she has been called!" insisted Old Manatook. "There are certain taboos she must follow. There is no choice."

More taboos! The idea struck Alaana like a slap in the face. Surely her burden was great enough already. The itching was unbearable, she was being eaten alive by lice, she couldn't play with the other children. But those prohibitions would expire after the five days were up. What were these other taboos?

"She shows the spirit light," continued Old Manatook, "and her *angakua* is strong."

"You never said she had it before."

"Hmmf. She didn't have it before. And that is peculiar. But she has it now."

"So you say."

No, wait, thought Alaana. She wanted to hear more about those extra taboos Old Manatook had hinted at.

"She's no shaman," said Kigiuna. "She's not going to wind up like Civiliaq and Wolf Head. I won't sit for that."

Old Manatook turned away so that Kigiuna wouldn't see a momentary weakness cross his dark eyes. From her place of concealment Alaana had a clear window on the old man's soul. The shaman had lost two close friends, he was alone, and perhaps for the first time uncertain whether he could protect the people all by himself.

Alaana feared for her father. She didn't want to leave her family, but if Kigiuna didn't do what Old Manatook wanted what terrible force could the shaman bring to bear? Was it possible to refuse the shaman in this? What would be the punishment? She didn't want her father to suffer on her account. She couldn't stand that.

When Old Manatook turned around to face Kigiuna he was calm and resolute once again. "The duties assumed by the shaman are not easy, the struggles which Alaana must undertake are dangerous. But necessary."

Kigiuna was unimpressed.

Old Manatook frowned. "This is senseless. We are not at odds with each other, Kigiuna. We are both trying to protect her. The spear has already been cast. She is changed. She must follow the taboos or she will die. That's simply the way it is."

"Die?" The shaman's statement gave Kigiuna pause. "Tell me. What are these new taboos?"

"She must not eat outdoors, and never the liver, head or heart of any animal. She is not to sleep through an entire night. She must wake up three times so that she may report her dreams to me in the morning."

Alaana was stunned. Three times during the night?

"Three times during the night?" said Kigiuna.

Old Manatook nodded gravely. "Every night. The spirits do not require her to move into my tent. That's usually just for convenience. But she must break the sleep in thirds. If you'll see to it, I will put up a special tent for training at the new camp, and she can remain with your family."

Kigiuna glared back at him. "I'll think about it."

With that, Old Manatook nodded politely and walked away.

Still kneeling in the snow, Alaana began to shiver. The welcome sunlight of spring was deceptive, making the weather seem warmer than it actually was. As soon as the sun sank to the horizon it was winter cold all over again. Kigiuna restacked the meat on the rack with sharp, angry movements. One thing was certain. It was not a good thing for her father to be arguing with the Anatatook's last surviving shaman.

Kigiuna, whose name meant 'Sharp Tooth', held no position of authority among the Anatatook, but he had a reputation for being more outspoken than most. There was no disguising the aggressiveness with which he attacked every chore, from hunting to eating to running his dogs. He smiled and joked often, but never seemed truly relaxed. He was always busy doing something — if not mending his equipment, he endlessly carved little bone toys for the children. There was not a child in the camp who didn't treasure some little thing he'd made for them.

Above all else he was proud and strong and the image that most often came to mind when Alaana thought of her father was Kigiuna, just returned from a long absence on a hunt, having crawled through the knee-high entrance tunnel of the *iglu*, raising himself up straight and tall despite obvious exhaustion, his parka barbed with icicles and his lashes encrusted with snow, and calling out, "I'm home."

And in the ensuing race among his children to brush the snow from their father's back, Alaana was most often the winner.

CHAPTER 5

SHE KNOWS

Inside the tent was not much warmer than out in the open air. Alaana's mother had left the lamp extinguished. She'd probably gone visiting with the other women. This meant she would come back all red-eyed from weeping. Most of the women, her mother among them, were walking about with sad, closed faces, and when they were together in groups they cried. Alaana wondered if the crying would last beyond the five days.

Her sister's soul hovered in the center of the room, halfway toward the hole cut in the skin roof for its passage. From the mussed hair, the round nose and crooked teeth to the spirit-parka and trousers, this was Ava just as she had appeared in life. Alaana ignored the actual body, pale and still riddled with blisters, which lay wrapped in soft skins on the side ledge. Mother had done what little she could to clean her face and straighten her hair but it struck Alaana as all wrong. Ava's hair had never been straight when she was alive and the crooked smile was gone from the face.

That wonderful, crooked smile lit up Ava's spirit-face as Alaana entered the tent. She asked immediately for news of the day's events. Alaana spoke directly at the ghost, telling how Mikisork's mother had accidentally slid on the ice while scolding the children for doing so.

Ava laughed at the image of Aolajut sliding on her rump, legs thrown into the air. The laugh was the same as it had ever been, a wonderful, joyous sound. Usually Ava's laugh brought forth an echo of similar laughter from Alaana. This time it had the opposite effect.

Alaana nearly broke down as memories of her sister came in a flood tide of tumultuous recollections. Ava dancing dangerously on lake ice which threatened to crack beneath her feet, felling a ptarmigan with a well-tossed stone, chasing Alaana up and down the hilly region near the tree line during the previous summer until the two of them fell down in the mud and slush, laughing, laughing.

Alaana faltered, her eyes glazing over. But Ava, who shared a mirror image of all those happy memories, continued laughing in her own familiar way. And if her dead sister could laugh, Alaana was determined not to cry.

"Are you afraid?" whispered Alaana.

"No."

"Not at all?"

"Should I be?" answered Ava. "The thing I was always most afraid of was getting sick and dying. And now that it's happened it isn't so bad."

Alaana considered her sister's words. Her greatest fear had always been that someone she loved would get sick and die, and now that it had happened it was even worse than she could have possibly imagined.

"Ava, I think I caused you to die."

"I don't think so, Alaana. There was this horrible old woman—"

"Civiliaq was doing a healing," Alaana interrupted. "He took the demon out of you but it didn't work. I think it was because I didn't believe."

"No," said Ava, shaking her head. "It wasn't you. This old

woman took me away. She brought me to a dark, scary place. Her eyes were so hungry, staring at me like she wanted to eat me. She said she wanted to be my new mother."

"I saw her too," said Alaana, shivering at the thought. She had suffered the touch of that same awful woman, only to be saved from death by the grace of Sila and Old Manatook. Now, without her sister, she thought perhaps it was worse to have survived the sickness than to succumb. No, she thought, that couldn't be right.

Of course if she were dead, she wouldn't have to bear the endless maddening itch of the lice. In the fading daylight coming through the skylight Alaana could see their tiny white silhouettes jumping around on the sleeves of her parka.

"Ava?" she said softly, "Would you be bothered much if I changed my clothes? The lice are eating me."

Ava chuckled. "No. Why should I care if you change your clothes?"

"No reason," said Alaana. Strangely, now that her sister had given permission Alaana thought better of breaking the taboo. It was said that if any taboo was broken during the five days the soul clung to its body, it might become an evil spirit, a *tunrat*, determined to wreak terrible revenge on the village. So Alaana decided to leave her itchy parka on until the end. She didn't want her sister to become a *tunrat*.

Ava asked, "Alaana, do you remember that time Maguan fell into the river?"

Alaana remembered it well. It had felt awful, almost as terrible as this. "I thought we would never see him again. I thought he would be carried down and away forever."

"But father and Anaktuvik brought him out, and when they laid him on the ice he was all blue and still. Remember?"

"I thought he was dead."

47

"Old Manatook breathed life back into him."

"I remember."

"But why couldn't he do that for me?"

Alaana didn't have any easy answer. The old shaman hadn't visited this house since Avalaaqiaq's death. "I guess it's different when you burn up with fever."

"I guess," said Ava.

"Maybe he was too busy," said Alaana, "saving all the rest of us."

"He did good," admitted Ava. "I'm glad you're safe, Alaana. And Maguan and Itoriksak."

They were quiet for a moment.

"I wish I could stay with you Alaana. But something is tugging at me, trying to pull me away. I don't want to go, but I can't hold out much longer."

"I know," whispered Alaana. Once Ava's ghost departed, she would be gone forever. Alaana couldn't bear never to see her sister again.

"The others are calling to me," Ava's ghost said.

Alaana could hear them. A chorus of muttering voices, whispering indistinctly from across the great divide. It was not a frightening sound. Rather there was a certain cadence to the mutterings that felt soothing and welcoming. On the other side of the open ceiling flap she thought she saw fluttering shadows against the fading daylight. "I can hear them too," said Alaana, "But who are they?"

"I think they're our ancestors. The father of our father is there. His name was Ulruk."

"Who are you talking to?" It was Kigiuna, having come inside to rinse his hands at the water bucket.

"Nobody," said Alaana.

"So now she's talking to herself?" asked Kigiuna. Alaana

found this a little funny since Kigiuna was in fact asking himself a question, as he often did. Her father was always talking to himself. Still, Alaana couldn't stand the look of frustration on his face.

"It's Ava," she said.

Kigiuna's nose wrinkled as he scanned the interior of the tent.

"You can see her?"

"Yes," said Alaana.

"Where?"

Alaana pointed to the spot where her sister's soul was hovering, knowing it would do no good. Kigiuna gaped at the empty air before him, obviously seeing nothing. "What's it look like?"

Alaana didn't really know how to answer. "It looks like Ava. Just like she always looked, but there's something more. Everything she was, everything she thought or wondered about, those things she loved. It's all there."

"What's she doing?"

Alaana could hardly keep from chuckling. There was no way she could describe the silly face her sister's ghost was making at that moment. "Smiling."

"I don't see anything," whispered Kigiuna in despair. "Has my daughter gone crazy? Has everyone gone crazy?" He turned away to wash his hands in the bucket.

Kigiuna hesitated. Before he went outside again he turned back to Alaana. "Does she know how we loved her?"

"Yes. She knows."

Dripping pink water from his hands, Kigiuna went back outside. His face was as helpless and sad as Alaana had ever seen it.

CHAPTER 6

TWO BURIALS

Alaana, again, sat alone. A flurry of activity animated the Anatatook people gathered at the fishing weir.

The freeze at the river had only recently broken up. A line of men were arranged single file on the rim of firm ice which remained on either side. The broad, flat stones of the weir rose only a hand's breadth above the level of the water. These stone walls led the spawning fish downstream into an enclosed central basin. Once inside the pocket, the salmon trout had no chance of escape.

These traps were as old as the tundra itself, having been built long before the Anatatook had even existed. Their origins were credited to the Tunrit, a race of primordial men who were the first to live on the world after the Great Rift. In their struggle for survival in a world of perpetual darkness, that long-dead race of heroic beings had engineered these traps and left them behind, a legacy written in water and stone.

The men went at it as hard and fast as they could, using double-pronged leisters to spear their hapless prey. Their frenzied activity had knocked some of the stones loose and Kigiuna and one of the other men were up to their waists in the ice-cold water fixing them back into place as fast as they could.

One intrepid fish jumped the wall of the central basin,

startling Oonark. He had enough troubles already. Having only one working eye made for a lot of difficulty spearing the fish. He tried to step out of the way as the salmon went slithering underfoot, but he wound up tumbling into the water. Everyone thought this very funny, including Oonark who waved cheerfully to the crowd before he hurried back to the camp to change his wet clothes.

There was much excited talk and laughter, with every fisherman working to catch as many as he could as rapidly as possible, spearing in any direction the confused fish might go. Several thrusts came dangerously close to her father, but there was little cause for worry. The hunters' aim was sure.

Itching lice, Alaana marveled at the stream of fish souls as they went up, darting this way and that as they climbed into the sky. The fuzzy pink balls of light looked as if they were swimming toward the heavens. Perhaps they thought they were still going upstream to mate.

The women stood behind the men, skewering the fish with long bone needles. When they held up the thong for drying, the fishmeat caught the sunlight in a bright flash of orange.

Maguan, who had a good eye for the leister, proudly represented their family in the spearing. He had tried to show Alaana the trick to it, given the way the water bent the view so that you had to spear somewhere below the fish in order to hit one. Alaana had been looking forward to helping string the fish this year, but mourning for Avalaaqiaq prevented it. Exceptions were made for the adults, who needed to work to survive, but a child in mourning could not work.

And then there were the ghosts. Men who had died of the sickness were standing aimlessly about, looking sad and forlorn. The shade of Kukkook was there, peering over his widow's shoulder. An elderly man with long crooked arms, his name stood for 'Big Crab'. In particular he had been renowned among the village for the strength of his urine. His morning flow was so dark and powerful it was used to cut grease when preparing skins and women prized it for washing the dirt out of their hair at summer's end. The ghost's movements were slow and out of time with the rest of the scene. He didn't seem to notice Alaana staring.

A few of the dead wives and children were there too. The ghost of Inuiyak had her arms draped around her husband's neck as he went about spearing the fish. Alaana could hear her moaning softly. As a girl she had been struck by lightning and survived, although her left arm had never moved properly after that. Alaana noted the ghost's left arm worked perfectly well now.

Alaana shut her eyes. She didn't want to look upon the dead any longer.

"Do they frighten you?"

Old Manatook stood next to her. Alaana flinched. If she must be left in the care of one of the shamans she wished it didn't have to be Old Manatook. Kuanak had been gruff, but he'd laughed as much as he'd grumbled. He'd always been at the forefront of any hunting party or whaling trip and any celebration of a good catch was not complete without his dancing and singing. Civiliaq had often entertained the children with amusing tricks and clever tales.

But Old Manatook was serious all the time. He seemed much more mysterious than the others, going off by himself for long periods on end. He and Higilak had no natural born children and had never adopted. If anything, Old Manatook did his best to avoid children as much as possible. Alaana and the others had always avoided him in return, even feared him. And it was much worse now, with that thing on his shoulder and that unearthly light in his eyes.

"Do they frighten you?" asked the old man again.

"A little," answered Alaana.

"Did they frighten you when they were alive?"

That was an easy question. "Of course not."

"So? Ghosts are all right so long as they aren't angry. Look again. They're only curious about the fishing, or drinking in the faces of their loved ones one last time. After another day or so they'll make their peace."

"Will we ever see them again?" asked Alaana. She was thinking of her sister.

"Their names will come upon us again. Someday soon someone will be born with powerful urine and they will name him Kukkook, and women will wash their hair and remember Old Kukkook. We must assure them that they will be remembered. This is important. In the end, that's all they really want."

"But these…," said Alaana, noting her question had not been answered. "When they go, wherever they go, will I see them again?"

"Perhaps. The journey to the land of the dead is a far one but a shaman's work carries him that way now and again."

This answer was somewhat less enlightening than Alaana had hoped. Old Manatook offered a reassuring pat on the shoulder. Alaana nearly cringed. All this newfound attention from the old shaman still made her nervous.

"There are many worlds and many great spirits," continued Old Manatook. "The Moon Man in the sky. Sedna tending her gardens of kelp at the bottom of the sea. Quammaixiqsuq, the lord of the lightning and his thunder sister Kallularuq. The many *turgats* that rule and represent the powers of the animals."

"And Sila," said Alaana.

"Ah yes, Sila," returned Old Manatook. "The mysterious Walker In The Wind. In the south they call him Silarssuk, the spirit of justice, though I hardly know why. I must confess to knowing but little of that one. I've encountered him only once."

Old Manatook paused as if unwilling to say more.

"Well, aren't you going to tell me?" asked Alaana.

"If you insist," said the shaman, a little smile curling the ends of his mouth.

"I was called to answer a plea from the far side of Big Basin. Many were sick and dying there. I went to do whatever I could. On my return, I crossed the sea ice alone in the dark of winter. I became lost in a storm of hail and snow.

"From the depths of the blizzard I called on Sila for aid. I called on him and he came to me. What I saw was this: although he was made of air, Sila had the form of a wizened old man, thin and much wrinkled, with long hair and a pointed beard the color of gray stone. He did not smile as his eyes came upon me, eyes that shone like stars, distant and cold. He puffed thoughtfully on a long-stemmed pipe, exhaling white clouds into the breeze. And little bits of things swirled all around him — stray feathers, dry leaves and spirals of snow.

"He seemed not nearly as impatient or uncontrollable as he's so often made out to be. He said I had saved lives on my journey, many of them children whom he loved best of all things, and he thought it unfair that I should perish in the attempt. With that, he blew the blizzard away from my path, creating a safe tunnel through the raging storm. He showed me the way home. And he was gone."

"A tunnel through the storm," repeated Alaana thoughtfully. She didn't doubt it. The old shaman was nearly as accomplished at telling a tale as his wife Higilak.

"So it went," replied Old Manatook forcefully. "But it's possible you may know more of Sila than I do." A little smile played out on his face, as if to remark at what a wonderful world it must be for a young girl to encounter a spirit with which even an old shaman was not familiar. "I don't completely understand what happened to you. When you first saw this spirit, you told me he had a voice that was all voices, a face that was all faces."

"I didn't see him, exactly," said Alaana. "He was like a gigantic spider's web, stretching out as far as I could think, touching everything, connecting everything."

"Hmmf," remarked Old Manatook. "That's strange. One's guardian spirit almost always appears human at first."

"He spoke as if he knew me. He told me, 'Though you had not the calling before, you will rise to it, Alaana.' " Alaana repeated the words with careful reverence. In them she had glimpsed a hint of destiny that thrilled her young heart.

"Called you by name?"

"Yes."

"It is very curious." Old Manatook turned to his left shoulder, where the strange creature of light had once again appeared. "On her first soul flight? Only one with enormous potential, I should think," said the shaman to his familiar. The creature responded with an indignant flutter of wings and a snap of its beak. "Sila is a potent spirit," replied Old Manatook cautiously. The shaman bent an ear to the creature, then slowly nodded his head. "I know. And she had shown no hint of it before. Very unusual. I don't understand it."

"If you don't, then how can I?" asked Alaana.

For a moment Old Manatook cut a more sympathetic figure. The winged creature went missing from his shoulder, and the pair of gentle eyes in his wide face glowed with kindness.

"Life is a long song," he said. "Sometimes it seems the more we learn, the less we actually know. Don't worry, little one. It is a mystery that needs unraveling. Perhaps we'll see the other side of it together."

With that, Old Manatook stretched his long legs and strode over to the river. At the weir he placed his hand on Old Kukkook's shoulder. Kukkook's wife had laughed at something another woman had said. It was a tiny laugh but it had upset the ghost.

Alaana watched the old shaman whisper comfortingly into the ghost's ear.

Kuanak remained kneeling before the *karigi*, his hands held behind his back as if still bound by the sealskin thongs. He was quite motionless now, the only sign of life being the movements of his lips as he muttered unintelligible words in low tones. His wife rocked him slowly from side to side. Her embrace made no impression on the shaman. Kuanak stared blankly ahead; he was far beyond seeing anything in this world.

Kuanak's eyes bulged suddenly, and a single unearthly word bubbled from his lips. Kuanak fell. Without a sound, he went face first in the snow. The end had come. His widow shrieked.

"She's gone," said Alaana.

Her sister's ghost had finally departed, surrendering herself into the embrace of the ancestors, headed for parts unknown. Alaana's gaze trailed after her to the hole in the top of the tent that marked her passage.

"Gone," repeated Kigiuna. His voice trembled slightly as he spat out the word.

He stepped toward his daughter's body where it lay wrapped in skins on the pallet. His steps were unsteady and Alaana wondered for a moment if he had not the strength to do what needed to be done. But there was no use doubting her father; Kigiuna had never failed them before.

Kigiuna peeled back the flap in the rear of their family tent, an opening which had been cut the day before in preparation of this moment. A dead body must be removed from the house by way of a hole cut in a wall, never taken through the doorway or it would linger and haunt the tent forever.

Kigiuna took Ava into his arms and carried her out of the

tent. He lay the body atop the little sled Ava had often used to carry broken slabs of ice up from the lake for water.

"Break it down," he said to Maguan, indicating their tent with a snap of his head, "and pack it up."

Kigiuna stepped over to where the rest of the family had been packing up their sled, but found their possessions scattered about the ground, in and out of the snow. Amauraq had thrown herself weeping down on the sled. She cradled Itoriksak in her arms.

"Stand up," he said. "Stand up!"

When she did not respond, Kigiuna kicked her. Amauraq turned around, still crying. She looked at her husband with a face tortured by extreme sadness.

"Get up," he said.

"How can we leave her here?" she sobbed. "How can we leave her?"

"What are you going to eat?" barked Kigiuna. "The snow?"

"I don't care," she wailed.

"Stand up!"

He was so strong and determined, he made Alaana believe everything would once again be all right. They would leave as planned, and there would be another day without Avalaaqiaq, and after that another and another. They would eat. They would sleep. And in time they would laugh again. All of this, clearly written in the hard lines of her father's face, an unlimited fountain of strength. And sure enough her mother saw it too. Amauraq stopped crying only for a moment, but it was time enough to stand up and see to the loose flaps on her parka. Her hair had come loose from its bun. She straightened it.

Kigiuna gestured at the sled. "Maguan, sort out these straps. Then help your mother get these things in their proper places."

Maguan nodded, putting on as brave a face as his father, and shoved a bundle of skins at Itoriksak.

"Come, Alaana," said Kigiuna.

Alaana took hold of the rawhide braces at the front of Ava's sled and helped her father pull, though it seemed to her she was actually doing most of the work. They passed the last of the others, gathering their things up and making their dogs ready for the trip to the next fishing area further inland. The happy bustle which usually accompanied such a move was absent, the quick tempo of excitement dulled to silence. The quiet was broken only by the yammering of the dogs as they milled about under the burden of backpacks, tent poles and cooking pots. A few of the men offered sad waves at them as they passed; all of the women averted their gaze.

It was a short pull to the little flat area, sheltered by a high rise of stone that made up a small cliff where the Anatatook buried their dead.

As they walked her father said, "Old Manatook tells me you are to learn to be a shaman."

Alaana didn't know how to answer. She knew her father was against it, and truth be told she was frightened of the old shaman and the glimpses into the spirit world that she'd already experienced. "I see things," she said.

"I know," said Kigiuna. "I know that you're scared." Her father let go the sled, turned and looked down at her. There was a cool panic in his eyes. "I can't help you."

Alaana was quick to reassure him. "It's not all bad. Ava..."

"Yes?"

"It's good I was able to say good-bye to her, to keep her company for the five days. She went off to a better place, I think."

Kigiuna grunted and took up the reins again. It was slow going along the melted trail and the toy sled creaked noisily. It was never meant to carry such a burden.

"Your father Ulruk was there."

"My father?" Kigiuna stopped the sled again. His face betrayed a series of deep emotions, going from sadness to happy recollection, then to a grim resolve. "We needn't worry about Ava then. She's in good strong hands."

Alaana returned her father's gloomy half-smile.

"When we get to the new camp, you'll be seeing a lot of Old Manatook. Do what he says. Try your hardest to please him."

Alaana nodded dumbly, aware that her father was ordering her to do something which he steadfastly opposed. She hadn't thought it possible anyone could convince her father to do anything against his wishes. Was this sudden change of heart genuine, Alaana wondered, or just meant for her protection against the threat of death?

Kigiuna took the body from the sled and placed it on the ground. The earth was frozen too hard for digging but there was a pile of large flat stones nearby. Alaana realized these had been prepared by her father ahead of time. They began to pile the stones carefully over the body. Kigiuna's face hardened to keep tears from coming down, but Alaana no longer felt an urge to cry. She no longer felt as if she were burying her sister. Having witnessed its passage, she knew Ava's spirit had already flown away, leaving the abandoned body behind.

The hillside was strewn with fresh graves. The Anatatook had lost many this spring. Their cairns mingled among the older resting places, memorials that stretched back to generations long gone. Alaana saw Old Manatook not far away, finishing off a grave of his own. She realized the old shaman was burying his friend, Kuanak.

Old Manatook did not notice her. He was busy with his own thoughts and grief. Alaana saw that Manatook was not alone. There were other things around him, shadowy shapes that glimmered and billowed in ethereal shades of light and darkness. She couldn't make them out clearly and thought better of staring too long at them.

When Ava's cairn was completed Kigiuna removed his mittens and put them among the stones. "Set your mittens here," he said to Alaana. "They touched her—"

Kigiuna choked back a sob. "They touched her. Leave them."

Then they left, careful to wipe away their footprints behind them so that death should not follow them back to the camp.

CHAPTER 7

A BRIDE FOR MAGUAN

"Can you feel the snow?" asked Old Manatook.

"Of course. It's cold and wet."

"Forget about that. That's just the water. Feel the snow. It's all around us. Feel it."

"I don't..."

"Relax. Reach out with your thoughts. Breathe this way." The old shaman demonstrated the pattern, a series of five sharp puffs followed by two extended exhalations, repeated endlessly.

They sat on a woven prayer mat in front of a small makeshift tent. A ragged sealskin tarp thrown over a few whalebone posts, it could hardly be called a tent at all. Old Manatook had put up two of these about twenty paces apart. They had come a long way to this bleak and desolate spot, far from the distractions of the river and the Anatatook camp. Trudging through slush and snow where there was no natural path, they had maintained absolute silence. The implication was clear; Alaana must leave her past and all family concerns behind, to come to a new place, somewhere she had never been before.

Mindful of what her father had told her, Alaana set about following Old Manatook's careful instructions. She would at least try to please him, although it was practically impossible to imagine what might make the crusty old shaman happy. His dour face seemed always weighed down by secret concerns and far-away troubles.

"Open your mind. Close your eyes. Breath this way." Old Manatook urged the tempo even faster, slapping the beat out on his thigh.

As she worked her lungs to the rapid pace, Alaana was seized with a profound sense of melancholy. She didn't want to be here, doing this; she wanted to be with the other children, with her friends. She wondered what they were up to right now. Last spring they had discovered a cleft not far from camp that made for a fun time sledding with a frozen rag of caribou hide. She could almost hear Mikisork's peals of delighted laughter. Or perhaps they had gone to the hollow beneath the bluff where lemmings nested this time of year. With her eyes closed she could easily envision Aquppak and Iggy gleefully chasing the little animals from their stony burrows with sticks and well-aimed stones. Or who knew what new excitement they might discover? So different from the close confines of dreary winter, spring offered a time for roaming and adventure.

Alaana's eyes began to burn and water but she didn't let the tears fall.

"Breathe!" urged Old Manatook. "Breathe the way I have shown you."

The extreme rhythm made Alaana feel lightheaded and dizzy, but she kept to the beat.

And then for no reason at all, everything suddenly changed. Alaana was seized by the overwhelming sensation that all was well, and even more than that, a feeling of unbridled joy. All cares were forgotten in the absolute pleasure of drawing in breath after breath of cool, dry air. It was strange to feel so happy without knowing why. She had no clue except a wisp of familiar musky odor, the mark of the old shaman. What had Old Manatook done to her? Altered her mind by force of will?

"The snow!" Old Manatook reminded.

And snow there was. All around her, everywhere, extending inexorably from horizon to horizon, nestled snugly beneath her bottom, and yes, even misting the air all around her. Even with her eyes closed she began to see it, the darkness of shut lids giving way to a panorama of blinding white.

The snow was ancient. Alaana realized this now for the first time. It had belonged to the world since its very beginnings, timeless and unchanging, distant yet ever close at hand. And, like all things of this world, it was alive. The snow was all of a piece, the embodiment of a single spirit that stretched on and on along the icy plains, across the river, atop the mountain, even blanketing the frozen shelf at the border of the sea.

The spirit of the snow was vast and unknowable, a venerable patriarch that watched over the land and all its creatures with a kind eye and a gentle embrace. Impossible to move or sway, it was possessed of a deep wisdom, having seen everything that had ever existed and ever happened, for all time. Every fall from grace, every flounder and lurch of progress, every triumph and catastrophe, through times of war and tranquility. If one could only get the snow to talk, what wonderful things one might learn.

The snow was ever asleep now, having seen so much, as an old man who was beyond having to work and sits proudly observing the activities of all his children and grandchildren, puffing thoughtfully at his pipe as he watches them, laughing slyly at their jests, and gratified at their triumphs. No force of this world could rouse that vast spirit to action nor break its profound patience as it draped itself over the land, a cherished companion, a beloved protector.

"Do you still think it cold?" asked Old Manatook.

"No," answered Alaana softly, "It's warm."

"Hmmf. And that's something the others can never appreciate. To them it is cold, and nothing but cold. But when you are out in the wild, on the long stretches, you need never be cold. Not while Brother Snow is close at hand."

The shaman struck Alaana forcefully across the face. In her dream-like state the slap felt like innumerable sparks splashing her cheek, droplets of water that fizzled but didn't really hurt.

Alaana's eyes flew open. She drew in a sharp breath that was surprisingly biting and chill. There was a little bit of snow in the air. She breathed it in and out.

"That was good, for your first time," mused Old Manatook. "Your spirit left your body completely, if only for a moment. And needing a considerable nudge."

Suddenly Alaana's cheek flushed hot where she'd been struck. She cast off the daze engendered by her dream of snow and returned her attention to her teacher. As Old Manatook's face came into focus, she realized his beard looked not so different in color and texture as the snow.

"Now let's take these tents down. If we hurry back, you may yet have some free time to play with your friends before nightfall."

Alaana returned to the Anatatook camp just in time to meet the arrival of her father and brother. Four days earlier they'd traveled to visit the bands to the south in hopes of finding a wife for Maguan. Now their sled made its triumphant return, pulling into the village in spectacular fashion, hauled by a fan of eight dogs.

In order to give the best impression possible to his new southern relations Kigiuna had borrowed extra dogs from his brother Anaktuvik's team. As he tramped alongside the sled, the slump of her father's shoulders spoke of the rigors of the soft trail. In spring, the runner tips caught in the snow at every rise or dip in the drifts and had to be hacked free and heaved along, making such a long journey exhausting.

Kigiuna looked upon the camp with a satisfied gleam in his weary eye. A grin parted his lips as the Anatatook came racing out to meet the sled.

Maguan, who had been riding alongside his new bride, jumped down and took up the lead trace at the front of the sled. He made a silly show of pulling the sled as if the dogs were not strong enough to tow it in. By this he meant his new wife was so heavy the team needed help to bring her to the village. It was an old joke, but it seemed particularly funny to Alaana as her brother was so skinny he could hardly be helping the dogs at all. In truth the sled was less heavy than it had been when they'd set out, loaded down with trade goods at the onset of the journey.

Alaana ran up close to the sled, dodging the big wheel dogs at the edge of the fan. She was eager to get a glimpse of Maguan's prize.

"Go! Get out of the way!" Maguan laughed. "A man is driving his new wife home." Although he had seen twenty winters, Maguan still wore his hair in a short boyish style. A scanty mustache grew only at the corners of his mouth, dangling at the edges of his smile. That smile was so vigorous and frequent it caused his cheeks to always appear full and his eyes narrow, but Alaana had never seen him as happy as he was just now.

A small crowd turned out to greet the sled, Alaana's other brother Itoriksak among them. Her mother was conspicuously absent. Many congratulatory claps fell on Kigiuna's broad shoulder. He shook them off and started unharnessing the team, taking particular care with his brother's dogs. Usually this chore fell to Maguan but Kigiuna took on the task so that his son could bask for a few moments in the admiration, smiles and well-wishes of the Anatatook.

Maguan announced his new wife as Pilarqaq, who came to them from the southerly band called the Tanaina.

Kigiuna suggested that Alaana and Itoriksak should be helping him and not gawking like they'd never seen a woman before. As she unlaced the straps, Alaana snatched a few stolen glances at the bride. Pilarqaq was the most beautiful woman she'd ever seen. Her broad cheeks held a rosy glow and her face was so wonderfully flat it seemed as if she had no nose at all, especially when viewed from the side. Alaana's heart raced. Her brother must be so happy. Pilarqaq was a miracle of feminine beauty, especially her long black hair which swept down over each shoulder in a glossy cascade. She wore a fancy parka laced with squirrel fur tassels that swayed with her every movement. Maguan's jest had not been too much of an exaggeration after all. His new wife was plump and very full-bodied, a sure sign that she came from a good family.

Alaana smiled contentedly as she led a pair of huskies toward Anaktuvik's kennel. She was amazed that Maguan had wound up with such a perfect bride. Because of the hunger times of past years, the mothers had not been able to keep all their girl-children and there were few young women among the Anatatook. Most men had to wait a long time to get a wife. She thought it almost impossible that such a beautiful woman could be unmarried and that her family would be willing to part with her. Things must have been better among the Tanaina. Credit fell squarely on her father's shoulders. Kigiuna had a solid reputation among the other bands.

Upon entering her new family's tent for the first time Pilarqaq looked askance at the floor of the *natiq*, the eating and living area in front of the sleeping platform. Alaana had never inspected it too closely before, but now she realized the gravel was strewn with discarded bones, frozen bits of fish entrails, cast-off scraps of shaved antler from her father's carvings and splotches of mud they

66

had all carelessly dragged in.

Amauraq noticed the young bride's discontentment. "Don't you use gravel in the south?" she asked indignantly. "Maybe it's a little warmer there, but it cuts the cold against the soles of our feet."

"Yes, we do," replied Pilarqaq quietly.

"Then… what?" asked Amauraq with a somewhat harsh, cutting tone. "I'm very busy here — I have to do all the sewing for my husband and children. Perhaps you'll have enough time to clean up the floor more often."

Pilarqaq nodded, her plump lips pouting in barely disguised resentment.

Amauraq brushed her hand along the top of her head, smoothing her hair. The movement was entirely unnecessary as she wore her hair drawn tightly back and draped over one shoulder in a long black tail. The style made her prominent ears seem even larger.

"You have lovely hair," she said to Pilarqaq. She proceeded to show her new daughter the soapstone lamp at the far side of the tent, which she would be taking care of from now on.

"We didn't put up much seal oil this year, so don't run the lamp at night," Amauraq said. "The men are warm enough. You know how to light it don't you?"

"Yes, Mother," returned Pilarqaq in a dry tone.

Amauraq showed her how to adjust the flow. "I use a little stick to open and close the wick, depending on how much of a flame is needed."

Pilarqaq indicated she was well-used to the process.

"I'm sure with enough practice you'll get used to it," Amauraq continued. "And we don't run the lamp too often in winter either. Kigiuna dislikes a wet *iglu*. He gets annoyed if the dome starts to melt and drip down onto his neck and clothes. Of course when you have your own place you may do as you wish, but Maguan is much the same."

Although she took pains to try to hide it, Pilarqaq was clearly uncomfortable under this barrage. Worry started to show at the corners of her mouth. Amauraq made matters worse when she tried to demonstrate the proper way to set up Pilarqaq's utensils on her side of the cooking area. Pilarqaq didn't have many cooking things of her own — only one pathetic soapstone teakettle, too small for family use and with two sizable cracks in it.

"Of course you are free to do as you wish," added Amauraq, "but I have a certain way of arranging it. It's what we're all accustomed to."

"Enough," said Kigiuna. "How about we eat? We've traveled far and we're *all* hungry." The emphasis he placed on the word 'all' made it obvious he meant to include Maguan's new wife as one of those needing comfort. Already he was showing fatherliness toward her. As everything else, he did this with characteristic intensity, making it clear he accepted Pilarqaq as his daughter in a profoundly genuine sense with nothing more than a smile and nod of his head.

Alaana felt the awkwardness of the situation begin to melt away. As always Kigiuna generated considerable warmth inside the tent, far in excess of his body heat alone. He playfully mussed his second son's hair, saying, "Itoriksak, run and fetch some water for the tea."

They had caught a pair of stray seal pups on the way up from the south and Maguan brought one in. He lay the fat, glistening carcass atop an old sealskin mat for the cutting. Kigiuna sat down on the sleeping bench. He closed his eyes rather than be pestered with questions regarding their trip, but Maguan talked excitedly while he butchered the seal. He told of the places they had traveled, the hardships along the way and everything they had learned about Pilarqaq's family.

Amauraq served tea and Kigiuna came to life with a few sips of the steaming brew. With a satisfied nod he turned to Pilarqaq, passed the ladle to her and formalized her acceptance into the family, saying, "Our daughter, have some tea."

"I apologize if the tea seems weak," said Maguan. "We've been using these same leaves since winter. Now that we're settled in here for a while, I'll show you a place a little way inland where you can go to collect some more."

"Itoriksak will show her," said Kigiuna matter-of-factly, "I'll need your help mending and setting the nets tomorrow. With the salmon already gone past, we have to act quickly or we won't have any tomcod this year."

Maguan nodded his assent, placing the seal liver on a flat stone at the foot of the *ikliq*.

Amauraq handed a blade to Pilarqaq. "You can borrow my knife," she said, placing an unwelcome twist on the word 'borrow'. Alaana had never heard such unfriendliness in her mother's voice before. Kigiuna said nothing, but seemed mildly amused by it.

With great concentration Pilarqaq cut the liver into even little slices. Alaana felt sorry for her. The poor thing's hand shook as she worked, struggling against that certain type of apprehension only the watchful eyes of a marriage-mother could cause. As she finished the task a deep blush spread across her broad, wonderful cheeks. Alaana realized this was the first time she was playing hostess as a married woman.

"Will you please have some portion of this seal my husband was able to catch?" she said politely. "It's not much."

This was false humility only; everyone knew it was a fine seal. She held the first piece, freshly pink and dripping, toward Amauraq.

Amauraq's face darkened as she slapped the piece of meat aside. "Stupid girl! Is this how they act in the south, without any manners at all? My husband shall have the first slice."

Alaana saw Pilarqaq's crushed expression, her eyes bulging wide as tears came into them, poised to run in a torrent down her cheeks.

"Enough!" said Kigiuna with a sharp glare at his wife. "Enough chatter, enough nonsense. Enough. Let's eat quietly and lay down to sleep."

As the sun lingered above the horizon for much of the night, there was still considerable light as they went to bed, even with the lamps both turned out. Kigiuna, seated on the platform, struggled with his mukluks, legs crossed, stepping down with his left foot while he yanked at his right boot with both hands. After such a long journey the wet hide seemed to have attached itself permanently to his feet. He called Amauraq over. "Come pull my boots off."

His pants came down next but instead of simply dropping his parka to the floor as usual, he had devised a new method of getting undressed, perhaps in deference to Maguan's wife. He stood up quickly, bending over so that the parka fell off to the front, covering his private parts from sight. With the same motion he swept the sleeping fur across his body and pulled his shirt over his head. An instant later he lay swaddled in the furs and ready for bed, grinning happily, and Pilarqaq had not seen a thing.

Alaana laughed, then turned away and wriggled out of her clothes. It was going to take some time to get used to the new order of things.

Making a pillow of his rolled-up parka, Kigiuna took up his sleeping position along the far side of the *ikliq*. In most households the wife occupied that spot, closest to the chill of the tent wall, leaving the man in a more snug central location. But as Amauraq was particularly susceptible to cold in the night Kigiuna assumed the significantly less pleasant position. It was a genuine display of kindness, Alaana thought, though her father made sure to remind Amauraq of his generosity at every turn. The rest of the family took their positions, Alaana directly beside her mother, then the empty space where Avalaaqiaq used to lay, then Itoriksak and Maguan, and

Pilarqaq along the farthest tent flap.

Just as they were getting comfortable Kigiuna asked if Pilarqaq needed to pee. Her father nudged Alaana with an elbow. Naked, she wriggled out of the cozy furs, crossed the room with her hands clasped over her privates, and dashed outside. The frigid air tore at her skin as she snatched the sealskin basin from the entranceway.

They passed the basin in order down the line, under the furs, and Alaana tried not to listen while Maguan's wife passed her water.

As she snuggled into the warmth of the bedclothes, a sense of contentment and familiar routine settled over Alaana, washing away all troubling thoughts of spirits, ghosts and cranky shamans.

"Sleep time," said Kigiuna at last. From the way he said it Alaana guessed he had recovered some of his lost energy. Sure enough, mother turned and tucked the caribou hide around Alaana to separate her from her parents while they were cuddling.

Alaana turned away, toward the empty place. Her thoughts went to her missing sister. She ignored what her parents were doing but wondered if Maguan was doing the same thing with his beautiful new wife. She couldn't help herself and listened, but didn't hear anything. What would it be like, she wondered, to sleep next to someone so strange and new?

CHAPTER 8

TIME UNBOUND

The next day Alaana and her teacher trudged in silence again to the far place out on the tundra. Old Manatook's huge huskie Makaartunghak pulled a small one-man sled loaded down with the tent poles and tarp.

"This is important," said Old Manatook. "The mind is all. The body is nothing. All that we accomplish we do with the mind."

The fierce glow in his eye spoke to Alaana as sharply as the shaman's slap of the day before.

"Liberated from the body, there is no place, no time, no lengths to which the mind can not go," said Old Manatook. "The drum and the rattle, the breathing and the chanting — these are merely tools with which to alter your way of mind. We use the body to liberate the spirit. It's not difficult once you know the way.

"But to heal," said Old Manatook, waving a finger in the air, "To heal, we must meet the minds of others. That is the difficult thing."

Alaana was overwhelmed. Her teacher was moving way too fast, speaking too many new words she didn't yet understand. "Way of mind...?"

"Hmmf," spouted Old Manatook with a pained expression on his face. "Lost you all the way back there, eh?"

"I'm sorry," said Alaana sincerely.

"You shouldn't be. Perhaps I lack the skills for teaching the young. I know for certain I've not the patience for it. Give me instead a raging storm to quell, or a herd of caribou to be lured to the hunt." The shaman stopped walking. He treated himself to a pair of deep, cleansing breaths during which his long face sagged even longer and his beard drooped and drew itself up again. Finally, as the clouded breath parted from his lips, he nodded in resolution. "Not easy for either of us. Still, it must be done. Way of mind, I suppose, means a way the mind works. No, better, it's a place the mind can travel. The body knows only one place." At this the old shaman kicked some loose snow up at Alaana.

"You exist. You walk on the ice and snow, you eat and drink, you touch another person. All of that is what we call *ijiq*, that which exists. Reality. The reality of the body.

"But there is more than one reality. You already know this. You see with your eyes, you hear with your ears that which others can not. You see the sparkle of the soul-lights, you hear the whispers of the dead. These things also do exist, but they exist in a different reality."

"Day and night," said Alaana, "They don't leave me alone."

"And they won't." The old shaman's eyes flashed. "The lost and lonely will always cry out to anyone who may hear. We must listen and help where we can." He called out to the dog and they resumed their trek.

"I wish things would go back to the way they were before," said Alaana.

"Yes," replied Old Manatook, indulging his student's fantasy, "And I would have Kuanak and Civiliaq at my side when the bad times come again."

"Fine," said Alaana, taking no insult. "And the sky would be normal again."

"What's this about the sky?"

"It looks all wrong now," replied Alaana. "It's the sun. The sun looks as if it doesn't belong."

"Hmmf. A ball of fire in the sky? Many's the time I've thought the same. It doesn't belong, but that's a mystery to which I have found none who could give answer. Perhaps when you go traveling the hidden pathways, it may one day be revealed. But those are places where your body can not go, which brings us back to the matter at hand. Only the unfettered mind can walk the shadowy lands of the dead, or visit the great *turgats* in their ethereal palaces, wander the chill bottom of the sea, or visit with the Moon Man up in the sky."

Alaana felt oddly reassured to learn her teacher didn't have an answer to the riddle of the sun. At least there was something he didn't know. And she was impressed at how easily he admitted his ignorance to her. She couldn't imagine he would have revealed such a thing to anyone else. Clearly, her status had changed.

"Hoo!" called the shaman, stopping his dog. He bent to the sled and swept the tent poles aside. "Sit!"

Alaana, feeling just a little resentful being spoken to as one of the dogs, settled herself on the sled. The old man crashed down beside her.

Seated so close together, Alaana noticed the deep lines etched at the corners of the shaman's eyes and the way they carved a network of ravines halfway down his cheeks. All this talk of traveling left her feeling dizzy. They were merely an old man and a girl sitting atop a ramshackle sled on the barren tundra. "It all sounds so... strange. Are you sure I can do this?"

"You already have," said Old Manatook. "You've walked in dreams. Under your sleeping fur at night, snug and warm. You close your eyes, the mind relaxes. Your spirit leaves the body behind. The mind wanders free. The soul goes traveling. What do you dream? Are you suddenly a grown woman with a family to feed? Are you a falcon, soaring through the sky? Do you travel to a distant land, meet strange people you have never encountered in ordinary reality?"

"But dreams aren't real," said Alaana.

"They exist wholly in the mind, yes. But how can you say they aren't real? You travel to a place, have experiences, and come back. Do you remember the experiences? Certainly. Are you changed by them? Again, it is so. Changed not in the body, but in the mind. And the mind is everything. And there we are back at the beginning again." Old Manatook chuckled softly and clapped his huge hands together, eminently pleased with himself. Alaana had never heard the man chuckle before. It was a dry, prickly sound accompanied by a sharp clicking of his large front teeth. Scary.

Alaana was afraid to admit that she still didn't understand, but the shaman read her expression easily enough.

"Sun and Moon, are you dull-witted, girl? If you set out on a hunting trip and come back, having caught nothing, having suffered no injury, your body unchanged, would you question whether the trip had been real?"

"I would have the memory of the trip," said Alaana.

"As upon waking you have memory of the dream.

"I would be hungry from the day's efforts," tried Alaana.

"And are you not hungry, having wakened from the dream?"

Alaana could pose no further objection and began to think there was little reason to doubt the shaman on the point. Those things she experienced in dreams might indeed possess a genuine, although ethereal, reality. Perhaps that was the reason for Old Manatook's insistence that she waken several times during the night in order to recall them.

"The Lowerworld and the Upperworld, the land of the dead, the dreamlands, the shadow-world. There are many strange places the shaman may travel. The human mind can not be confined by space or time."

"Time?" said Alaana. "Surely no one may move through time?"

"Oh, surely not," said Old Manatook with forceful exaggeration. "Surely not!" He mopped his brow with an oversized, gnarled hand. He turned away, his attention drawn to his left shoulder.

His words stung, and Alaana thought perhaps her ordeal had come to an end, that the old shaman would wash his hands of her and send her home in disgrace. She wondered if her father would be pleased or angry.

Alaana struggled to see the thing which had appeared on the shoulder. Its outline shone bright white, almost blindingly so, a perfect match to the old shaman's spirit. The exact form was hard to define, its contours shifted like smoke. A pair of thin, sharp wings undulated in constant motion, and there was a pointed snout. More than that she couldn't tell. Nor could she hear its whispered reply.

"I am not!" answered Old Manatook. He scowled ferociously, but thoughtfully, and bent an ear again to the creature. "Then the girl and I are both the same. Too old and set in our ways. What's to be done about it now?"

Without awaiting an answer, he waved his hand roughly across the space occupied by the mysterious creature. The form of light became indistinct as if it were a footprint drawn in the wind-blown sand, and disappeared. "It might work," he mumbled.

"Now listen here," he said to Alaana in an angry tone. "When you say something is impossible, you practically make it impossible. You must never speak that way. We can get nowhere with that. Understand?"

Alaana nodded.

"It's as simple as this: Everything is possible. You mustn't doubt that. You are never to doubt that.

"Now, if I were to say that we were going to embark on a journey through time, right here, right now, would you allow for the chance that such a thing might be possible?"

"Yes," said Alaana, nodding her head.

Old Manatook's gaze was penetrating. A dubious smile indicated he thought Alaana was perhaps less than honest in her enthusiasm.

"Such a thing might be possible," said Old Manatook enigmatically. "That is all I am asking for you to admit. Look here."

He gestured at the tundra laid out before them. Glistening wetly, the vast plain of snow and ice stretched out the length of several days' travel. Mountains of gray rock broke the surface in a ragged clash against the azure sky. A few clouds drove languidly toward the horizon, aligned in thin white streaks, giving a sense of gentle motion.

"This rock has sat on this spot for hundreds of winters." Old Manatook indicated a large round boulder that lay just ahead of them. He yanked off one of her mittens and pressed her hand against the cold surface of the stone, causing her to lean so far forward on the sled she thought she might topple headlong into the slush. Alaana gazed at the rock, its gray surface worn smooth by time and weather. She saw the spirit of the stone as it lay sleeping, a faint glimmer of gray light buried deep inside.

"The snow has been here forever," continued Old Manatook. "It moves and flows forward, it shifts back. It dances on the wind then comes to rest. And yet it appears much the same as always. The hillside cuts the same outline against the sky, eternal and unyielding. Our world does not change much."

The shaman's words had a certain rhythm, an undulating

cadence that made Alaana feel uneasy. They caused a buzzing in her ears, much like the swarming of mosquitoes in summer.

"If you stood on this very spot ten winters ago, what would you see? Would the view look any different than it does to you this morning? Would the air not smell the same? Can you be sure, at this moment, that we have not traveled back through time to visit the same place ten winters past? Is there not some little doubt on the matter? Hmmm?"

Before Alaana could make up her mind to answer, the old shaman drew her attention to a dark smudge against the base of the hillside. "What goes there?"

The shadow wriggled and elongated to become a caravan, emerging through a low mountain pass. A string of sleds came into focus, a weary band of travelers. Familiar sounds carried across the distance — the clatter of equipment, commands shouted at the dogs, the snap of a whip, the slosh of a hundred padded feet through the snow.

Alaana began to recognize some of the people.

"It's the Anatatook!" she said. "All packed up and on the move. But where can they be going?"

A momentary panic seized her. Why should the village move now? Were they abandoning her?

"Look closely," suggested Old Manatook.

The foremost sled came into view, pulled by a fan of hearty gray huskies. At the helm she could clearly see Kuanak, old Wolf Head himself, leading the train of pack-sledges forward. It was impossible. Kuanak was dead and buried.

And there were Higilak and Krittak chatting with the other old women, Kanak and his sons, and Civiliaq holding court over a handful of children. Kigiuna and Amauraq paced alongside their own sled. The sight of her father amazed Alaana, for this was a figure cut in a day when times were hard, his face decidedly leaner, his step less certain. Maguan trudged beside him, a skinny young boy hauling a pair of packs too large for his shoulders. A young Itoriksak rode atop the sled. Next to him, fastened with a seal thong so that she might not fall was Avalaaqiaq. She smiled and waved at no one in particular, merrily singing a song as they traveled. Alaana's heart sank at the sound. She remembered the way Ava was forever singing some nonsensical little song and taking such great pleasure in it. How she missed her dear elder sister.

"And who might that be?" asked Old Manatook, "Snug in her mother's *amaut*?"

Alaana realized that the passenger traveling in her mother's pouch must be herself, practically a newborn infant. This was the Anatatook as they had appeared ten years ago, on their way to the spring campgrounds at winter's end.

"If they should come upon us standing here, what a shock it will be to them," mused Old Manatook playfully. "Perhaps we should go." He mumbled a command in the secret language of the shamans, words which Alaana did not yet understand, and the vision faded away.

Old Manatook pressed Alaana's hand against the cold surface of the stone again. The buzzing sound resumed. "And if we had stood on this spot twenty winters before that? What would we see? The same sky, the craggy hillside unchanged, the snow. And the same band of travelers?"

A new caravan approached, at first undistinguishable from the previous one. Dogs, sleds, men and women, clatter and rattle, and casual trail talk softly spoken. These too were the Anatatook, she was certain. But also different. Though they trod the same track through the valley, there were few faces she recognized and many she did not. Old Manatook drove one of the lead sleds, standing tallest among them. Perhaps at this earlier time he might be properly called simply Manatook, his hair a deep brown only lightly speckled with white. Higilak walked at his side, rendered once again young and beautiful.

"There's someone you should meet," remarked Old Manatook. He indicated a man of middle age at the head of his sled and family. He bore a striking appearance, striding forward with a bearing that radiated great wisdom and strength. He pulled at the traces, lending aid to the dog team but using only one arm. The opposite arm was missing completely from the shoulder.

"That is Ulruk," said Old Manatook. "Nestled there in his woman's *amaut* is his third son, Kigiuna. Take note. You must know all your ancestors, for they are the ones who keep the way open for your return when your spirit travels between the worlds."

"His arm...?"

"Torn away during a brown bear attack. That *aklaq* made a nasty mess of him. I remember binding the wounds myself."

Alaana's grandfather threw back his hood. Large patches of his hair were missing, having failed to grow back after the beast had ripped open his scalp, leaving ugly scars across the top of his head. He bent to his eldest son, whom Alaana recognized as her uncle Anaktuvik, and made a funny face at the child to cheer him up. When grandfather's craggy face came back up, he was laughing heartily. He took a moment to look about him, drinking in the sight of the tundra with glittering eyes, and resumed pulling the sled.

"Enough. I had no desire to meet myself then, and I certainly don't just now," said Old Manatook and again he muttered words that dispelled the scene.

"What about a hundred winters?" asked Alaana.

"Or perhaps a hundred hundred," said Old Manatook with a satisfied smirk. "Might such a thing be possible?"

With a mumbled command, the shaman pressed Alaana's hand even more firmly to the chill surface of the old stone. The rock buzzed with an intensity that flooded Alaana's ears. The sky grew darker, but not with the deliberate pace of nightfall. This darkness came with a thunderclap as if an approaching storm had suddenly shut out the light. "A hundred hundred," muttered Old Manatook. "The stone is still here. Two hundred, three…"

The darkness was nearly complete. A choking, smoke-thick darkness which smothered all light and hope. Alaana would not have been able to see anything if not for the benefit of her spirit-vision. The many and varied soul-lights stabbed brightly at her from the purplish gloom. The place even smelled different. The air was heavy with animal scents, the stink of old blood, the smell of pungent decay. She heard all sorts of strange twitterings and rustlings and murmurs, the language of ancient beasts long forgotten.

Three gigantic figures emerged from the shelter of a cave. A series of low, throaty rumbles passed between the animals as they moved. Their bodies were massive and square, with shaggy coats rippling gray against the astral darkness. Their heads swayed back and forth between hunched shoulders, sweeping enormous fluted tusks across their path.

A smaller version, a mewling calf, shifted uneasily beneath its parent's stocky legs as the three passed by. The largest one, whom Alaana assumed to be the mother, began to sing.

"The *mamut*," whispered Old Manatook, "How they sang! If only we could learn the power songs of these great animals. But they are all gone. Long, long gone."

The song of the *mamut* was a series of deep sounds, produced by long, powerful trunks and profoundly sensitive souls. There was a faint echo to it, as if it came from far away. A song of toil and strife, of long lonely treks across lands of desolation and darkness, and a stoic struggle against the inevitable pull of oblivion.

To Alaana the eerie sound drove home the sense they had traveled far. She felt cast adrift, insignificant and alone.

81

A shrill trumpeting blast interrupted the song.

"Something frightens the *mamut*," whispered Old Manatook. "There. Do you see it?"

The great beasts hurried in their ungainly manner, stomping away with thunderous footfalls. What could such magnificent creatures possibly fear? She could make out a shaggy shape circling in the darkness. Alaana shrank back behind the smooth round stone. It was the most horrific creature she had ever seen. Perhaps twice the size of a man, it resembled most closely a bear, but there was a lithe smoothness in its movements, a cunning and thoughtfulness that no bear could ever possess. Its eyes glittered with unnatural fury, set above a sharply elongated snout in the manner of a wolf. The soul of the beast struck Alaana like none she had ever witnessed before. Jagged and primal, it blazed a violent crimson, alive with savage energy.

The wolfbear broke cover, but the *mamut* had already taken up a frantic retreat. The predator circled cautiously, weighing its hunger against the risks of a full-on battle with fearsome tusks and huge trampling feet. Alaana's mind teetered between confusion and panic. Was this merely a vision, or dangerously real? That beast looked like it could rip them apart in an instant. So far it had not seen them, and Alaana was suddenly glad for the darkness.

A low whistle came from the rear and a man appeared. Taller even than Old Manatook, the spirit-vision revealed his outline clearly in white-hot soul-light. It burned with fierce energy and drive. The head was disproportionately large for a man, and his body obviously well-muscled below the rough furs. A pair of wizened eyes darted in deep pools beneath a heavy brow.

"The Tunrit," whispered Old Manatook. "Risen from the mud after the Great Rift. The first to walk this world, they were so much more than men."

Alaana marveled again. So this was a Tunrit.

Actually there were two of them. As the first distracted the wolfbear another circled around behind, hefting a huge spear. The shaft was almost as wide around as a man's neck, the tip a hunk of chiseled stone.

"He's so big..." whispered Alaana.

"Shh! Watch."

The wolfbear lurched toward the Tunrit with a swipe of a paw sporting five claws each as long as a man's head. Despite its massive size the creature attacked with amazing speed. At first Alaana thought the Tunrit had gone down below the force of the charge until she noted the man's soul-light still burning bright. He had disappeared into a narrow pit under the ground and rolled to safety beneath a flat rock. Alaana realized the entire escapade had been anticipated in every detail. This was all an ambush, set by the men.

The wolfbear stood confused for less than a moment, but the second warrior launched his spear. His aim was certain, but the animal's foreleg knocked the spear away. It seemed never to stand still. With a terrifying growl loud enough to rattle the ears and drive the mind to complete dissolution the beast lunged at the Tunrit. In an instant it was on top of him, ripping and tearing. Alaana thought the titanic hunter certain to be killed.

But in an amazing act of speed and cunning the Tunrit slithered out from under the animal's flank. Suddenly astride the great beast, his knife struck unerringly into the back of the wolfish head. Without a moment's hesitation the other Tunrit pressed his attack, driving his spear for a fatal blow.

"Enough, surely," said Old Manatook as he waved his hand to blot out the scene. The death cry of the animal, a sound Alaana would never forget, tore at her ears. The sound stretched and faded, giving Alaana the sensation of a startled rabbit fleeing the scene down a long burrow.

The strange buzzing sound signaled their return to the present but Alaana was not satisfied. She had learned the cadence of the vibration and matched it with a low humming of her own, deep in her chest. She visualized the buzzing sound as a tether, a chord linking past and present. What would happen, she wondered, if she gave that chord a yank? How far back might it take them? She tugged.

Suddenly an incredible light engulfed them. Alaana slammed her eyes shut but the light persisted, a multicolored rainbow bursting behind her eyelids. An oppressive warmth coexisted with a bitter, freezing cold. There was no earth beneath their feet, no sky above. Alaana's head spun around as an overwhelming desire to plunge into sleep came over her, and she realized she was already asleep, dreaming she was awake. She was a fledgling eaglet suddenly tossed out of the nest above a terrifying, gaping abyss. She was awash in the lightness of being, a dizzying rapture of endless possibilities, gasping for breath, soaring, expanding uncontrollably. She was an arrow, notched in a bow tensed on a hair-trigger, a mere thought away from taking flight, from becoming an animal — wolf, fox, owl, bear — it didn't matter. Wings sprouted from her back, a pointed beak to the fore, she went up and down and around, joyful and free, spinning, spinning, so totally alive, so totally free.

All sensation collapsed into a single feeling, one definitive emotion that dominated the rest, filling her heart until it was fit to burst and she could stand it no longer. Unbridled freedom. Alaana could go wherever she wished, be whatever she wanted — she could fly without need of wings, unconstrained by form, unconstrained by time.

"Sun and Moon!" hissed a rough voice.

And then she was back, seated on the sled atop the icy plain, her hand pressed against the round stone.

Her return came as a thunderclap that left her heart throbbing painfully in her chest.

"Manatook?" she said.

"Yes," answered Old Manatook. Alaana thought the shaman's voice wavered weakly. "The Beforetime," he announced, having recovered himself.

"I felt it," said Alaana. "It was..." She could find no words to describe it.

"Yes, it was," agreed Old Manatook. "And dangerous too. Having felt such bliss, even for an instant, a person can not help but be changed. I hadn't intended for that to happen. Again, things slip out of my hands when you are involved!"

"I was flying."

"Yes, yes."

"I could do anything. I could be anything."

"It was a time of great spiritual energy. A time when all the magic words were first formed."

"Were we really traveling in time?" asked Alaana in amazement.

"Were we?" returned Old Manatook. "Is such a thing possible?" He smiled broadly, flashing oversized teeth.

Alaana nodded with conviction.

"Aha!" Old Manatook clapped her on the shoulder. "Is such a thing really possible?"

"Yes," said Alaana. "Yes."

"Hmmph," said Old Manatook. "Or perhaps my old friend, the spirit in the rock was merely sharing a few of his memories with us? Hmmm? Think on it."

The old shaman took a deep breath and scanned the horizon. "I suppose that's enough for today."

CHAPTER 9

WALRUS ON THE ICE

"Wake up! Wake up!"

Alaana snapped awake at the little *tunraq's* shrill call. She grabbed the amulet where it lay beside her head on the platform.

"Ssst!" she whispered, "before you wake my whole family."

The amulet lay cupped inside her palm, a tiny auk skull with dead eyes and a downy tuft of tan feathers at the top. "Wake up!" it screeched again. Its eyes bulged in time with its call, then receded back into the depths of the sockets. Its name was Itiqtuq, which meant simply 'Wakes Up.'

"I'm up!" Alaana hissed. She looked to her family. Her father was a notoriously light sleeper, attuned to any stray yap or yammer from the dogs in the night, but he had heard nothing. This call was for Alaana alone.

She must now try to remember what she'd been dreaming, but when the auk screeched in her ear, she couldn't remember anything at all. It seemed like only a few moments since the *tunraq* had interrupted her sleep for the first of three times this night, though the gathering light outside the tent said it had been much more. Morning would be here soon. She felt as if she hadn't even had time enough to dream.

Alaana looked to Itiqtuq, but the amulet provided no

inspiration. The silly little thing had gone dead again. Its function was only to rouse her, again and again. Nothing more.

She was no good at this game. She didn't often have dreams at all. Still, Old Manatook said she must try. She thought perhaps she might have been dreaming of Avalaaqiaq. She thought of her lost sister often enough in the night. Itoriksak lay beside her now, but it was different. Ava used to poke and pinch playfully at her, trying to surprise her during the night, and Alaana would rake her toenails along her sister's calves to tickle her legs. Itoriksak, being older, was much too serious for any of that.

Alaana's stomach grumbled, making a sound that seemed nearly as loud as Itiqtuq's shrill cry of alarm. Had she been dreaming about food? Yes, she felt certain of it. There had been a taste in her mouth just a moment ago. She rolled her tongue around, but nothing remained. Of course, it had all been in her mind. Caribou liver cooked in the pot. That was it. As a shaman-in-training she had been forbidden to eat the liver of any animal, but her mouth watered at the thought. Caribou liver cooked in the pot. What possible usefulness could there be in telling that to Old Manatook?

The sun was coming up fast and she had little chance of getting back to sleep now. Besides, it was too noisy. Little bits of souls were all around her, even in the tent at night. The sleeping skins whispered in the darkness, the lantern had stories to tell, the very walls of the house had tongues. Even the soapstone pot had something to say.

And Maguan's wife was snoring again. How could someone with such a tiny nose be so loud?

As Alaana sat awake, her thoughts turned to that brief glimpse of the Beforetime she had experienced just the day before, which had itself seemed like the most powerful of dreams. Compared to that flash of paradise, that unlimited bounty of light and wonder, what were the pathetic wanderings of a sleeping mind?

So many things were changing. With brilliant light came darkness as well. Every day a parade of dangers and gloomy portents crawled before her very eyes, dark and peculiar things she could not before have imagined and didn't want to know.

Her father stirred beside her, mumbling in his sleep as the spring dawn came in a rush.

"Where's the tea?"

These were always the first words out of her father's mouth every morning even before he got out of bed. Amauraq, having come fully awake on the instant, rose from the sleeping platform and set about breakfast. Kigiuna was always one of the first men to rise in the camp and usually the first out to see to the day's work.

He brushed unruly locks of greasy black hair from his face. As he stood up to get dressed he launched into a typical morning monologue, talking as much to himself as anyone else.

"The fishing nets are in rough shape. I don't remember them being so ripped up last year. Someone must have been sloppy putting them away."

He went on and on as the rest of the family began to stir.

"It's hard work braiding the nets," he said. "My fingers are too clumsy for that type of work. The children are better at it than me. Alaana goes off again with Old Manatook." The heavy sigh that followed sounded somewhat like the whimper of a kicked seal. "*Ayurnaarmat*," he said, meaning it could not be helped.

To Alaana this did not sound like an enthusiastic endorsement of her training. She agreed with Kigiuna. She didn't want any part of it. She was better off staying home. And yet her father still kept forcing her to go.

"Itoriksak, get up. Get up! Mending today."

A small groan came from her brother's throat, as he began to come awake. Alaana remembered the feeling, still half asleep, her father's voice urging them on, getting them all started for the day.

"Come on, Itoriksak. You can help us putting the nets in the river. Let's hope you don't fall in!" Kigiuna started laughing to himself. It was such a nice, warm sound. "That would be sort of funny, us fishing you out with the nets. Bad for the nets, though." He laughed again, as if seeing the comical picture in his mind.

"Maguan. Up! I don't care how snug and warm you are beside your new wife. Married man or not, let's go. She's another mouth to feed now, you know, and maybe more than one in a short while."

Kigiuna laughed again. He was in a good mood. He had a special fondness for fishing. He loved springtime as much as he despised winter with its bleak stretches of inactivity and tedious seal hunts. And having so recently lost his eldest daughter, Kigiuna seemed altogether pleased to have Pilarqaq around. She clearly admired her new marriage-father and doted on him whenever he was in the tent, spoiling him with hot tea and good things to eat, and warm smiles.

Maguan groaned and sat up. Alaana did the same, poking at the lazy Itoriksak until her brother stirred to swat the offending hand away.

"Come on. We've a busy day ahead," said Kigiuna with a smile. "Let's eat!"

"Do I have to go?" Alaana asked her mother. "I want to stay and help mend the nets."

Amauraq made a soft purring sound, then smiled. With her hair pulled back, her face appeared even more lean and narrow, but the smile fit snugly beneath high, proud cheekbones. "You want to be with Maguan and Itoriksak. You don't even want to play. You're growing up fast, Alaana. I'm pleased."

"Good. Then I can go with them?"

For a long while Alaana thought her mother wasn't going to answer. She continued picking the scraps of their breakfast from the gravel on the floor, a housekeeping activity she had newly undertaken since Pilarqaq had come to live with them. Alaana wondered if she could consider her mother's silence as a tacit agreement.

"I don't think Old Manatook would look too kindly on that," Amauraq said at last. "I'm sure he's waiting for you already."

"Well, I don't want to go."

"Your father says you must go." There was a note of finality to this statement that brooked no argument.

"He says one thing, but thinks another," Alaana suggested.

Amauraq stopped fussing over the gravel and Alaana feared some massive rebuke was on the way. She had practically called her father a liar. Instead, her mother grabbed her with both arms and hugged her close. "My sweet baby," she said. As much as she hated being called a baby, Alaana did enjoy the hug.

Her mother said, "You always know what people are really feeling, don't you? You're always smiling when someone around you is happy, even if you don't realize it yourself. I never could hide anything from you, and I suppose neither can he."

"I think Father is afraid."

"Maybe he is," Amauraq said. "But you mustn't be afraid. There is a strength inside of you. I know because I put it there. Listen.

"When my mother's father was an old man his sight began to fade. After a while he couldn't see any more. His name was Quipagaa.

"When his eyes went dark it was too terrible for him to bear. He was lost to us. He wanted to die, saying the burden of life had become too heavy. He asked my mother to take his life but she wouldn't do it."

Alaana listened carefully, drinking in every word. Amauraq did not often tell stories.

"At last he went out in the snow. We cried and cried. He lay down in the snow. Many days went by. After a while my father went out to look for him but he was covered over.

"But Quipagaa did not die. The spirit of the eagle came to him, saying, 'Quipagaa! Do not despair! You shall see again! With my eyes you shall see the ocean and the mountains! You shall see your children again and your little grandchildren!'

"He came back to us and it was true. He could see again. But it was backward. He could see the lights inside of things instead of outside. The same way you do."

Amauraq's words startled Alaana. She hadn't told anyone about the spirit-vision except for Old Manatook. She didn't want anyone to know. The last thing she wanted was to be treated any differently than the other girls. But she should have known; her mother's sharp eyes never missed anything.

"It's terrible," she said, "I see things I don't like. I hear things all the time."

"You mustn't be afraid. Remember about Quipagaa. He could see again! His eyes were very bright like stars and in them lived a happy expression and a great blazing stare. And suddenly he could dance all night long again, as he used to when he was a young man. After that I swear the old man could make anyone do anything he wanted. But," she laughed, "he never made anyone do anything at all."

Amauraq's gentle brown eyes glistened with fond recollection.

"Then one day there sounded a great rumble and the ice mountain went crashing down into the pass. Our people were trapped. There was no way to get through. None of the hunters could find the way. Not one of the young men could do it. But Quipagaa found the way out for us. He saw it as from above. He

91

saved us from the hunger and the cold that would have ended us. A few days later, he died. But he died a happy man."

"Well I don't want to die!"

"Alaana!" Amauraq took her hands tenderly, rubbing them as if they were cold. "You won't die. You will become the shaman."

Alaana couldn't believe her ears. This was the last thing she expected to hear from her mother. Mother's fears, and they were many, were well known to the entire family. She was always so overprotective of her and everyone else. How many times had mother chased after her, insisting she wouldn't let her go out without the double parka in winter, or urging her to change wet clothes that weren't even that wet, or to remind her about every little taboo?

Amauraq feared the spirits more than anything else. On winter nights when the wind howled she insisted the spirits were angry and wouldn't let the children outside the *iglu*. Kigiuna proclaimed it was just the wind, but not even he could sway her. And when all was said and done, they stayed in.

Yet here she was urging Alaana along the most dangerous path imaginable. She could hardly understand it.

"Aren't you worried about the spirits?" she asked.

"All the time," her mother answered. "But I believe in you. You will become the shaman and you will protect us all. Don't you see? You'll protect us all. The family and the Anatatook and everyone else. We need you."

Amauraq gave her hand a squeeze. Her mother's gaze was warm and there was not a hint of doubt in her eyes.

"When we lost your sister," she said, "we gained something too. You gained something, Alaana. A mother knows. There is a balance to things. There has to be. If something is taken away," she said sadly, "something is also given."

Alaana recalled the things Sila had said. Justice. Balance. She thought her mother must be very wise to understand all these things, without even being told.

"Whatever you do with that gift, Alaana, you do for your sister. You do it for our poor Ava. She died for this." She stopped for a moment, putting her hand tight against her mouth, a far-off look in her eye.

"Now go and do your important work with Old Manatook."

"Pay attention!" snapped Nunavik.

Alaana sat up straight, her legs crossed on the prayer mat, her hands on her knees.

"To receive messages on the wind," continued the shrill voice of Nunavik, "is a skill that can be learned like any other skill, unless you are too thick-headed to listen, which just might be the case."

"I'm sorry," said Alaana.

"Don't apologize! Do not ever apologize. My blood, but you are dense aren't you? Concentrate!"

Alaana ran her eyes around the inside of the little tent, one of the pair Old Manatook had erected out in the wilderness for their practice sessions. There was nothing much to see. The interior was an empty cone of old caribou leather, a tight space barely large enough for herself and Nunavik.

Nunavik frowned, at least as much as a bull walrus could be said to have frowned. His gigantic, whiskered cheeks puffed out even further than usual and his long, yellowed tusks drew themselves back toward the folds of blubber at his chin. Nunavik was very old and very fat, with golden skin that bulged with a strange luminous glow as if constantly bathed with reflected sunlight. It was always dawn breaking across his craggy skin.

Nunavik was the first *tunraq*, or spirit helper, Alaana had encountered. Old Manatook had handed Alaana the amulet, a slender piece of walrus tusk inscribed with runic symbols, saying,

"This is Walrus On The Ice. Listen carefully, but don't pay too much attention to him. He's very sensible. He'll help you. He knows all about everywhere."

Alaana could not see the golden walrus within the talisman. She perceived only the tiny remnant of a soul that would be present in any tusk, in this case represented by a peculiar golden sparkle. But when she held it Alaana experienced a smell like no other. It was the stale walrus smell of festering blubber and rank mildew, of half-eaten fish stuck between massive teeth, but there was also a waft of something ancient, something which had plumbed the great depths of the ocean, that knew vast spaces of star and sky, and had walked with spirits great and small. "You can't see him unless he wishes it," explained Old Manatook, "The amulet is just a pathway; the spirit is on the other side. You can't see it, but you can feel it."

"I can smell it!" Alaana had said, wrinkling her nose.

"Now concentrate!" barked Nunavik, and Alaana's thoughts returned to the present. "What is needed is an intense concentration of thought. Thought! How a mere child can be expected to do that, I'll never know."

"I can do it," said Alaana.

Nunavik's tiny black eyes narrowed. "Perhaps you're too young, too stupid and starting too late."

"I can do it," said Alaana firmly.

"Better," remarked Nunavik. "Now let's get started in earnest. Old Manatook is sitting only ten paces away. All that separates us are a pair of flimsy tent skins. He is not simply thinking the word, he is sending it! There's a difference. You have to learn how to listen, how to receive. It's not a passive activity like hearing a bird song or a crash of the ice, or your mother calling her little baby in to supper. You have to work at it.

"You have to envision the intervening distance as strands along the spirit of the air. You can't see them, but you feel them with your mind. Feel the message, sense the word, coming at you along the strands. Picture Old Manatook's face, those deep, inscrutable eyes, that flat ugly nose, the unkempt ragged rat's nest of a beard..."

Alaana chuckled softly.

"Concentrate, girl!" urged Nunavik, hardly aware he had said anything the least bit amusing. "Tune yourself to the passing of his message, like the spider on the web. The strands shake and twitter. It's a word! He's reaching out to you right now. Feel it. *Feeeeel it!* Oh what's the use, it's like talking to a plank of wood! You're not getting any of this are you?"

"I'm trying," said Alaana.

"All right, listen to your Uncle Walrus. There's a trick I know. One must achieve a certain one-pointedness of thought necessary in order to receive. Of course you don't understand any of that, I know. It's a concept. But it can also be a game. The key to achieving the trance of one-pointedness is to completely remove all other things, emptying your mind (as if it isn't empty enough already), to a state of complete blankness. Now listen. There's no sound here. Complete silence."

It was so.

"Now make things disappear. Get rid of the tent – it's no longer around us, we are out on the open plain. There is no we — I'm no longer sitting beside you. I no longer exist. The distant mountains lose their colors and their forms, breaking into tiny fragments, crumbling away, they fall to dust and are gone. See? There is only the bare ground alone, only the snow so white it seems not even to be there. It all fades away. Subtract the stones and the earth, take away the sky, until there is nothing left."

Alaana dutifully nodded her head although she still saw everything as before, tent and walrus included.

"There is only pure, boundless space," said Nunavik in a

hypnotically soothing voice which sounded not like him at all.

"You exist in a vast plain of nothingness, an emptiness of the mind — in your case this should be fairly easy, allow your usual dumb stare to come over your face, now it suits our purposes. One must get rid of the moods, the joy, fear, sadness, rid yourself of the memories of any person or thing or event that has ever happened or ever will."

"Does that include you?"

"Of course that includes me. We got rid of me long ago. Haven't you been listening to anything I've said at all?"

Alaana didn't answer.

"Well, answer me girl! Haven't you heard a word I've said?"

"I can't hear someone who isn't here," replied Alaana.

Nunavik let loose a full-throated roar. He was not in the least amused. "Now concentrate!" he said. "Feel the word coming to you through the strands of the air. The word will arise within you; you will feel it, having emptied your mind of all ideas of your own. The word will come."

"It's a type of food, isn't it?"

"I'm not here to give you hints, girl."

"It's some kind of meat. . ."

"No, it's not."

"It's a piece of equipment for the hunt…"

"Perhaps," said Nunavik. "Concentrate! You make too much of this. It's not a guessing game. You don't have to figure it out, you simply have to receive. Old Manatook's doing all the work."

A moment later he added, "Unless you count all my time and effort. It's hard work straining my patience like this. And what do I get for it? A headache. And none of the credit. But I suppose there's nothing unusual in that. Getting anything yet?"

Alaana shook her head sadly.

The old walrus inflated his huge bulbous chest, then let out a frustrated growl. Alaana expected a blast of foul-smelling air to rush past her face. Of course there was none. The Walrus was spirit only.

"Relax your mind," said Walrus On The Ice. "That's the problem with the young, they never can concentrate on any little thing."

"How old *are* you?" asked Alaana.

"Never you mind that! I was young and foolish once too. You could well learn a thing or two from my story."

"You're not here to tell me stories."

"No. No, I'm not. I've much better things to do with my time and so do you. I don't know why I do that crusty old shaman these favors. He owes me his life, you know."

"I don't."

"Oh, now that's a story, that one! Hah! Let him tell you about it sometime, you won't hear any of it from me." His flippers danced in front of his golden face in what Alaana imagined was a walrus' show of modesty. "But maybe this is an idea. A proper story might relax your mind. What is there to lose, I've tried everything else?"

Nunavik's tiny eyes widened in their sockets. "Let Uncle Walrus sing you a song! It's a song of triumph and tragedy, although not in that order. It goes more like tragedy, more tragedy, triumph, tragedy, mild comedy, and a sort of triumph again. Its end is unwritten, but I suspect it will not conclude on a high note."

Walrus On The Ice let out a deep braying laugh, but his eyes held a strange expression of sadness.

"My father, whom everyone called Big Bellow, was famous for his tremendous lungs. You could hear his bull roar far away, far out of sight, over the ice. Yes, but even he was surprised when he taught me to dive deep. No one could believe it, the way I could

97

dive deep down. I became a sensation, diving down and circling below the glacier as the other young bulls chased me along the top of the ice. There aren't so many great amusements for us walruses, you know. Still, after a while they grew tired of waiting for me to come back up.

"And each time I went, I stayed below a little bit longer, and went a little bit deeper. Each time there were new marvels for me to behold, new friends, new dangers. I went deeper and deeper. Once I saw a sea turtle as large as a beluga whale. I discovered strange types of fish that light up the murky depths like stars in the night sky. At last I came to the very bottom, to the place where Sedna dwells."

"You saw her? What does she look like? Is she horrible?"

"Ackk! The most horrible woman you could ever imagine. Her hair is wild and dark, strewn with strands of seaweed and kelp that writhe like snakes; her flesh is a scaly green and bathed with sea slime. Her eyes are like knives; her mouth is cruel, her lips thin and blue, forming a crusty cave in which reside the teeth of a barracuda."

"Is it true what they say?"

"What?" asked Nunavik, with an irritated flash of his head at the interruption. "That she was the daughter of two giants with such an uncontrollable urge for flesh that she tried to devour her parents in their sleep? Or that she was a young beauty forced to marry an elderly neighbor, who by some trick turned out to be a monstrous carrion bird, leaving her no route of escape except into the salty deeps? Or perhaps, as some say, she was a poor orphan girl mistreated by her community and cast into the sea by the other children, who cut off her fingers as she clung desperately to the side of the kayak?"

"Which story is true?"

"All of them. Every story is true, I suppose. Looking at her, it is easy to see that she is cruel and terrible, quick to rip open your chest and tear your liver with her teeth, but in her eyes can also be seen the tears and desperation of a young girl forced to marry, beaten and rejected. All the great spirits and *turgats* that we know, they all came into being at the moment of the Great Rift, fashioned out of those who inhabited the Beforetime. So who knows? Perhaps in the Beforetime, where dreams were reality, she was all those things, lived all those lives. It doesn't matter. On this side of the divide she is Sedna, the Sea Mother who controls the supply of game animals from the ocean.

"Now listen! Great whirlpools guard the entrance to her house, a palace of glittering coral at the bottom of the sea. No living creature might reach those brilliant gates but my lungs were prodigious, and my flippers young and strong, and I wanted to see. I had to see what came next, what lay just around the corner. And I spied her there, on her bed of kelp. Her husband, Kktakaluk, is an even more hideous creature — a giant sea scorpion, blood red in color and twice the size of a man."

Nunavik snapped a flipper in the air in fair imitation of a sea scorpion's spiked claw. Alaana laughed, though a bit nervously, the image of the gigantic deadly creature alive in her mind.

"There was a daughter," added Nunavik. "Coming of such parentage you might think she would be ugly and cruel, but it was not so. She was beautiful, such a fragile and delicate thing. She had no cruelty in her, only loneliness. A profound loneliness as deep and as relentless as the sea itself. I could see it in her face, in the hesitant way she moved, so vulnerable and shy and demure. How could I help but fall in love with such a creature? They kept her locked away, visible to me only through a crack in the coral wall. I longed to talk with her but by then my lungs were fit to burst and up I must go. Up for air and down again, and again, but never enough air for squeak or squawk or whispered hello.

"And so it went. I dared not think she could return my

affections — a craggy thick-skinned walrus with a flat head and beady little eyes! Get that smirk off your face, girl! I was a good-looking walrus, but what a homely creature I must appear to her. That's what I meant. One time as I peered into her chamber our eyes met and I would have... Acck, but the father scared me off, venomous devil. He is cruelty personified. Those claws! Snipped a piece of my hind flipper clean off."

Nunavik leaned far forward, raising his tail with a flourish. Sure enough, there was a sizable piece missing.

"After that I was afraid to go back. Anyone would have been. You can understand that?"

Alaana nodded.

"Well, understand this," continued Nunavik, "I did go back, Kktakaluk be damned. I went back again and again. Always he was there — talk about a flat head and beady eyes — with those claws and that enormous deadly tail."

Again he exhibited his damaged tail. "There seemed no way around him. They kept her there, imprisoned for her protection, they said. She didn't see it that way. There's another one young and foolish..." The walrus' eyes, small and beady as they were, glossed over for a moment and Alaana realized it was painful for him, talking about his first love.

"One day she escaped! I don't know how she did it. But I know why. She was coming up to find me. She must have been, I suppose, simply curious," he said with a sigh. "Searching for me or not, she found instead the fishermen of the North. She became entangled in their nets. Poor helpless creature. To them she appeared monstrous; their eyes could not see the charming, delicate and gentle being that I had found.

"Now comes tragedy and more tragedy. They killed her, of course. And Sedna flew into a monstrous rage of whipping gales and smashing storms. The Sea Mother's revenge was ruthless. No longer would she allow the game animals up to the surface to feed the men.

"My sorrow was beyond the telling, and my terror even greater than that. The souls of all the sea creatures are Sedna's playthings. It seemed inevitable she would discover my part in this disaster and then... one can not even imagine what torturous end her wrath would bring to me. There was no place I could run. There was no place for me to hide.

"That's when I met Kaokortok, a broken-down Tungus shaman who had stranded himself at sea. He'd been carried off on a piece of ice which broke away while he was hunting seal. He had never had much luck on the water; his guardian spirit was the vole, you see. Really he was the most pathetic sort of shaman I've ever met, and I've known quite a few.

"Many days he drifted until, starving and weak, he drew his belt-knife with the brilliant idea of ending his miserable long-suffering life. I told him to stay his hand, the ridiculous fool. Land was only a few feet away. I nudged his floe toward the iceberg as best I could and tossed him a few fresh-caught tomcod. In his gratitude he did me a service. He hid my soul in my left tusk, the very one that you hold now in your greasy little paw. Those carvings you see there were done by the shaky hand of Kaokortok. The man was a complete idiot, and came to a bad end shortly thereafter, but his spirit cage was a good one. He hid my soul from the wrath of Sedna.

"The men began to starve, but Sedna would send no more food to them. The people grew mad in their starvation and hunted whatever seal and walrus they could find to utter destruction. I saw all my friends and family destroyed, killed and eaten, every one, even though it wasn't their time. I wanted to die along with them myself but I thought of old Kaokortok lost at sea with the belt-knife in his shaky hand. What an inspiration, eh? At least I knew what I didn't want to do.

"But what to do?

"Alone on the ice, soulless, steeped in tragedy. I sat on a rocky cleft overlooking the sea.

"Where had I gone wrong? What had brought me to that place? I had dived too deep, I had touched upon things that should not have been seen by mortal eyes. I had went too far, asked too many questions. But I resolved, there and then, sitting on that miserable rock, to stumble blindly no more. No mortal creature of the sea was meant to witness what I had seen, to meddle in the affairs of the Great Spirits. And yet I had done so. Something within me had made it possible. I would push it as far as it would go. I would learn all there was to know about magic and the spirits and all the other worlds.

"And so it began, my odyssey into the—

"Oh, but wait. I wasn't asked here to fill your head with stories about me, as enlightening and instructive as they might be to an empty-headed girl. The strands. The word on the wind. Concentrate!"

But Alaana could not concentrate. Nunavik's wondrous story had sparked too many new ideas. Alaana thought of Sedna and giant sea scorpions, of storms and spells, of the ill-fated romance Nunavik had so long ago suffered, and Maguan's recent marriage.

"I wonder how it'll be when I'm married?" she asked.

"Marriage is not a certainty for shamans," replied the golden walrus.

"Why not? Kuanak and Civiliaq were married, and Old Manatook too. They all have children, except for Old Manatook and Higilak but they're too old for that."

"People fear what they don't understand," said Nunavik grimly. "Now get back to the task at hand. I'm not here for idle chatter. Concentrate on the message, *ungarpaluk*." This last word was twisted sarcastically, a nickname Nunavik had adopted for Alaana which meant 'The Little Harpoon'.

"Harpoon," said Alaana, with sudden inspiration. "That's the word, isn't it?"

Nunavik's eyes bulged, his golden face reddened. "You guessed that from what I said!"

"I'm right," trilled Alaana, "I'm right." Glee rang out in her voice. "And now that we've finished early, I can go and help mother repair the nets."

"Not so fast," said Nunavik. He paused, probably to confer across the spirit of the air with Old Manatook, then said, "There is a new word. Try again."

CHAPTER 10

THE WEDDING FEAST

There were no lessons for Alaana the next day. It was time for Maguan's wedding feast.

Their family tent had been linked with her uncle Anaktuvik's to form one large enclosure that would better accommodate all the people who happened to visit. Pilarqaq had laid the floor with broad, flat stones to cover the messy gravel. People came and went all day, passing in and out of the tents, staying for a while and eating their fill, then going away only to return some time later. Of the eight families that made up the spring encampment, four or five families were present at any one time. The women, having shaken off their outer garments, settled on the platform toward Kigiuna's side of the enclosure, eating and snuggling among the furs. The men took to the other side, sitting cross-legged on the skins covering Anaktuvik's floor, eating and smoking their pipes. The men paid no attention to the women unless the talk coming from their side grew too loud, at which time Kigiuna would object.

He wouldn't speak to any of the women directly, but merely called out, "Hurry, men. Grab your slings and bows! The auks have hatched on the cliffside! I can hear their squawking from all the way over here!" The women would respond with a moment of shocked silence and then, with a ripple of laughter they would start up all over again.

The children took possession of the region between the two camps. The press of body heat rendered the tent quite warm. Discarded parkas littered the floor and the smaller children made a game of crawling under and between them. The older youths stood in a cluster at the choicest spot, the cooler region near the tent flaps. Alaana positioned herself directly in the middle, where she could hear some of the women's gossip but still be close enough to watch Maguan. The mood inside the tent was so relaxed and joyful, Alaana felt happier than she had ever felt before. She was so very proud of her brother.

And the food! Heaping trays kept coming in the door as each hunter eagerly showed off the best his house had to offer. A competition was struck up in order to see who could bring the most — from fresh marrow melted into huge yellow cakes, to bittersweet willow greens and steaming walrus and seal meat. After a steady diet of fish over the past season the satisfying taste of meat raided from the stores was a welcome treat.

The women passed out lumps of sweet tallow and handfuls of fish eyes. Alaana chomped merrily on the salty treats, and she and Iggianguaq made a show of swallowing the tough kernels inside rather than spitting them out as Mikisork did. They remarked, quite falsely, on how delicious they were, just to watch the expressive oval of Miki's face curdle with disgust.

"My mother says a boy's not really a man until he gets married," she said.

"And a girl's not a woman until she bears her first child," said Iggy completing the saying. He then made a variety of groaning noises and rubbed at his stomach in an approximation of giving birth. Given the oversized nature of Iggy's belly, Alaana thought the act fairly convincing.

"Well, I can't wait to have mine," Alaana said indignantly.

She puffed her cheeks and pulled her shirt out in front.

"Even if they look like Mikisork?" Iggy asked, twisting his expression into an exaggerated imitation of Mikisork with narrow cheeks and flared nostrils.

"Well, I don't care," said Alaana with a sulky curl of her lip. She thought Miki was handsome enough.

"Hey!" said Miki, who didn't find the joke very funny either.

Iggy flapped air out of his mouth. Mikisork was well-known for his flatus.

"I don't mind that either," she insisted, "He's good-natured and kind."

Alaana had been promised to marry Miki ever since the day she'd been born. As Miki was one of the sons of the headman, Tugtutsiak, her father had thought this a very successful arrangement. Alaana had no quarrel with it either. She had looked upon Miki as her betrothed all her life, and he had always acted with a special affection toward her. She liked him a lot. Her father was very good at arranging marriages.

The feast was likely to extend for several sleeps. A few of the guests already dozed contentedly, having fallen asleep right where they sat. In the summer, when it was nearly always light outside, the days spilled together. Each household kept to its own sleeping schedule; and the children were free to play as long as they liked, or until exhaustion claimed them.

"How do you feel?" Kigiuna asked the groom. He clapped Maguan on the shoulder, then slapped him lightly on the cheek.

"I am happier than any Anatatook man has ever been before!" said Maguan, his face aglow.

"This is what they all say," remarked Kanak. "At first."

"I'm not surprised," said Kigiuna. "Pilarqaq is a true beauty. Your reputation is on its way up, my boy."

On this day it was Pilarqaq's joy to be hostess and the mother of the house. Amauraq had been relegated to the background where she must toil over the pots and stews, leaving the serving to her son's new wife.

Maguan's bride was unique at the gathering for she held the attention of both the women and the men. Her impressive parka with its squirrel fur tassels made it seem the other Anatatook women went around dressed in miserable rags. Her luxurious hair flowed loosely about her shoulders and down her back.

Pilarqaq held aloft a plate of boiled meat, and spoke the ritual words, "Enjoy the meat, my guests. I trust you will all eat your fill. Hurry, hurry! Empty the pots quickly so that we may load them up again."

She said nothing else to the men, going among them only to serve lumps of boiled walrus. She presented an impressive piece to Maguan, held at the end of a pointed sticker of caribou antler. The new wife politely licked the bloody juices dripping down the meat so that they wouldn't mess up her husband's shirt or run down his fingers too much.

Alaana had seen women do the same at every ceremonial dinner, but she sure hoped Miki didn't expect her to do that for him. She had asked her mother about it once. Amauraq had said the men worked so hard for everyone, fishing and hunting all day in the cold, that she saw no harm in showing them a little respect.

Maguan stuffed the food into his mouth. Taking a lusty bite between his teeth, he sliced off the bulk of the slab and passed it along to Kigiuna. And so went the meat from Kigiuna to Kanak and then to Anaktuvik and on and on down the line. The meat was followed by a choice slab of blubber that disappeared in much the same fashion. When the blubber had gone halfway across the room and all present seemed to have adequate amounts of blood and grease smeared on their faces, Maguan called out to Pilarqaq for a new slab of meat.

Itoriksak passed around a little seal skin basin full of drinking water. Melted from snow in the same pots used to boil the meat, the water had a light brownish color and little globules of animal fat bobbing about on the surface.

Tugtutsiak entered the tent, followed by his wife and three eldest sons. He was headman among the Anatatook and the captain of the whaling boats. He tossed a large sealskin bag full of mussels onto the floor in front of the groom.

Tugtutsiak was a short but powerfully-built man only a few winters older than Kigiuna. He was distinguished from Alaana's father in that he owned only one face. That face held eyes which gazed always far away and a hard-set mouth whose lips pursed in grim determination. He smiled only rarely and Alaana had never heard him laugh. She supposed this was because Tugtutsiak, more than anyone else, lived in a state of constant worry over the food supply. It fell to him to wrestle with important decisions of when and where to move the camps, based on his dealings with the shamans. He anxiously awaited their negotiations with the spirits in regard to the caribou hunts, and of course, the whaling trips. Tugtutsiak had a deep love for the sea and whaling seemed to be the only joy for him, although this too was dangerous work.

Mikisork yanked at Alaana's shirt. "Wrestle me," he cried, "wrestle me!"

He offered a crooked wrist. Alaana, preoccupied with a wonderful bit of seal meat, brushed him off.

"Wrestle me!" he insisted in a high, happy voice. Alaana intertwined her wrist with his and they began to pull and laugh and pull. Mikisork and Alaana were fairly well-matched, even though Miki was definitely a little bit stronger. There were so few girls in the village Alaana had grown up with mostly boys for friends and had gotten pretty good at wrestling. In the end Miki fell forward, giggling, and let her land on top. Not content with such a suspicious victory she threw her arms around his neck and kicked him playfully in the ribs. She was not as gentle as she might have been and Miki, practically strangling, called out for help. As ever, Iggy came to his friend's aid, peeling Alaana from Miki's back and tossing her among the parkas. Iggy went straight for her weak spot with an onslaught of tickling under the armpits.

Alaana knew that Miki had let her win. He was always so concerned about everybody else's feelings, even in such little matters. That was one of the things she liked best about him. Aquppak never let anyone win at anything, and neither would Iggy. She glanced at her intended where he sat joking with the other boys. He was such a gentle soul and not all full of himself like the others.

Old Manatook entered the tent, bringing a seal so freshly killed it was not even frozen in death yet. No one knew how he could catch one all by himself, so far from the shore and in the middle of summer. Such questions were not asked of him. And if there were fresh claw marks on the animal's neck, nobody spoke of it.

Once the old shaman joined the party the men grew talkative and excited. Old Manatook had boundless energy for such an old man and on this day, as on many joyful occasions, he put away all seriousness, any whiff of dark spirits left behind, and he sang and danced with a carefree abandon. He truly was a marvel. His eyes dazzled. He stood a head taller than the rest of the stocky, broad-shouldered Anatatook men. Only the few eldest among them had any gray among their uniformly dark hair, and none the pure white of Old Manatook.

Alaana was glad to see him acting so relaxed and happy in contrast to his usual cranky nature. Raising the people's spirits was one of the shaman's duties, whether it came easily to him or not. She could not imagine herself in that same role. Not now or ever.

The men told a variety of stories and jokes, many reserved

especially for the occasion of marriage. Kanak, seized with the spirit of the day, sang this song:

"What dowry shall I offer, for my bride, for my bride?
A walrus hide, a walrus hide!
And not some flimsy patched-up thing
Bring me the hide, tall and wide, tall and wide.
You lonely young man with no bride,
Sing with me, sing with me!
I'll let you lay with my walrus hide!"

Kigiuna slapped his hand on his knee to get their attention, then launched into the familiar tale of how he had, years ago, got his wife Amauraq. Alaana had heard the story before, but she listened again anyway. She liked the way her father told it.

"She tried to hide in her family's tent, playing shy," Kigiuna said. "I had been courting her the entire summer and winter was fast approaching. You know how difficult it is to drag a woman from an *iglu* in winter — there's only the one narrow entrance tunnel. A summer tent is much easier. Clearly, it was time for action. I had arranged it all with her father beforehand of course, but still I must abduct her properly as any decent groom would.

"I tried to catch her when she came outside to pee, but she was quick! She'd dart back in, fast as a fox. She was determined, too. I think she could've kept it up forever. But I had resolved not to break camp without a wife. I ripped my way into that tent," and on this part he demonstrated a great feat of strength tearing the caribou flaps asunder. "And burst in. Children ran screaming before my feet. Amauraq tried to hide under the sleeping furs, but I tore them away." He smiled slyly as he glanced over at the other side of the enclosure to see if he might catch the eye of his wife, but the women were busy with their own business.

Alaana was familiar with her mother's version of the tale and it differed considerably from this one. The way she told it, the

110

entire affair was her idea.

Kigiuna continued, "I started to yank her away but she grabbed the tent pole, resisting with all her strength. Oh, but I pulled hard and fast. The whole tent shook, ready to come down on our heads. My marriage-mother screamed!"

Here he broke out laughing again and had to stop. He imitated the shrill screams of the lady in question, and everybody laughed. "I pulled Amauraq, she pulled the tent pole, the whole thing ready to come down. She chomped down on my hand! That's right, she bit right through the skin and into the meat of me. I pulled some more, and wouldn't you know she was never going to let go, that tent pole ripped right out of the ground, tore the tent cover in half. I roared and charged at her like a mad bull, rolling her along the ground and outside of the tent. In the open air, we had room to maneuver and a proper audience as well. Her family cheered her on, urging her to make a good show of it; my relations spoke for me. She still had the tent pole in her hands. She swung it at me. Oh, it was some fight! She clawed at my face like a wild woman, but I got her up on my shoulders. She kicked her way loose. I pulled her up again. She got loose again, sending me crashing into the meat rack. But I got hold of her a third time and that was the end. It was the happiest day of my life. Oh, did I forget the part where she tore out some of my hair? That too!" He shook his head gaily. "But I got her on my sled and the game was over at last. If you ask me, Maguan, you had it way too easy."

"It pays to have friends in the south," said Tugtutsiak dryly.

"And a sizable dowry to part with, I'll bet," added Kanak.

Kigiuna declined to comment. He leaned back, rubbing the last remnants of blubber from the greasy beard and mustache that framed his mouth.

Tugtutsiak's uncle Krabvik, who was old and crazy and had a face like a slab of dried fish, began to sing:

111

"Who will carry my pretty sister?
Her face is flat, her hips are fat.
Who will care for my pretty sister?
Her knife is dull, but her tongue is sharp.""

Alaana had a hard time deciphering all the words. Krabvik's teeth were mostly gone and he was laughing hysterically at every line. He went on:

"Who will marry my dreadful sister?
She has no fingers, she can not work.
Who will bed my monster sister?
She has pointed arms, she has pointed legs.
Put her on the sled, take her to bed…""

Alaana supposed there must be a final line of the song, but by this time Krabvik became so consumed with laughter his delivery ended in a gurgle as he fell sideways with glee, unable to finish. If there was more to the song they would not hear it this night.

Tugtutsiak's wife Aolajut passed around another platter of fish eyes and sweet tallow lumps. But this was nothing compared to what came next. Not to be outdone, Anaktuvik had disappeared into the meat locker outside his tent and brought back the most festive food of all. It was a *giviak*. With a great sense of ceremony he hauled the frozen carcass out before the men.

It was the body of a small seal, emptied so that only the skin and blubber remained, creating a special type of a sack. Two winters ago the thing had been stuffed with auks, tiny birds that flock along the sea cliffs. Alaana recalled when she and her brothers had run along the scree at the base of the cliffs, making crazy noises to flush the little birds out and into the waiting nets of the women. The birds had to be carefully prepared for the *giviak*. Most importantly they must be killed a certain way, by crushing the breastbone with pressure from the thumbs at a particular place just above the heart.

Anaktuvik sliced open the belly of the sac with his long

hunting knife. This proved hard work as it was still frozen, but he went at it with gusto, cheered on by the men. He dug out frozen chunks of pink meat and cured feathers. The men attacked these treats without any help from the women. The women were hardly aware of the *giviak* at all. Alaana could tell by the looks on their faces that they were deeply immersed in one of Higilak's romantic stories.

Maguan flipped a frozen tidbit to Alaana and she shared it with Iggy. She chewed it slowly, crunching and spitting out whatever bits of feather and bone came loose as it thawed in her mouth. The taste was sensational. The blubber had seeped into the bird meat as the *giviak* lay buried all summer, creating an incredibly pungent taste.

To Maguan went the ultimate prize, the frozen lump of blood which collected around the auk's crushed heart. Still frozen, he popped the crimson oval into his mouth and then laughed delightedly, falling off the mat and into a swoon, rolling about on the floor muttering, "Delicious, delicious."

Kigiuna laughed.

Anaktuvik went back to the carcass. Now sufficiently thawed, he went at it again peeling entire birds from the compressed mass, passing them out to the men.

Kigiuna took one of the little birds in his mouth. Securing the legs between clenched teeth, he brushed off the fermented feathers in a trickle of downy snow that fell across the front of his shirt. With delicate motions of his teeth he separated the skin and turned it inside out. Remarkably, he tossed the meat aside. He was only interested in the skin. He sucked the skin into his mouth and pulled it out against his raking teeth, stripping off all the delicious bird fat.

Alaana and Iggy had seen enough. They scrambled toward the place where the bird had landed among some carving tools stored at the side of the tent. Alaana greedily took a bite from her half. This thawed version tasted considerably different than before. The soft, oily bird-meat now carried an intensely sour taste. Alaana's mouth watered as it never had before. She desperately wanted more. Iggy rolled his eyes with delight, but there was so little and it was soon gone.

Tugtutsiak belched loudly and that got all the men going. Soon a contest broke out to see who could express his appreciation longest and loudest. Kanak won the day as he burped and broke wind ferociously at the same time and everyone laughed.

Alaana felt herself growing tired. A belch of her own brought forth the sensational sour taste of the *giviak* once more, startling her back awake.

She noticed her father had fallen asleep. Like most of the men Kigiuna slept very little during the long days of summer, preferring to spend as much time as possible out on the hunt, banking stores for winter's long night.

Iggianguaq, having achieved the impossible and gorged himself to satisfaction, had closed his eyes. He lay on the floor, his head nestled atop Miki's bare ankles. Filled to bursting with food, Alaana felt her own eyes closing. She had a supremely contented feeling. Times were good when food was plentiful.

She wished she could keep this feeling always in her heart. It was a feeling of warmth and love, of safety and security within the community. Alaana thought the wedding feast a remarkable success. It was good Pilarqaq had joined their family.

CHAPTER 11

MORE SECRETS

As Alaana peered at the figure on the platform, she began to feel afraid. Putuguk lay unmoving, his eyes closed, his face relaxed as if he were merely asleep, as if all one would have to say to him was, "Heya! Wake up! Get going!" and he would snap out of it. But his skin had taken on a dull gray color and his breathing was rapid and shallow.

"My father doesn't speak," said Tikiquatta. "He doesn't move. He can't eat or drink."

Word of Putuguk's illness had already spread throughout the Anatatook camp but Tikiquatta, kneeling beside her stricken father, repeated the details. "He suffered pains in the head and eyes for three days and a great fatigue as if some heavy weight were bearing down on him. Finally he lay down to sleep and did not wake up."

To the large group packed inside the *karigi*, the daughter's despair transformed the sad story into a call for action. An expectant silence fell among them as they sat in a loose circle around the platform.

Alaana felt sorry for the old man. He had long been a fixture in the camps. Many people disliked Putuguk because he had grown weak and could no longer work, but he had several children in his household including her friend Aquppak and two small grandchildren. In light of Putuguk's inability to keep his family fed without help from the others, her father felt some sense of responsibility toward them. Kigiuna said that so long as Putuguk could still keep up with the sleds during the seasonal movements of the band, he was as much an Anatatook as any.

Putuguk had seen more than his share of misery. His wife died young and his son and daughter-by-marriage, who had been Aquppak's parents, were dead as well. Alaana thought maybe he had simply had enough. That was the way with old people sometimes, wasn't it?

All eyes turned to the shaman.

Old Manatook lay a reassuring hand on Tikiquatta's shoulder. The shaman cut an impressive figure under the bright summer light spilling down through the tent's smoke hole. The sunlight lit up his blood-red parka as if he were robed in a sheath of fire. "Trouble has come here," he said in a powerful, commanding tone of voice. "We shall have it out!"

Old Manatook inhaled sharply. The mixed scents within the crowded tent spoke to him of frequent meals of fish and seal oil, the musk of recent lovemaking, and the pungent aroma of Tikiquatta's fear. He bent to snuffle at Putuguk's cheek, but his nose discovered no clue as to the nature of the illness. He undertook a full inspection of the body, in full view of the people.

He lay hands on Putuguk's temples, taking a measure of the body heat. He pressed a thumb against the lower lid to gaze into the man's left eye, where the soul could best be seen. The eyeball was motionless, indicating the sufferer had not gone wandering to the dreamlands. His soul-light was still present within, but had grown dim and inconstant, as the last flicker of a dying ember.

"We will have it out!" he said again.

He selected a small drum from the row of masks and drums

arranged behind the platform. The drum had a round head of stretched fawn skin no larger than the palm of his hand. A thin line separated the surface into two equal parts representing the worlds of the living and the dead. Though small, the drum had a strong connection to the Underworld, and had always proven reliable. Old Manatook pressed the beater into Alaana's palm, taking a moment to instruct her on the proper rhythm for the ceremony.

"You will lead them in the chant," he said, "*Halala, halalalee, halala, halaalalee!*"

Manatook drew five fragments of crimson stone from his pouch. He arranged these helper spirits around Putuguk's body, ignoring their pitiful cries, and knelt before the platform.

The shaman emptied his mind and let the people's emotions fill it back up again, tasting the mood of the crowd. Restless movements and stray chatter had all been banished by the repetitive chanting. Their minds were now full of well-wishes for poor Putuguk, coming even from those that thought him old and lazy.

There remained a few pockets of resistance and discontent, most notably a familiar lack of commitment from Kigiuna. The presence of even one person who did not share the same outlook as the others was disruptive. Manatook considered having Kigiuna removed, but he was confident he could heal Putuguk despite Kigiuna's lack of support. He worried that expelling Alaana's father would have a negative effect on the girl's concentration. No matter, he thought, perhaps a lesson was in store for them both, father and daughter.

Now to begin. His questing eyes roamed the room. "Word wants to come up!" he said. "Who here has broken faith with the spirits?"

Tikiquatta, still kneeling beside her father, made a small, desperate squeak.

"Yes, Tiki?"

117

"It is — this is my fault. It's surely all my fault." Speaking hesitantly, Tikiquatta confessed how the bottoms of Putuguk's *kamiks* had worn through. "Rather than mending the holes," she said, "I was lazy and neglectful of my father."

Tears streaked her face.

Tikiquatta had always been regarded as very pretty; her light brown hair was the fairest among all of the Anatatook. But she had been widowed twice at a young age, and was considered very bad luck by all the men. Yet for all the hardships she had endured they had never before seen her fallen so low as this — sobbing fitfully, her head resting against Putuguk's chest as Old Manatook bent to inspect the man's feet. After a long moment the shaman pronounced that she was not to blame as there were no signs that evil spirits had entered from his boots, but Tikiquatta could neither be consoled nor wrenched from her father's side.

Putuguk's cousin Mequsaq also claimed responsibility. He stood up, saying, "Three sleeps ago, I had a nightmare in which I stabbed a man through the chest."

Old Manatook's formidable eyebrows rose up. "Was it Putuguk?"

"No, it was someone else." Mequsaq hesitated. His face had a distinctly fox-like appearance, especially about the eyes which were keen and narrow and the nose, which was short and sharply pointed. He looked uncomfortably around the room, his eyes resting on Alaana for a brief, searing moment before he revealed, "It was Kanak."

"What was the reason for this?"

"In the dream, he took my wife by force. But I know he wouldn't steal my wife away. He's my friend. He's not a bad person."

Old Manatook noticed a tell-tale flash from Kanak's eyes, and thought it best to quickly draw attention back to himself. He raised

118

his arms to quell the rustling crowd. "This is a very troubling situation," he said, aiming his words in Kanak's direction. "But for now let us put it aside. It has no relation to Putuguk's problem." He also caught a guilty look from Tugtutsiak's wife. "And you Aolajut?"

"Yes, I... I have done something, but..." She nudged her head in Alaana's direction.

"She understands," said Old Manatook. "I have made it clear these things are never to be spoken of again. She knows."

"She shouldn't be here," said Tugtutsiak forcefully. The headman had a deep, resonant voice that carried a lot of weight. "A healing is no game for young girls to play. Women are not allowed on the hunt, for fear their presence will cause insult to the spirits. Many times you've told us so. And unmarried women are not allowed in the *karigi*, for the same reason. You risk poor Putuguk's life with this nonsense. If she is leading the chant, what chance does he have?"

Manatook now faced a sea of discontented faces. The headman's words, raising doubt in everyone's minds, did more to risk failure than the presence of the girl. With his spirit-vision the shaman could see that Alaana's soul now held the *angakua*, the special light of the shamans. But the people, blind to the spirits, were not so easily convinced. Generations of tradition spoke against her. "Putuguk has every chance," Manatook reassured them. "He will be healed if the people wish it so. Believe it!"

Manatook turned again toward the headman's wife, "Now tell us what happened."

Aolajut hardly seemed reassured, but went on. "Not long ago I lay with my husband." She lifted her eyes, having expected some reaction from the people, then realized more needed to be said. "It was the night before the caribou hunt. We knew it wasn't allowed..." She looked incredibly pained and embarrassed, then

119

added, "Twice in the same night."

Tugtutsiak's stolid face flushed red. Alaana looked quickly away.

One by one the people confessed their transgressions in hopes of aiding the stricken man. Alaana came to know a great deal about stinginess, bouts of bad temper, and other cruel acts she had never even imagined.

More secrets! With each confession Alaana drew herself further down into the folds of her parka. Every stray look, each pained expression drove her deeper.

Formerly she had been banned from the spirit-callings as were all children, but now that she had assumed the role of shaman-in-training everything had changed. She was charged with learning the Way as demonstrated by Old Manatook. She recalled the time she had snuck beneath the tent skin, so eager to learn what the adults did inside the *karigi*. Now she envied the rest of the children under the tender care of the storyteller in the companion tent. At this very moment her friends sat captivated by one of the old woman's heroic tales, shielded from malignant spirits by time and distance, comfortable in their belief that stories were merely stories. She wished she could be with them. She felt certain she did not belong here, not dressed like this. The tall head piece she wore, with its representation of a snowy owl resting atop a spirit pole, was straining her neck.

Worst of all was the way her father turned quickly aside when their eyes met, so that she might not catch his disapproving glance. Gone was the affectionate softness with which that gaze had always warmed her in the past. Most of the other adults, even the women, peered at her in the same distasteful manner, making Alaana feel thoroughly unwelcome.

Now it was her mother's turn to confess. Amauraq admitted to speaking unkindly of her son's new wife, though she immediately pointed out that the criticism was well-deserved and stemmed from Pilarqaq's own rampant vanity.

"It seems," Amauraq added loudly, speaking less out of remorse than a desire to advertise Pilarqaq's shortcomings to the whole of the Anatatook, "that she values her constant preening above doing any useful work. She spends more time coming her hair than anything else."

Pilarqaq put her hand to her luxurious, neatly braided hair. Although she would not dare speak openly against her husband's mother, her face flared deep purple with rage.

In his turn Kigiuna shook his head and said, "I haven't done anything." The eyes of the crowd circled around, dosing him with disapproval and suspicion. He glared back at them. He would admit to nothing.

CHAPTER 12

"I STRETCH FORTH MY HAND"

At a sign from her teacher, Alaana broke off the chant.

"Enough is said," proclaimed Old Manatook. "I have decided to use the *qilayuq* method — the head lifting."

To this end he tied a sealskin thong around Putuguk's brow. Again he looked into the left eye at the last flickers of Putuguk's soul-lights. He smiled slightly. "As I had guessed," he said, "there is another spirit hidden here. It runs from my sight. It fears me."

Putuguk groaned softly. As the spirit buried itself deeper, his soul faced an increasingly deadly stranglehold.

Old Manatook applied pressure to one of the crimson stones with the heel of his boot. The spirit within howled, a hideously inhuman sound, audible only to the ears of the shaman and his young student.

Some years ago Old Manatook had attempted to imprison the soul of a rival shaman in a fist of red stone but the strain had caused the rock to shatter. The rival had escaped, but small pieces of his soul had been trapped within the fragments. They cried out endlessly for their master, each with a different mournful tone. Old Manatook found their emotions useful in attuning his own mental state. He prodded this one and that, eliciting eerie wails in various pitches that drew his mind into closer alignment with Putuguk's soul.

When he was ready, he said, "Angry spirit, why do you trouble this man?"

The question was loudly uttered, fired up into the air, aimed at nothing in particular. There was no answer.

"He is a good man, a father, ever faithful to the spirits, always fair in his dealings with others."

No answer.

"Did he do something? Did he give cause to offend?"

Standing beside Putuguk, Old Manatook took hold of the thong. The unconscious man would reply by head weight alone. The head lifted easily. The answer was no.

"Did Kanak's boastfulness cause you to come here?"

The head went up. No.

"Was it the laziness of Tikiquatta?"

No.

"Have you come from the Underworld?" The mention of such a dreaded realm brought a frightened murmur from the crowd. "Stay with me," he grumbled, shaking off their fears.

The head lifted easily. No.

"The shadow world?"

No.

"The Outer Darkness?"

No.

"Are you one of us?"

The head was heavy. Yes!

A collective gasp erupted throughout the room.

Old Manatook looked back at them. His face revealed a surge of confidence. "What human name had you when you lived among us, I wonder? Which one of us? Are you Iakkasuq?"

No.

"Is it Old Kukkook?"

123

No.

"Avalaaqiaq?"

The sudden mention of her sister's name shocked Alaana. She had very nearly come to accept that the face she had gazed upon with such joy day after day had left her forever, that a voice so familiar and dear to her heart was finally silenced, never to be heard again. Always remembered as smiling and cheerful, the idea that Ava might have been corrupted, that her twisted soul had brought suffering to Putuguk was too dreadful to bear. Thankfully, the answer resounded quickly.

No.

Old Manatook kept on. "Is it my dear fallen brother Kuanak?"

No

"Nalungiaq?"

The head could not be lifted. Yes!

This revelation was met with a mixture of sighs, groans, and lamentations from all those gathered inside the tent. Alaana saw Old Manatook's intensely white soul-light flare around his eyes as they blazed with triumph.

She fondly remembered Nalungiaq, who had been a close hunting partner to her family and always kind to the children. He had been murdered by Yupikut raiders shortly after ice-melt of the year before.

"Ah, Nalungiaq, why do you pass among us again?"

No answer. The name laid bare before him, Old Manatook at last glimpsed the offending spirit lurking behind Putuguk's left eye. "Hmmf," he said. "No matter. I shall have it out!"

He turned to the semicircle of Anatatook who sat before the platform. One guilty face leapt out from among the rest.

"Mequsaq!" said Old Manatook. "How have you offended Nalungiaq?"

Mequsaq's hands flew to his cheeks. "Me?" he protested feebly. His eyes darted wildly in his face, then settled full upon Old Manatook. "It is me!" he said, as if he'd suddenly found a revelation. "We had no newborn child in the family. So when Nalungiaq was killed I gave his name to a pup in the litter…"

"And?" demanded the shaman.

Mequsaq's narrow eyes bulged slightly with realization of his error, his jaw sagged. "But the pup died, and I gave no more thought to the matter."

Old Manatook glanced at Alaana. Alaana nodded. She understood. If a name was not passed on within one year of the death, it may turn into *agiuqtuq*, a twisted spirit causing sickness and death.

"Now we come to it," said Old Manatook. As he stretched up his hand, the wide sleeve of his red parka settled at his elbow. Alaana noticed his wiry forearm, the pale skin frosted with fine white hair, tensed as if he were drawing something tremendous down out of the sky.

"I stretch forth my hand…"

Alaana noted the way the shaman spoke the words as if with great effort. Old Manatook's ability to carry the audience along and inspire them had a decisive effect on the people. The correct pitch of voice and intonation, the confidently erect stature, the proper gesture, the blood red parka. It was all there, as Old Manatook spoke these words:

"I stretch forth my hand,
Through fear and woe
Through hope and sacrifice,
We seek the way — Guide us!
Those who lay beyond, guide us.
I put forth my foot,
To step across the divide!"

125

As Old Manatook stood before the people, one mukluk raised above the packed snow floor, his eyes seemed to lock gaze with all of them at once. He held that expectant pose, ready to take that fateful step on their behalf, as the heart of every person in the room skipped a beat. Then he launched into a complicated invocation, his head and arms swinging in wide circles almost too rapidly to see. Alaana tried to follow his meanings but couldn't understand half of the words; she did not yet understand all of the secret language of the shamans.

She alone saw the change in Old Manatook's aura. Like sunlight reflected off the snow, his soul had grown bright enough to burn the eye. The old shaman went wild, frothing at the lips, the violent jerking motions of his head sending spume flying across the *karigi*.

The people were roused to sympathy for poor Putuguk, suffering under the torments of the revengeful name-soul of Nalungiaq. They knew the sufferer was in good hands with Old Manatook. Alaana felt it too. With renewed gusto she led them in a reprise of the chant: *"Halala, halalalee, halala, halaalalee!"*

Kigiuna repeated the words of the chant, though they engendered little feeling within his own heart. He tightened the muscles of his face to mimic the enraptured expressions of those around him. He shook a balled fist in time with the rest of the crowd, so no one would realize he stood apart.

He wished for Putuguk's recovery as much as any of the others, perhaps even more. After all, he was one of the few who supported the old man's family with gifts of food and supplies. Yet on any ordinary day, many of the people in this tent spoke in low tones of Putuguk's inability to provide for himself, his unsociable manner, his rough treatment of Tikiquatta. To Kigiuna, all of this, their earnest chanting and posturing, were gestures that rang somewhat false.

Kigiuna glanced at Alaana, who sat near the head of the platform. A seriousness of expression transformed his young daughter's face, which was not what anyone would consider pretty in the first place, into a distorted gloomy mask. Prior to the death of her sister the girl had always been a sort of a carefree spirit, and it saddened Kigiuna to think that innocence had so quickly been stripped away. Alaana wore a ceremonial parka that was yellowed and ill-fitting and bunched awkwardly about her arms and shoulders. A faded curl of grey pelt lacing the neckline suggested the dress had formerly belonged to Wolf Head. To Kigiuna, his daughter's distorted outline was symbolic of the misguided direction the lives of the Anatatook, and his family in particular, had taken under the stewardship of Old Manatook.

It was clear to him that Alaana felt much the same. Anyone could see that her new-found responsibility sat as awkwardly on the girl's shoulders as her too-large outfit.

The voice of Amauraq, as she sang out beside him, was one of the loudest in the tent. Kigiuna thought his wife listened too much to the whispering of the old women, who proclaimed spirits at every turn. But while her behavior and reputation were his responsibility, he had no desire to dictate her beliefs. Let her chant and sing, if that's what she wanted.

Let them all chant and sing if it made them feel better.

And there was Old Manatook, leaping and cavorting around the platform. As he cried out to his guardian spirit Tornarssuk for inspiration, he lapsed into a fair imitation of a white bear. His growl was impressive, nearly indistinguishable from that of an enraged animal. The shaman's face contorted terrifyingly, making his eye teeth seem to have grown longer.

And there was Alaana, at the head of the platform, driving the people on. Kigiuna had always presumed that Alaana shared his sense of skepticism toward the mysteries of the spirit world. His daughter had always pestered Civiliaq with questions on the matter, much to the cocky shaman's unending irritation. She had even accused Civiliaq of a false healing right there at the sick bed of her sister Avalaaqiaq. And now, there was Alaana, drum in hand, leading the chant.

CHAPTER 13

A GILDED ARROW

Alaana led the chant to a fever pitch. The crowd became more and more desperate for the release that only a cure for Putuguk would allow. She felt the strength of the people flowing into Old Manatook. Their heartfelt cries spurred him on, whipping his mind into a frenzy, surging in a flood tide, carrying him into the trance state.

"Tornarssuk! Tornarssuk!" he cried.

He channeled their enthusiasm across the link so that it might strengthen Putuguk's troubled soul. The time of liberation was at hand.

"Tornarssuk! Tornarssuk!" he cried, again and again. "My guardian spirit, the master of the polar bears, is never far from me. Acting through me, Tornarssuk will reach deep within Putuguk and rip out the offending spirit."

Again, Old Manatook intoned the ritual words. This time he spoke for them all:

"We stretch forth our hands,
    We put forward our feet,
    Guide us. Guide us!"

Alaana sensed the rise and flow of energy within the tent, as a fish must feel the eddies and currents of a tidal pool. The tide swept forth from the people, raging toward the shaman who directed the flow into the heart of the stricken man. Old Manatook was the center. His back was turned to Alaana, a silver portal swirling all around him.

Alaana's ears were filled with a great rushing sound that drowned out the voices of the people. An entrance to the realm of the spirits gaped before her. The grotesque moaning and sighing of the long-dead called to her from across the divide. On the other side a frightening impression of the great spirit Tornarssuk loomed over them. A gigantic figure covered in matted white fur and bathed in starshine, seething with unbridled power and fury. Carrion-breath that stank of fresh kill. Enormous teeth and pointed black claws.

She stared up at the immensity of the spirit. All the air left her lungs. Surely this was not something that the eyes of human beings were meant to look upon. Her heart pounding, she struggled for breath. The gigantic spirit-bear swung its huge black eyes down toward her, eyes that glittered with the light of stars.

Old Manatook's voice rang in Alaana's head saying, *"You should know this spirit. Trust me. Just take the step."* One step. But what frightening and unknowable things awaited her on the other side? It felt too much like falling from a great height into an unknown abyss of utter darkness. How could she trust Old Manatook would be there to catch her?

Her head dizzying, Alaana swayed on the verge of passing out. It seemed too much like death. To proceed voluntarily toward death, to take that fateful step, was too difficult. And then it was too late. Old Manatook had found the solution already. The deed had been done.

The cause of the trouble, having been extracted from Putuguk's soul, lay writhing in Old Manatook's outstretched hand. From the elbow upward, the shaman's arm appeared blanketed with white fur, and clutched in the black claws of his fingertips was the *agiuqtuq*.

The sight of it caused Alaana to retch in horror.

"I see nothing," whispered Kigiuna. He nudged his wife's shoulder. "Do you see it?"

"Of course not," replied Amauraq curtly, irritated that he had interrupted her rapture. "Something like that, surely all eyes must be blind to it but the shaman's."

Old Manatook held his trembling hand on high, clenched in a position resembling a claw. Though the fingers wrapped themselves around empty air, the old shaman stared intently at the hand as if it throttled some venomous catch.

Alaana's face had gone deathly pale. Kigiuna started to rise from the ground. If not for Amauraq's restraining hand pressing hard on his shoulder he would have rushed to his daughter's side. He shook off her grip, but the warning lingered. Not here, not now. He held himself in place.

His little girl was wide-eyed with terror. But of what? There was nothing there! What did she see? What was happening to her? The chanting, the lifting of heads — those things seemed harmless enough — but he would not stand for Alaana being tortured with fear over things that most likely didn't even exist.

He stood up.

Alaana gagged as the bitter taste of bile rose in her throat. Not more than an arm's length away, the *agiuqtuq* was the most horrible thing she had ever seen. It writhed and twisted at the end of Old Manatook's arm, threatening at any moment to break free of the shaman's grip. A quivering shape composed entirely of blood, resembling nothing that had ever lived on this earth, it moved with the desperation of a mortally wounded animal, thrusting its crimson tentacles first one direction then another.

Old Manatook tightened his grip on the corrupted name-soul. In his opposite hand he took up a gilded ceremonial arrow, pointed at both ends. He slammed the base of the arrow into the driftwood platform beside Putuguk's head. Then, with a sharp, confident motion he impaled the *agiuqtuq* onto the upturned barb of the arrow. He stepped back, and Alaana could see his shoulders trembling slightly in the aftermath of the effort.

Impaled on the stick, the name-soul no longer seemed quite so terrible. Drawn forth by Old Manatook's hand, brought out into the world, exposed and alone, it shrieked and trembled. The *agiuqtuq* was afraid. In a horrifying way Alaana recognized the essence of Nalungiaq within the shifting mass of red jelly. Nalungiaq, who had always been good to her, offering a gift or a joke, and smiling down with kind, soulful eyes. Poor, dear, Nalungiaq.

Old Manatook lost no time. He yanked the arrow from the wood, lifting the ceremonial bow, and notched the arrow.

"This dart will speed Nalungiaq's name on its way to the Moon," he said, "where it shall reside until it sees that I have made amends for the improper treatment it has received from his family."

He shot the arrow up through the vent hole. Alaana noted the angle of flight carefully. The arrow had been aimed so that it would come down far from the camp, out of the way of the dogs and tents.

A few of the men grunted encouragingly as the missile was released. All eyes went to Putuguk. Old Manatook, perhaps knowing the result already, gazed instead at the faces of the crowd as they flushed with relief and happiness.

Putuguk sat up on the platform, rubbing at his eyes with the heels of his hands, and a great cheer rose up within the *karigi*. The excitement nearly burst the tent skins.

***

To Alaana's delight a celebratory feast followed the spirit-calling. Unfortunately she couldn't stop to participate. She had shaman work to do.

Evening was drawing near, but it was still warm enough that hoods were thrown back to reveal smiling faces. Children ran back and forth outside the *karigi*. Women cut up arctic char fresh off the drying rack, passing out the morsels of red meat as fast as they were grabbed up.

A satisfying feeling of harmony filled the camp. Laughter rang out and gossip was exchanged on light-hearted subjects that strictly avoided the sensitive disclosures of the spirit-calling. Several joyous singers competed for the attention of the crowd but, judging by the cheers of the men, Tugtutsiak's deep, melancholic voice won the day.

The air swarmed with clouds of summer mosquitoes. Alaana sidestepped Maguan and his friend Ipalook, who were doing an energetic dance that incorporated the swatting of the annoying pests as part of the routine.

A group of women, a few of them heavily pregnant, tended a big pot of caribou ribs. They had a real fire going under the cooking pot, a rare sight, using dried willow shoots gathered the previous spring. The tantalizing smell of sizzling snow goose filled the air.

Putuguk stood near the pot, talking with his daughter and Kigiuna.

"How do you feel?" Kigiuna asked.

Putuguk smiled with the few half-rotten teeth that remained to him. "Tired, old, barely able to walk."

"Good," returned Kigiuna, smiling. "All is well again. We were worried."

Putuguk looked around at all the happy faces. "It's good that people still care."

"Of course we do," said Tikiquatta, "You should have seen

133

them, Father. All in the *karigi*. All worried for you. And Old Manatook transformed himself into an enormous white bear, right there in front of all of us."

Kigiuna clicked his tongue against the back of his teeth, indicating that women should not intrude into men's conversations. He snickered at Tikiquatta's silly, wide-eyed expression. He thought Old Manatook's impersonation of a bear hardly ranked as a transformation. "But what happened?" he asked of Putuguk. "What did it feel like?"

"I didn't feel anything. I was asleep."

"But you wouldn't wake up…"

Recognition creeped over the old man's eyes. "I remember a bad dream. A bad taste in the mouth."

"What kind of bad taste?" asked Kigiuna.

"I don't know. It's not important. I woke up."

"And the dream?"

Putuguk's craggy face sagged under a dreadful far-away look. "A dark shape was over me, pressing me down. It was like thick black smoke, choking my air, and a huge hand with fingers as wide as tent poles, holding me still, wanting to crush the life out of me. It chills me to think on it too much. I don't want to remember."

"Leave him be," urged Tikiquatta. "He shouldn't speak of it. Do you want him to fall ill all over again?"

Kigiuna took offense at her tone but Putuguk said, "She's right, she's right. Just a bad dream in the night. All is well now."

Aquppak ran up to his grandfather. Having begged a choice rib from the stew pot he presented the steaming prize to Putuguk.

Alaana headed away from the camp, passing close to the kennel. The dogs had all burrowed into the snow bank under the kennel posts to escape the raiding mosquitoes. They howled for their share of the food. Alaana chuckled, thinking she much preferred their noise to Tugtutsiak's horrible singing.

134

Sometime later, Kigiuna circled the outskirts of the camp. His daughter's trail was not difficult to find. The soft, wet snow melted a little more each day, erasing most of what had gone before, but was still deep enough to set new tracks.

He made his way down a slope toward a shallow valley to the west. He saw no one out on the plain. The onrush of dusk limited visibility, and there were too many hillocks and rocky escarpments between the camp and the distant cliffs, already in deep shadow, where sight of the girl could be lost.

Kigiuna kept up a brisk pace. Usually a long walk across the barren, windswept tundra went a long way toward soothing the irritations of camp life, but even that small enjoyment was impossible for him now, so worried was he about Alaana's disappearance.

It didn't surprise him that Putuguk could remember nothing, as if his ordeal had never happened. Maybe nothing had happened, just a bad dream in the night and a foul taste in the mouth. But what had caused that taste? Had Putuguk eaten tainted food? Or had something been put into the food to make him sick? It occurred to him that all of this could perhaps be Old Manatook's doing. Poisoning Putuguk, and then creating the illusion of having cured him to make himself look important.

It wouldn't do to voice such suspicions in front of Putuguk or Tikiquatta, so Kigiuna had stilled his tongue, swallowing his own bad taste in the mouth. He was already disliked by some of the families. People had distrusted him ever since he was a child because of his blue eyes. Add to that a few lapses of temper in his younger days, certain rash actions and loud words which had earned a reputation he'd never been able to shake. It didn't seem to matter how freely he laughed and joked with the other men or that he did more work than any of them. They still thought him hotheaded and as much as he fought to hide it, he knew his temper occasionally seeped through the cracks in his smile.

For the same reason he dared not oppose Alaana's training. Old Manatook's influence was a force more powerful than the tides, and more dangerous. If one angered the shaman it was too easy to become outcast. And to be outcast was to starve. No man can hunt seal by himself, unless he knew precisely which air hole it would come up.

And also there was that thing the old shaman had said, his warning that Alaana might die if she didn't complete the training. Kigiuna was not certain enough of his skepticism to hold forth in the face of such a threat. How could he be certain in disbelief? There would always be the nagging doubt that he was missing something through some fault of his own, a lone skeptic left out of the mysteries the others could all comfortably share. What were the stars in the sky? Why did the sun hide itself for half the year? Some things were not meant for anyone to know. But of course that didn't stop certain others from pretending they had all the answers.

He came to a stream of run-off cutting across the valley. The water was ten paces wide and knee-deep. He had no desire to wade across but, stooping to examine the footprints carefully, he found Alaana had crossed here on her fool's errand and not yet been back. He removed his *kamiks* and trousers and set forth across the icy stream.

On the other side, he took advantage of a convenient rock to dry his legs. As he sat rubbing the cold away, he had a stray thought of his own father, who had perished in water during a whale hunt. Kigiuna had been only six winters when his father, Ulruk, had left for the hunt, cheerful and exuberant as ever, and had never returned. The sea had swallowed him whole.

Kigiuna laced up his boots, jerking the thong tight. He felt a little bit like a seal in a stewpot. Tugtutsiak held too much influence over the Anatatook and enjoyed exerting his power, perhaps a bit too much. And the shamans were just as bad, slinging their omens and portents.

The ice and snow, the sharp bite of the wind. A belligerent seal, a charging musk ox. These things were real. The hunt was tedious enough, the struggle for survival difficult enough without invisible spirits adding to men's troubles. It seemed the shamans never really prevented anyone from getting sick, and by his count just as many died as got better. If a shaman could hunt and pull his own weight, as Kuanak had always done, then that was a man he could respect. Otherwise, Kigiuna believed the importance of shamans was overstated and often abused.

The Anatatook's former shaman, Civiliaq, had been the worst in that regard. It was widely held among the band that he could fly through the air. At every sighting of a strange light shooting across the night sky he later proclaimed it had been himself, soaring across the heavens. Kigiuna noticed he always took off and landed out of sight of ordinary people, usually from behind one of the tents.

Civiliaq also claimed he had once fought off three Tsungus in an ambush by removing his right arm and using it as a weapon. No one had directly witnessed this marvel, but nearly everyone believed the story and several people claimed to have relatives among the Tsungus who would swear to having seen Civiliaq detaching his limb and putting it back on again. Ridiculous.

And now Old Manatook was filling Alaana's head full of this sort of nonsense. Kigiuna felt a renewed urgency to find his daughter immediately. He wished he had set out earlier — now he could see only a little way ahead in the dusk and would have to stoop and follow the trail closely, making for slow progress across the plain.

He noticed a dark spot moving toward him in the gloom. He thought perhaps it was Alaana but dared not call out to her on fears that it might be a wandering bear. He stood still for a moment, but the figure was quickly approaching. Indeed it was Alaana.

The girl approached her father.

"Let me see," Kigiuna said. Alaana produced the gilded arrow she had been hiding behind her back.

"I would have thought this would be on the Moon by now," said Kigiuna dryly.

"The arrow is still here, but the spirit has flown on its way." Alaana spoke the words hesitantly, in a slightly apologetic tone. But, Kigiuna realized, Alaana wasn't reluctant to explain her own actions; she was sorry for her father's disbelief.

Without touching the thing, Kigiuna bent to sniff at the arrow. Then he took it, turning it over until satisfied it was just an arrow. He wanted to point this out to Alaana, but he knew what she'd say. He wanted to ask what Alaana had seen on the end of that stick, but was afraid of what he would hear, of the earnest look of devotion that would shine in his daughter's eyes, that same rapture he'd seen in the *karigi*.

Kigiuna threw the arrow down. The weighted point plunged into the snow, standing the arrow upright where Alaana could easily find it later. He pressed his daughter's chilblained fingers in the warmth of his own hands for a silent moment. Then, with a commanding jerk of his head, he said, "It's late. Come inside now."

CHAPTER 14

SPIRIT OF THE STONE

Alaana pumped her legs hard, putting on a burst of speed. She caught up to the ball, corrected her course and kicked it again.

"Come on Iggy, you can make it," she called over her shoulder.

Iggy whooped in dismay, the sound trailing along behind. He had no chance of winning, being so fat and slow, but as usual he plugged away with good humor. Foot races almost always belonged to Aquppak. But this time, Alaana thought she might have a fighting chance to win.

Not even the freezing slush oozing down into her *kamiks* could dampen her spirits. It was good simply to be able to run free. The summer was the only time for it, with the snow only ankle-deep and soft as beaver pelt. She drew in deep gasps of the chill air. Old Manatook had gone off on some secretive journey, as he frequently did, offering no details about how long he'd be gone. For Alaana this was a welcome break from the endless recitations of lore, listening for messages carried on the spirit of the air and drumming, drumming, drumming, and none of it going well. She didn't want to be out on some dreary plain with Old Manatook. She wanted to be right here, doing just this. Having fun with her friends.

They were halfway across the course now and approaching

the thin pole of driftwood that marked their goal. Alaana was leading Aquppak by a few paces. If only her ball would last out the race. Already the seams were splitting, with tufts of caribou hair spilling out. She tried kicking it a little more carefully, but a ridge in one of the drifts sent the ball bouncing off the wrong way. She darted after it.

Her advantage this day was the fact that Arlu, one of Anaktuvik's dogs, had attached himself to Aquppak. Arlu meant 'Killer Whale'. The dog had earned the name because of the big black spots that adorned his white coat and because of his ferocious character. Several times already Arlu had gotten between Aquppak's legs, threatening to bring him down.

In an earlier time Anaktuvik's dogs would have been chasing Alaana, but no longer. All the pack animals had acquired an aversion to her; they shied away when she came near, would not get into harness if she held the traces, and their dislike stopped just short of growling at her as if she were a stranger. Old Manatook had said, "It's the taint of Sila. The dogs can smell it on you. Sila is not evil, but he is powerful and unpredictable. The Walker In The Wind is the spirit of chaos, of winds blowing both this way and that, of blizzards going forward and back and around again, of something over here briefly and then over there. He represents the fury of the unknown, but dogs are simple creatures. Such chaos their hearts can not abide."

Alaana had suggested that Sila also stood for justice.

"Perhaps," Old Manatook had answered, "but what do dogs care for justice?"

That the dogs could smell Sila on her was a good sign, said Old Manatook. It proved that the connection was still strong. There had been reason to doubt it. Apart from their initial contact during the fever Sila had not yet shown himself to Alaana again. And that was worrisome. A shaman may use helper spirits, but a guardian spirit should be the strongest contact a shaman possessed.

Soon would come the time of Alaana's initiation. If Sila didn't show himself in full support of her, Alaana could not become a shaman. Alaana thought maybe failure would be for the best. As intriguing as it was to learn of this new world of spirits and magic that had opened up before her, she had no real desire to commit her life to such work. The shaman walked a lonely path, apart from all others. There were no half measures when it came to the initiation. It was all or nothing. And if she should fail, her father's objections and worries would be laid to rest, smoothed over like a pallet of fresh snow, and forgotten. The Anatatook could find another shaman, and she could go back to being a normal person again.

Alaana and Aquppak were both nearing the pole, running practically side by side. Arlu beggared off as Aquppak gained on Alaana. Now it was just the two of them, faces pink from exertion, the mist pumping in and out with each breath. This was not the time for gentle kicks, decided Alaana and she belted her ball as hard as she could. It was a good ball for kick racing, larger than most, made of soft sealskin scraps, some dark brown, some tan. Her mother had been sewn it with loving care, the colored pieces forming an intricate pattern. Alaana didn't care how pretty it looked, she only hoped the stitches would hold a little while longer. But at the last moment the ball burst against a sharp ridge of crust, spewing the hair in a spiral out into the air, and dashing her chances for a rare victory.

Aquppak danced around the finishing pole, out of breath and laughing. He made a loud victory sound like the hooting of a night bird.

"Hai! That was great! Nobody can beat me," he said. "It's like I have wings." Aquppak stuck his arms straight out like a bird gliding this way and that.

Alaana was only mildly irritated by his silly capering. "I

almost won," she pointed out.

"Sure, with your dog snapping at my crotch!"

"My uncle's dog."

"You can't beat me Alaana, and you never will."

Alaana bent to pick up the deflated remains of her kick ball. "It was a good race."

Aquppak uprooted the driftwood pole, hefted it as a spear and sent it flying across the open space. "So I said," he replied, smiling. "A great race."

He kicked a thin line of slush at Alaana's knees. "Don't worry, I'll still let you tag along behind me any time."

Alaana kicked some slush back. She hadn't expected to win anyway. It was enough to be with her friends doing normal things for a change instead of sitting in a darkened tent with Nunavik or tramping some long way across the tundra so Old Manatook could show her where to find and harvest some obscure root, herb or berry that was no good for eating.

"Come on, Iggy," urged Aquppak, "You can still make it." He did a pantomime of running in ridiculously slow motions.

Iggy made no move to get up. He had plopped down in the snow far behind, claiming exhaustion. Alaana trudged along behind Aquppak as he went to retrieve the pole. They caught up to Iggy at the crook of the river where a group of other children were gathered.

Mikisork and his cousins were playing at shaman. One of the older boys was in the center of the group spinning himself around and around. When he finally stopped, his eyes had gone crazy in his head and he could barely stand, he was so dizzy.

"I've gone out of my body," he announced. "I'm flying! Nothing can touch me!"

He spun some more, making a wobbly arc before the others.

"Everything's gone," he said, shakily. "Everything's gone."

He fell to his knees, retching. The children cheered.

"You do it Alaana!" said Iggy. "You'd be great at it."

With a low grunt, Alaana refused. The game was truer than they knew. The spinning did produce an altered state of perception. To Alaana, spinning around was one thing she could no longer do. The motion played havoc with her spirit-vision, causing flashes of light both agonizingly bright and painfully dark.

"You'll never be the shaman," said Tugtutsiak's third son, Oaniuk, "You won't even spin around." His starkly dismissive tone stabbed at Alaana. It was such a simple thing to them. Spin around and be the shaman.

Alaana's eyes met Mikisork's. He shrugged as if to say, "What does it matter?"

Iggy said, "Let's play feats of strength."

This was Iggy's best game. He was stronger than anyone else in the circle. Alaana and the others hunted about the river bank for stones of various sizes, arranging them in order of increasing weight. The boys took turns trying to raise the stones above their heads. Alaana made a poor showing of it, Aquppak didn't even try, and second place went to Oaniuk. Iggy beat them all. The boys cheered him as he growled like a bear and swung his hands, shaped into claws, in the air.

Then Alaana had an idea. She remembered something Old Manatook had shown her a few weeks ago on one of their long tramps inland. They had walked for three days to get to a certain spot where star anise could be found, a plant whose aroma was particularly pleasing to the spirits of grazing animals such as the caribou. Old Manatook planned to teach Alaana the secret of finding the star anise in the dark by its scent alone.

After a long day spent scrambling over rocky ground they came to a huge ledge of soapstone. Old Manatook ran his hand along the glistening, smooth surface of pearly gray. He regarded the mound carefully. The rock was scarred where the Anatatook men had worked on it.

"I was thinking," he said to Alaana, "perhaps your brother's new wife might appreciate a nice soapstone pot."

Alaana, who was still out of breath from climbing up the hill, nodded her head absently.

"Let's see your knife, girl," said Old Manatook.

Alaana obliged, pulling out her little knife.

"My father made it for me," said Alaana, "It's a good knife."

"So it is," said Old Manatook. Fashioned from the rib-bone of a brown bear, wound around with a sealskin thong for a handle, the blade had a fair cutting edge which tapered to a neat point. Kigiuna, who was good with working antler and bone, spent a lot of time making tools and small toys for the children.

"Good enough," mused Old Manatook.

"For what?" asked Alaana. She had caught her breath and was eager to get moving again. The sooner they reached their destination, she reasoned, the sooner they could start back for home.

Old Manatook slapped the mound of soapstone. "Let's make your sister a nice new cooking pot. Cut off a big piece." He inspected the rough areas where the stone had been worked before and demonstrated to Alaana where she could cut off a sizeable chunk, large enough for a spectacular pot. By using the existing contours, it could be done without having to cut through too much stone. "Right here, I should think," he said, pointing out the exact location, "and come around to here."

"Now? Do it now?"

"Why not?"

"That's going to take a long time. What about the star anise?"

"It can wait," said Old Manatook. He settled down in a crooked niche in the rock-wall and closed his eyes. "Let me know when you're finished."

Alaana had no experience cutting soapstone. That was something the men did.

Did Old Manatook think she couldn't do it? With an exasperated sigh Alaana took up the challenge. She had seen her father do it, with long steady strokes of the blade, back and forth leaning down on the knife.

It was hard work. After a long time she had only etched a little groove in the soft stone. She blew the shards off, and watched them drift to the ground. They were long and thin like hair. At the base of the stone she saw something move.

She heard a tiny cry which sounded like, "Ooort."

Looking closer, she saw something move again. It was a small lump of gray soapstone, quite round, that seemed to have tiny arms and legs. She reached for the thing. It reacted with a start, but couldn't roll away fast enough, propelled only by such delicate limbs. She picked it up, finding it pleasantly warm in her hand.

"*Weyahok*," it said in a small, squeaky voice, "*Weyahok*." The word meant 'stone'.

Alaana couldn't see any mouth from which the sound might have come. The creature had no face.

"Is that your name?" she asked. "Stone? Or is that what you are?"

"Girl like," it said.

Alaana chuckled. "You like me, or do you mean I like you?"

Weyahok purred softly. It was the sound of tiny bits of gravel rustling down a slope.

"Put that silly little thing down, and continue with your task," said Old Manatook. He was balanced in the rock niche in a very odd position, his back along the ground with his long legs sticking straight up in the air, and Alaana had no idea what he might have been doing. His eyes were closed.

145

Alaana did as she was asked. She noticed Weyahok had climbed up onto her boot and nestled itself comfortably in the bend of her ankle.

When the bulk of the day had passed Alaana became too tired to continue. Her arms were aching. Old Manatook inspected her progress.

"That's a good start," said the old shaman. "I suppose you'll be able to finish it tomorrow."

"Tomorrow?"

"Yes, when else?"

They camped for the night in the lee of the cliff. Alaana was ravenous from the exertions of the long walk through the slush and the cutting of the stone. After a warm meal she fell right off to a welcome sleep, although Old Manatook wakened her several times in the night to hear about her dreamings. Alaana groggily related those she could remember, concerned mostly with trudging uphill and endless sawing at a gigantic mound of unyielding soapstone.

Next day, Old Manatook offered no help on the cutting. He sat cross-legged and in deep thought, gazing out along the countryside. Their vantage point allowed a striking view of the winding peaks and valleys and frosted hilltops of the area. At times he mumbled a few words, as if catching up on some bit of pleasant news or conversing with old friends. For Alaana the work had become slow and difficult due to painful blisters along the sides of her fingers. She might have brought her mittens had she known she was in for this type of work. The fatigue of her arms and shoulders was a dull ache punctuated with fire at every stroke of the knife. Her blade had become so worn there seemed not much point in using it at all. Finally she gave up.

"Knife's too dull," she announced, upset at having ruined the knife. Old Manatook took it from her without a glance. He stooped to inspect the progress on the stone. "Half a day more and you'll be through," he said dryly.

"Not with that knife," said Alaana.

Old Manatook handed back the blade. It was every bit as sharp as before. That was a neat trick, Alaana thought, and at least a useful one. But how had he managed it? Alaana might have asked, except the old shaman never answered such questions directly. Old Manatook caught her inquisitive look, and offered this enigmatic statement, "In time."

The shaman's estimate proved far off the mark. Perhaps he hadn't taken into account Alaana's tortured arms and shoulders or her raw fingers. At last, after working the rest of the day with breaks only for meals, the big piece of soapstone began to sag. With a triumphant blow Alaana snapped it off from the rest of the mound.

She offered the piece to Old Manatook for inspection. Now that the bulk of the day was gone; they'd have to make camp and sleep again before setting out after the star anise. At least there was no shortage of food, as Old Manatook had caught a pair of snow hares for their supper.

"It's a rough job," said the old shaman. "And poorly shaped for a pot. I suppose you might work it into a small lamp or some such, after a fashion. You'll have it done before year's end, I'm sure."

Alaana was undaunted. Pilarqaq might enjoy a new lamp of her own just as well as a pot.

"There is perhaps an easier way," mused the old shaman. At that he braced his long legs before the soapstone mound and, pushing up the sleeve of his jacket to the elbow, extended his gnarled hand.

To Alaana's surprise and fascination, the shaman's hand passed into the surface of the stone as if it were made of water. Old Manatook moved his hand around as if rummaging through a sack of old hunting equipment. At last he withdrew a perfectly-formed soapstone cooking pot of an elegant design.

"How?" asked Alaana in amazement. "How did you do that?"

Old Manatook smiled, his black eyes beaming beneath their snowy brows.

"How? I merely asked the spirit of the stone to give it up. He's a nice enough fellow when you get to know him, you know."

Alaana turned the pot over in her hands. "That's a nice looking pot," she said.

The little bit of the stone spirit still within the pot thanked her for the compliment.

"Let me show you something," Alaana said to the group of children at the river. She kneeled before the largest of the stones, one which not even Iggy could have hoped to lift.

"What are you going to do with that?" asked Oaniuk sarcastically. "Crawl under it?"

"You'll see."

Alaana could see the spirit within the stone, a dim feather glow deep in the heart of the rock. *Wake up*, she said to it in the secret language of the shamans, *Wake up and let me in*. The spirit was fast asleep and didn't wish to be disturbed. Alaana felt a momentary panic, thinking this stunt was not going to work. Once more she would be made to look foolish in front of everyone, especially Mikisork. He watched with keen attention, a slight smile of expectation crossing his lips. Alaana smiled back.

Wake up, wake up. She nudged the spirit of the stone with her mind, but again there was no result.

I'm coming in, she thought. *Just for a moment, I'm coming in.*

Alaana's hand passed into the surface of the stone, disappearing to the wrist. The other children gasped in astonishment, hung in silence for a moment and then burst into a babble of excited chatter.

At the same time, Alaana felt the mass of the stone collapsing around her hand. The spirit within the stone had no patience for being used in this manner, and Alaana knew what she had attempted was wrong. A shaman should never act in this way.

Alaana screamed with pain. Her hand, trapped within the stone, was being crushed. She couldn't pull it out.

"What's wrong?" shouted Miki.

Alaana couldn't answer. She glimpsed Miki's horrified expression through her own slitted eyes.

Let me go, she thought, *let me go*. It was no use. Her fingers felt ready to pop from their sockets.

She sunk her other hand into the pocket of her parka and clasped the carved tusk of ivory. *Nunavik*, she pleaded, *help me!*

"Oh, what have you gotten yourself into now?" answered the mystical walrus.

"Get me out!" screamed Alaana, in a terrifyingly pained voice. The shouts of the children, who could hear Alaana but not Nunavik, took on a panicked tone. Mikisork screamed. Iggy grabbed hold of Alaana's arm and tried to pull it loose.

"I can do nothing," said Nunavik, "Except to have cautioned you not to proceed with this foolish endeavor in the first place, had you bothered to ask."

Alaana grabbed Weyahok, who rested also within her pocket.

"Ooort! Help!" said Weyahok.

"Yes, help!" moaned Alaana. Her hand felt as if it was being crushed to jelly.

The little stone spirit flew into a panic. "Girl hurt. Ooort! Help! Brother Stone, nice stone. Nice."

That's it, thought Alaana. Suddenly realizing her mistake, she reached out again to the spirit in the stone. *Brother Stone*, she

149

thought contritely, *I shouldn't have disturbed your slumber.* It was all she could do not to scream again. She thought, *Please move aside and let me pass.*

The spirit in the stone purred sleepily.

Please, thought Alaana. *Please!*

The stone released its hold on her. Iggy, still tugging mightily, overbalanced and flew backward, landing atop Oaniuk. The older boy pushed him away, saying, "Get off. Fool!"

Remarkably Alaana found her hand whole and uninjured. The few children still at the scene seemed suddenly embarrassed by their own panic and fear. They looked at Alaana as if she'd been playing some type of cruel trick.

"Thanks Iggy," said Alaana, clapping her friend on the shoulder. "You really are a strong man."

Alaana met Mikisork's eyes, finding them the perfect mirror to her own. His cheeks, as hers, were wet with tears. She held up her hand to show it wasn't hurt and tried to smile. By the time she had wiped the water from her face Miki had already turned and run off, a tiny figure fleeing toward the camp.

Alaana stooped to retrieve Weyahok, who had fallen from her hand during the ordeal.

"Girl hurt?" Weyahok asked.

Alaana did not answer.

When Alaana returned to her family's tent, she found a tiny bracelet tossed onto the snow near the entrance. It was a tricolor bracelet made of strips of walrus, seal, and caribou skin braided together. She recognized the bracelet. She'd given it to Mikisork as a token of friendship.

Her mother's sister Otonia was visiting their tent. Seated on the platform at opposite ends of a kayak cover they were mending, they didn't notice Alaana.

"There's just something not right about that girl," Amauraq was saying.

"Oh, you're only being jealous," returned Otonia, "because she's so beautiful."

"Well, she's more interested in fussing with her precious hair than doing any real work, that's for sure."

"Her good looks are her husband's pleasure," remarked Otonia. "And Kigiuna's too. A well-kept young wife makes the reputation of the house."

"Tttt!" said Amauraq. "I just wish she'd put down that comb and skin some fish bellies once in a while."

"Jealous!" chided Otonia. "She seems nice enough to me. A nice quiet girl."

"Quiet? You should hear the inside of this tent at night. She snores like a bull walrus!"

The two sisters, having the identical soft trilling giggle, shared a moment of laughter.

"She can't sew worth a lick," added Amauraq.

"She'll learn. You'll teach her."

"I've tried. She's clumsy, I tell you. Her fingers are too fat for the work maybe."

"Oh, that's just you making her nervous, I think."

"I might make her nervous, but I doubt I'm making her stupid!"

Otonia chuckled. "Amauraq, you've got such a mean streak. I'll teach her, then."

"Fine. And you can feed her, too. She'll eat our stores flat, I tell you. And I'll not sleight the children to keep her in fat."

"You're terrible," said Otonia, still laughing. "Terrible, terrible. So mean!"

"Well, it's not as bad as all that I suppose," returned Amauraq. She stopped to bite off the line of sinew she'd been

151

sewing. "But I just think she's hiding something. She's beautiful, yes, but why wasn't she already married? And why were the Tanaina so eager to let her go?"

"The dowry—"

"The dowry wasn't so much as you may think. She can't even look me straight in the eye, I tell you."

"Oh, stop that. Maguan seems so happy…"

"Yes," admitted Amauraq with a smile. "He's a good boy. He's always been very lovable. Just like Itoriksak and…" She paused where Ava was concerned, then continued, "and my little Alaana."

Amauraq began to cry then, and Alaana knew it was because of Ava. She couldn't listen any more. She went outside.

She was determined to see Mikisork. Alaana made her way to his family's tent, hoping Miki would be inside. Tugtutsiak's tent possessed a rarity — a thin wooden plank for a door. The plank was not connected in any way to the skins, so Alaana moved it to the side and stepped in. Alaana stood in the entrance, silently shifting from foot to foot until the women noticed she was there.

Miki's mother, Aolajut, and a few of her cousins were seated in the center of the tent, busy cutting patterns out of a sealskin hide. Aolajut noticed Alaana at the entrance. She offered a dry smile.

"I was looking for Miki," Alaana said.

"Miki is doing work now," Aolajut said coldly, "with his father. It's long work. I don't think he'll have time to play with you anymore." As she spoke, Aolajut looked at Alaana without any emotion whatsoever.

Alaana didn't know what to say.

Aolajut added, "Tugtutsiak has already spoken to your father, but you might as well know. I'm sorry but he's called off the marriage."

Alaana was stunned. "What?"

152

"You and Mikisork won't be getting married. That's final."

Alaana couldn't believe it. Her first thought was that they could run away together. But no, out on the tundra there was no place to run. Two young people could never survive alone, and her father and Tugtutsiak knew everyone in the other bands. It was hopeless.

"But why not?" she asked.

"Don't you know? You're not stupid."

Alaana felt as if she'd just taken a wet slap in the face.

Aolajut continued, "What kind of wife would a shaman be? What kind of a mother? A woman has to mend the clothes and cook the food and look after the children, not chase around fighting evil spirits."

"The men shamans do their work."

"It's not the same. A woman doesn't send her soul flying outside of her body. What if you were with child? How would your soul leave your body then? What about the baby?"

"I don't know."

"There's a lot of things you don't know. People don't always marry who they're supposed to. Tugtutsiak is a very important man. He'll find another wife for Mikisork. If Old Manatook says we have to have a woman for a shaman, then so be it. But not in my house. Not for my son. I'm sorry." She turned back to her work.

Alaana was desperate to speak to Miki, but she remembered the frightened look in his eye that afternoon. And then his tears. Mikisork's face had already spoken with a fullness of its own. They had shared so many good times together, darting through the camp on secret adventures, playing with the dogs or pretending to be caribou, holding sticks to their foreheads as antlers. All of that was gone now, washed away in an instant. Miki was afraid of her.

And Tugtutsiak would find another wife for him. Just like that. Alaana felt as if she were a tiny auk, captured along the cliffs,

153

and someone had pressed their thumbs into her chest, crushing her heart.

She stood by the entrance for a few moments more, but no one offered her tea or said anything else to her. She went away.

She decided to try and sharpen some of her father's tools. It might not take too long, she thought, if the tools were willing and provided she asked the spirits inside them very, very nicely.

CHAPTER 15

FIRST JOURNEY

Kigiuna pressed his face into the caribou fur as he hauled it from the sled, wiping the frost from his cheeks. The short hairs, stiffly frozen, grazed roughly against his skin.

He lay the pelt down on the pile. The sleds were loaded high with caribou carcasses still thick with summer fat and the dogs were tired and irritable after the long pull. They snapped at each other between the sleds, which had been arranged in a semicircle before the meat rack.

Kigiuna felt little better than the pack animals. The men had been on the trail for ten sleeps, following a herd of caribou as they made their southbound migration before the freeze-up. His entire body was stiff and half frozen. All feeling had gone from his legs and hands, but his shoulders were on fire from driving the team.

The other men finished racking the meat and walked over to him.

"What's this?" asked Tugtutsiak.

"I've separated the furs by family," explained Kigiuna.

Nuralak, who was the leader of the other major family group in the community, nudged one of the piles with his boot. His long face was impassive, but he was clearly not pleased.

Kigiuna shrugged, struggling to control his irritation. How

dare they question his intentions? "The distribution is fair."

Tugtutsiak refused to even look, while Nuralak glanced cursorily and said, "I suppose."

"These are set aside for Putuguk's family," said Kigiuna, pointing to a few he'd reserved for the old and infirm hunter. "Three full hides, two white bellies, six legs. Isn't that what you would've done?"

"It is," said Tugtutsiak. "Just the same, it's not your place to divide our kills."

Kigiuna's anger flared despite his best effort to maintain a carefully crafted neutrality of expression. "I only wanted to get it over with quickly, so we can put away the dogs and go home."

"As do we all," commented Nuralak. "Let's say no more of it."

Tugtutsiak grunted softly.

"It was a great haul," said Kigiuna, even though there was substantially less meat than in previous years. He threw his hands in the air in a victory salute favored by the men, smiling broadly. Once again he found himself playing the fool to chase away whatever suspicion had been caused by the intensity of his emotions. To the Anatatook, an angry man was a dangerous man, a man to be watched closely, a man who could never be trusted.

"A great haul," agreed Tugtutsiak, in his usual smugly dismissive tone.

"I've seen better," said Old Manatook, who had suddenly appeared behind them.

"Here. We've set aside some furs for you and Higilak," said Nuralak, gesturing toward the pile Kigiuna had made for Putuguk.

The shaman waved them away with his hand. "No need. I've more than enough," he said. "Let's not forget Putuguk."

"There's plenty of meat," said Tugtutsiak, although he also knew it wasn't true. "We'll feast well tonight."

156

"Ahh, a warm meal will be welcome," added Nuralak with a sigh. "I've forgotten what my wife's cooking tastes like."

"I think we should store this meat here," said Old Manatook. "We'll be moving inland in two sleeps."

This sudden change of plan surprised all the men. Kigiuna wondered what might have happened while they'd been away.

"Store the meat?" asked Nuralak. "Why? Surely we'll find more caribou near the bay?"

"I'm not certain," said Old Manatook. His hesitation seemed slightly embarrassing. For a brief moment he appeared awkward and very old as he outlined his plan. "We leave a full half of the meat here. As soon as the hunters have had some rest, we move. Perhaps we can catch the herd on the far side of Big Basin."

"Why go so far south? So early?" asked Kigiuna sharply.

"If we miss the herd, we'll starve next spring. Our stores are low as it is."

"Let's send a scout," suggested Kigiuna. The reason Old Manatook wanted to store so much food suddenly became clear to him. It was a protective measure, just in case he was wrong. He didn't know where to find the herd. "Kuanak always used to go and scout before any big move."

"That was when there were three of us," said Old Manatook calmly. "Now I've too much to do all at once."

"We can send Maguan," offered Kigiuna. "He knows the way."

Old Manatook shook his head. "We can't wait. The omens are clear. We must move in two sleeps to catch the herd at the crossing."

Kigiuna looked to the other men for their opinions. A wrong move could be a terrible mistake. Nuralak's word carried a lot of weight, but he said nothing.

Tugtutsiak had final say on the band's movements. "We shall

157

do what he says," the headman said with finality. "Old Manatook is usually right about such things."

"Usually, but not always," grumbled Kigiuna. "If he's wrong—"

"Are you questioning my judgment?" asked Old Manatook, speaking in a perfectly calm tone.

"*Mitaanginnaqtunga*," said Kigiuna, indicating that he'd been simply joking. "Of course no one can be correct every time." He stepped away so that he didn't have to say anything more. He directed Maguan to pile their share of the skins on their sled and drag it to their tent while he saw to the dogs. As he unhitched the cross beam, his team followed eagerly behind, knowing their next meal would be delivered at the kennel.

"Omens," mumbled Kigiuna as he walked. He had no desire to follow nebulous signs that nobody but the shaman could see. Even Kuanak, who was a shaman himself, had always relied on scouts.

Kigiuna yanked at the traces to keep his lead dog, Tiggat, from following some stray scent. He gave the line an extra jerk, eliciting a startled yelp from the big dog. He told Tiggat, "Old Manatook says the omens are clear, but he acts as if he's unsure."

He put the dogs in their places, shouting at them to stop their jumping about. "*Qaluk, qaluk*," he said, assuring them they were about to be fed. By the time he tied them all up, Alaana had arrived with the food bag.

"Maguan told me he brought down two bucks," Alaana said excitedly.

Kigiuna took the bag and began tossing chunks of old trout to the dogs. They tore into the fish, powerful jaws crunching half-frozen meat. "He did well. He's got a good eye for—"

Kigiuna was surprised when Tiggat nipped at his hand, breaking the skin. He swung the food bag into the big dog's nose.

Tiggat whimpered at the blow and bowed his snout halfway to the ground.

Kigiuna stepped forward and kicked the dog in the ribs. It was difficult to gauge how hard he struck since his feet were still numb from the cold, and he felt unsatisfied. He gave the dog another shot, envisioning Tugtutsiak's smug expression as his foot connected. He wanted to give him one for the old shaman as well, but Alaana spoke, saying, "You don't have to hit him!"

Kigiuna faked another blow with his boot, pulling up short. Tiggat, whose head was already bruised and bloodied, flinched away. "Everyone beats their dogs," Kigiuna said. "Otherwise they wouldn't behave."

"Old Manatook doesn't whip his dogs."

"Is this what Old Manatook's been teaching you these days? How to be disrespectful to your real father?"

"No," Alaana replied, the word a frustrated whisper.

"Then what goes on in those tents on the hill?" Kigiuna spoke sharply.

"I can't speak of it."

"Is that so? I seem to remember a girl who was all too eager to break the rules before."

Alaana's eyes went wide. "I want to tell you. But I'm forbidden to talk of it, or something terrible will happen."

"That's what he says?"

"It's true," said Alaana, shaking her head. "I know that it's true."

Kigiuna snickered and resumed tossing the food at the dogs. A sizable piece landed directly in front of Tiggat. The big gray huskie looked mournfully at it but did not eat.

"He's been acting up all day," Kigiuna noted, now eager to change the subject.

"He's sick inside," said Alaana. "He's going to die."

159

Kigiuna looked askance at his big boss dog, squinting one eye. If what Alaana said was true, he saw no sign of it.

He leaned down and sniffed at the dog, but there was no reek of sickness. He turned to Alaana. "How do you know this?"

Alaana shrugged. "He told me."

"Shamanic knowledge is experienced, not taught," said Old Manatook. "Each to his own, I can only guide you on your journey."

"I understand," said Alaana.

"Laughable," quipped Nunavik.

"I'm ready!" insisted Alaana.

"One hopes as much, *ungarpaluk*," said Nunavik. The walrus leaned back thoughtfully, pausing to pick some remnant of a ghost fish from his front teeth with the edge of a flipper. "Be careful. There is a certain overpowering joy to the trance state. You must be able to resist it and keep going. Remember the objective of the journey is to bring back knowledge and power in order to help other people. It is a serious purpose."

"These realms are entered not for play, but knowledge," said Old Manatook.

"Is there an echo in here?" snapped Nunavik. "Didn't I just say as much?"

Old Manatook huffed. "And you've said more than enough. Quiet now. We need hear the drum, not your shrill, weedy little voice."

Alaana and her teacher sat side by side in the *karigi*, the special tent used by the shamans of the Anatatook. The air was moist and stuffy since the vent hole had been covered to dim the light. Still, midsummer could not be kept out. It took advantage of leaky edges, it crept in through the seams of the caribou hide, it crawled under the flap.

Alaana felt warm, wearing a light, tan-colored parka of short-haired caribou. Old Manatook was stripped bare to the waist. In stark contrast to the mostly hairless bodies of the other Anatatook men, his chest was frosted with curly white hair.

The sunlight made their task more difficult, but Old Manatook thought it important that Alaana embark on her first journey from this place, set right in the middle of the Anatatook camp, as a reminder that her power belonged to the people.

He rummaged among the drums and the masks arranged along the sides of the tent. The instruments came in all shapes and sizes, trimmed with animal bones and fur tassels. Every drum had its own beater, ranging from a slender shoot of whalebone to Kuanak's prized drumstick, covered with the skin of a wolf's tail. Each housed a companion spirit, revealed to Alaana's eyes in varied colors and textures depending on their powers and purpose.

Most of these belonged to Old Manatook and had been crafted over the many years of his lifetime. The equipment of Wolf Head and Civiliaq was arranged carefully off to the side. The helper spirits which had inhabited the drums had fled upon their masters' deaths, but the masks might still be used later, perhaps by Alaana, when she learned how.

"Deep breaths," said Old Manatook. He placed a large round mask over his face. The mask was made of wood with a rich brown color and had at its center a round hole that almost resembled a mouth. A series of concentric circles, cut deep into the wood, radiated outward from this central void. Eye slits were placed along the curve of one of the ripples. Behind them Alaana saw Old Manatook's smoldering eyes, alight with blazing soul fire.

The mask was old, very old. Alaana could sense its ancient power. The seasoned wood had a faint smell of crisp mountain air, charged as if caught in the moment just after it had been sizzled by lightning.

161

Allowing the drum to speak, Old Manatook said nothing more. The large oval drum had a deep bass note, a voice from far away, calling Alaana to surrender herself, to abandon all thought and care, and drift down and down. The rhythm was dull and unvarying, the pace exactly that of a heartbeat in deep slumber.

Old Manatook stopped abruptly.

"And this is important," said the old shaman. "Beware fanged reptiles at any cost. Anything with fangs must be avoided."

"And any spiders or swarming insects you may encounter," added Nunavik. "Pass around them or go back if they stand in your way."

Old Manatook grunted softly, indicating that Nunavik's interruption held some merit. "I should have mentioned the spiders. But the snakes are the main thing. They are to be strictly avoided. We won't be staying long in the Lowerworld anyway. We'll just traverse the tunnel, have a glimpse at what lies beyond, and return."

He took up the drumbeat once again. "Relax and let your mind drift. I'll show you the way. Success in journeying depends on a state of mind exactly between exerting one's self too much and not trying hard enough."

"I will beat the drum throughout your journey," said Nunavik, "keeping the way open for your return. When I make a string of five sharp raps, that is the signal for you to know the journey is concluded. You will then return."

"Deep breaths," reminded Old Manatook as he took up the rhythm once again. Alaana was tired and hungry, having fasted for an entire day in preparation for this exercise, and soon felt her head sway with dizziness. She let the voice of the drum take hold of her, its invitation so deep it rattled her body, numbing her consciousness, blotting out everything except the hoary voice of the old shaman.

"Visualize the tree stump. Do you remember? That trip we

took to go and look, the place where I coaxed the soapstone pot from the cliff face?"

"Yes," said Alaana. Her own voice sounded far away. "I remember."

"The hollow tree stump we found. You thought it strange, one solitary stump out there all alone, as wide around as a man is tall. Remember?"

"Yes."

"That memory shall be our portal. Visualize the stump. It shall be our entrance to the Lowerworld. We need not travel to the stump; its spirit can be brought here."

His words were soothing, soporific.

"Here it is before us."

And there it was. In the center of the *karigi* the gigantic stump had appeared. Alaana could feel its presence, so old and revered, rimmed by flaking, ancient bark. Now hollow and dark, but not empty. Never empty.

Still kneeling on the ground, Alaana peered down into its black depths. What mysterious recess lay there untended and undiscovered? She smelled rich dark soil, whose depths sheltered unimaginable creatures of myth and fable.

"The stump's roots go deep," said the old shaman, "See them slither and stretch like serpents, tunneling under the snow and ice, beneath the wall of everfrost where men can never go. We may wander there, not in body but in mind, yes, that is the way. Just like the roots, we go delving into lands of forests and rivers and lakes unknown, of strange creatures and peoples that dwell in another place, in another way."

The stump transformed into a gaping tunnel, a whirlpool of churning snow and earth being sucked down and away.

Alaana didn't need to be told what to do next. Her spirit, which had already drifted apart from her body, surged forward. The way opened before her, and she stepped into it.

Her *inuseq*, her spirit-form, fell down a long tube. Concentric rings of light and dark flashed by, their pulsations in time to Old Manatook's quickening drum beat. Alaana was uncertain whether she moved along the tunnel or if the body of the earth was flowing past her in the opposite direction.

The tunnel melted away, fading into a gray and dimly lit landscape. She caught a glimpse of a vast sea, with two rivers leading away in opposite directions. And then she was in the water, afloat in an ineffable sense of joy, an awe of the mysterious and fascinating world that lay opened before her, full of impenetrable secrets and profound truths.

Bliss! Her spirit, having left the body behind, roamed free. Anything was possible.

The sea was composed not of water but tiny crystals of all tints and hues — emerald and pale blue, tan and brown and radiant white — as if pure light had been captured in each grain. The crystals, smoothed by eons of ebb and flow, bathing her in truth and wonder. All her questions could at last be answered, all her troubles washed away by the endless scouring of the crystals. She was almost lost forever, but for the echo of Nunavik's warning. One must be able to resist this enchantment. Alaana wasn't sure she could turn her back on this, that she didn't have the strength in her to do so, but the deed was already done. The thought alone had been enough.

Another vortex opened beneath her, a slender whirlpool that took her down and down, spinning her *inuseq* in a dizzying spiral.

Her spirit-form took on a sudden weight and, with a grand thump, Alaana landed solidly in the Lowerworld.

CHAPTER 16

A VISIT TO LOWERWORLD

In the absence of any natural light, normal sight was impossible. But even plunged into a realm of total blindness Alaana had the power to lighten the dark, to see what others could not perceive. The spirit-vision rendered everything in shades of gray and purple which she found oddly disorienting. No sky hung above, just a ceiling of rock that marked the roof of a cavern. She could still hear the beating of the drum in the distance, echoing softly as it came down the tunnel. She felt lightheaded and uncertain.

"Manatook?"

"I'm here, Alaana, though you may not look upon me directly. I am merely a guide on this, your first journey." The old man's voice sounded strange, having taken on a peculiar muffled quality that echoed within the cavern. Alaana couldn't see her teacher. There was only a shape of blurred white hovering near her, wavering and indistinct as if someone were flapping a sheet in front of it.

"How much time do I have?" she asked.

"Hmmff. Time. You will have exactly as much, and not a moment more. Begin."

The cavern had a floor of dark gray stone strewn with tiny crystals, little bits of shell and bone, nut-cases and twigs. Alaana picked up a particularly fine, blood red crystal. It was roughly the size of her thumbnail. She slipped it into the front pocket of her parka.

Deep cracks lined the cave floor. Alaana felt one of her *kamiks* yanked from her foot. The laces had all been neatly cut. A thin black hand was struggling to draw the boot down into the crack, but the *kamik* was too wide for the slender opening and bounced away. Alaana lurched after it, but before she could grab it another slender arm shot up out of another crack, again in pursuit of the *kamik*. It groped blindly, knocking the boot further away.

"Heya!" she yelled.

The boot continued to move as more spindly, bone-like appendages emerged from the cracks and tried to force it down into the floor. Alaana dived after it again and again. In the end she almost reached it, but her desperate grab missed its mark and the boot was dragged under and gone.

She went down on her belly and peered into the impenetrable dark of the crack. After a moment she realized she was looking directly into a set of beady little eyes. The creature in the chasm twitched and its outline suddenly became clear. It looked like a hideously emaciated caribou, all ribcage and spindly legs ending not in hooves but thin-fingered hands. It looked as if it had been charred in a fire, the fur crumbling away like charcoal. On a slender neck sat an ungainly head crowned by a pair of stunted, thorny antlers. The nose twitched fitfully, the nostrils flaring above a slit mouth whose frown told of unspeakable sadness. But the eyes that stared back at her were not the large glassy orbs of an animal; the eyes were distinctly human.

"Manatook?"

"These are the *lumentin*. The souls of hunters who have taken caribou out of turn, without the permission of the *turgats*. Here their souls are merged with that of their prey in a perpetual torment. Mindless things, or so they seem. Leave them be. At the moment they appear content with only your boot."

"But if I've lost my *kamik* in this world, what will happen to my real boot?" asked Alaana.

"Thunder and lightning, child, they are both real! You have carried the spirit that resides within your boot to this place. If it does not return with you, you will find your physical boot much the worse for wear. With its spirit gone, the sealskin will be dried and shriveled away. You must heed this lesson well. If your *inuseq* were to be trapped in any of the other worlds you travel, your physical body would suffer much the same."

Alaana shivered, recalling what had happened to Kuanak. She looked into the rift again but the *lumentin* had retreated into the shadowy depths. She reached for the opening.

"Don't!" said Old Manatook. "Leave the *lumentin* alone. Give no more thought to them. They are more mischievous than dangerous, at least on this side. But these cracks extend to the Underworld on the other side, and they have a much different existence in that world. If you meet them in the land of the dead — beware their dark power."

"But isn't this the Underworld?"

"Certainly not. Would I be so foolish as to bring a novice to the Underworld on her first spirit journey? This is the Lowerworld."

Alaana glanced around the cave. Of the seven worlds to which a shaman's spirit might travel, five were aligned vertically. Both the Lowerworld and the Underworld, home of dread spirits and demons, lay below the physical realm of Nunatsiaq. The Upperworld and the Celestial realm of the Moon and stars hung above. The other two worlds, the dreamlands and the shadowworld, were more intimately connected. She had only Manatook's descriptions of the Underworld to go by but if there was some distinction between that dreaded realm and this place, she couldn't

167

find it.

"Ah, I see the cause of your confusion," said Old Manatook. "Perhaps it would be better if you went outside of the cave."

"Outside?"

The fluttering wraith with the old shaman's voice drifted toward an opening in the cavern wall some fifty paces away. Without his guidance Alaana might never have spotted it. It was just as dark outside.

As she passed through the arch of stone that described the opening, she merely passed from one cave to another. She entered a vast world-cavern. The sky was again made of gray stone, but that roof could hardly be seen at all because of the trees. There were trees everywhere. Trees!

Alaana had seen very few trees in her lifetime, excepting a lonely conifer or a dwarf pine or two, standing near the tree line at the far reach of the tundra. And even those, stunted by wind and snow blast, grew barely to the height of a child. But here, there were trees! An impossible number of trees, outlined in the pale moonlight of the spirit-vision. Etched by stark contrasts of purple light and deep shadows, Alaana could almost believe them carved into the rock of the cavern itself. That notion was quickly dispelled by the rustling of leaves as a squirrel leapt among the high branches. Joining overhead, branches and leaves intertwined like hands clasping, to form an arched canopy. Alaana was disappointed there seemed to be no such thing as scent in this place. She could only imagine the richness of fragrance she might smell among that varied and wondrous foliage.

She passed among the trees, noting the individual character of each. Here was one whose trunk was three trunks woven together like snakes, caught frozen in a race to the top of the cavern. Another forked into two competing stalks like rival brothers whose leaves, waxy and polished, gleamed silver in the twilight. And here

168

was another from whose mighty trunk wild branches flared at odd angles like flame. Here was one with purple leaves whose trunk was five trunks, a loving family whose boles spread up into the cavern far above.

An incredibly broad tree blocked her way. Its bark, thick and hoary, sculpted by time into an abundance of rough knots, shone silver in the pale dream-light. Standing beneath this giant, with its massive arms spread above, great and wide, until they flayed out like a tremendous fountain, Alaana was struck by the sense of a venerable patriarch, old beyond guessing, who had stood with grim forbearance as the paltry lifetimes of men flew by, generation after generation. Alaana thought she glimpsed a pair of wizened eyes peering at her from a deep cleft at the base of the trunk, but when she moved closer they were gone.

Something stung her bare ankle, as if she'd been stabbed with a pin where her foot went without a boot. She saw a rustle among the clutter of twigs and leaves that littered the rocky ground. A small figure darted through the underbrush to take shelter behind the mighty oak. It moved with a strange, waddling gait. She remembered the admonition against snakes, but she didn't think it was a snake.

"What was that?" she asked.

"Oh, just some foolish little creature looking for attention," replied Old Manatook.

"That's some rotten way of showing it," said Alaana. She pulled a thin needle of bone from the heel of her foot.

"Hmm-hum," said a little voice, "Play with us?"

Alaana circled slowly around the tree but the creature matched her progress, keeping the trunk between them.

High up on the massive trunk, a tree squirrel groused loudly down at her. It was dressed in a miniature parka. Having ridiculed her thoroughly, it fled back up among the boughs.

The creature that had been playing hide-and-seek with her peeked around the side of the tree. The strange little man stood only about as high as her kneecap. He had large friendly eyes beneath bushy brows, a nose so small as to be insignificant, and sharply peaked ears set quite near the top of his head. A tuft of gray fur ran in a strip along the top, to match the patches of scruffy growth on his cheeks. He was dressed in a gray parka made from some short-haired animal, belted at the waist, with a tail like a squirrel tacked to the rear.

"Hum-hum, visit with us," said another little voice. Alaana spun around to find another of these creatures standing just behind her. Before she could start toward it, the little man dove backward and disappeared into a hole in the ground. Alaana brushed away the twigs and dead leaves. It looked like a small squirrel hole going down between a gap in the rock. She paused with her hand poised above the burrow.

"Do squirrels have fangs?" she asked. "Didn't you say something about fangs?"

"You've nothing much to fear from those *ieufuluuraq*," said Old Manatook. "But there might just as easily be a snake down in that pit, you know."

She withdrew her hand. When she turned around there were four *ieufuluuraq* behind her. They all jumped back half a step. They stood frozen in wary poses, tiny noses twitching, watching for her next move. Laid out just in front of them was her lost *kamik*.

"Mmm-hum. Come. Come."

Alaana found the little men charming enough but Old Manatook had said that every journey between the worlds had a distinct purpose, whether it be apparent or not, and that it was up to the shaman to find out what it was. She doubted she'd been brought here to frolic with these little things, as much as she might've enjoyed it.

170

A long wailing cry rang out across the cavern, so twisted with anguish it seemed entirely out of place, though Alaana felt hard pressed to imagine any world where such a tortured sound might belong. The four very little men scampered quickly away. With a flash of bushy tails they were gone. The terrible screech has left a near-total silence. The only sound was that of the distant drum beat as Nunavik held fast to his duty, keeping the tunnel open.

"What was that?" asked Alaana.

"I don't know," returned Manatook. "From top to bottom, from the Outer Darkness to the smoldering center of the earth, I've never heard anything like that."

"What should I do?"

"You might start by putting on your boot."

Alaana slipped on her boot but couldn't fasten it. The laces were scorched where the claw of the *lumentin* had cut them.

She wandered for a time among the great trees, marveling at their size and complexity and the way they grew directly out of the bare rock.

The ground curved lower, running from a mild decline to a steep slope. The trees thinned as she reached the shore of an underground lake. Alaana was impressed by the enormity of the cavern that housed the Lowerworld. She wondered what other marvels lay in wait for her in this world devoid of light yet full of trees, where the sky might be more solid than the ground, where squirrels dressed as men, and men might be squirrels.

The lake lay quiet and serene, its waters untroubled by wind or wave, nor current feeding in or flowing out. There was no sound at all, excepting, over there, in the distance a quiet splash. A sploosh. Yet another splash. Alaana saw a figure in the lake, wholly unaware that it had been seen, frolicking in and under the water.

"Manatook?" she whispered, but the shaman seemed to have left her.

She made her way to the shore, surprised at how the rocky ground simply ended where the lake began, without any beach. She got the impression that the lake didn't belong, that it had perhaps been transported to the spot from somewhere else. From this closer perspective Alaana saw that the figure in the lake was in fact a young woman. From her lips came youthful giggles and mumbles of pleasure as she enjoyed the caress of the waters. Although she was a little embarrassed at watching unannounced, Alaana didn't turn away. Somehow this chance encounter felt right.

"Heya!" she called out.

The figure dipped under the water. Alaana, who hoped she hadn't startled the other girl into drowning, kept watching for her to come back up. She resurfaced right near the edge of the pool only an arm's length away. She was young and perfectly formed.

As the water dripped away from the girl's body, Alaana beheld the wrinkled flesh of an old woman, at least as ancient as Higilak the storyteller. The woman, walking with a pronounced stoop, went directly past, saying nothing. She bent and took an old skin from its place among the rocks and draped it over her bony shoulders. She deftly manipulated the skin, folding it over this way and that until she was completely clothed.

"Why don't you come inside and share a cup of tea?" she said, still facing away from Alaana.

"Do you mean me?" asked Alaana.

The woman turned. "Of course, you," she said kindly. "Who else but you? Dear child. You should call me Weeana, though it's a long time since I've heard that name spoken aloud. I'm not sure I should like to hear it again." She seemed momentarily confused, and remained staring at Alaana.

"Perhaps that was a mistake," she finally said. She gave Alaana an intense look, as if trying to see beneath the surface and determine her true nature. Alaana felt uncomfortable beneath her probing stare.

A wave splashed up from the side of the lake, breaking the old woman's reverie. "What would you call me, child?" she asked.

"Weeana."

"Ahh, it sounds not so terrible after all. Least ways, not coming from your lips. Darling girl. Come for tea. My house is just over here."

She led Alaana to a small house of packed earth and stone further up the shore. The entrance had no door and they passed into a room that could have been the kitchen in any Anatatook house. There were cooking things strewn about and a sizable larder heaped with fish and mollusks. From a large pot Weeana ladled some dark green tea into a pair of drinking cups and carried them into the sitting room. They settled onto neatly braided cushions of tall brown grass set atop slabs of bare stone. Alaana noticed the interior of the walls were packed with earth and sediment and a fair amount of worms could be seen working through them.

"It's a good house," Weeana said, "on a peaceful shore."

"Are you alone here?"

"My husband can not enter this house," she said plainly. "And my children... Well, that is a long tale and one which does not concern you, I'm sure. Have some tea."

Alaana took a sip of the tea. It was tasteless. She couldn't tell if the drink were hot or cold, and questioned whether she was really drinking anything at all. Of course, her body was only spirit and not flesh and blood. She listened carefully for a moment, making sure she could still hear the reassuring beat of Nunavik's drum.

"Now I'm wondering why you asked me that," Weeana said.

"What?"

"You asked me about my children. That was the first thing you asked. Even before you drank the tea."

Alaana peered down at the cup. Now she wondered if there

were something in the brew, and whether or not she should have partaken of it. Old Manatook was nowhere nearby. What kind of trouble was she getting herself into?

"I didn't ask anything about your family," said Alaana. "I was just curious about the house. I didn't expect to find a house here. I didn't know there were people down here at all."

"But what did you expect? I can't breathe underwater, you know."

"I didn't expect anything."

"Ahh," she said, "That explains much."

Weeana twirled the tea with her little finger and watched it spin in the cup. "As I said, I've been here for such a long time. It's so unusual for me to entertain guests, and you are an unusual sort of a guest. You're not a shaman. What errant breeze blew you my way, I wonder?"

Her comment confused Alaana. There was no such thing as wind or breeze in the great cavern of the Lowerworld. "If you're talking about Sila—"

"Shh! I don't mean anything of the sort. I'm simply trying to protect my family, as any mother would. I've a right to be suspicious, clearly, with the way you keep asking after them."

"I don't mean to be any trouble." Alaana plunked her cup down on the stone. "I can just go, if you like."

"Go? Without hearing my story? I don't think you can."

Alaana tried to stand up but it was exactly as Weeana said. She couldn't rise from the cushion. She wanted to cry out to Manatook for help but decided against it. It might not be wise to speak the old shaman's name in this company. Weeana seemed most preoccupied with names.

The old woman jabbed a finger at her. "Aha! That proves it! That proves it indeed." So saying, she flung her hand up in the air with a quick, sparrow-like gesture. She had completely forgotten the

174

tea, which splooshed out against the wall.

"Prove what? Let me go!"

"I'm not holding you here, child. I have no such power over you."

Alaana boiled with frustration. "You let me go, or Sila will come and—"

"Shh! No, not that one." She waved her hand at the air. "They say there is one who answers the prayers of the lost and the lonely. That he resides in a hidden place, somewhere deep within the earth. Some say that he is himself lost and alone. The First among the shamans."

"I've heard this legend from my teacher," said Alaana. "His true name is unknown."

"Yes, and that's for the best I think. Names have power."

"We call him the Long-ago Shaman," said Alaana.

"Call him what you will. But understand this. Many times in my despair I have called out to him. And you are the answer."

"No, I'm not. You're wrong. Let me go!"

"It seems I may only accomplish that by telling my tale. Listen.

"My father, who was named Qasiagssaq, was a lazy man. He was a poor hunter, having no patience to sit long on the ice when he might be safe and warm at home. His great goal in life was to marry me off and acquire a hard-working son-in-law who would see to his needs. My father had two sons already, but they were both equally as lazy as he, and the elder quite stupid and the other quick to anger. Who would want to marry into such a family?

"My father decided to marry me off to some wealthy foreigner in order to get a rich dowry. And so came a parade of suitors to our house, old men and those with many wives already, and ugly men with cruel eyes and sharp tongues and I would have none of them. And every time Qasiagssaq beat me for

175

disobedience, I would go and swim in the lake. For the water, to me, was not icy and cold but warm and consoling. The lake washed away my blood and my bruises both. In the evenings I would sit by the shore and sing. And as I cried, my tears mingled with its waters.

"And so I came upon the spirit in the lake, for lakes as you might already know, are as alive as anybody else. Oh, he was such a gentle soul. There was no anger in him, no violence, only serenity, only peacefulness, a love of life and the simple joy of being. And as I felt his warm embrace, how could I not fall in love?"

Alaana noticed a tiny spider-woman peering at her from around the corner of the stone on which the old woman sat. The spider strung a strand of web across a delicate niche in the stone and crawled back out of sight.

"My father grew so angry and frustrated at my refusal to marry he left me there when the camp moved on, thinking I would die abandoned and alone. To starve without food or anyone to take care of me. Did I say, he was a very stupid man?

"Of course the spirit in the lake was happy to take care of me, feeding me with fish and krill in abundance. He took me from that place and brought me here. For it was only a matter of time until someone would have come — my father or some wicked traveler, a murderer or a rogue, or a caravan of traders. Upon finding me, what would they do? You're young. Perhaps you don't know such things. They would come and the lake would not be able to protect me.

"Taamnapkunami, the spirit of the lake, took me to wife. And lo, these many, many years I have known a quiet happiness here in this place. You really should meet him. You must! Tell me, are you a good swimmer?"

"I do well enough," replied Alaana. This was a falsehood, for she had never swum in a lake in her life. Icy water was hungry and unforgiving, and no place for children. But it must have been the

176

right thing to say since it bought freedom for her limbs. She felt the invisible bonds restraining her arms and legs release.

Weeana brought her to the lake. The old woman made a gleeful sound as she dove in. In the water she was graceful and lithe. Wet, her hair appeared two shades darker than its formerly soiled gray color and her face, relaxed and at peace, seemed to shed its wrinkles and worry lines.

Alaana was apparently expected to follow the woman in. She thought instead of running the other way, but somehow she knew the lake wouldn't hurt her. And she really wanted to meet him.

She dove in, only to flail about in the water, awash in sudden panic at the fact that her feet couldn't touch bottom. Again she felt neither hot nor cold. She soon learned two convenient and reassuring facts: that she had no need to propel herself by strength of limb where thought alone would suffice, and that her *inuseq* had no need for air.

"You've an odd way of swimming, that's for certain," observed Weeana as she bobbed at the surface. "Awake! Husband, awake!"

She splashed wildly at the water, throwing spray halfway across the pond. "Oh, snoozing again I'm sure. It's rude, that's what it is. Taamnapkunami! Wake up!"

Suddenly, a brilliant luminescence surrounded Alaana, bathing the entire lake, the water, sea plants, the fish all in ghostly sea-green light. Alaana, realizing she was perceiving the soul of the lake itself, was stunned by the vastness of it.

"Welcome," said a voice deep and mellow. Its tone rang playfully of everlasting youth and effulgence. Alaana felt the water tickle at her spirit-form, a sensation both pleasant and strange.

"Mmmmmm. You'll forgive me," said the lake. "Since I have taken leave of my friends the river and the stream my waters are still. I grow so sleepy. I used to wander about a little and flow free. I used to come and go, ebb and flow and come and go. Before I took that woman to wife. Ah, but I've no regrets. That's the way of married life, isn't it?"

"I guess so," said Alaana.

"Welcome," said Taamnapkunami. "It's a girl! Haven't seen much of anyone in a long time, or was it just yesterday people used to come and swim here? I remember, I remember. Kayaks and nets, and hooks and lines. Makes me itch just thinking on it."

The lake tussled Alaana again, its bubbling laughter lifting her to the surface to deposit her beside Weeana's paddling form.

"Mmmmmm, unless I'm mistaken she's one of your people Weeana, my love."

"Anatatook?" she Weeana.

"You're Anatatook?" asked Alaana.

"It's long ago," she said.

"Your father, girl?" asked Taamnapkunami.

"Kigiuna."

"His father?"

"Ulruk."

"And his?"

Alaana thought for a moment. "Patagona."

"Mmmmmm, Patagona, Patagona. Didn't your father have a brother named Patagona, my love?"

"That's a common name," Weeana said.

"Yes, but that Patagona, some Patagona swam inside me. I'm certain he splashed here as a child."

"It's the fate of our children that brings this visitor to us, husband," said Weeana. "It is most important, I think, that she should see them. Would you let her see the children?"

"Why not?" said the lake. "As it is, I believe she's already family."

The lake took Alaana in eager hands and pulled her under.

Humming with fatherly pride, Taamnapkunami's idea of gentle seemed like a wild ride to his passenger. Alaana swooped this way and that, nearly crashing into every cod and flounder on the way down. It grew no darker the deeper she went, for all the way was still lit by Taamnapkunami's mellow light.

Somewhere near the bottom, their course took a sharp turn and they entered a large underwater cave. Here, affixed to the rocky wall, were huge orange sacs resembling salmon roe. There were at least half a dozen of them, each with something indefinable moving around beneath the oily membrane.

"Here are my beautiful little ones," said the lake. "My lovely babies. Careful you don't get too close, dear. Here I keep them in secret so that they may remain safe."

"There is no day or night in the Lowerworld," said Weeana. "There pass no moons, no seasons. Here, in the stillness of the lake, changing so little, it seems the lives of others flow swiftly by."

They stood at the entrance to the house, gazing back at the placid surface of the lake.

"The problem is this. Time passes ever more slowly for my children, for their sire is the lake itself. While he is eternal, I am not. I'm already old and growing frail. Who will take care of our children when I'm gone? Taamnapkunami will look after them until they hatch, I'm sure. But what then?"

"But what are they exactly?" asked Alaana.

"I don't know," the old woman returned gleefully. "They are not human, but that needn't be considered a shortcoming in this place. I only believe, as any mother would, that they are something wonderful. Something needed."

She patted Alaana on the hand. "Mark my words. They will be needed. But what do *they* need? That is the question you have come here to answer, I think. They will need someone greet them when they hatch, if I can not. When they come out into the world, a friendly face to meet them. That's all I ask."

"I can do that," said Alaana.

"Done!" Weeana said.

No sooner were those words spoken, Alaana realized the drumbeat in the distance had changed. The steady drone was gone. Hear now, the five long beats. Nunavik was calling her back.

Reluctantly Alaana allowed herself to be drawn away. Her return through the tunnel was swift and easy. She sped upward along the tube with no effort at all, as if the physical reality she had left behind was greedily drawing her soul back to its bosom. Almost immediately she returned to the *karigi*.

Old Manatook, having taken off the big wooden mask, was already putting away the drum. Nunavik bent close to Alaana, his flat, golden head moving rapidly about. The wide spacing of his tiny black eyes and the drooping tusks gave his face an overly concerned look. The Walrus On The Ice sniffed at her so closely his whiskers tickled Alaana's cheek.

"Well," he said, "you seem to have made it back all in one piece."

It took a moment for Alaana, lost in a sense of discovery and awe, to shake off the idea that she'd been dreaming. By now she had learned enough about traveling to know that she had not been asleep.

"That is, if you still have your tongue in your head," said Nunavik. "Can you speak? You might thank me for bringing you back safe and sound, after all."

Alaana found her voice. "It was incredible! There was this house and an old woman and a lake and—"

"You're welcome," said Nunavik.

"For what?" asked Alaana playfully.

Nunavik growled and shook his head, then shuffled off to the corner of the *karigi* to sulk.

Alaana turned toward her teacher. "But Manatook, where did you go? Why did you leave me alone?"

"I went looking for the thing making all that hideous noise."

"What was it?"

"I don't know. I couldn't find it. Perhaps it's not meant for me."

"You shouldn't have left her," said Nunavik.

"She made the return journey well enough."

"Oh, did she?" Nunavik shook a golden flipper in the air. "Did that all by herself I suppose? No thanks to anyone else? If the Old Walrus had gone wandering off, chasing after some mysterious noise or other, what then? Of course, goes without saying that wouldn't happen. That's taken for granted."

"Are you finished?" grumbled Old Manatook. "It's Alaana I want to hear from, not some cranky old bull. Girl, tell me everything."

"She promised them something," said Nunavik.

Old Manatook's eyes flashed. "You didn't? Not that crazy old woman?"

"I only said I would come back again," said Alaana. "There's no harm in that is there?"

"Beware obligations incurred in the other worlds, child," said Old Manatook, "They are as real as any. Take care you don't let them become too numerous."

"And what's that there?" asked Nunavik, jabbing a flipper toward Alaana's boot.

"Hmm?" said Manatook as he bent to pluck something from Alaana's *kamik*. It was the tiny spider-woman she had seen in Weeana's house. But as the old shaman held it up, Alaana could see that the poor creature had become bent and twisted, appearing now more like a bloated louse with a deformed face.

"Poor little thing," said Old Manatook. "Take her back, Nunavik?"

"What? You expect me to tramp all the way back to the Lowerworld now, as if I haven't been beating the drum all day keeping everybody safe. Just for this foolish little thing? Oh, I see. Too much trouble for your tired old bones, I suppose. So why don't we get the old walrus to do it?"

"Have a nice journey," grumbled Manatook.

He deposited the little creature onto a golden flipper. Nunavik looked sympathetically down at his new charge. "Well she is rather pathetic, isn't she? And of course you need your rest, Manatook. One trip is more than enough for a man of your great age and decrepitude. Wouldn't want you to strain yourself."

As if in response to Nunavik's tirade the tiny deformed spider-woman let loose a pitiful squeal of fright and madness.

"Come on, little dear," said Nunavik. "Let your old Uncle Walrus take you home."

With that, the walrus and the little creature both vanished.

"Now is time for you to tell your tale Alaana, and leave nothing out."

Alaana peered into the front pocket of her parka, looking for the brilliant red gem she had secreted there. She wanted to show it to Manatook, but now she found it had crumbled away to thin gray dust.

CHAPTER 17

TURGATS, TARRAKS, AND GHOSTS

That night, Alaana stirred restlessly under her sleeping furs. The men had all followed Old Manatook out on the hunt along the caribou trail. They were all gone —Kigiuna, Maguan and even Itoriksak. With only Amauraq and Pilarqaq beside her on the platform, the tent seemed empty and cold, the sleeping furs poor protection against the chill of night.

Mother acted so very differently when Kigiuna was away. She did not run the lamp at night. She said little, ate little, spending most of her time brooding and doing her work quietly. Even now Alaana thought she was probably not asleep but lost in worry, every so often releasing a sad little sob.

Pilarqaq was most definitely asleep and making quite a bit of noise as she snored contentedly.

Alaana thought of Mikisork, who had hardly spoken a word to her since the day her hand got stuck in the stone. He wouldn't even listen to her. And he wouldn't look at her.

So be it, she thought. What did she care about some silly little boy like that? She had other friends. And besides, she had more important things to do than run foot races and wrestle with children. She had done an amazing thing today. She had actually sent her spirit traveling outside of her body. She couldn't help but be intrigued by all she had experienced — the squirrel men, the old woman, the talkative lake, and their mysterious children. And Old Manatook had capped it off with a promise to show her how to journey to the Moon. There was so much wonder in the world. Having glimpsed the Beforetime, she could almost believe that anything was possible.

All her life she'd heard tales of the miraculous things shamans could do. Perhaps it wouldn't be so bad to be counted among them. As long as she didn't end up all gloomy and careworn like Old Manatook, or like Kuanak with the palsied hand and the one blind eye, or poor Civiliaq, gutted by a demon in the Underworld. Did none of them end up happy?

With a sigh, she drifted off to sleep.

But sleep for a shaman-in-training was not the same as for a carefree child or a normal woman. There was little rest in it. As her mind relaxed, her spirit strode boldly forth, stepping across into the world of dream. Walking in the dreamlands had changed now that she was tasked with reporting every dream to her teacher. To help remember the details when she woke, she paid strict attention as they happened. She remained aware that she had left her body behind, as most people were unaware. In this way the idle workings of her sleeping mind transformed into true journeying.

This night she dreamt of a barren wasteland of dried, cracked earth. The snow had all burned away, leaving the ground hard and brown. The sky blazed with the colors of sunset.

Suddenly she felt the sting of fiery acid against her ankle. An ebony hand reached up through one of the cracks. Her spirit-flesh burned. The hand yanked hard, pulling her down to one knee as it drew her toward the crack in the earth.

She glanced down into the blackened abyss. It was one of the *lumentin,* a leering demon surrounded by a smoky haze. Desperate, hateful, it wanted to pull her under, to destroy her. Alaana struggled against its deadly grip, trying to brace her other foot against the hard ground but the earth was so dry and brittle, crumbling away, and the crevasse grew even wider. It was inevitable that she'd be dragged down.

Another demonic hand reached up and pulled even harder. Alaana felt a rising panic. All was lost.

A shadow crossed the grasping arms and the demon's grip faltered. A moment's hesitation was all she needed. Alaana kicked free.

She rolled over, hugging the ground.

"Step carefully, little bird."

Alaana looked up. Civiliaq stood over her.

"Civiliaq!"

The bare-chested shaman smiled and nodded. All in all, he looked little worse for having died. Clean-shaven as always, his glossy black hair arranged in a pair of neat braids that fell on either side of his smiling face. Alaana noticed the intricate designs that covered his arms and bare chest were drawn backwards, as figures most often appeared in the dreamlands. His tattoos looked even more fabulous than ever, etched now in deep purple and black against the shaman's pale spirit-flesh. A big, black raven spread its wings across his bare chest, having just pounced atop a snake that circled his narrow waist. A ring of protective amulets hung silently, stitched into the skin across his neck. Serpentine loops and circles of mystic design covered his broad shoulders and ran down and around both arms. Most impressive of all, a pair of large feathered raven's wings, which had been merely tattoos in the waking world, now extended from the backs of his shoulders.

"Civiliaq? How can you be here?"

"I walk again in dreams, as does anyone your mind may conjure."

"Oh," said Alaana, rising to her feet, "I forgot where I was."

185

Civiliaq smiled affably. "You are asleep. And you dream of me! I'm flattered, little bird." He reached a hand down to pull Alaana up.

"I never thought I'd see you again," said Alaana, taking his hand. It felt solid enough. Civiliaq gave her fingers a hearty squeeze as she rose to her feet.

"You miss your old friend Civiliaq," said the shaman. His smile drifted away. "Of course I'm not really here. My soul is trapped in the Underworld, where I am debased and tortured for trying to help you and the others."

"I'm sorry…"

Civiliaq bowed his head slightly. "You don't have to be sorry. After all, it wasn't you who betrayed me. It was not you who damned me."

Alaana knew he was talking about Old Manatook. She'd never been told exactly what happened when the three shamans had fought the fever demon, but she'd figured most of it out for herself.

Civiliaq's wings flapped twice, very slowly. "And that's why I've come. To help you. Your education is woefully incomplete so far. There are things Old Manatook is not showing you. Squirrel-men and golden walruses are all well and good, but there are too many things he is keeping from you." Civiliaq gestured with the single black feather he held in his hand, pointing it toward the crack in the blasted earth, toward the *lumentin*.

Alaana shrugged. "I suppose he'll show me in time."

"In time, or not at all," returned Civiliaq, "and such a misjudgment may very well lead to your destruction. There are things I must show you. Terrible things. I don't want to frighten you but I feel it's my responsibility. Remember, I've always been a good friend to you. I've always protected your family."

Alaana nodded. For all his haughty conceits, Civiliaq had never done anyone harm.

"Fine," said Civiliaq, "This is a good place for a lesson. We have everything we need." He raised both hands above his head, as if drawing down the clouds from the sky. The shaman's face hardened with intense concentration as he worked his fingers in the air, drawing a picture out of dreamstuff. The ground covered with white snow again. The air took on the chill of winter.

"Look upon Kayoutuk, shaman of the Tungus."

Alaana gasped. She saw a vision of a man running — a shambling horror, his skin flayed off, dripping blood, his guts opened up. Intestines looped out and trailed down in a bloody mass which he trampled underfoot in his mad rush forward.

The man moaned in hopeless torment. He stumbled blindly onward, seeing nothing as he passed directly in front of Alaana.

She cringed, stepping back. It was the most terrible thing she had ever seen. "What happened to him?"

"He made one mistake," answered Civiliaq, "as did I."

Alaana turned her head. "Take it away."

"Not until a hard lesson is learned. One mistake is all it takes. The shaman's dance is a way of prayer. Its purpose is to pay homage, to give proof of your sincerity to the power of the spirits and beg their aid. But their sympathy may so quickly turn to anger. The form of the dance is important. Kayoutuk made one single misstep, perceived as insult by the *turgat* he had been meaning to impress."

"But what spirit?" whispered Alaana.

"Look up and see."

Alaana raised her eyes to see an enormous figure striding toward them across the flats. This was Erlaveersinioq the Disemboweler, a gigantic figure of death, whom the Anatatook also called the Skeleton Who Walks. Instead of ears, the yapping maws of a pair of ferocious dogs sprouted from each side of the *turgat's* head, their fangs dripping ichor and blood. The spirit's eyes, dead in

187

their sockets and as large around as summer houses, looked down upon Kayoutuk as he stumbled along the bloodied snow. As the eyes swiveled around, Alaana prayed they wouldn't come to rest on her.

Thump, thump, thump! The great spirit's every footfall shook the earth. Alaana felt each step rumble through her. She had the urge to bolt and run but Civiliaq stood fast beside her, showing no fear.

Erlaveersinioq's mouth was a bloody rent, filled with more rows of dagger-teeth than anyone could count. Alaana imagined the torture of being swallowed down that long, horrible throat. Screams of women and children rose from its depths, and blood dribbled down the chest in a heaving torrent. As it walked along, six slender arms, the color of midnight blue, clawed violently at the air.

"It could have been any of them," explained Civiliaq. "They don't tolerate failure. The *turgats*, the great spirits, they are so far above us. Even the most powerful shaman is nothing to them. We beg favors from them and sometimes they look down and give us a little. But just as likely they can be temperamental, spiteful and cruel. They can crush us in an instant."

"Please," said Alaana, glancing away. She couldn't look upon it any longer.

"I don't show you these things to frighten you, but to help you," explained Civiliaq. "Open your eyes, little bird. There is nothing to fear."

Alaana gazed again at the empty tundra. She let out a long sigh, shaking her head to recover herself.

Civiliaq's hand clamped hard on her shoulder.

"We're not finished," he said.

"I don't—"

"Shhh. More to see, more to learn. If the Anatatook happen to travel to the other side of Big Basin, you might encounter this one. Iakka, shaman of the Yakut people."

Civiliaq's hands moved around again, forming another vision from the dreamstuff. He used the black raven feather as an artist's brush, adding detail to the scene. Alaana saw an abandoned village take shape around them. Half buried in snow, only the tops of the tent poles and meat racks could be seen. A sense of grim foreboding came over her as the expanse of haunted wasteland came to life.

"Iakka," said Civiliaq, "a shaman who became a *tarrak*. A dark, angry spirit. He abused his power and became a sorcerer, commanding his will upon others, twisting their souls, forcing them to do his bidding. He made them do little things at first but the temptation was too great. In time the Yakut people were marched about like puppets at the whim of the sorcerer. But in the few moments of free thought left to them, communicating in whispered tones and hand gestures, the men decided what to do. The sorcerer must be killed even at the cost of all their lives, this was their solemn vow. They planned their trap in desperate, stolen moments and then they sent a score of arrows into his back. He lies there still, covered by the snows of years gone by."

The coal-black tail feather of the raven pointed to a mound just in front of Alaana, the tips of several arrow feathers just piercing the snow cover.

"His spirit is a different matter," said Civiliaq, "not so easily disposed of."

"What happened to it?"

"It's still here. Can't you feel it?"

Alaana shuddered. She did feel the old shaman's twisted spirit, still possessing the village it had consumed. It had taken root among the shattered tents, the wrecked meat racks, the broken kennels and the corpses of the people and dogs he had killed. Their ghosts had become a part of him and they did not rest easy. Like nettles under the skin they writhed and twisted, stabbing at their murderer.

"Iakka's soul is still here," repeated Civiliaq. "He suffers in eternal damnation and misery. Sometimes the wind blows his screams across Big Basin. I've heard them on cold nights. Haven't you?"

Alaana nodded. She had! "Oh, it's real," she said. "It's true." All around her the mingled screams of the murdered and the murderer rang out, piercing her very soul. She put her hands over her ears.

Civiliaq nudged one of the girl's hands down with a sharp elbow. "Of course it's true."

"I don't want to wind up like that! Not ever!"

Civiliaq frowned. "Of course you're not eager to learn this, but I wouldn't be your friend if I let it pass without due warning. The dangers of being the shaman are great."

"My mother said it was a gift."

"What do mothers know of such things? You must be careful, little bird. A dream so quickly may turn to nightmare. Too often without warning. That's what happened to me. We can't finish your lesson without a visit to your dear old friend Civiliaq, and the demon that torments me still."

Alaana cringed at the memory of the fever demon. To this day she lived in fear of that hideous old hag. A row of gray figures wandered in the mist behind Civiliaq, all victims of the sickness. All children. She closed her eyes.

"Don't look away," barked Civiliaq. "Let me show you what they've done to me."

"I don't want to see," said Alaana. "Not that! Not her!"

"But you must see. If I was destroyed by a single doubt and a feckless friend, what chance do you have? You are riddled with doubts. You can't hide that from me. Not here. I worry for you.

What will become of you, little bird? You are so full of doubts. And remember, you have the same deceitful friend as I."

"Old Manatook?"

"Old Manatook. We three went down, and he came away alone. Think on this. Have you ever seen his true soul-shape? I'll bet you haven't. Don't feel bad about it. Neither have I. There are things he hides even from his fellow shamans."

"I don't—"

"You don't know!" snapped Civiliaq. "I tell you he is not what he seems. That's for certain. Who knows where he goes alone on his long journeys to the north? Do you?"

Alaana shook her head.

"And why did he not end the fever demon? He didn't kill her, just pounded her into the snow. Why did he leave her alive to torment me, abandoning me, trapped in the Underworld? She has clipped my wings! My ties to Tulukkugaq – the Great Raven – are severed. He cannot help me now. He cannot hear my cries!"

Alaana noticed that the wings sprouting from the shaman's back had been stripped away. His tattoos began to smolder, sending curls of gray smoke up from his body.

"No one can help me. I am adrift and alone. Same as you."

Alaana didn't know what he meant by that, but she dare not ask. Her head broiled again with the fever as if the demon had taken hold of her once more. She felt dizzy and weak.

Civiliaq went on, "I am trapped in the Underworld — I dare not show it to you! But of course I must." He raised his arms to the heavens once more. The sky darkened.

"No. I don't want to see any more!"

"I'm sure you don't. You'd rather stumble blindly forward doing just what he tells you to do. He killed my father, did you know that? The shaman that trained me, I mean. As true a father as I ever had. Manatook slit his throat, murdered him right in front of all the people. Let us have a look at that instead!"

"No!" said Alaana. "I won't!"

"You will!" fumed Civiliaq, flecks of spittle flying from his lips.

In the dreamlands, the power of the dead shaman was too intense to resist. Alaana felt helpless before him. There was only one thing she could think to do.

"Itiqtuq!" she called out. "Itiqtuq!"

She felt the amulet warm inside her palm, a tiny auk skull with dead eyes and a downy tuft of tan feathers at the top. "Wake up! Wake up!" it screeched.

With a startled groan, Alaana sat up. She was breathing hard and fast.

Her mother had heard her shout and turned toward her.

"You've had a bad dream, Alaana. That's all," she said. She brushed the hair from Alaana's forehead. "I shouldn't wonder with your father away. It's over now. Go back to sleep."

Alaana settled back down under the furs, though she felt not at all reassured.

Her mother sighed. "It was only a dream."

But Alaana knew differently. Her mouth was so dry she could hardly swallow. Itiqtuq squawked once more, reminding Alaana that she had been instructed to relate all of her dreams, in detail, to her teacher in the morning. How could she tell Old Manatook about this? It was impossible. The things Civiliaq had shown her, and the things he'd said, were all true. Maybe Old Manatook couldn't be trusted. Alaana wished there were someone else she could talk to about this. But there was no one.

CHAPTER 18

"IF SHE IS TO BE THE SHAMAN..."

Tugtutsiak tilted the sealskin pouch, spilling the dried leaves across the flat surface of the gray rock. Old Manatook reluctantly bent forward to sniff at them. He detested the smell of tobacco.

He scented nothing out of the ordinary, stirring the crumbling brown leaves with the tip of his finger until satisfied. The soul-lights within the plant were quiet and at peace, without sign of disease.

"It's clean," he said. "There's no taint." After their recent trouble with the fever demon, Old Manatook personally inspected all trade goods that came from the white men.

Tugtutsiak separated the tobacco into two small piles, offering one to Nuralak. He drew out a small pipe made from the hollowed flute of a walrus tusk, and thumbed the bowl full. He gestured toward his pipe as if expecting the shaman to provide the spark. Old Manatook ignored him, gazing instead at the scenery.

Behind the bluff on which they sat lay an expansive view of the whole of the Anatatook camp. Several families had just recently returned to form the combined winter camp on the sea ice. The people below bustled with eager activity. It was a time for greeting friends and catching up on news, exchanging gifts and pleasantries.

Tugtutsiak gazed out upon the opposite slope. A pair of huge shimmering bergs rose on either side, reflecting blue from the sky.

His gaze trailed all the way down to the gleaming ice-foot that frosted the beach. Dark blots speckled the ice, each one young a seal basking in the sunlight. Tugtutsiak watched them roll and frolic, knowing the bellies of the Anatatook would not get any of them until the ice was ready to take a man's weight.

His attention was recalled, as always, to the rolling sea. "I never tire of looking at it," he said. "How far does it go, Manatook? Have you ever reached the end of it? Can anyone?" The headman gestured toward the open sea with his unlit pipe. He craftily waved it where Old Manatook could not help but notice, but the shaman ignored him.

"We'll have to start hunting seal right after the freeze-up," Tugtutsiak continued. "Our stores of caribou meat are low."

"That was a poor hunt at Forked River," said Nuralak.

"The herd is thinning," said Old Manatook. "They graze farther to the south every year."

"Or perhaps," said Tugtutsiak, "Perhaps you chose the wrong place for the hunt." He struck his flint against the stone, without effect.

"Perhaps," admitted Old Manatook.

Tugtutsiak repositioned the shred of dried moss on the rock. "You should understand. I have certain expectations of you. We've done well in recent years. Some people forget the hard times when their bellies are full. But I don't forget." He struck his flint again but got no spark.

"All this is known to me," said Old Manatook gruffly. "I'm not so old that my memory is dulled." He paid attention neither to the headman nor to Nuralak, who had taken up the flint. Instead he kept his eyes on the people below. At this distance their soul-lights appeared like tiny insects, and yet he could identify each and every one of them. "The loss of my brother Kuanak goes hard on me."

"Your brother?" said Tugtutsiak loudly. "Kuanak was my

sister's husband, my traveling companion, my hunting partner. My brother."

"We shamans are linked together," said Old Manatook firmly. "The bonds go deeper than you can imagine. Kuanak and Civiliaq and I, we were more than brothers. When I lost them, I lost parts of myself."

"And now there is only you to guide us," said Tugtutsiak. "With parts missing."

This rebuke stirred a wave of anger deep within Old Manatook. He repressed the urge to shed his skin, to rage and growl and settle the headman's complaints in primal fashion. These powerful men would flee from him like babies. But he was a man of many secrets, one who must not let his true nature be known to his loved ones, or to anyone at all. "I am well aware of the trouble," he said, "I don't need you to point it out."

Tugtutsiak held his gaze. The headman was firm in his convictions and seldom backed down to anyone. Not even, thought Manatook, a charging polar bear.

As the sole remaining shaman, Old Manatook was hard pressed to meet the needs of the entire village. Kuanak had been most gifted at bargaining with the *turgats*, the powerful spirits who controlled the supply of game animals. Civiliaq had been adept at healing the people and settling their disputes, despite his tendency toward self-aggrandizement. Manatook was the eldest, yet least important among the three. He had been free to come and go as he wished, a situation which suited him perfectly well. He often had important errands elsewhere, obligations to the north that did not involve the Anatatook at all.

"We had three shamans when you first came among us," noted Tugtutsiak. "Before you killed Klah Kritlaq..."

"Hai!" shouted Nuralak, having brought forth a spark at last. He lit both pipes and leaned back against the cliff, shoulder to

195

shoulder with Tugtutsiak, for an extended bout of contented puffing. The stench of burning tobacco assaulted Old Manatook's nose.

The shaman turned aside to face bitter recollection.

Killing Klah Kritlaq had been one of the most difficult tasks he'd ever been called upon to perform. Civiliaq and Kuanak stood idly by while Manatook did what needed to be done. Having been trained by Klah Kritlaq he was like a father to them; they would not raise their hands against him. And yet Kritlaq endangered them all. He had been driven mad by dark forces — his thoughts twisted to the point where he had begun seeing demons at every turn, accusing the people of unwarranted corruption. In the end he had become too dangerous, tainted beyond reason or redemption, using his power to force them to do his bidding.

"And now we have only you," said Tugtutsiak at last, not having lost his train of thought for all the smoking and the long silence.

"I can only do what I can," said Old Manatook. "I will plead with the spirits again. Perhaps — though I can not promise it — perhaps we may get one last chance at the herd before winter."

"Perhaps we can get another shaman," said Nuralak rather coldly. He laughed as if he had simply been joking, and added, "Why should you have to do so much by yourself?"

"If only it was such a simple thing," said Old Manatook. "I should well appreciate the help."

"What do you know, Nuralak?" asked Tugtutsiak. "You go often to the south."

"There is not much hope for it," Nuralak returned, blowing out smoke. "There are fewer and fewer shamans about these days. Everywhere I hear the same."

"How is Alaana coming along?" asked Tugtutsiak.

Old Manatook hesitated.

He was reluctant to recount the many troubles he had encountered in Alaana's training, uncertain as he was about it all. The girl had been called late, by an enigmatic and fickle spirit who had shown little interest in her since. And worse yet, Alaana lacked the dedication necessary to succeed at the task. Four moons had come and gone, and they had made precious little progress.

Were these difficulties a result of the reluctance of the pupil or the faults of the teacher?

He could not talk about such details to these men. And yet, he wouldn't lie either.

"It's early yet for her," was all that he would say.

"A girl," said Tugtutsiak, blowing out gray smoke. "We can't depend on her. Isn't there anything else we can do?"

Kigiuna looked up from his carving.

It had been a clear, dry day, probably one of the last before the storms and snows of freeze-up. As the sun dipped toward the horizon it left a rosy corona where it kissed the crusts of ice and snow. Kigiuna shivered. Such dramatic sunsets only reminded him of the long winter to come. They had been sitting idle too long. The cold had begun to creep into his bones.

"You did well in the hunt, Maguan," said Anaktuvik, who sat beside Kigiuna under an overhanging shelf of gray sandstone. He leaned back contentedly against the rock face. "I think married life agrees with you."

"I've no complaints," replied Maguan. He rolled his eyes playfully.

"Well I do," said Kigiuna. "The meat stores are still half empty. Old Manatook chose the wrong place to intercept the herd."

"Can any man know which way the wind is going to turn?" mused Anaktuvik in an easygoing tone.

"He's the shaman," replied Kigiuna. "He's supposed to

know. That's what he tells us, isn't it?"

Anaktuvik was not concerned. "They bleed red just like the rest of us."

"And so he'll starve right along with us?" snapped Kigiuna.

"No one's going to starve," said Anaktuvik. "Nunatsiaq, our beautiful land, will provide." He wore a sparse, curly beard which differed from Kigiuna's only in that it clung to a face which, although several years older, seemed much less lined with worry. Kigiuna envied his elder brother, so full of optimism, eyes closed above a gentle smile as if he might at any moment drift off to sleep, where a pleasant dream awaited him.

Maguan said, "Perhaps Tugtutsiak will get a whale this year."

Kigiuna snorted. "Perhaps I don't want to rely on Tugtutsiak."

He scratched a mouth onto the face he was cutting into a long ivory chit, using an iron nail pulled from a piece of driftwood he'd found on the beach. It was the only thing he owned that had belonged to the white men. The nail was extremely useful for fine detail work, such as decorating the hair pin, one of a pair he was making for Amauraq. He thought she would like a smiling face on the pin, but his disgruntled mood was souring the result. The smile looked more like a leer. "I worry about empty stomachs during winter's long night. I worry that the dogs might starve or Putuguk will face hardship or be left behind."

"All will be well," said Anaktuvik. His eyes popped open. "What's come over you, Kigiuna? You never used to brood like an old woman."

Kigiuna stabbed at the carving. His brother was right. It was impossible to keep secrets from him. "It's Alaana."

"What about her?"

"I don't want her to become a shaman." There. He'd said it. He felt no guilt at the admission. At least his words were safe in his

198

brother's ears.

Maguan turned to his father in surprise. "Alaana will be a great shaman for our people, Father. A great woman. Think of the honor we'll have, with a shaman in our family."

"Our status will rise among the hunters," observed Anaktuvik.

"I don't care about any of that," snapped Kigiuna. This was not strictly true. He would've liked nothing more than to elevate his status among the band. Ever since the days of his impetuous youth he'd been marginalized, viewed with suspicion and held at arm's length by the men in power. But there were some things he wasn't willing to sacrifice for status. "Alaana doesn't sleep well. She's restless throughout the night. Every night."

"You should have renamed her after that fever," observed Anaktuvik. "Why didn't you?"

"Old Manatook said not to. He said the spirits called Alaana by name and she should keep it."

Anaktuvik grunted softly. "It's no good to keep the same name after you've almost died. Everybody knows that."

Kigiuna dragged the nail along the surface of the flat stone on which they sat. "What if Old Manatook is wrong? Just as he was with the caribou. What if Alaana doesn't really have the calling? I don't think it sits well with her."

"It doesn't sit well with you," said Anaktuvik.

"No, it doesn't," admitted Kigiuna. "It's too dangerous."

In a dismissive tone, Maguan said, "I'm sure she's fine."

"You're sure she's fine?" seethed Kigiuna. "Well, that's a relief! That's a great comfort to me. As long as you're satisfied, why am I wasting my breath talking?"

Maguan's eyes bulged slightly, then shrank back from his father's withering look. He got no help from his uncle who, eyes closed again, pretended to be on the verge of sleep.

"If only the Anatatook could hunt our prey with sarcasm..." mused Anaktuvik in a sleepy tone. "You would be the headman, Kigiuna."

"Very funny."

"Why don't you ask Old Manatook?"

"I don't want to ask Old Manatook," spat Kigiuna. "He's the cause of all this trouble."

Anaktuvik frowned. "You shouldn't talk that way about the shaman. What have you got against him?"

"Father never trusted him. It cost him an arm."

"That was a long time ago. Old Manatook had newly come among us."

"Do you remember when he murdered Klah Kritlaq?" asked Kigiuna.

"That old sorcerer was crazy. He was dangerous."

"I was right there when Manatook killed him," said Kigiuna. He remembered it well. The day Old Manatook killed Klah Kritlaq was to have been the day of his manhood ceremony at twelve winters. His ceremony had been delayed an entire season because of the events of that day.

Klah Kritlaq had always been mean and formidable. All of the Anatatook children, Kigiuna included, found him terribly frightening. There was something about the old shaman's eyes, the way they seemed able to jump from their sockets and cut into you, that sent a shiver through his soul.

The fight began with the two men standing in the middle of the camp, locked in an intense stare. At that time Manatook had been in his early middle age. Klah Kritlaq was old but not feeble; he was still able to wrestle most of the men to the ground. The staring match went on for some time until at last Manatook looked away. No one could stand long under Kritlaq's cutting gaze.

Kritlaq laughed softly. It was a quiet snicker, but with such a malicious character that Kigiuna was tortured by nightmares of that sound and the old shaman's dreadful yellowed eyes long after he was dead. Kritlaq drew out his blade. He carried a short ceremonial knife only. Manatook had a killing blade of slivered bone, long and sharp.

Manatook charged. Unlike in the stories, there was no thunderclap, no flying through the air, no bolts of otherworldly energy. Simply two men fighting each other in the space between the tents. Kritlaq was savage with his blade, slashing Manatook in several places. Manatook held back for the killing stroke; he seemed cool and careful compared to the mad fury of the other. When the opening came he sent his long knife deep in the belly. Kritlaq hung on the blade, yellow eyes bulging. Manatook pulled the knife out and slashed across Kritlaq's neck with one deft motion, severing the necklace of charms he wore. The charms fell to the snow, and Klah Kritlaq fell with it, stone dead. It was the first time Kigiuna had ever seen a man killed. He didn't even understand why they were fighting.

Anaktuvik stood up. "It was a good, clean kill. It was necessary."

It was hard for Kigiuna to reconcile that statement with the recollections of his boyhood years. The viciousness of that stabbing. Kritlaq's chilling death rattle. The cold predatory look in Old Manatook's eyes. That was not the first time Manatook had killed a man, he was certain of it.

"Now he's the only shaman left," he said, "spending so much time with Alaana."

"Time to go inside," said Anaktuvik. "Maguan is right. Alaana will be fine. If she has been called, she must answer. What can we do? Life isn't for worry," he said with a smile, "Life is for life."

What else was there to say? What else was there to do?

201

Kigiuna picked up the hair pin. Despite his bitter mood he had shaped the expression on the face into a smile for Amauraq. He realized the features on the carving wore the face of his brother.

It was getting dark. Time to go inside.

CHAPTER 19

SHE THAT MUST WALK ALONE

The whip cracked above Alaana's head. Her shoulders felt as if they were being ripped from their sockets. On hands and knees in the snow she was cold and wet, and laughing so hard she could barely breathe.

The whip cracked again, almost too close for comfort. "Come on," shouted Aquppak, "Get moving, you mangy pup!"

It was no use. Alaana let the traces go slack. The sight of Iggy's rump, directly ahead of her and waggling crazily, was too much. She could not stop laughing and signaled for Aquppak to take his lash elsewhere. Perhaps he could tame Iggianguaq.

"That's no fun, Alaana," said Aquppak. "It's no race if you're lying down in the snow."

Their game, a race across the snow-plain pulling their little toy sleds, had gone totally wrong. First there had been some confusion as to the direction of the course, which left the children running in messy circles with tow lines crossed and hopelessly tangled. After that, Iggy's impersonation of an overly enthusiastic lead dog was too comical to bear. Alaana and Aquppak had both broken down laughing.

"It's no good race anyway," said Alaana. "Nobody can beat Iggy."

And that was true. The toy sleds hauled heavy stones as passengers and all the stones were roughly the same size, which meant Iggy was certain to win.

Aquppak, who characteristically refused to play at any game where there was no chance for him to win, refused to pull a sled. Instead he had a thin whip of sinew and acted as team driver, snapping it above their heads.

"It's his fault," said Alaana, stabbing a finger at Iggy. "Get him!"

Aquppak lunged for Iggianguaq. Still acting the part of a wild dog, Iggy broke loose from his traces and met Aquppak's charge. The whip forgotten, the two boys went tumbling in the snow, Iggy growling and snapping in a grand imitation of the most ferocious huskie anyone had ever seen. After he knocked Aquppak aside, he turned crazily playful, his tongue flopping in the air, still romping gaily about on all fours, splashing up fresh snow.

When the crazed boy-dog began tugging at Alaana's clothing with his teeth, Alaana thought she might burst from laughing.

"Come on, then. If that's the way it is, let's wrestle for real," said Aquppak, brushing the powder from his face.

Iggy whooped with glee. Outside of meal times, wrestling was by far his favorite activity. He pushed the heavy stone off his makeshift sled and, turning it over, unwrapped the sealskin which held the spars together. He set the skin out over a flat place on the ground, saying, "Who wants to lose first?"

Alaana shot a glance back at the camp. Thick brown smoke was still trailing out of the *karigi*. Inside Old Manatook was communing with Tekkeitsertok, the spirit of the wild caribou, trying to arrange for another hunt. The smell of burning incense was thick in the air as it wafted throughout the camp. As she was not yet a full shaman, Alaana wasn't allowed to witness the bargaining with such great *turgats* as Tekkeitsertok, but she felt certain the rite was nearly done. When Old Manatook emerged from the *karigi* he would report his results to the headman, and then he and Alaana were to continue her training.

"Fine," Alaana said. "I have just enough time to beat you once or twice."

Iggy chuckled. Alaana had never beaten him at wrestling in his life and never would.

Iggy centered himself on the mat and stripped down to his pants, tossing his parka off to the side. He was already so wet it didn't matter. He puffed himself up, baring his chest dramatically, but this to Alaana was a bit comical too. Iggy was so fat he had bigger breasts than some of the girls.

Iggy made a ferocious noise and extended his crooked elbow. Alaana linked arms and they were off. They spun around, neither one pulling their hardest or the match would be over too soon. The sealskin mat sunk into the slush, and as they stomped this way and that, icy water welled up over the sides. Alaana began pulling in earnest. Iggy matched her strength, moaning and groaning with mock strain. Alaana yanked downward, trying to get under her opponent and nudge him off balance but it was useless. Iggy's legs were too strong. He hauled Alaana up, but as he swung her around to the side he slipped on the mat's slick surface. Caught standing at an odd angle, Iggy wobbled for a moment then went down. Alaana slapped him on his bare chest. She was the winner.

Alaana had never won before. She thrust her arms outward in imitation of a grizzly.

Iggy was slow to stand up.

"You cheated!" he said. "You vexed me."

"I did not," laughed Alaana.

"You did!" His tone was sharp. Iggy wasn't joking. "You took the strength out of my legs, you made me slip!"

"I didn't."

Iggy stepped close to Alaana but Aquppak slid between them. "It's all right, Iggy. You slipped and fell. That's all."

"No, she cheated! I felt it."

"I didn't!"

"I feel sick," said Iggy. His eyes went wide with horror and revulsion. He could hardly stand up and his face was pale. He took a shaky step toward Alaana, an angry look on his face such as they had never seen.

"What have you done to him?" asked Aquppak.

"He's joking," said Alaana.

"I am not!" Iggy spat the words as if he had a foul taste in his mouth. He staggered forward and vomited into the snow.

"I didn't do anything!" Alaana said, stepping back. Or had she? She wasn't certain and there really was no use in saying the same things over and over. She could tell from their faces. No one believed her.

As tears blurred their horrible, accusing faces, she ran off.

Maguan smiled handsomely, extending his foot for all to see. "New boots."

Itoriksak and his friend Ipalook both leaned forward to see, nearly butting their heads together. "Pilarqaq made them from scraps of sealskin left over from last winter."

"Do they fit right?" asked Itoriksak. The sealskin sole was so crookedly sewn that Maguan had been walking on the side of the boot rather than the flat of the bottom.

"Sure. It's a nice piece of work, too. Look at these tassels." Maguan rotated his foot to better show off the tiny leather tassels, several of which had already been torn off by crusts of ice trampled underfoot.

"They don't seem even," remarked Ipalook.

"The snow doesn't mind," said Maguan.

"I think they're fine," said Alaana.

"There. You see? Here's a young woman who appreciates good work." So saying, Maguan gave his sister a playful little kick with the boot she had just been inspecting so closely. "And someday Alaana you'll make a pair just as nice as these."

"I hope," said Alaana softly. The young men all laughed, but Alaana remained sour-faced.

Ipalook sorted through the collection of long bones set out before him. Ipalook was distinguished by a face that was completely ordinary. Straight black hair, small dark eyes, a thin-lipped mouth. He looked like every Anatatook who had gone before and every Anatatook since. His expression was serious, but then again his attitude was always serious, so different from Maguan's lighthearted demeanor. Maguan was always happy, and seemed especially content since his marriage. Even in her current dark mood, Alaana felt good just to be around her elder brother.

The four of them were settled in a secretive nook in the shelter of a pair of peaked rocks, free from prying eyes, just outside the camp. There were two groupings of whale bones laid out on the mat — a pile the men had already agreed upon and another pile of cracked and yellowed bones whose usefulness was still under consideration. Ipalook held one up. "We might make a spar out of this."

Maguan took the piece and turned it over. He ran his hand along the inside slope.

"We'd have to shave it down to size," suggested Ipalook.

Maguan nodded. He brushed thoughtfully at the thin threads of mustache hanging at the corners of his mouth. "This will be just fine. It'll be the third rib on the left hand side." He smiled with a faraway look as if imagining the boat they were planning to construct. "We'll have the best boat on the water," he said. "Just you wait and see. We'll have an even better boat than Tugtutsiak."

"If you ever get enough whalebone for the frame," said Itoriksak.

"I'll get it. I'm hoping this season he'll land another bowhead, and we'll get a few more pieces."

"Scraps left over from Tugtutsiak's hunts," muttered Ipalook.

"I don't care," returned Maguan. "I'll take those scraps and put them together and we'll have a grand boat. He thinks he's the only one can bring in a narwhal. He'll see what we can do."

"We'll show him," said Itoriksak, shaking his fist in solidarity.

"You'll have the best crew," said Alaana.

Maguan nodded, smiling.

"If only we could find someone who knows how to fit the joints together," said Ipalook, "beside Tugtutsiak."

"I'm thinking on it," Maguan assured them. "Tugtutsiak doesn't matter. There's a better way to do it than even he knows. I just haven't thought of it yet. There's plenty of time."

"Can I be on the crew?" asked Alaana.

"Of course not," said Ipalook. "You'll be sitting on shore, waiting, with the rest of the wives."

The mention of marriage brought a scowl to Alaana's face. Ipalook didn't know her wedding had been called off.

Maguan was quick to try and soothe her hurt feelings. "Soon you won't have time to bother with any of this. You'll be too important, and whaling's too dangerous to risk the shaman."

"That's right. You should be playing with your friends now while you can," said Ipalook, "instead of bothering us."

"She's not bothering us," said Maguan.

Alaana kicked absently at the snow. "The boys don't want to play with me anymore. They're afraid of me."

"Oh, don't mind them," said Maguan. "Everyone's a little scared of the shaman, I guess."

"Even Iggy's turned against me too. They all have."

208

"Don't worry about it," said Maguan. "There comes a time when boys won't play with the girls any more. It doesn't matter."

It did matter, thought Alaana. The girls avoided her too.

"Here, look," said Maguan, holding the whale rib up in front of her face. "It has to have a certain type of curve, but you can't shave too deep or it becomes too weak there in the center. It takes a long time and it's hard work, but we'll get it done."

"I can help," Alaana said. She could see the little flicker of blue within the rib, a tiny spirit — all that remained of the proud soul of the whale from which it had come. The spirit seemed friendly enough. She thought she might get the bone to assume the desired shape with a little nudging of her own.

"Okay. Sure," said Maguan. He handed Alaana the shaver, a thin flat piece of hard gray stone attached to a short handle of antler. "I'll show you how."

Maguan demonstrated his technique, taking long firm strokes with the dull blade. Rather than shaving off slivers of the bone, it seemed he was perfectly content to merely wear it down slowly by degrees. He nodded his head and smiled at Alaana. "You give it a try."

She took the tool, immediately dismissing the idea of altering the bone's shape by use of anything outside of good, hard work. There was too much joy in doing it this way, the normal way. The shaver was another matter. There was a dull gray spirit inside the stone blade. She reached out her thoughts and easily convinced it that it desired a sharper edge for itself.

Alaana worked the bone as Maguan had shown her. "That's it," said Maguan, pleased. "You have to lean into it with your shoulder."

Suddenly their father called out to them. Maguan stood up. "We're here."

Kigiuna came around the edge of the tall rock.

"Maguan, what are you doing there? Stop fooling with that silly boat and come and do some real work. Old Manatook just came out of the *karigi*. He says the caribou will cross the rapids in three days. That's our last chance for the year. We need to work on the kayaks, not waste time on this foolishness."

"Yes, Father," said Maguan.

Kigiuna's eyes alighted on Alaana. "And what are you doing here? Aren't you supposed to be with Old Manatook?"

"Yes, Father."

"Then you should be moving your legs in the direction of the camp." His words were sharp; he meant what he said. But Alaana noticed his fist tensed up before he spoke, as if he were angry at himself.

Alaana headed back toward the practice tent but had no intention of meeting with Old Manatook. She felt awful. Her brother's words rang true. Everyone feared the shaman. She had seen the frightened look on Mikisork's face often enough of late, as he went out of his way to ignore her. And even the adults all looked at her differently now that she heard their darkest secrets as revealed in the spirit-callings. Seldom did anyone speak to her at all, except for her family. All of this, and she was not even a shaman yet. Far from it. She'd only been studying with Old Manatook for four moons. It was turning out to be the very worst year of her life.

Alaana turned away from the camp, following a break through the ice which wound its way down toward the river. She sat among the large, rough boulders that framed the bank, once again struck by the incredible natural beauty of the site. The water, as always, sparkled perfectly clear, shimmering as it moved along, weaving its way between the rocks in the center of the stream. Sitting at the water's edge, she was fascinated by the delicate patterns of ice that gathered around the rim of the stream. They floated on the surface, forming fragile webs with long thin fingers, probing into the water only so far until they broke off with the flow.

The spirit of the river was vast and mellow and the cool blue color of ice at midnight. Whenever Alaana had a chance she came back to it, a steadfast friend whose babbling waters always had a gentle story to tell. The river didn't worry about anything. It had no concerns as it rushed along other than that it should wind up where it was headed, a journey that inevitably brought it back around to exactly where it had come from in the first place. Alaana offered a tentative hello, knowing this was the last she would see of it for awhile. The band would be moving to the rapids very soon and after that they would make for the winter camp along the seashore.

The river said nothing in return. The spirit had grown lazy, its waters sluggish and choked, thick with tiny pieces of ice. The big freeze was coming. Soon the river would be laid to silent rest under a blanket of ice. It was already asleep. Farewell, thought Alaana, until next year.

"Play?" said Weyahok. "Play?"

"Not now," answered Alaana in a low grumble.

She felt the little piece of soapstone take on weight in her pocket, growing heavier and heavier until she had no choice but to pull it out. "Stop!" said Alaana, "You'll tear my pocket apart."

"See me," said Weyahok, "See me."

Alaana opened her hand. Weyahok wasn't much to look at, just a small irregular lump of waxy gray stone.

"Why not make yourself nice and flat," said Alaana. "That's the perfect shape to be."

Weyahok was eager to oblige, especially if flat really was the best shape to be. Alaana judged the results as adequate for her task, if a bit lopsided. She hefted the little stone, drew her arm back and let fly. Weyahok skipped three times across the surface of the river before it caught a bad hop against the side of an ice-cake and sunk down. Alaana could see her little friend down in the depths of the river, sprouting tiny arms and legs and making its way along the bottom. Eventually it came up the bank and rolled to her feet.

"Throw Weyahok again? Throw Weyahok again!"

Alaana did as she was asked.

"And what are you doing here all by yourself?" asked Nunavik. Alaana's hand must have brushed against the piece of walrus tusk when she had drawn Weyahok from her pocket, calling Nunavik to her.

"Thinking," she replied.

"Well, you seem to do that quite a lot for a person of such little sense. Keep at it. You must learn to crawl before you can run."

Alaana laughed. Certainly the single best thing that had happened to her this year was her friendship with the golden walrus. "Nunavik, have you ever been married?"

"Ackkk! Certainly not. In my many travels and many years I've found out one thing of which I am certain — love may be foolishness, but marriage is madness."

Alaana laughed again.

"Good friends are infinitely better than good lovers," said Nunavik. "And a lot less trouble. But you shouldn't be sitting here alone. Old Manatook is at the *qaqmaq* waiting for you. If you don't show up he's bound to be angry."

"He's just my teacher, not my friend."

A frown flattened the golden walrus' already flat face, puffing out his huge round cheeks. "I've made a great number of friends along my way. From the smallest of creatures to the greatest. But my best friend was also my teacher. She was a sparrow, and also a great shaman."

"I didn't know the sparrows had shamans."

"There were a few. Now there are fewer than ever. I went to her to learn the secrets of the sparrows."

"I don't see how that could be," said Alaana. "You can't fly."

"Can't? Don't be ridiculous. Every soul can fly. We would meet in the Upperworld and she would teach me. I never could do much sparrow-magic, though. Not built for it. Most of it involves feathers."

Alaana nodded knowingly, then said, "Don't souls have feathers, if they want?"

"Clever girl," laughed Nunavik. "Not on my glorious golden hide, they don't! And a beak?" Nunavik tilted his face to show off his profile, which consisted principally of a pair of gigantic cheeks, a flat upper lip and the great hoary tusks. "Some things are beyond imagining."

The walrus had a particularly raspy laugh.

"Beaks," he continued, "And wings, and talons. Definitely not for me. Still, good things to know about. Be sure and learn as much as you can, Alaana. The world is a much more dangerous place than you care to know."

"Maybe I don't want to know," said Alaana. "Maybe I only want to laugh and to rest easy and to marry, and not be left out."

"Ah, that's something I know quite a bit about," returned the Walrus On The Ice, "sitting alone by the seaside."

Alaana was reminded of Nunavik's tale, how because of one mistake the walrus had witnessed the death of everyone he had ever loved. Another life ruined by the spirits.

"Why must it be that way?" asked Alaana.

Nunavik grunted softly. "That is what it is to be *angatkok*. It's an old word. *Angatkok*. It means 'He That Must Walk Alone'"

"What's the word for 'She That Must Walk Alone'?" asked Alaana.

"There isn't any."

"I don't want to walk alone," she said.

"Who does?" answered Nunavik.

213

CHAPTER 20

THE SEEN AND UNSEEN

"That girl! She tried to hide from me today! She actually tried to hide from me. Does she think I don't see her wherever she goes?"

"I think she knows." Higilak spoke softly, as counterpoint to her husband's shouting. She had rarely seen him so upset.

"She knows?" raged Old Manatook. "What did she think? That I would come running after her? Is that what she wants?"

"Doubtful. More likely she just wanted some time alone."

Old Manatook huffed, pacing back and forth before the *ikliq*.

"Come, now," Higilak said. Their narrow tent was barely tall enough for him to stand, and her husband was flitting about like a trapped moth.

"Skipping lessons. Keeping me waiting. She's wasting time, she's slow to learn and she rebels at every turn." The leathery skin of Old Manatook's face reddened with frustration. "She fights me."

"Shhh. They'll all hear you."

"I don't care if they hear," he said, though in a much quieter tone. "A stubborn child, that's what she is. I should take control of her mind..."

"The way you control mine, and make me love you?" She smiled coyly. He didn't notice.

"I never tampered with your mind," he said coldly.

"You never needed to," she replied warmly. "At least stop lurching back and forth." She motioned him toward the platform. "And you shouldn't have to tamper with Alaana."

"I can't anyway," he grumbled. "Outside influence on her mind will taint the training. It's no good. The spirits always know." He sat wearily on their bed, his anger spent.

Higilak cast off the sleeping furs. Naked, she felt the sudden chill of the night. She shuffled forward on the platform, putting her arms around her husband's neck from behind, pressing her breasts against the warmth of his back.

"So what then am I to do?" he asked. "You spend more time around the children than anyone else. What do you think?"

"Children rebel," she said simply. "They can't always be controlled. Every father knows that. The most important thing is patience."

"Sun and Moon, I don't have the patience for such games. I don't have the time. Not when I'm needed by the Anatatook and elsewhere also. Before, I could come and go as I pleased but now — and trying to instruct that child on top of everything else — it's too much."

Higilak began to fiddle with the back of Old Manatook's shirt where the soft fawn skin was laced together, but he drew her hands gently aside.

"Sometimes I think she's more trouble than she's worth," he said dejectedly.

"She was always different," Higilak said.

"She was?" asked Manatook.

Higilak suppressed a chuckle. Her husband could see across all seven worlds, yet he missed so much in this one. Most of all where children were concerned.

"Yes," she said. "That child asks questions. All the time. She was forever interrupting story time, when she wasn't sneaking out on some errand of mischief."

"Hmmf. Her father should have taught her better."

"It's not the father's fault. It's her nature. She's inquisitive, thoughtful—"

"Stubborn."

"Her stubbornness will take care of itself. In time it will work in your favor, you'll see. You've only to point her in the right direction and watch her go. If you would only calm down and consider what *she* needs."

"She needs a good solid thump on the backside."

"Think again."

Old Manatook growled softly. "I have no ideas. I was shown the Way a long time ago, in a place very different from this. It was Kritlaq who instructed Civiliaq and Kuanak, not me. Children! Give me an enraged bull walrus. Give me a demon, a handful of demons. With claws the length of my arm! Give me anything but a petulant child. I am no good with them and I don't know how to teach them."

Higilak sighed. "Little girls and grown men are not so different, my love. Her problem is the same as yours, I think, and perhaps that's no coincidence. Your heart is divided. It always has been."

"And it always will be," he said firmly, plunging them into silence. There were certain things that they did not speak about.

"I know," she said. "Where you go and what you do is your business. I know your heart, and it always comes back to me."

After the destruction of her village Higilak had met Manatook, a stranger who found her wandering alone on the wastes. Soon after they married, the two adopted the Anatatook as their own. She was happy with these people, especially the children. They grew up knowing her voice, her wistful smile, and her love.

And, judging by the joyous light in their eyes, all that she gave was returned in kind. Higilak was perfectly content among the Anatatook. But Manatook was a man of frequent travels and long, mysterious absences.

"You have never fully committed to the Anatatook, my husband, spending so much time away. It's a whole lifetime we've been here—"

"I can't spend all my time with the girl. I can't." Old Manatook felt the weight of his responsibility smothering him like a fateful shroud. He had obligations elsewhere; for too long he had been neglecting his work to the north. Others depended on him and he would not let them down or see them fall, with important matters left unfinished. Already he was long overdue for a return to his true home. He would have to leave again for an extended period once Alaana was ready, but when would that be?

"Fathers must accept a certain responsibility," said Higilak. "The freedom to roam is the first thing that is lost."

"I didn't ask to become her teacher," said Old Manatook. He was torn in so many directions at once. He felt Higilak tighten her embrace as if she meant to hold him together. He turned to face her. She was the one constant in his life, the one thing he could always depend on. His one true love. For a moment he considered how best to voice these sentiments to her once again, but she interrupted whispering, "You must protect her."

"I will see it through," he said firmly, "but I can only do so much. She has to walk the road herself."

"Have you made it clear to her what's at stake?"

"That she will die if she doesn't pass the test? No. It can't be done that way. She has to want it, not embrace the Way out of fear."

"Then ask yourself, what will get her to walk that road? Why do you walk it?"

217

***

"Wake up! Wake up!"

Alaana slapped at the amulet.

"Awwwk!" it squeaked.

She thrust her hand over Itiqtuq's furry little beak, even though she knew by now the amulet had no power to disturb her sleeping family. Silenced, the tiny bird-eyes bulged rhythmically for a few moments more, then went dark.

Stupid thing, thought Alaana. She hadn't yet even been asleep.

How could she possibly sleep? It was quiet enough, through the long night on the far side of summer. Her family was abed and asleep, but all she could do was toss and turn and stew in her own misery.

She had successfully avoided Old Manatook for the entire evening, returning home only at her mother's call for supper and saying nothing to her family about her exploits of the day. Now she felt badly about it. Surely the old shaman could have found her at any time if he'd wished. And Nunavik had said Old Manatook would be angry. But who would be more angry, Alaana wondered, Old Manatook or her father? She was not looking forward to Kigiuna's reaction when he learned his order to attend the shaman had been so blatantly disobeyed.

There was no way to sleep. She kept seeing Iggy's face, flushed with anger and fear. Iggy had practically wanted to kill her, all for losing a wrestling match. And all the others had fallen right in line, taking Iggy's side. The more Alaana thought about it, the easier it was to see that aside from her brothers, she had no friends at all. And they weren't really friends, they were her brothers.

"Alaana!"

Alaana nearly jumped out of the sleeping furs. She couldn't see anyone in the darkened tent. Still, there was no mistaking that

218

gruff voice.

"Manatook?" she whispered. "Are you in here?"

"Certainly not!" came the reply. "I'm lying snug in my bed, same as you."

"Really?" she said, still casting about for any sign of her teacher in the shadows near the tent flap. "What? Then, how…"

Old Manatook offered no answer except a moment of silence to let his student figure things out for herself. There was only one possibility. The old shaman did not lie. He must be communicating to her in the secret language of the shamans, from halfway across the camp. It was difficult for Alaana to believe. She'd never received such a message before, despite their rigorous training. She sat up on the *ikliq* and listened intently.

There was nothing further. Then she recalled her teacher's words. The trick was not to try too hard, to just relax and receive. She'd finally learned the lesson, when she had least expected it.

She blew out a deep breath, lay back on the bunk, and forced herself to relax.

"Good!" said Old Manatook. "Now let's have done with all this silliness and begin. You've missed your lessons today, girl. And I will have my due, even in the middle of the night. I'm waiting right above you. Rise up."

"Where?"

"Right above you, in the air above the tent. Rise up. Use what Sila has taught."

"I don't want to," said Alaana. She wondered briefly if her pout and the contentious snap of her head carried across the strands of the air as well as her words.

"Don't be foolish, child. You can not turn away from the gifts Sila has given you."

"I don't want them. Sila can take them back."

"There is no choice."

"I don't have to use them."

"You've been called. To deny the spirits is to endanger us all."

"I don't care," she projected. She squeezed her eyes shut but it was too late. She was crying again.

"Rise up, girl," growled Old Manatook, "Or I swear I will rip your *inuseq* out your body by force!"

The connection broke, leaving Alaana to the silence and the dark. She was painfully aware of one undeniable fact. The old shaman did not ever lie. She cringed, imagining icy spirit-hands yanking her soul from her body.

It was better to try and do as he asked. Separating spirit from body was simply a matter of surrender and relaxation. A seemingly impossible task when one was heartbroken and reduced to tears, with the threat of violent dissolution hovering in the air.

Alaana wiped her face with her hands, took a deep breath and gave herself up to greater forces, letting go all worries and cares. Her soul rose into the air, leaving her body lying motionless on the sleeping ledge as she passed through the tent roof and into the night sky.

The sky was black, mist-laden and jeweled with stars. A gentle snow was falling. Flakes of white trailed down, growing as they came to meet her but offered no chill kiss as they passed through her spirit-form and continued on their way.

She felt a sudden rush of exhilaration. Set free from the pull of the earth, her spirit soared. She felt the lure of sweet oblivion, and thought how easy it would be to release herself completely. And fade away.

Suddenly her spirit-form, untouchable by any earthly force, was shaken by the rough hand of Old Manatook. Alaana paid no attention to her master; the sight of the mysterious stars completely consumed her. Viewed through her spirit-vision they looked brighter and more fantastic than ever before.

"They do lift one's spirits, don't they?" said Old Manatook.

"What are they?"

"I don't know," said Old Manatook.

"Looking down, do they see the earth? Do they see us?"

"Who can say? There's a strange thing about them. You may travel toward them for days or years — you can lose yourself in trying, but go as far as you want, you will never reach them. You get no closer to them at all."

Her teacher's *inuseq* appeared beside her. Blurred and obscured, it hovered in the night sky like a gossamer shadow in white. Alaana couldn't help but remember the suspicions Civiliaq had raised.

"The lesson begins," added Old Manatook. "Now look down."

Alaana turned her gaze away from the stars.

"Look at the camp," said Old Manatook.

Summer was gone. The gentle nightly snows no longer melted during the day, leaving a crust of white clinging to the tents and sod houses, glazing the camp in twinkling starlight. Arranged below them were all the structures that made up the Anatatook camp, but more than that, Alaana found she could see inside the tents as if the skins were inconsequential things made entirely of air. She saw her friends and family, all asleep in their beds.

"Shamans walk between the worlds," said Old Manatook. "You see everything in two aspects at once. Look closely."

Alaana noticed that the souls of the sleepers had also gone wandering. As she adjusted her gaze, she could see what each of them was doing on the other side of the curtain of sleep, in the world of dreams.

"In this way your sight is doubled," said the voice of Old Manatook, "your world divided. This is what it is to be *angatkok*.

221

Your thoughts must at all times follow two separate tracks at once."

Looking down into her tent Alaana saw her dear brother Itoriksak dreaming that he was a seagull, drifting over the frozen ocean. The wind carried him on his way, blissful and carefree, as Sila had once lifted Alaana.

In Amauraq's dream, she held a baby. The sight of her so happy, beaming lovingly down at the babe in her arms, warmed Alaana's heart. Was the dream child Ava or herself? She couldn't tell. Did it matter?

Maguan and Pilarqaq, she discovered, did not sleep. They were awake and snuggling, and Alaana looked quickly away.

Her father mumbled softly; he was troubled in his sleep. Alaana looked deeper. Her father was lost in the dreamlands, battling shadows. Standing alone in the shifting darkness, Kigiuna faced uncertain opponents. He swept his spear in a wide circular arc but could not hit them; they were smoke.

A yawning chasm opened up before him, intent on taking his family away. From the depths came a sound like the roaring of rapids, a jumble of unintelligible voices, moaning, wailing. Kigiuna stepped back from the brink but it was no use. The land itself began to lift and tilt, threatening to bring them all sliding down into the darkness.

"Manatook, how can we help him?" asked Alaana in a near panic.

"I can only offer this," said the old shaman. He reached out his arm, then quickly pulled his fist closed as if catching a fly. Slowly he uncoiled his spirit-fingers and blew on his palm.

Kigiuna's eyes popped open. He sat up in his furs, searching about in the darkness of the tent. Reassured that his family were all still present and unharmed, he sat back on the *ikliq*, but did not sleep again. He looked over at Alaana, who lay sleeping beside him, and sighed.

222

"I can not make his troubles go away," said Old Manatook. "That is, I think, for you to do."

The two of them hovered over the village in the quiet night.

"There is more to see," said Old Manatook.

Alaana cast a wider net, peering into the tents of some of the other families. For Higilak, who lay asleep beside Old Manatook's earthly body, it was also a dream of children. Sitting amidst a circle of eager faces, each hanging on the very next word of her tale, she pretended they were all her own. As she filled their ears and minds with her story, so they filled her heart with an equal measure of hope and wonder.

For Tugtutsiak it was the ocean. Alaana supposed it must always be the ocean for him. He stood on the deck of his *umiak* in heavy sea, eye to eye with an enormous bowhead as it churned the waters. He anticipated an exciting chase and a successful kill, the admiration of the other men, the satisfaction of a well-fed camp and whale oil burning in all the lamps.

His wife Aolajut sat awake, softly consoling her sister who still wept over the loss of her dear husband Kuanak. In their tent also was Krabvik, the headman's uncle, also awake. He rolled a pair of small seal skulls across the floor, for Krabvik was old and crazy and held to a mistaken belief that the skulls held the souls of his long-lost children. Alaana chuckled at the sight of him and the endearing way he spoke to the bones at night.

In his tent Kanak dreamed of the hunt. The scent of caribou thick in his nostrils, the tension in the sinew of the bow and the muscles of his arms and neck sang with anticipation. For his adopted son Iggy, it was the sweet taste of the fruit of such a hunt. Caribou meat, boiled and roasted, liver and loin. Even after Iggy's betrayal, Alaana couldn't help but smile at her friend's mouth-watering delight at the thought of such a meal.

Up above the settlement, watching all the people she so loved, their dreams and aspirations, their worries and fears all laid bare in their sleep, Alaana was struck with an incredible sense of awe. How she loved them, every one of these people. Each heart held its own world of stunning hidden beauty.

Old Manatook brought the lesson to an end, saying, "These are the people you will protect. They have no other defense against the spirits, no chance of finding food in a blizzard, no hope of survival traveling alone in this harsh land. You are the guardian of their well-being, maintaining the balance, straddling both the physical and spirit worlds. The shaman is a man — a person — who lives in loneliness. The others know only one place, one reality. You are one of them but apart from them. You transcend them, yet walk among them. But although you travel freely between the seen and unseen worlds, you are here, you must always be here, in your heart.

"That is what it means to be the shaman."

"Wake up! Wake up!"

Alaana opened her eyes. This time it was not Itiqtuq rousing her from sleep but the firm hand of her father. "The day has already started," Kigiuna added. "It's time to eat."

Alaana noticed her father did not look any the worse for all his night terrors. His jaw was set, his blue eyes sparkled, and he was ready to begin the work of the day.

The smell of boiled fish heads was strong in the tent. Mother set the pot on the gravel floor as Alaana pulled on her underclothes and heavy parka. Maguan and Itoriksak, finding the stew still too hot for eating, warmed their hands over the pot. Pilarqaq sat cross-legged near the foot of the sleeping platform, chewing Maguan's boots to stretch and soften them after a night's hardening.

"Aquppak!" said Amauraq. "I didn't notice you there."

The boy had come in while they were making ready for the

day, and as was the custom, waited patiently in the doorway for someone to notice him.

"Do you have anything for Putuguk?" he asked in a low voice. Aquppak hated to beg, but he frequently visited the tents in the early mornings looking for charity.

When his parents were killed in a snowslide, Aquppak had been adopted by Putuguk who was actually his grandfather. The boy was constantly embarrassed by the old man's weakness and inability to provide for the family. His sister Tikiquatta had been widowed twice and was left with two young daughters of her own, one from each marriage.

"I'm certain we do," said Amauraq. "Kigiuna put something aside just this morning." She began rummaging among the food stores, half buried in the snow floor near the doorway. Alaana thought it was taking a long time to find something that had been put aside just that morning, but eventually Amauraq held up a fat, fresh trout.

"Will Tikiquatta have time to flay it, or should I?" asked Amauraq.

"Oh, she'll be fine."

"And what will you do today, Aquppak?" asked Kigiuna.

"Setting out a trapline for fox. Want to come along, Alaana?"

"Can't," she replied. "Got to study with Old Manatook."

Aquppak said his thanks and scooted out the tent flap, nearly colliding with Amauraq's sister Otonia on her way in. "That's a rich broth I smell," she said.

"There's plenty," said Kigiuna. "Sit with us."

"Aiyah!" shouted Amauraq, who had gone to straighten the now-vacant sleeping furs. "What's this?"

She came back holding up what looked like a clump of straight black hair. No sooner had she walked to the center of the tent, she rushed back to search again among the furs. Kigiuna, sipping from the ladle of steaming soup, followed her movements with a curious eye.

"Liar!" said Amauraq at last. "Cheat!"

She hurled this accusation at her daughter-in-marriage. The *kamik*, wet with saliva, dropped from Pilarqaq's mouth.

Amauraq charged toward Pilarqaq, then drew up short and ran at Kigiuna. She thrust the hairs under his nose. He interrupted his meal for a tentative sniff.

"It's the hair of a musk ox," Amauraq said sharply, before he had even an opportunity to comment. "From the back of the mane. I was wondering why there was always a stink in here."

Amauraq helped herself to another big sniff of the stuff, then waved it in the air above her head. "Oh, such beautiful, wonderful hair you have Pilarqaq! Oh, how long and lustrous and fine, Pilarqaq! Cheat!" She rushed back toward Pilarqaq, leapt at her, took hold of the hair in the middle of her head and began tugging at it. Several strands did come off in her hands but whether they were made of the damning musk ox mane or if they were Pilarqaq's own, plucked from her scalp, Alaana couldn't tell. Pilarqaq screamed and swatted her away.

Kigiuna, one hand clamped over his mouth, was hard pressed to keep from laughing. His face grew redder and redder.

Maguan found this not funny at all and rushed toward his beleaguered young wife. He wrenched her by the arm and pulled her outside.

"She's going to get a beating for this...," said Itoriksak.

"He'll throw her out, I'm sure," commented Otonia.

Amauraq said, "He'd better. Oh, my poor Maguan."

"A scandal for certain," returned Otonia. "It's no wonder she was unmarried among the Tanaina. I can only just imagine what Krittak will say."

"And think of the dowry," said Amauraq. "Kigiuna, how can

you stand it?"

Kigiuna brought the ladle to his lips and slurped noisily. All the while his eyes regarded his wife across the top of the ladle.

Amauraq was beside herself. "What a disgrace! I won't have that thief in this house a moment longer."

"That's not for you to decide," said Kigiuna sharply.

That being said, the whole lot of them rushed to the tent flap. Amauraq took a moment to pick up Pilarqaq's comb, a fine piece of carved ivory and her most prized possession, and snapped it in half, throwing the pieces on the floor. Only Kigiuna remained behind. He refused to be parted from the soup.

"Was that too much, do you think?" she said to Kigiuna. She was hard pressed to suppress a little laugh.

"I haven't seen a performance like that from you since I dragged you out of your father's tent to marry you."

"Teach her a lesson," said Amauraq.

Kigiuna sighed. "It took me a long time to carve that comb."

A small crowd had already gathered outside. Having heard shouts, the Anatatook smelled a good fight. They came running from their tents in anticipation of Maguan's first public thrashing of his beautiful spouse.

All eyes went to Maguan as he stood before his bride. He inspected the top of her head, parting the hair with his fingers. He spoke to her in hushed tones. She said nothing, but tears tracked down along her wonderful broad, flat cheeks. With a disapproving murmur from half of the crowd, and a sigh of relief from the other half, the two came together for a loving embrace.

Maguan then brought his wife back into his tent. Pulling her hastily by the arm, he sat her down beside the soup.

Saying nothing, Kigiuna passed her the ladle.

CHAPTER 21

LIGHT AND SHADOW

Tiggat was dying. Left alone at the kennel, the big dog lay curled into a ragged ball of tawny gray fur, his tie-in line trailing limply to the post. All the other dogs were gone, the men having taken them to the sea ice to sniff out the seal holes.

Alaana reached down and stroked Tiggat's forehead. Her fingers ran along the misshapen skull, passing over a thick, warty growth beneath the fur. "Rest now," she said. "You're a good dog."

Tiggat whimpered weakly. A restless movement of his head sent his snout deep into the ground snow. It pained Alaana to see the big dog brought so low. Tiggat had long been the boss dog of her father's team. So proud and strong, he dominated the pack, immediately taking fight to any newcomer hitched to the sled. With a ferocious growl, standing stiff-legged and bristling, Tiggat could whip any other dog in the camp.

Although fluttering weakly, the big dog's soul-light still shone a dauntless orange-yellow. Alaana reached out with her mind and tried to soothe the dog's flailing spirit in his last few moments. Tiggat's eyes rolled balefully toward her. As ferocious as he was with the other dogs he had always been affectionate and gentle with the children, even letting them pull his tail or sit on his back.

The huskie's soul surged, rising up out of the stiffening body. Animal souls didn't often remain with the body after death, and this one hurried away, running up into the sky as the mighty dog used to run, bold and strong.

"Goodbye Tiggat."

Now Alaana was once again left alone. She would leave Tiggat's body where it lay. Kigiuna would see to it. The fur would be skinned and someone would wear it as a shirt. The meat would be frozen and, once the familiar odor of Tiggat was washed away, the other dogs would eat it.

Alone again. Alaana bristled at the concept. Old Manatook was busy elsewhere and her father and brothers were out testing the ice, marking out the seal holes for the season's hunting. Most of the women had gone to help, leaving only a few behind to look after the children. And the children, it had been decided in a mutual wave of distrust, wanted nothing to do with her.

Gazing at the camp in the glow of the spirit-vision Alaana witnessed something new and wonderful in the air around her. With the onset of the winter freeze, the spirit of the frost mixed with the spirit of the air to create a sparkling gleam that danced on the currents of the dry wind. She smiled as she watched the frost play.

Alaana recalled the day Sila had lifted her high above the Anatatook camp, above the entire world, and shown her its wonders. In her darkest moments she always returned to the memory of that one flash of absolute clarity. The moment when she learned how people, animals and all things of this world were connected, each radiant with light and spirit.

Sila had opened up a wonderful world for her, but she was losing an entire world too. The ordinary world was slowly being crowded out. Maguan had said the other children avoided her because they were jealous of all the marvelous things she could see and do. But the opposite was true as well. She found she was very much jealous of them, jealous that they didn't know and needn't see all the terrible things which danced before her eyes in the shadows of the spirit world.

"You are an arrow loosed from Sila's bow," Old Manatook had told her. "Free yourself from hesitation and doubt, and fly true."

Alaana frowned. Even Sila seemed to have abandoned her. The great spirit had not returned since that very first day. Spirit of justice be damned. This was all his fault. He had dumped all this trouble into her lap and then gone away, leaving her alone. And lonely.

"Alaana?"

Aquppak stood before her, calling her name. She snapped back to reality, imagining how foolish she must have looked just then. What kind of silly expression had been written across her face?

"Heya," said Alaana. "Not playing with the others?"

"I don't feel like playing," said Aquppak, his words rife with frustration. "I wanted to join the men out on the ice, but Putuguk won't let me go. He says I'm still too young, that I have to wait until next year."

He suddenly noticed Tiggat. "I think your dog is dead."

"I know," said Alaana.

"It's not fair," said Aquppak. For an instant Alaana thought he was still speaking about her dog until he added, "I don't want to wait till next year. I want to get my seal and have my ceremony. I want to be a man."

The killing of his first seal had been the most important rite of manhood for Alaana's brother Maguan, as for any Anatatook hunter. A yearly festival was held where the bladders of the slain seals were inflated, painted with colorful designs and hung from the dome of a large ceremonial snow house. Old Manatook hung animal puppets from the ceiling as well, effigies of seals and walrus and whales, which flapped and moved by way of concealed fishing lines. At the yank of a cord, these puppets paid tribute to the souls of the hunted animals as the men sang and danced for three sleeps.

On the final day, Kuanak had stood atop the *iglu* and rendered an impassioned speech honoring the great *turgats* who had provided the band's nourishment and the valiant new hunters who had achieved their first kills. The bladders were gathered and the hunters followed the shaman down to the sea. A very young Alaana had watched Maguan take his turn, ripping open the bladder to release the soul of the departed seal beneath the water. Alaana had raced up for a closer look but saw nothing unusual.

But now in possession of the spirit-vision the memory of that day was colored with a new light; she clearly observed the souls of the seals, vivid purple balls of light in the water, as they circled and danced, then sank back down into the depths to be reborn again.

The new hunters rode back to the settlement in a short procession of kayaks. Alaana had run along the banks of the river, waving to Maguan as he went by. Her brother had looked no different at the time except for a foolish wide-mouthed grin, but now with the memory shaded by her new vision, Alaana could see how Maguan's soul had actually changed. A newfound confidence and virility sharpened the hue. Maguan had become a man.

And next year Aquppak would have his turn. And also, in her own way, would Alaana. From what little she had been able to glean from Old Manatook's' mysterious hints, the ceremony for a young shaman was different, an initiation held out in the trackless wastes. She wasn't looking forward to it.

"That's what I want, more than anything," said Aquppak. "To hunt, to provide for my family. I won't have to beg for Putuguk anymore. I won't have to wear cast-offs and dogskin

231

clothes. I'll make a name for myself among the men."

"I know you will," said Alaana.

Aquppak put on his most serious, manly expression. "And I will, too. I'll be the best."

Alaana smiled, joining in her friend's fantasy. "You'll be the headman, I'll bet."

Aquppak beamed handsomely. "That's right. Who needs sour old Tugtutsiak? And grumpy Old Manatook? I'll be the headman and you'll be the shaman. We'll be in charge of everything."

The two of them got carried away laughing. And it was good to laugh. Alaana had almost thought she'd forgotten how.

"But what about now?" she asked.

"Oh, that's what I came to tell you. Three days ago, I spotted a falcon's nest up on Dog-Ear Ridge. I didn't tell anyone." A winsome smile puffed his cheeks and he winked. Alaana was impressed at being included in so important a secret.

"This is our last chance before winter to get up there and try to get that falcon," Aquppak explained. He held up his *kiipooyaq*, with its three strands of sinew each tipped with a slant-cut segment of ox tail bone. Alaana remembered when Kigiuna had made it for him. Aquppak brandished the weapon. "That falcon won't have a chance."

Alaana glanced at the peaked outline of Dog-Ear Ridge, a rugged cliff of sandstone speckled with ice and snow. "That's a long way to go for such a small chance."

"Small chance?" Chuckling, Aquppak began spinning the threads, getting one bone-tip swinging in a southerly direction and another the opposite way. Alaana took half a step backward. Although Aquppak was fairly adept at the game of *chuk chuk*, he did occasionally hit himself in the face. When Aquppak tried to get the third strand going in an independent direction, a move that almost always resulted in something or someone getting inadvertently hit, Alaana cried out, "Enough, enough."

"I'll go alone if I have to," said Aquppak.

Alone. Alaana took her friend by the arm. "You don't have to go alone."

"Good," replied Aquppak, with a mischievous glint in his eye. "If we're going to run things around here together, we might as well get started."

They'd been climbing the cliff face for most of the day and now the sun had reached its highest point, still only a little bit above the horizon. Alaana took a moment to appreciate the slight warmth it brought to her face, and how beautifully its light glittered on the ice below. Soon they would have only twilight days without a sun, and then the long winter night.

A treacherous wind came roaring up the slope from the sea. It whipped around the cliff face only to rush back out, all too willing to blow unwary children off the ledge. The intense cold of winter had already declared itself but didn't bother Alaana much with her hood pulled over. Except for the foot. On the way up she'd stepped into a deceptively deep pocket among the rocks and some wet snow had trickled into her boot. Even the long climb had failed to warm her foot. It chilled her entire leg, but she didn't have the heart to turn Aquppak back.

The wind whistled in the heights. It cast a fine spray of drift into her face, reminding Alaana of her fickle patron Sila. But no, she thought, it was just the wind. Sila wouldn't even stoop to insult her with a faceful of snow.

The view of the sea was exquisite. Just beyond the base of the knoll a great white berg stood silent guard over the lazy, ice-covered waters. Beyond the cluster of snow houses in the bay, the white wastes of the north extended as far as the eye could see.

233

Alaana had witnessed many extraordinary landscapes on her soul flights above Nunatsiaq, but this was different. This time she'd paid for it, working her way up the slope, step by step, hauling herself over the rocks. The spectacular view was all the more sweet for having worked so hard to gain it.

"Look," said Alaana, pointing toward the ocean. "You can see them all from here."

At this distance she couldn't pick out her father or brothers among the figures spread out over the sea ice. Most of the men wore identical coats and dark sealskin leggings. Some were busy testing the strength of the ice, while others worked the dogs or squatted before the seal holes, hacking clear the openings. Old Manatook, however, was easy to identify. Taller than the others, he hurried among the men dressed in his faded white parka and pants of polar bear fur.

"I don't care about them," said Aquppak. "I want to find that bird." He faced the other way, gazing up at the crest of the Ridge. "I saw it two sleeps ago. It has to be here."

"How much farther?" asked Alaana, rubbing at the mukluk covering her frozen foot.

"Not much. Let's move on."

Progress from this point was difficult. Jagged outcroppings rose straight up from the uneven surface, leaving gaping ravines between them, narrow but very deep. The children had to leap across each gap and pull themselves up among the rocks on the far side. Aquppak huffed and fretted, clearly annoyed at not having chosen the best route of ascent.

Alaana's arms grew tired from climbing over the sharp edges, her legs trembling with exertion. She recognized this site as the place where the murres roosted in springtime. Earlier in the year she and her mother had come to these cliffs looking for fresh eggs atop the rocky ledges. She remembered their wonderfully salty taste,

234

cracked open and devoured right on the spot.

Alaana's sluggish foot slipped and suddenly snow and sandstone shales started to flow underfoot, carrying her down into the ravine. She dug her heels in the snow but couldn't slow down. She grabbed desperately at the stones as they flew by but only tore her mittens and skinned the flesh from her fingers and palms. With a startled cry, she plunged into one of the clefts.

Her rough downward slide ended painfully with one leg wedged between a large stone and the rock face. She succeeded in freeing her leg and pulled herself over the top of the stone, but could find no way to scale back up the steep slope. Handholds were few and treacherous with ice. It was far too dangerous to climb, and certain death yawned below.

Alaana was afraid to move or she might start sliding again. She called out for Aquppak but he would never be able to get down to help her, or climb back up if he did. Her only chance was a small opening in the rock face directly above the ledge. Alaana carefully stretched up to get a look, catching her breath at every bit of loose shale she sent plummeting into the chasm. The opening led to a short tunnel through the cliff. In a hopeful sign, the dark rock was speckled with creamy bird droppings throughout, indicating there probably was an opening at the other end.

She wriggled into the tunnel, passing through to a narrow ledge on the other side. The ledge hugged the cliff face as it wound its way upward. A bulge of the rocks above the ledge obstructed any view higher up. Beside the ledge was a steep and dangerous gap.

"Aquppak!" she called again, but it was no use.

The ledge was narrow, and the overhanging rocks forced Alaana to crawl slowly on her belly, knees and elbows. Following a steady upward course, the ledge curved out of sight. It seemed her only way up.

She crept slowly forward, pulling herself along amid a trickle of shale and bits of loose ice. The muscles in her arms had already been spent on the climb up but, digging down deep, she found the strength to continue. But after rounding the turn, it became obvious that the ledge had been a mistake. Ahead, it narrowed and narrowed until it merged into the overhanging rock. With no handholds in sight, she could go no further.

Alaana's breath caught in her throat. She needed to go back down but she was facing the wrong direction. It was impossible to turn around on the narrow ledge. Peering over the edge, she had a good view all the way down into the drop below. Any mistake promised a deadly fall to the bottom.

Her mind raced, frantically trying to conceive of some way the rock itself could be induced to help. Surely the spirit of the mountain didn't want her to die here. But she could neither calm herself nor slow her breathing. The thought of death was too sharp in her mind, the rising panic quickening the pace of her heart. She couldn't achieve the peace of mind necessary to communicate with the spirits.

She felt nauseous and dizzy, her situation all but hopeless. She couldn't turn around. Her only chance lay in trying to back up along the ledge, going blind. Perhaps if she went very, very slowly. But the ledge was slippery with ice, a condition that had not caused much difficulty on the way up, but became an unbearable problem when trying to return in the backwards position. She could think of nothing else but slipping and falling. Falling and then being dashed against the rocks below. She had never felt the pull of the earth so strongly; it seemed intent on dragging her down to her death.

"What kind of trouble have you gotten yourself into, little bird?"

Alaana turned her head as far to the side as she dared. A vision of Civiliaq hovered above her. The shaman's dirty boots were close in front of Alaana's face, stepping on empty air.

Civiliaq looked much the same as Alaana had last seen him, his black raven wings burned off, his ornate tattoos smoldering. But the shaman's spirit-form was so insubstantial Alaana could see the outline of the opposite rock face through his body. He was not smiling.

"Help me! I'm stuck here."

"So I see," replied Civiliaq.

"Help me!"

"That I can not do," said Civiliaq sadly. "I am still trapped in the Underworld where Old Manatook has left me. You remember? What you see is only a shadow of my spirit, projected here at great exertion. Even down below, I still worry over you, daughter of Kigiuna. And I sensed you had fallen into trouble."

"Isn't there anything you can do?"

"Perhaps mighty Tulukkugaq could help, but I have lost all connection to the Great Raven, my spirit guardian."

At mention of the raven Alaana recalled something she had seen last year when hunting these cliffs for eggs. One of the murres, having fallen from the cliff, lay stranded on the ice. A crafty raven, grown tired of living off scraps, gazed eagerly at it. The little bird, unable to take flight from such a flat surface, hopped lamely away. But its feet soon froze, rendering it defenseless, and the raven made a quick meal of it.

"It's all I can do to appear here before you," continued Civiliaq, "and warn you of danger. And soon I fade. It's no use. Why don't you call upon your own guardian. Sila, isn't it?"

"That won't work," said Alaana desperately.

"And why not? You still have his light. I can see it."

"It won't work," repeated Alaana, with neither the time nor inclination to explain. She felt the rock face ready to give away beneath her at any moment. "It just won't."

237

Civiliaq nodded his head in a sort of painful acquiescence but when his face lifted again, his eyes held a thoughtful shimmer. "There's only one chance then," he said. "If I had your light, I believe I could manage some way to get you out of this dilemma."

"Then you can have it," said Alaana. "I don't want it. I never did."

"Well, I can't simply take that burden from you, little bird. You have to give it to me. Yes, that might solve your problem. You have only to let it go."

Release the light? Was such a thing possible? She thought about it. Her spirit was, she realized, like a fist holding tight to Sila's gifts. She had only to release that hold, relax the fingers and open up the hand…

"Then here it is," said Alaana. "Take it from me."

"That I can do," said Civiliaq.

Alaana began to relax the ties that bound her to Sila. Civiliaq's spirit-form bent closer, peering intently at her. The shaman's eyes flew wide in surprise for an instant, recoiling slightly backward. He shook his head in disbelief.

"What did you see?" asked Alaana. "Just then, what did you see?"

"Don't you mind that. We haven't much time. Let me help you. Give me the light now. Hurry!"

His outstretched hand reached eagerly toward her. But something about the greedy light in Civiliaq's eyes gave her pause. She drew back the fist, coiling herself once more around Sila's gift.

Now that it was hers to give away, she realized just how much she desired to keep it. She thought of her family and all the other brave people of Nunatsiaq. If she gave the light away, what would the Anatatook do for a shaman? Old Manatook was old and getting older all the time. Who would take care of them, if not her? Not Civiliaq. He was already dead.

She had been entrusted with this responsibility, with this destiny. She alone.

"What's wrong?" demanded Civiliaq. "Why do you delay? Hurry before the demons get their claws into you."

"Demons?"

"Yes, surely you can hear them."

Alaana cocked her head to the side. It was true. A tormented wail was rising up from the depths of the chasm.

"You should hurry," urged Civiliaq. "It's not safe here. Don't you hear them? They're coming up."

Alaana hesitated. She thought Civiliaq's sudden panic played false. "What demons are these?"

"The *tarraks* of the abyss. This is an old place, a place of death. These rocks are tainted with blood, this chasm can not be separated from the tragedy that happened here. Always the past seeps into the present. *Ayarnaarmat.* It can't be helped."

Civiliaq thrust out his open palm, the fingers curling upward as they awaited Sila's gift.

Alaana shook her head. "Tell me."

"We waste precious time with stories. You see those rock piles below? They fell from these cliffs years ago. A gigantic landslide splashed down into the water. A party of Tungu women had climbed up here to get eggs from the ledges, leaving their men idle back at the camp. But as the women were gone, the men broke the taboos. And in so doing they brought the cliffs down. The women were crushed and buried as the cliff rocks fell on them. When their cries rang out from beneath the rocks, the men came looking. But the men couldn't get them out. They could only listen to the screams of their lovers as they went on and on.

"Over the years, the spirits of these women became demons. Hunger drove them at first, as it drives all of us. Pain and loneliness corrupted them. They have no need for physical food; they feast on

239

the naked souls of unwary travelers. I tried to warn you. Now it's almost too late. Only with your power can I hope to fend them off. Hurry. Give it here!"

As the terrible sounds drew nearer, Alaana envisioned the angry *tarraks* clawing their way up the ravine. Three women, rotten hags with the same hungry eyes as the fever demon that had tormented her last spring. Dry, cracked lips smacking. Long, clawed fingernails scraping the rock.

And yet, before Civiliaq had mentioned them, Alaana had heard nothing.

"Last chance, little bird," barked Civiliaq, "Before you feed the hungry demons of the cliffside."

But it was Civiliaq who seemed too eager and hungry. She knew that look in his eyes. Every Anatatook knew the look of hunger.

"You're lying!" said Alaana. "Let them come."

Slowly, with infinite caution, she began to push herself backward. It felt as if her arms were lifting her entire weight with each shove. By the time she'd gone halfway back along the ledge, she was nearly exhausted. To make matters worse, she misjudged the edge with her right leg and kicked away a clump of sandstone. The loose stones clattered down the drop as her leg swung over the ledge, threatening to drag her down. At any moment she expected a withered arm to reach up from the abyss and latch onto that leg with hideous strength and pull.

With a desperate lurch, she swung the leg back up. The jarring motion almost sent her tumbling to her death, but she held on with all her strength.

Once she had reassured herself she was still among the living, Alaana felt around with the tip of her boot.

She was still held tight in the icy grip of fear, helpless to call upon any sort of spiritual aid. She had knocked too much of the ledge off and it was now too narrow to continue her retreat down the slope. She had no way to proceed.

The apparition of Civiliaq had vanished, taking the shrieks of the demon-women away with it but Alaana's dilemma was no less dangerous than before. She lay very still, unable to calm herself down.

"Alaana!"

She opened her eyes. A length of sinew dangled just above her shoulders.

"Take the line," said Aquppak. "It's steady up at this end. You can climb up."

Her heart still pounding, Alaana threw off her mittens and rubbed her hands along the grit of the rock face to warm them. She took the line in both hands and swung free of the ledge. It was not such a long climb, but her arms were already tired and weak. As she neared the top, her strength was all but gone. She wasn't going to make it. Again she thought the rope might be convinced to help, or perhaps the wind, but she didn't have the presence of mind to make the attempt.

She cried out, certain she could go no farther, nor maintain her hold much longer. Aquppak's arm came swinging down. "Take my hand." Dangling dangerously close to the edge himself, the boy hauled her up with both hands.

Alaana hugged the snow-strewn rock at the top as she rolled over onto her back. It had never felt so good to feel solid ground.

Only one thought was in her mind. She had very nearly died. If not for the quick action of Aquppak in climbing down after her, she would have.

As her friend helped her to her feet, she felt a great love for Aquppak. The boy was a true hero, having saved her by the strength of his arm and a willingness to act without hesitation.

"You saved my life."

Aquppak shook his head, saying in an offhanded way, "It's nothing. The hunters do that kind of stuff all the time."

"I won't forget it."

"Fine," said Aquppak, smiling handsomely. He glanced up toward the peak of the ridge. "You think we can still get that bird?"

Alaana thought that in all likelihood the falcon had already followed the snowbirds on their southerly quest for warmer climes, but she wasn't going to say so.

CHAPTER 22

TAKE UP THE RATTLE

Ivalu, who was Ipalook's wife, would not look at anyone. She sat on the edge of the sleeping platform, hunched over, her head in her hands. Her hair hung loose and wild.

The air in the *iglu* stung Alaana's nostrils. It was rife with curls of wafting smoke from the sputtering seal oil lamp and stank of urine and rotting meat. Old Manatook stood beside the stricken girl, with Alaana next to him. Behind them in the small circular room were Ivalu's parents and Maguan's constant friend Ipalook. A pair of newborn pups darted about underfoot, their white fur dusted with black soot.

Ipalook said, "My wife hasn't left the *iglu* in three sleeps."

Ivalu's father, Ogpingalik, looked upon the scene with typical Anatatook stoicism. In contrast her mother, Misana, couldn't hide her worry or her tears. Misana added sadly, "She lost her child, un-named and only half-formed. She passed the poor little thing in the snow outside the camp. She won't even tell me where."

"She won't go outside, and she can't stand the light," added Ipalook. He absently kicked one of the puppies out of the way. "Two days ago she spoke of terrible pains in the head. Now she says nothing."

Misana brushed her daughter's forehead, tenderly sweeping

back a wayward clump of hair. "Other women have come visiting. They've tried to help but it's no use. They all have children of their own, and it's twice now that Ivalu has failed to bear her fruit."

"She won't do any work," said Ipalook.

"Enough," said Old Manatook. Standing tall in the *iglu*, he drove his fist up at the dome to crack the seal.

"*You see?*" he said to Alaana in the secret language. "*What affects one begins to affect them all. They don't even have enough sense to clear the vent hole.*"

He punched again at the ceiling and a few pieces of ice spattered down, revealing a clear night sky behind the veil of smoky air drifting upward.

Ivalu's family exchanged concerned glances. They didn't understand the shaman's words and assumed they had some deep and mysterious significance. Even Ogpingalik, who was deaf in both ears, looked impressed.

Old Manatook bent over the stricken girl, gently lifting her head by the point of her chin. The broad oval of her face was completely blackened with accumulated soot from the smoky house, with the exception of a pair of tracks that ran straight down from the corners of her eyes where her tears had washed the grit away.

"Ivalu," he said.

She did not answer.

"She doesn't answer," said Ipalook.

Old Manatook shot him a withering glance. "I can see that."

"She looks right through us," said Misana, "Or else down at the ground. This isn't normal."

"Of course it's not normal," Old Manatook huffed. The shaman bent down the lower lid of the girl's left eye and gazed inside.

The old shaman urged Alaana closer with a jerk of his head.

"*The problem is obvious,*" he said privately. "*A simple thing. Come and look."*

Alaana stepped up. She knew the method by which a shaman, gazing in the eye, could make a direct inspection of the soul. With intense concentration, she looked beyond the obscuring veil of the iris and entered the dark abyss of the pupil. A scintillating corona of light rushed forward to meet her, brilliant colors unknown to the eyes of those who dwelled in the Anatatook world of white and gray. Streaks of indigo and violet, verdant green and shimmering gold flashed by.

And at the end, gleaming and radiant, the naked soul-light of Ivalu was there. All the things that made up her life's essence, her dreams and aspirations, sorrows and fears. A dazzling spectacle. Alaana wished she could spend a lifetime studying all its depth and beauty.

"I can't see anything wrong," she said.

"Hmmf. You must first know what to look for. It's a power intrusion from the shadow world, taking advantage of her sadness and grief. There's a shadow on her soul. Look there, underneath the part that belongs to Ipalook."

Alaana pressed forward again, looking for any smudge that marked an intrusion. She concentrated her effort on those fragments of souls which had so touched Ivalu's own that they had made a place for themselves within the very heart of her being. A piece of Ipalook was there as well as, Alaana was surprised to find, a little bit of both of the unborn she had lost. And hidden among them, a shadow.

"A simple thing to take care of," added Old Manatook. *"But we must first have things right inside this room. Take up the rattle."*

Old Manatook provided one of his best rattles, a single root of heartwood carved into an elegant cage containing a handful of polar bear teeth. Alaana had been given no instruction as to the proper cadence for this ritual. She took up what she supposed to be a natural rhythm.

The seal oil lamp flared up, flickering intensely for a moment and then went out. There was a startled gasp from the family.

"*What you would not long ago have considered a contemptible trick, serves a noble purpose,*" said Old Manatook. "*Look at their faces. Now sense what they are feeling.*"

Starlight alone lit the room. Filtered through what was left of the smoke it touched the faces of Ivalu's loved ones, revealing a mixture of awe, reverence and faith. Their minds were becalmed, confident in the shaman's power to heal.

"*Ivalu senses it,*" said Old Manatook, "*They give her strength.*"

The shaman's fingers reached out toward a particular area of the girl's forehead just above the brow where the bones of the skull came together. This was an important entrance and exit point for harmful spirits.

Old Manatook began to hum. His power song for Tornarssuk filled the ice house, a slow deep cadence that spoke of long lonely treks across the ice. Old Manatook paused between each refrain for a slow breath, an expression of quiet rapture over his face. Alaana was amazed at the transformation. In this new light the craggy lines of her teacher's gloomy countenance had become a serene ideal of dignity and faith.

Alaana felt a twinge of jealousy. She didn't know any power song for Sila. Old Manatook had searched for such a song on his many journeys, but to no avail. There were no other shamans in the northlands who could claim the Walker In The Wind as their guardian spirit. All Old Manatook could say was that Sila must teach her the song directly. Alaana despaired she would never learn it.

Ivalu cocked an ear. "What is that sound?" she whispered.

"A song of healing, my love," said Old Manatook. "A song of my guide Tornarssuk."

"So beautiful," she murmured.

Ipalook and Misana exchanged an enthusiastic glance of approval. Even Ogpingalik, who was completely deaf and could hear nothing at all, began to smile.

Old Manatook knelt before the girl, gently touching her face, still humming his power song. He instructed Alaana again, saying, *"In order to free her mind, you must take her troubles as your own. It's the only way."*

"I feel your pain and sorrow," the old shaman said loudly. "It's a terrible thing that has happened to you. But you do not stand alone. I walk the same path, in the dark places in your mind, and I am not afraid. I will take your burden and cast it far away. Help me in this."

As Old Manatook established the connection, Alaana began to sense the change. The shaman's mind was softening, flowing outward, shaping itself to match the outline of Ivalu's soul-light. Alaana found it fascinating the way Manatook's immensely powerful mind sought not to dominate but instead bent to the will of the sufferer. Ivalu's spirit rose up to meet him. Their heartbeats aligned, their minds joined.

Alaana caught an echo of the girl's pain. She saw the stark image of Ivalu's bloody miscarriage as it was cast steaming atop the white snow, slowly sinking into the melting mound. It was so cruel and unfair.

Ivalu had dared to hope. She had dared to hope that despite what had happened before, this child would live; that she would hold the baby in her arms, soft and warm. That she would name the baby Tertaq, a name that had long been in her family, and that she would cuddle him and love him. She had dared to dream. Only to see it all come to nothing, a red splotch on the snow. Alaana felt the crushing sadness in her heart, suffering every bit of her pain.

"Tornarssuk will remove the dark thing inside her," Old Manatook announced.

The leather-wrapped handle of the rattle tingled in Alaana's hand. She glanced at it, seeing the spirits flare within the bear teeth. She wanted desperately to feel the power of Tornarssuk for herself, but she could not — that boon was reserved for Old Manatook. She realized she had stopped working the rattle. A wry smile crossed her lips. Old Manatook did not need her help; the rattle was irrelevant. Nevertheless, she took up the rhythm again.

Old Manatook pressed his lips to Ivalu's forehead at the juncture of the bones. He alternated blowing air at the fontanel and sucking in.

"Ahh, I feel the darkness and the pain that has come."

His tall frame, bent over the sitting girl, seemed to sag under the weight of the strain. Alaana realized this was once again for show only. Old Manatook had nothing but confidence and strength.

"Great Bear, take this evil away."

Alaana felt a rip tide of energy tear through the room. The hand of Tornarssuk swept down, snatching the malicious shadow and carrying it away. She felt as if the entire *iglu* must blow apart with the power of that great clawed hand, but the spirit was concerned only with Ivalu, and in a moment it was done.

Ivalu moaned softly. Her eyes flew open.

"It's done," announced Old Manatook. He turned to Ipalook, saying, "I can do nothing for her grief. That is your responsibility. But her spirit is healed."

Misana rushed to give her daughter a heartfelt embrace.

"Thank you, *angatkok*," said Ipalook sincerely. He turned to Alaana and clasped her hand warmly with both of his own. He bowed his head slightly. "Thank you."

Alaana was taken aback. Ipalook, the longstanding friend of Maguan with a sour disposition, had so often teased her in the past. This reaction was the last thing she had expected. Alaana was embarrassed at having been thanked. She'd done nothing but shake the rattle, and even that had been completely unnecessary.

CHAPTER 23

BLACK FACE

It was not yet the deep winter cold, the cold that renders every breath a painful chore and sucks the life from the body. Nor was it the stinging midwinter cold that eats relentlessly away at hand and face wherever it may find them. But the wet cool of summer had become the dry, hard cold of early winter with breath clouding all day from start to finish.

Old Manatook seized the first opportunity, as soon as the fresh ice made such distant travel possible, to take Alaana on a long journey. They had been at it for two days, traveling east and then north. With a team of three well-fed dogs eager for the run, their sled flew across the tundra. Makaartunghak, Old Manatook's gigantic gray huskie, pulled mightily at the lead with two smaller dogs in swing positions. The team would've been an even four but Old Manatook's other dog, Yipyip, insisted on riding on the sled. Yipyip, a coal-black mixed breed, sat beside her master on the front stanchion. The little dog rested her head on the shoulder opposite where the winged creature often resided, giving a balance of black and white to frame Old Manatook's face.

The sled sped along the hard pack, crossing a wide basin between the glaciers. With no trail to follow they advanced erratically, their path winding around a chain of small frozen lakes.

Old Manatook kept mostly silent, concentrating on the way before them. The fresh ice could be treacherously thin where swift water ran below, and often bent and creaked beneath their runners.

The fast-moving dogs churned up clouds of snow. Wherever the spray struck Alaana's parka it stuck, fringing her garments with frost and tiny icicles. She didn't know their destination, the point of some mysterious errand which Old Manatook said he had put off for too long already. Alaana knew this territory only through the tales and recountings of others. She was determined to memorize all the landmarks as they passed. More than any other Anatatook she must know the region, she had been told, for when the *angatkok* went traveling it was most often alone.

Sometimes she ran along behind the sled to warm up. Drifting snow, tossed about by the brisk arctic wind, swirled at waist height, only occasionally rising high enough to swat her face. Alaana kept her nose tucked into the flap of her hood to prevent the ground blow from freezing the skin off her cheeks.

The sky deepened from cool blue to gloomy indigo. Night was almost upon them. Old Manatook pointed out Black Face, a ridge of dark stone that rose far above the tundra, its surface covered with a delicate white tracery of frozen run-off from above. They kept close to the sheltering rock, safe from the northerly winds.

Yipyip curled herself in Alaana's lap as if seeking warmth there. Actually her motivation was the exact opposite. The mysterious little dog blazed with her own inner fire and Alaana wrapped herself around its pleasant warmth.

"Hooo," said Old Manatook, ordering the dogs to stop. Black Face opened before them, a heel of rock thrust out from the cliff like a petulant jawbone. An arch of ancient stone marked a cave entrance.

"This is an old resting place," said Old Manatook. "We'll stay here for the night."

Alaana hopped down from the sled and began to untie the gear. She was eager to set up the tent but Old Manatook placed a restraining hand on her shoulder. He sniffed at the air like a hound.

"Wolverines are about and they're hungry," said the old shaman, his eyes scanning, his nose drinking deep. "Eight or ten of them. They have our scent already, and they intend to attack."

Alaana scanned the view to the south. The flat expanse of tundra showed no signs of life or movement. The many jagged rocks scattered about the base of the cliff would provide the wolverines an opportunity to approach unseen.

"We should go," she said.

Old Manatook shook his head. "This dampness in the air foretells a storm. Makaartunghak is worth three wolverines in a fight. We can handle them if necessary, but if they should tear down the tent in the middle of the night we'll have real trouble. We'll be better off inside the cave."

Alaana refastened the thongs she had already untied, then took hold of the traces. When she tried to lead the dogs inside, Makaartunghak balked at her efforts. He much preferred a warm burrow in the snow to the cold stone interior of a gloomy cave. The big dog, pulling back with all his prodigious strength, was too much for Alaana to handle.

"I'll take them," said Old Manatook. "You'd better see what you can find growing among the rocks to use for torch and fuel. Without a good fire, we won't last the night."

Alaana dared not venture too far from the entrance. Just outside the cave mouth she found a few clumps of short heath growing between the rocks and the tips of upland grass peeking out like stubble above the crusted snow. She thought she saw shadows slinking nearby as she picked her way among the stones, but the light was fading quickly and she couldn't be sure. In any case there was no doubt of the wolverines. By now their smell was thick all around. Her heart pounding, she pulled the frozen grasses up by the handful, pausing just long enough to scrape some dry moss from the stones.

Old Manatook had prepared a place for the fire. In the darkness he'd found an old log set aside long ago. The wood was ancient and hard enough to pass for stone. As Alaana arranged the log and the grasses, the wolverines began a chorus of starved, frustrated cries outside. A dark shape flitted across the cave entrance.

Makaartunghak, who had been set loose from the traces, darted forward. He crouched just within the cave opening and hurled his own wild bark out into the night.

Old Manatook commanded him, "Stay here!"

Makaartunghak glanced unhappily at his master, then snapped his head back to resume his watch. Old Manatook tossed a slab of dried fish at him but the big dog ignored the food, aiming a series of low growls at the cave mouth.

The other dogs were content to huddle at the side of the cave, bickering over the last scraps of the meal of minced salmon Old Manatook had given them. Yipyip, a black shadow, slipped outside.

"Heya!" said Alaana. "Yipyip!"

"She'll be fine," said Old Manatook.

"I hope so," said Alaana. "I've been thinking. There must be a way to convince the souls of the wolverines to leave us alone."

"You may ask, but it won't work. Hunger speaks loudest of all things."

"Can't you force them? Compel their souls to go away?"

"No," said Old Manatook. Alaana could see little of her teacher's face in the dark except for his eyes, which were alive with soul fire. "That is the difference between a shaman and a sorcerer, and a sorcerer is but one step from a demon. We ask. We cannot

253

do more. Now, start the fire."

"The smoke will choke us in here."

"I think not," said Old Manatook. The dark silhouette of a finger passed before Alaana's face, and she followed it upward to see a star-lit vent hole at the top of the cave.

The spirit within the log was ancient and drawn thin, a dim glimmer barely clinging to this existence. It said it had once been a tree and been quite happy at it, but had now been only a log for a long, long time. Ages had passed since it had thought much about anything at all, but it admitted to being at least curious to see what it would be like to be smoke instead.

Alaana asked the tiny spirit within the dry moss to spark into flame, and offered apologies to the grasses.

The fire caught and flared up.

"That's good," said Old Manatook. He had upended the sled beside the hearth, and already begun draping his wet clothes over the runners to dry. Old Manatook was the oldest man Alaana had ever seen. Naked, he looked as if his skin did not fit him well; it sagged and wrinkled in odd places like a loose shirt that he might simply shirk off at any moment.

Alaana stopped in the midst of unfastening her parka. The far wall of the cave, bathed now in warm amber light, had caught her eye.

Men from ages past had marked the wall, blowing powdered paint over the backs of their hands to leave behind the outlines of broad, thick-fingered palms.

"This is a Tunrit cave," said Alaana. Now she understood the unlikely vent hole, which had been carved out of the rock ages ago by men of legendary muscle and sinew.

Figures of the Tunrit were drawn in dark silhouette against a brown ochre background of cracking paint. Bulky men with overlarge heads, carrying arrows and spears. The Tunrit had lived here in the dark days of the world's beginning, leaving behind the marks of their hands on the wall in silent memorial of their struggle to survive in those wild times. It seemed to Alaana that the cave still echoed with their voices, cries of determination and strife, glad shouts swelling up after a successful hunt, and the melancholy laments of all that had been lost to them.

The ancient paint was chipped and flaking away, etched by moss at the damp fringes. The paintings must soon be erased completely, but how soon? Having stood for thousands of years, how fast does time eat them away, Alaana wondered.

She thought the paintings both crude and beautifully evocative. The long-tusked *mamut* marched there, outlined in white and gray, tremendous shapes with humped backs and powerful limbs. Other strange beasts with bony faces and odd-shaped horns stalked among the shadows, their long snouts and crushing jaws ready for a charge at the Tunrit hunters.

Smoke swirled before the paintings, and the shifting firelight made it seem as if the animals had come to life, tensed and ready to leap out of the rock wall itself. At the lower edge of the wall Alaana noted a strange figure. More finely rendered than the others, it stood apart. A tall Tunrit, dressed in a long gown of matted grasses. His face was empty except for two sooty black circles that represented eyes. But strangely, as the flickering firelight touched the cave painting it seemed as if the eyes glowed red to match the burning embers of the hearth.

"That figure on the wall…" said Alaana.

"A Tunrit Sorcerer," explained Old Manatook, without looking up. He was busy giving his feet a vigorous rubbing-down before the fire.

Alaana felt a wracking chill and turned away. She shook off her wet clothes and hung them out to dry. She sat naked before the small fire, grateful for the log's generous gift of warmth. Old

255

Manatook handed her a slab of dried fish with two lumps of caribou fat draped over the top.

"Where is this place we're going?" Alaana asked. "Won't you tell me?"

"Hmmm, I suppose I shall have to at last." With the harsh yellow highlights and deep shadows thrown across his face by the shifting firelight Old Manatook looked even more dour than usual. "It's a foul place. A place of great danger, Alaana. Murdered souls fester there. There was a war, and people killed in their sleep. I'm no storyteller, so I'll just come out with it. If my Higilak were here she could make you see it clear and feel the true horror of it. But perhaps this is not a tale you want to know too well."

The dogs crept close to the fire, all except Makaartunghak who held his position at the entrance in answer to the frustrated cries of the wolverines. The huskies settled around the old shaman, their noses low to the ground, as if they too would hear the tale.

"It happened like this: A man from Uwelen was traveling to the south with his wife, and came upon a rival band. A stranger in their camp, he was killed by a man in need of a wife. When this news reached Uwelen the man's relatives sent out a revenge party. They were confident of success. They had many excellent archers among the Uwelen and good spearmen as well. When their enemies saw the party approach they sent out their own hunters. The two groups faced each other across a field of ice, and the drifts grew red with blood. In the end the men from Uwelen took back the woman who had been stolen.

"They returned home from their war victorious, but found they had lost all. In the absence of the strong men, Yupikut raiders had set upon the village of the Uwelen. They took the women and slaughtered the old men left behind to guard them. Children's bodies lay strewn in the snow, the dogs nibbling at their faces. Such is the cruelty of the Yupikut.

256

"It was too much to bear. Some men fell dead on the spot, their hearts bursting with grief. Others killed themselves or turned against each other, adding to the toll of tormented ghosts. Some had the idea to reclaim the women, but in truth once the Yupikut got finished with them their husbands couldn't want them back. They went after the Yupikut anyway, knowing they would be killed."

Old Manatook turned his head toward the cave entrance. The smaller dogs had approached Makaartunghak and begun sniffing at his still-uneaten slab of fish. With a swipe of his massive paw the big dog sent them creeping back to the fire.

"We shamans come here to Uwelen whenever we can, so that the evil does not spread and threaten us as well. It's a long time since I've passed this way. I fear we've neglected Uwelen. There are too many tasks to do and too few shamans in Nunatsiaq nowadays."

"Ghosts and more ghosts," said Alaana with a sigh. "It seems as if there are ghosts everywhere we turn."

Old Manatook nodded. "This is a harsh and unforgiving land. Nunatsiaq provides for us, but only what we wrestle from its grasp. And also it takes. It takes. Many come to a bitter end among the ice and snow. Even good people are driven to do terrible things when their bellies are empty and the cold claws at them and the sun closes its golden eye and goes away."

"I think it's a beautiful land." replied Alaana.

"Yes. That too."

"It doesn't matter how hard it is," added Alaana. "We survive. Just take a deep, deep breath and feel it fill you up. That's the most beautiful thing of all."

"Now you've got it." Old Manatook actually smiled. The emotion did not sit well with his face. His cheeks bulged oddly as if the wrinkled flaps of flesh might fall off at any moment.

"You'll do the task tomorrow," he added. "But remember the danger. These ghosts thirst for nothing but revenge, and they no longer care who they seek to punish. To be lost in the spirit world is a terrifying fate for these mortal souls. Without our help they become confused and wander the wastes, like a foul breeze in the night, killing women and children in their sleep. Their names remind them, ground them to their past. Do you remember the chant? Do you remember all the names?"

"Will the names bring them peace?"

"Peace is dearly bought for those who die in such anguish. Better shamans than I have tried. If we were all to work together, it might be done. But such a gathering is not possible. For now we can only soothe these tormented souls and send them back to sleep for a little while." Old Manatook shook his head. "That's the head and the hindquarters of it. Now let me hear the chant."

Alaana sat up straight, careful of the dogs beside her. With a warm, furry body to either side she had begun to feel very comfortable and sleepy. She shook herself awake, and began to recite:

"Those from Uwelen, how they sang,
Those from Uwelen, how they danced,
They fished under the blue sky,
They slept in the black night.
These poor souls, who stir around us,
Let them not fall into sorrow.
A thousand times the starry sky has turned,
And still they wander, lost and lonely.
You are not forgotten.
You may sleep without care.
We remember.
Just so, just so, what are your names?
Ituituq, Kajorsuq, Qanorme,
Nerugalik, Nontak, Tassiussaq,
Guide your families to their rest now.

Go off to the sky and be free.

Everything is swept away.

And gone."

"That's good," said Old Manatook. "But the power of these old songs fades after being used again and again. This one is almost worn out. The last two lines must be delivered in the secret language of the shamans." Old Manatook hesitated. His left eye squinted as he struggled to remember the verse. "It is this: *Iluquaan sanfiyaqtuq pavva iqsisaaqtuq. Tifitkaa.*"

Alaana was not yet an expert at the secret language of the shamans, but thought the translation sounded flawed and said so.

"Tornarssuk save me from this insolent pup!" grumbled Old Manatook. "The translation stands. That's it. If I remember correctly, and I do." He squinted again, and Alaana thought she'd never seen her teacher looking so old and uncertain. "I think."

"Will the chant be enough?"

Old Manatook muttered a curse. "Of course not! The chant is almost irrelevant. You must call on the power of Sila."

Alaana leaned into the fire and rubbed the chill from her shoulders. "I don't understand," she said. "Why was I chosen by Sila? He said I would restore the balance, but what does it mean? The balance of shamans?"

"Possibly. Or something more." Old Manatook threw up his hands. "You must seek these answers from Sila. You must call on him for aid whenever you are in need. As I do with the Great Bear."

Alaana settled back down among the dogs. "Tell me again about Tornarssuk," she said, eager to lead the conversation away from Sila.

Old Manatook smiled, which was a rare thing indeed. "He is the tireless master of the white bears. Born in the time of the Rift as were all the great *turgats*, he has watched over the world for a long,

259

long while.

"This frail human body," continued the shaman as he gestured toward his bare, sagging chest, "cannot endure the presence of such a great power for very long. So he comes only when necessary. We have an understanding. A part of him waits for me in lonely places. I know that if I am in need, he will always help. This gives me confidence. You must have the same confidence if you are to go forward."

The shaman stretched his legs with a weary groan. He went to the rock ledge where he had stowed their food and supplies out of reach of the dogs, and came back with one of the tent skins.

"How did you first come to know him?" asked Alaana. She arranged the broad tent skin over herself and the two dogs like a blanket.

"He has been with me as long as I can remember. Many times I have visited the crystal palace which is his lair deep within the earth. He has always helped me, walked with me. He is my friend. He is my guardian. As a shaman, all my power is but a small fragment of his own; I am less than a child to him. But he is kindly, he smiles broadly. His attack is swift and brutal when need be, yes, but he seeks always for harmony. Not just for the bears, but for all things. That is the measure of his great wisdom."

Alaana felt her eyes begin to close. It had been a very long journey. "Sila..." she said sleepily.

"Yes?"

"He spoke to me," said Alaana in a hopeful tone. "He called me by name."

Old Manatook was unimpressed. "The dawn has come many times since then. The sky has turned half a year. Has he come to you since? Or does he remain unseen? I worry that your relationship with Sila is not as clear or strong as should be."

"I have the spirit-vision, his gift to me."

"Yes. Growing dimmer all the time."

"As you said it would."

"I did."

"And I have the *allaruk*..." The spirit trance. That haunting moment of clarity was still strong within her.

Old Manatook said nothing more. Alaana turned away, annoyed at having to justify her relationship with Sila to Old Manatook when she hardly held much faith in it herself. If Old Manatook didn't believe in her connection to the Walker In The Wind, then why the training? Why were they here?

"This is a test, isn't it?" she asked. "A test to see if Sila will come to me?"

"Yes, yes. It's not an easy thing. It's not a fair test, but few tests are fair. In any case, you will succeed. Sila will come when you call, most certainly."

Now it was Alaana's turn for an angry silence.

"If you truly reach out to him," said Old Manatook. "If there is need. Yes, he will come if there is need. Of that you can be sure."

"But what if I'm not strong enough? What if I can't? I'm not like you."

Old Manatook snickered dryly. "Silly girl, even I'm not like me."

"Manatook, what do you—"

"Hooo," said Old Manatook, as if silencing the dogs. "You're tired. Go to sleep."

With Alaana fast asleep in the cave, Manatook cocked an ear to the sounds of the night. There was surprisingly little noise outside. Naked, he stepped over the shaggy form of Makaartunghak where the dog slept at the cavern entrance.

The old shaman sniffed at the frosty air. The wolverines had been and gone, perhaps seeking out some careless snow hare or other nighttime creature. A gentle breeze drifted down from the northland, carrying the traces of a distant cooking fire. Yupikut raiders most likely, he thought, as he caught the scent of freshly cured bearskin, which that band most often used as garments. And what was it they were roasting? He sniffed again. Fresh-caught fox.

He bowed his head, arms outstretched, palms forward. He settled into the one-pointedness of mind necessary for receiving messages on the wind. The pulse of his heart slowed, his breath stilled to a whisper.

A distant voice spoke to him in the secret language of the shamans. "*You are sorely needed*," it said. "*You are called and yet you do not come.*"

Old Manatook felt his heart skip a beat, almost losing the concentration of the trance.

"*I am teaching the girl*," he sent back. "*It doesn't go well.*"

"*You are called*," insisted the voice from the north.

"*I thought you would understand*," said Old Manatook. "*It was you who taught me the Way. And now I teach her. I thought you would be pleased.*"

"*There is no time to waste*," insisted the other. "*Our Great Work must go ahead.*"

Old Manatook growled softly in the back of his throat. "*But the Anatatook have no one else.*"

"*Let them fend for themselves. You waste too much time with those men. Your own kind need you now.*"

"*I understand*," sent back Manatook. "*I will come as soon as I am able, Father.*"

CHAPTER 24

DISCOVERING THE WAY

Another half day's travel brought them to the lower reaches of the basin. A mild snow had fallen all day, drifting gently down then blowing back up. Alaana spent the entire journey sitting on the sled, chilled to the bone. This type of weather was more exhausting than she had ever imagined, leaving her too tired to run after the sled to warm up.

The dogs trotted down the slope at breakneck speed, joyously slipping and sliding as they went. Old Manatook tugged sharply at the traces. He seemed tireless for such an old man. At the bottom of the bowl they came to an ice-bound river. The river must have had broad shoulders in the summer as it gathered the run-off from the entire region. Even now it stubbornly continued to flow, oozing between the rocks in a slender tongue where the wild water defied the frost.

Old Manatook punched a hole in the rim ice with the butt of his snow knife and cool water bubbled up for the dogs to drink. Alaana drank as well, filling her sealskin water bag. The water tasted fresh and satisfying, and not the least bit salty.

"The spirit of the river is in good humor," said Old Manatook. "Soon he lays down to sleep. But he will grant us a favor. He is willing to answer a question."

Alaana couldn't see the *inua* of the river for all the ice, but river spirits were always better heard than seen. She listened intently for the master's voice, but the sloshing of the water obliterated all other sound.

"I can't hear its voice."

"Concentrate," suggested Old Manatook. "Use the *tunraq.* That's what they're for."

Alaana fished the small sphere of soapstone from the front pocket of her parka. "Weyahok, take a question to the river."

"Weyahok," the stone replied.

"Yes," said Alaana softly, "I want you to ask the river: Why was I called to be the shaman?"

Alaana felt the piece of stone shudder in her hand.

"Ooort! Weyahok know not nothing! Never nothing knew never!"

"There's a mouthful," chuckled Alaana. She gave the stone a reassuring squeeze. "Stay calm. Go and ask the water." With that, she flung the stone into the center of the stream where the stretching fingers of ice had not yet clasped across.

A moment later, Weyahok came rolling back along the surface of the ice. Alaana warmed the *tunraq* in her hands, awaiting its answer. Weyahok delivered a single word: "Justice."

"Justice?" she asked the little spirit. "Are you certain?" But Weyahok, struck uncharacteristically silent, would say no more.

One word. Not much of an explanation. But Alaana thought she knew what it meant. The people in the south believed that Sila stood for justice. Maybe he didn't think it was fair that women weren't allowed to be shamans. She remembered what he'd said, that she would do great things, that she would restore the balance. Maybe he thought it was time for a woman to be the shaman.

They crossed the river ice carefully. Alaana followed Old Manatook, who checked frequently for thin ice. A deadly drop could lurk beneath a deceptive covering of snow. Once across, they went back again, carrying the sledge between them and calling the dogs to follow.

They had to climb a rough scramble of rocks on the far side of the basin, coaxing the dogs at every step. When they came to flat open spaces they hitched up the team again. Even then, the fresh fallen snow hindered their progress. Old Manatook had to dismount every so often to clear away the bunched-up snow clogging the runners.

They arrived at Uwelen near dusk. The village was marked by a tall grave post looming above an old burial platform. The carven image of a grinning skull looked down on the passers-by. Remnants of crimson paint clung in the recesses, giving the impression that the face was both crying and dribbling blood. This represented Erlaveersinioq the Disemboweler, The Skeleton That Walks — a spirit who loved murder and death above all other things.

Alaana felt a chill, remembering the vision Civiliaq had shown her. The towering figure with huge, dead eyes, that listened with the snouts of rabid dogs for ears, and spoke in women's screams. The silent skull atop the post delivered its message clearly. This was a place not to be traveled by men.

Not to be traveled by mortal men, thought Alaana, but shamans were required to pass. And she, not even a shaman yet, was expected to stumble blindly forward, armed with nothing but a chant.

Beyond the marker lay a pitiless desert of snow. Low tussocks of black rock, where there might have been a marshy expanse in summer, were now locked with pools of dirty gray ice. Straggly reeds had tried to grow up and caught in the ice, grimy under a coat of frozen slime. In the midst of this barren, gloomy plain a mournful rampart of stone rose, bare and bony, as a watchtower above the desolation. That stony pillar, said Old

Manatook, was Alaana's destination.

Their visit had been timed poorly. The sky was already growing dark. A distant wind gusted across the plain, carrying the stench of decay and the hissing and snarling voices of the long dead.

Old Manatook pressed the palm of his hand to Alaana's nose, which had gone dangerously white with frost. Alaana felt the shaman's warmth spread across her face, flushing her cheeks.

"Are your ears troubled by the conversations of the dead?"

Alaana nodded.

"A shaman's greatest weapons are courage and determination," said Old Manatook, "but above all he must have faith. Do you believe you can do this thing?"

Alaana looked deeply into her teacher's eyes. She knew that to balk now would mean more than simple embarrassment and disgrace. Her fate was out of her own hands or even those of Old Manatook. This was no time to turn back. There were things required of her, by forces greater than any human being. She could not deny the will of the spirits, the sacrifice of Avalaaqiaq, the needs of her friends and loved ones.

"Don't worry, I'll do it," she said.

Old Manatook's lips drew into a thin line between the folds of his beard, an expression which for him might be considered a smile. "Here dwell wrathful and dangerous spirits. Tread lightly and travel with half-closed eye. Make a straight line, placing one foot directly in front of the other. Heed not the laments of the dead. When you reach the pillar, do what you must. You go alone."

Alone? Alaana hadn't realized this was for her to do alone. The old shaman's bushy white eyebrows raised slightly. Alaana realized how openly her own face must have betrayed her fear. She straightened her bearing, composing her features into her best imitation of her master's grim resolve. Old Manatook wouldn't have brought her this far just to die. Clearly he believed she could

266

accomplish this task, and so she would.

She stepped forward, treading carefully among the jagged black rocks. Nightfall brought a gray fog, drifting in twists and curls as it flowed in the low places between the tussocks. The Moon, now only two or three nights from the full, was high in the sky and lent an eerie silver glow to the surface of the roving mists.

The air grew decidedly colder and sharper. It bore a bitter reek, here one moment, gone the next. As Alaana passed over the wide flats of ice, she heard lingering traces of what had once existed here — the familiar sounds of camp life now strangled and twisted, the voices of children whose play echoed only in joyless laughter and spates of ominous giggling. In the gaps where no gray twilight fell on black stone, tent posts and buildings could be glimpsed in the shadows. A meat rack, a kennel, standing for a moment then gone.

Pressed by a growing fear, Alaana marched onward. Mindful of Old Manatook's instructions she squinted her eyes, but it did no good. The crawling mists lurched upward here and there to outline eerie burial mounds clogging the plain in endless rows, an obscene phantom graveyard amid the desolation of Uwelen. There was no doubt of some great nightmare lurking close. Alaana couldn't shake the feeling of an invisible hand, cold and dead, clutching at her throat. What wicked horror awaited her at the end of that shaggy arm?

At the rampart's base lay a flat stone the size of a spread tent-cover. As she stepped on it Alaana felt a glimmer of relief and newfound confidence. The choking grip relaxed and drifted away. Her throat was dry, but she dared not moisten it with the cursed snow that rested here.

She braced her back to the stone tower, quelled her thundering heartbeat, and began the chant.

"Those from Uwelen, how they sang,
   Those from Uwelen, how they danced."

Even as she spoke, she knew the chant wouldn't be enough. Old Manatook had made it clear she must call on Sila for aid. That was the true point of the test. But now it came to it, she resisted reaching out to the great spirit for help. Sila had first appeared to her as a kindly old man but that wizened face which had bestowed upon her the gifts of the shaman had never reappeared. Having turned her life upside down, Sila had left her quite alone. And that made her angry.

"They fished under the blue sky,
    They slept in the black night—"

A desperate howl rang out from somewhere on the twilight-frosted plain. This came from no phantom; it was a sound most definitely grounded in reality. A most dangerous sound. It was the call of the wolverine. A sudden wave of horror and uncertainty came crashing down on Alaana. Her chant could have no power over the living, only the dead.

Puffs of mist shot upward here and there between the rocks, marking the passage of wolverines. How many?

Wolverines were usually solitary creatures, only moving in packs when hunger drove them to ultimate desperation. How many? And what was she going to do? She had only a small hunting knife with which to fend them off. She fought the urge to run, for that would only bring certain death in the form of deadly claws digging into her back or a ravenous snout at her throat.

The laments of the dead rose from the snow-covered ruins of the village, combining to form a nightmarish voice whose message was a cry of unending pain and suffering. There were ghosts here, that was certain. Even the wolverines knew it. The puffs of sooty mist picked their way around the phantom graves, approaching not in a direct line but in an uneven and faltering path, as if they too were frightened by the tortured presences which infested this place. But as Old Manatook had said, hunger spoke loudest of all.

The mumbling of the dead grew more forceful but at this moment Alaana feared the living more than the dead. Tufts of brown fur revealed themselves between parting puffs of smoke. The wolverines would soon be upon her.

Alaana drew her little hunting knife. If she killed the first one that charged, she wondered, was there a chance the others would flee?

A black snout burst through the mist, followed by a pair of dark, ravenous eyes under a sloping gray brow as one of the wolverines came shooting toward the platform. Another cut through the mist and another, teeth bared, jaws slavering with anticipation. Alaana held out the blade, its tip quivering. The beasts snapped and snarled as they broke from the gray mist, gathering in numbers before they might strike. She could almost believe them a pack of malevolent demons bred in the ruin of Uwelen.

Suddenly a low growl burst across the plain, louder and deeper than any wolverine could possibly muster. It was the roar of some huge predator protecting a kill. A luminescent figure rose up from the mist. The monster seemed to be made of gathering fingers of moonlight. It loomed large, a creature with the size and outlines of a polar bear. Moving quickly it passed in front of Alaana, cutting across the wolverines' line of attack.

The bear's massive paws swept the mist, knocking aside one attacker and then the next. The hissing snarls of the wolverines gave way to terrified yelps. The mist danced and heaved, flung in stringy tendrils with each killing stroke. Another terrific growl, even louder than the first, sent the last few wolverines darting away.

Alaana's fear was every bit as great as their own.

The bear turned to face her. Its eyes were ablaze, reflecting some distant unworldly fire. Alaana felt lost in space and time, trapped alone in a vast sea of nothingness, empty except for those huge glowing eyes.

The shape blurred, transforming into the figure of a man, tall and thin, dressed in a shabby white parka. What was this deadly wraith now come before her? Its face hung waxy and pale, stretched and sagging at the chin as if it were nothing more than empty skin, the eyes lifeless in their deep, craven sockets.

"Those from Uwelen, how they danced," rasped Alaana.

"They fished under the blue sky,

They slept in the black night.

These poor souls, who stir around us,

Let them not fall into sorrow."

As the phantom drew closer, Alaana fumbled with the remainder of the chant.

The ghost's life history reached out for her as surely as the long, bone-white fingers that groped toward her face. This man was a murderer, an outcast from his band, who had beaten his wife almost to death, an evil man who had been caught up for his sins and skinned alive.

"Ituituq, Kajorsuq, Qanorme,

Nerugalik, Nontak, Tassiussaq,

Guide — guide your families to their rest."

Alaana stumbled again, her back pressed hard against the cold stone of the pillar. It was useless, she knew, because the last lines of the chant were all wrong. Old Manatook's translation was indeed flawed and worthless, and would avail her nothing.

She grabbed for her knife, but the ghastly spirit knocked it away. This then, was the end. She sank to her knees in total despair.

"Hmmf," said the ghost, "I had hoped the words I've been pouring into your ears these past few moons would have at least done you some good. I hate to think so much time and breath had all gone to waste."

Alaana blinked. Old Manatook stood revealed before her.

270

"Get up!"

"I'm sorry," she said quickly, "I thought—"

"I know full well what you thought," said Old Manatook. "It's clear I've put too much faith in you."

"It's the chant," said Alaana, shouting above the rising wind. "There's something wrong with the chant."

"The fault is with you," said Old Manatook sharply. His tone rang with disappointment.

"I can do better."

"And you shall have to. The ghosts have not yet been made to go away."

Alaana, who had hardly allowed herself a sigh of relief at the appearance of her master, saw now that the phantoms of Uwelen had risen in earnest. Moving in eerie silence, a ring of horrific figures surrounded the stone pillar, permitting no chance of escape.

The ghosts of Uwelen were unlike any she had ever seen. Corrupted by centuries of anger and hatred, these were twisted souls indeed. Dressed only in whatever rags that still clung to them, they marched on long, bowed legs. They reached out with long bony arms, withered and dead, strung with flesh that had been robbed of all blood, bleached of all color and vitality, barely held together by a thought. They stared with dead eyes, dark and empty vessels that could suck the life, or perhaps the very soul, out of anything they might encounter.

Slain husbands draped ropey arms across the shoulders of their mutilated wives, not in kindness or comfort but cold resignation. Fathers and uncles clung to sons and daughters in unending remorse and desperate horror. And saddest of all were the ghosts of the slaughtered children. Seething with helplessness and fear they cowered behind the adults, who could offer them neither warmth nor protection.

"What shall we do?" whispered Old Manatook.

Alaana shrank from the ranks of the advancing wraiths, finding them too dreadful to look upon directly.

"It's been much too long a time since any shaman has passed this way," said Old Manatook. "Thunder and lightning child, what shall we do?"

"Those of Uwelen," said Alaana forcefully, "how they sang!"

She welcomed her teacher's deep, resounding tones as Old Manatook joined her in the chant.

Darkness filled the hollow, seeming to have spilled in from all sides as much as fallen from above, as storm clouds overwhelmed the Moon. Alaana's spirit-vision showed the ghosts in lambent detail as they pressed closer, their bloodless faces stretched and elongated by misery and an eternal hunger for vengeance.

"They won't get us," said Alaana. "They'll stop."

"We are here only to placate them," reminded Old Manatook. "You see, the chant already gives them pause. They hear their names, they remember their humanity."

"It will work," said Alaana.

"Yes, it will. Again. Those from Uwelen, how they danced. They fished under the blue sky, they slept in the black night…"

Despite his encouraging words, Old Manatook despaired of their chances of driving Uwelen's ghosts away. He felt the starry eyes of Tornarssuk upon him, as the benevolent *turgat* gazed down from his celestial palace. But the great spirit would not come to their aid unless called and Manatook, remaining calm and steadfast in the face of the advancing horror, held back the call. He knew he could count on help from Tornarssuk on an instant's notice. But they had come here to learn if Alaana could expect the same of Sila.

His young pupil's relationship to that great spirit was not all it should have been. Alaana had received the calling at a late age and under unusual circumstances. She had shown not the slightest inclination for shamanism prior to her encounter with the fever demon. And though her *angakua* had been very bright at first, that spirit light had become progressively dimmer over time. It was all wrong. Manatook felt he must be missing some obvious fact, but what? The answer lay somewhere beyond his experience.

They delivered the last few lines of the chant in the secret language of the shamans, lines which now sounded to Manatook as if they might indeed be flawed. It didn't really matter. The content of the chant had little bearing on the outcome, so long as the names were correct. He kept careful watch on Alaana as she recited the lines. No longer did the girl stutter and trip over the words. Good. The girl's state of mind was clear. She was certain the chant would work. Faith was restored. A lesson learned, perhaps, but their lives were still in jeopardy.

"Again," said Old Manatook. "The spirits begin to falter. But it is not done. Put aside your resentment. Ask Sila for help. You mustn't think ill of your guardian spirit." Again Manatook held Tornarssuk at bay.

"I don't think ill of him," said Alaana.

"You do," snapped the old shaman. "I can feel it. And if I can feel it, the *turgats* certainly can as well."

The ghosts stepped closer and Alaana realized they were, each and every one of them, looking directly at her.

"This is no good, Alaana. The shaman can not hesitate. Is Sila with us or not? Are you going to do this? Or not?"

"I'm going to be the shaman. I've already agreed to that."

"Going to be the shaman? That's not good enough. You have to *want* to be the shaman."

"I do. I want to help."

Alaana's *angakua* began to burn more brightly, and the ghosts again halted their advance. Manatook sniffed the crisp night air. All was still. There was no trace of the mystical winds this night, no taint of Sila.

273

"Again," said Old Manatook. Alaana launched into the chant once more. This time he allowed the girl to go it alone. Her voice was confident and strong. He felt the power rising as Alaana's spirit burned so very brightly.

With a mixture of amazement and satisfaction, Manatook saw the character of the spirits begin to change. Tortured expressions melted away as icy, pale faces were replaced by pink skin and warm living flesh. The twisted mouth drew closed, the eyes sparked back to life. The ghosts glanced sidelong, looking as if they had just wakened from a nightmare. They turned toward each other and saw friends and neighbors, tribesmen and loved ones.

Old Manatook had come to this place many times before and, with Kuanak or Civiliaq beside him, had performed the same chant and the same ritual. Always the souls of the tormented, temporarily soothed and satisfied, went back into the ground, back to the phantom burial mounds in the mists of Uwelen. But this time, under the steady hand of Alaana, the spirits began to glow. Infused by the girl's power, they shot up into the night sky in a stream of white light. It was just as the chant had ordered them to do. Go off to the sky and be free. Everything is swept away. And gone.

Alaana fell to her knees. Her face was as pale as crusted snow but she was smiling.

"We did it," she mumbled, shivering. Old Manatook knelt beside her, putting his arms around the girl to help warm her.

"You did it," said Old Manatook. "The ghosts of Uwelen have gone across the divide, to the distant lands. They will trouble Nunatsiaq no longer."

"And they will be safe," said Alaana. Manatook thought this an odd thing to say, unless Alaana had meant safe from becoming demons.

"Yes," said Old Manatook. "So you see? The chant was not false after all."

"It was flawed," said Alaana softly.

"Really? Then how then could we succeed?"

"Because I knew that you were with me. I had faith in you."

Old Manatook grumbled in surprise. "I did nothing. I didn't call on Tornarssuk."

"Then who?" asked Alaana. "Was it Sila? Did you see him? Did you see Sila?"

Old Manatook would not lie to his student. "No."

"I don't care," said Alaana. "It doesn't matter, so long as they're safe."

"It does matter," huffed Manatook. "I had hoped for you to learn the importance of faith today. Without faith in your spirit guardian the chant will not work. Nothing will work. You were slow in learning this lesson, and now I find your faith is misplaced. You had faith in me, but I did nothing. All your faith must be in Sila."

"I felt something," said Alaana, weakly, "but I didn't see him." Alaana closed her eyes. "He didn't come."

"That's because you did not ask properly."

Old Manatook turned away. Sila had not come. This miracle had been achieved by the power already within Alaana, raw power which had now been greatly depleted. Worse yet, the strength and luster of Alaana's *angakua* was fading rapidly. Something must be done about that, too. The girl lay shivering in his arms, exhausted. She might have died from the exertion.

Old Manatook wrapped her in a loose tent cover, and Alaana fell off to sleep. He carried the girl back to the sled.

The old shaman looked out over the snow-covered ruins of Uwelen. The night was now quiet and still. Not surprisingly there were no signs of the pack of wolverines. After all that had happened here tonight, they wouldn't be back.

Gazing into the clear night sky, Manatook was tempted to call upon Sila himself. He had done so once before, trapped in the blizzard, and the Walker In The Wind had saved him. But this was different. One might beg assistance from *turgats* in time of need, but for a man to call upon such a great spirit to explain itself? That was definitely not the Way. His appeal would be ignored, or otherwise lead to his instant demise, crushed under the heel of the wind.

"If there was need, Sila should have come," whispered Old Manatook to his left shoulder.

"I told you this wouldn't work," answered Quixaaragon. The creature of white light flapped its scaly wings indignantly.

"And how did you know?"

"I just knew."

"Hmmph."

For a spirit helper, Quixaaragon was neither very servile nor responsive. The *tunraq* did not answer to the shaman's will, and was just as likely to give orders as take them. They had met many years ago when the spirit had stumbled across Old Manatook, a traveler in the dream world, and attached itself to him. Quixaaragon was a wayward fragment of a dream, but Old Manatook had never discovered for sure whose dream it might have been and had long since given up hope of finding out. A curious relationship had formed between the two of them, but Old Manatook found Quixaaragon to be as wise as he was ancient, and its advice always sound. It had taken a keen interest in the development of Alaana.

"It would have worked," insisted Old Manatook. "That pack of wolverines spoiled it. They drew me out, forcing my hand. They would have killed her."

Quixaaragon said nothing.

"I had to reveal myself to her," fumed Old Manatook. "But I don't think she understood anything."

"You'll have to tell her some time," remarked Quixaaragon.

"Not yet. I don't care if the girl knows, but not the rest of

276

them."

"Not even after all these years?"

"No. Not even after these many years."

"Is this vanity, Manatook?"

"No," snapped the old shaman. "It is love. And something I will not justify to you. The point is, the test was spoiled. Once I came into it, everything was ruined. We can't know what might have happened. Would Sila have left Alaana to die?"

Quixaaragon snapped its pointed beak at the shaman's broad, sloping nose. "Do I need to answer that? Of course he would have."

"Maybe. Or maybe Sila saw that I was there, and there was no real danger." It was hard to tell. The *turgats* cared very little for lesser creatures, only intervening if called on in a very specific way.

The little dragon tilted its round head up at the shaman and said, "The proper question is – would Sila have failed to come if correctly called?"

"Would he? You tell me. You act as if you know everything."

"Only bits and pieces. Fragments and echoes. I am only a wandering bit of a dream after all."

"A very powerful dream," mumbled Old Manatook thoughtfully.

"An ancient one. And my memory for things is not always as clear as it used to be, if it used to be at all. I falter, seeing only ripples in the pool. I am incomplete. Sometimes I think I am merely a weapon, searching for my target."

"Well, point yourself somewhere other than me if you please."

"Not to worry, old friend," returned Quixaaragon. "But I am certain of this: the girl must not die."

"Sun and Moon, this is all my fault, my failure. Now the test has spoiled its own purpose. Alaana knows Sila didn't come. Doubt has been raised where there should have been confidence. And look at her now, so weak and helpless, her light almost gone. I've done her no good at all. I should have taught her better. I should have led her away from her resentment, not let it fester like this." Manatook took his face in his hands. "What must I do?"

"Try again. Find a way."

"Good advice, as always." Old Manatook looked down at the thing perched on his shoulder but instead of smiling he bared his large white teeth. "I still don't have an answer. Would Sila come if he was called?"

"Maybe he's not always able to respond. Maybe his situation is not so different than your own. Your people call you home and yet you remain here, with her. You promised to go to them, if there was need."

"How can I go? I can't leave her like this."

"That's your choice."

Manatook waved his arm at the *tonraq's* head, but his fingers passed through the white smoke. "Leave me be."

Quixaaragon's form dissipated but its voice lingered, saying, "Let me ask you this: Are you going to succeed in her training or aren't you?"

It was a trick question, but an incisive one. At once Old Manatook realized there could be only one answer.

"Of course I am going to succeed," he said.

CHAPTER 25

SIEEAKTUQRUK

"Wake up! Wake up!" squawked Itiqtuq.

Alaana could barely force her eyes open. "Let me alone!"

With a sudden start she realized she'd spoken out loud. She dare not turn to face her father, a notoriously light sleeper, for fear of finding him awake and staring back at her. She just wanted to sleep. She was so tired.

Itiqtuq pinched her on the cheek with its beak. Alaana smacked the little auk skull away.

"Awwwwrrk!"

She didn't want to remember the dream. It had been a bad dream. It was all bad dreams for her lately. The ghosts of Uwelen haunted her, even after she had set them free. Small fragments of their suffering, thrown off in their moment of release, clung to her soul, coming out at night as she slept.

The list of names took on new significance. Nerugalik, an old man, had been strangled and stabbed by Yupikut raiders. Tassiussaq, a young girl, pushed down into the snow and roughly used. Nontak, her father. Insane with grief, he had opened himself with a long hunting knife.

"I expected you to comfort them," Old Manatook had said, "not release them." The old shaman told her that nothing could be

279

done about these haunting echoes except perhaps an undertaking to the dream world to try and sort them out. He promised they would go when they found time. Meanwhile, the bones of those who had gone before peopled her memory, their tortured voices rang out in her dreams. Determined to ignore them, Alaana pulled the sleeping fur closer against the chill of the night.

Itiqtuq pecked at her again. It had never done that before. The dream. The dream. It had been a bad dream, but it had not been about Uwelen. She must remember.

Itoriksak on the ice. The seal hunt. The images came rushing back to her. Her father had been there.

Itoriksak walking along the new sea ice. An ominous sound cut the frigid air, the rumbling of unsteady floes grinding against each other. A moment of fearful expectation always followed such a noise, as all awaited the thunderous crack that must surely come. The soft green ice fractured at Itoriksak's step, directly below his boot. His leg went plunging in. An instant later the ice sheet pulled back, crushing the leg at the thigh. She heard Itoriksak scream. That scream, so shockingly frightful, so vivid and gut-wrenching — that was what had set the dream apart. Alaana recalled the moment vividly. As the merciless ice pulped Itoriksak's leg she glimpsed her father's face, contorted with horror and fear. And then her brother fell under. Itoriksak. Dead and gone. Swallowed by the icy sea.

Alaana shivered, the memory having grown so painful and fresh. She turned toward Itoriksak, who slept beside her on the platform. Undisturbed, her brother's face appeared serene in repose.

She reached over and gave his shoulder a reassuring squeeze, a gesture mainly intended to comfort herself against the lingering horror of the dream. She couldn't bear to think of anything happening to Itoriksak.

Itoriksak murmured softly. All was well. So tired. Alaana

drifted back to sleep. Please, she thought, let there be no more ghosts tonight.

"Why didn't you tell me this right away?" demanded Old Manatook. His angry words echoed along the vast emptiness of the windswept tundra.

Old Manatook held his snow knife in hand, having just sliced through the well-packed drift along the pressure ridge. He was halfway through assembling their practice *iglu*. Alaana had once asked why they couldn't simply ask the snow to shape itself into the house the way they did with the soapstone. Manatook had replied that the spirit of the snow lay spread out across all of the land and was so vast and sleepy it could never be roused to action. It had to be worked by hand. This was no great inconvenience, after all. If the snow was firm enough, they could raise the *iglus* in a very short time.

"Well? Don't just stand there. Answer."

"I didn't remember," she said. "Itiqtuq helped me and I did remember, but then I was so tired. I forgot again."

"This was not something to forget! If it was as vivid as you say, this dream is important. This was *sieeaktuqruk*, a Big Dream."

"What does it mean?" asked Alaana, suddenly alarmed at having made such a dangerous mistake.

Old Manatook threw the snow knife down so that it embedded in the drift, handle upward. "Come now," he said. "Have you lost your senses so completely? Every old woman can explain dreams."

The shaman sat cross-legged in the snow. "It means your brother is going to die today!" he said. "Stay here."

Old Manatook hummed a deep note, and his eyes rolled back into his head. That was all it took for him to perform the *ilimarpoq*. His soul took flight.

Alaana watched as Old Manatook's *inuseq* shot up out of his body. For an instant the shape of it struck her as wrong, as if it were substantially larger than a man. But she had only a glimpse before the contour of the shaman's soul blurred itself so that she could no longer see the outline clearly, and flew away into the dark winter sky.

She was left to wait by herself. To wait and worry for her brother.

She closed her hand around the walrus tusk amulet.

"Nunavik?"

"Yes, Alaana," replied the Walrus. "From the pitiful tone of your voice I take it you've gotten yourself into some new trouble?"

"I don't know. Maybe. I mean, I think so."

"I see. Well, walking about in a daze like that, what do you really expect? Out with it."

"I think I may have caused something terrible to happen to my brother."

"Oh," said the Walrus. That single word fell hard as a stone. Alaana remembered the story Nunavik had told her. The Walrus had brought a singular doom upon all of his family and friends by meddling with the spirits.

"Oh," said Alaana.

"Perhaps it's not too late," said Nunavik. His tone was both urgent and grim. "Alaana, if there is anything you can do to save your brother, you must do it without hesitation."

Old Manatook opened his eyes. So distracted, Alaana had not seen the shaman's spirit-man return.

She grabbed her teacher's elbow. "Did you warn them? Is Itoriksak all right?"

Old Manatook jumped to his feet. "Of course I didn't warn them. How could I? They can't see my spirit-man the way you can. But I found them. And yes, your brother is still alive. We must

282

hurry."

It was a long run across the tundra. Though Old Manatook's legs were much longer than Alaana's, she had no trouble keeping up. She would run until her heart burst if needed. They chased across the frozen wastelands, climbing over the pressure ridges carved in the snow during the night before. These obstacles, put in their way by the night wind, suggested to Alaana that Sila was working against her, but she didn't truly believe that. This was her fault alone, for not saying something sooner. How could she have been so careless?

We'll make it, she told herself. We will.

Old Manatook found his way unerringly through the darkness, leading them on a direct line toward the party of seal hunters he had scouted out on his soul flight. Breathless, they reached the edge of the bay. A series of dark figures in the gloom far out on the ice marked the men waiting for their prey.

Alaana and Old Manatook charged out onto the frozen sea. Kigiuna and Itoriksak sat working the same hole, with Anaktuvik and Maguan not far away.

"Get off the ice!" Alaana shouted, "Get off the ice!"

She waved both arms as she ran toward the men.

"Don't run!" hissed Old Manatook.

She felt the vibration of the ice below, aware that it might collapse under her at any moment. But she didn't care for her own safety. She only wanted to safeguard her brother. "Itoriksak! Don't move!"

Kigiuna stood up, annoyed. "What's all this fuss about? You're making enough noise to scare off every seal in the bay."

"I had a dream," panted Alaana, "Itoriksak is going to fall in."

"A dream? That's all?" Kigiuna looked disgusted. He scowled first at Alaana and second at Old Manatook. Then he glanced nervously around the bay to see who might have heard the

283

commotion. The other hunters had all looked up from their holes. How could they not? Silence was paramount on the seal hunt. Maguan and Anaktuvik, who had been manning the two nearest holes, began to walk toward them. Old Manatook gave them the hand sign to be careful on the ice.

Old Manatook said, "It was a Big Dream."

"Alaana has nightmares all the time," Kigiuna said coldly, looking at Old Manatook as if the entire situation was his fault. "So what of it? Dreams aren't real."

Old Manatook was resolute. "Kigiuna, you should not mock what you don't understand."

"What's happened?" asked Maguan, who arrived just ahead of Anaktuvik. "What's the problem?"

"Itoriksak must go home," said Alaana. "If he's on the ice today, his leg will go in. He'll fall under!"

All eyes went to Itoriksak. He quickly answered, "I'm not afraid. I belong out on the ice."

"That's right," said Kigiuna. "We'll be careful. We're always careful. What else can we do? If we don't bring in the seal, we don't eat."

"You may dismiss this at your own peril, Kigiuna," said Old Manatook, "But I won't allow harm to come to this one if I can help it." He took Itoriksak by the arm.

"You won't allow?" fumed Kigiuna. He reached out for Itoriksak's other arm, but Anaktuvik stopped him, saying, "Where's the harm in it, Kigiuna?"

Kigiuna stomped his foot down on the ice, as if to demonstrate its reliability. But it was no use. They were all against him. "Fine. If you insist, he'll stay off the ice today. We can manage without him." He turned to go back to his seal hole.

"It's not that simple," said Old Manatook. "Something else must be done."

Kigiuna turned back around, alarmed at the foreboding tone the old man had used.

"What now?"

"This was not an ordinary dream. This was *sieeaktuqruk*. It can not so easily be sidestepped. If he does not fall in today, the crack will be there tomorrow."

"We'll be careful," insisted Kigiuna.

"You can't be careful enough. The crack will appear, no matter how solid the ice. Alaana has dreamed it. It cannot simply be avoided."

The other hunters now crowded around, listening carefully to the conversation and commenting to each other in low tones.

"Quiet!" said Old Manatook.

"What can we do, *angatkok*?" asked Maguan. "Surely there is something you can do to help."

Old Manatook nodded slightly. "A dream like this can not be avoided, but it can be prevented. Alaana?"

Alaana frowned, inhaling deeply before she gave voice to the reply. "We have to make the dream come true."

"That is correct. And how?"

Alaana shifted uncomfortably. Although she knew the answer, she did not want to say it. Her father was looking at her as if she was a traitor to the family.

"And how?" insisted Manatook.

"We must break Itoriksak's leg by ourselves."

"What?" said Kigiuna, much too loudly. "Listen to crazy people speaking without meaning! Has all good sense left your minds? Break his leg?"

Alaana stood firm. "If we don't do it, he'll die. I'm sure of it. I had the dream. I'm sure of it."

Kigiuna jabbed a finger at Old Manatook. "I won't allow it! A broken leg! Not because of a silly dream."

The shaman stepped forward, pressing his chest to the tip of Kigiuna's extended finger. "I warn you. Don't stand in the way. If you care nothing for your son's life, I do."

This was the last straw. Kigiuna lunged forward. Old Manatook didn't react, as if he already knew what would happen next. Anaktuvik grabbed Kigiuna from behind and spun him around. He pulled his brother backward in a protective hug, pinning his arms at his sides. Anaktuvik whispered in Kigiuna's ear, "Control yourself. Everyone is watching."

Kigiuna knew what his brother meant. A single negative word from the shaman and his entire family could be cast out.

Old Manatook sat down on the ice, his feet tucked under his buttocks. He gestured to the space across his thighs.

"I haven't done anything wrong," said Itoriksak.

"I know you haven't," said Old Manatook. "Accidents happen out on the ice, or on the hunt. The spirits have nothing to do with it. You are fortunate your sister has given us the chance to prevent this trouble."

"Prevent?" Itoriksak glanced apprehensively down at his leg. "But Alaana's only a child. She could be wrong…"

"You're wrong, Itoriksak," said Maguan. "She's not just a child. Alaana is someone very special. She has a greatness in her. We're blessed to have a sister like her."

"I have to be clear on this," said Old Manatook. "Our efforts will not succeed, Itoriksak, unless you believe it is right."

Itoriksak's brow knitted as he looked again at Alaana. It was difficult for him to see his younger sister as anything but a child.

Maguan caught Itoriksak's eye and nodded his encouragement. "Be strong, brother. If Old Manatook says it's needed…"

"*Vaaa*," said Itoriksak at last. He avoided looking at his father. "Let's get it over with." He laid the lower portion of his leg across Old Manatook's thighs.

Kigiuna struggled against Anaktuvik's grasp. "Anak!" he growled. "Let me go!"

His brother wouldn't let him move, saying, "A broken leg will heal. Don't destroy your family."

Old Manatook said, "It has to be you, Alaana." He handed her his snow knife.

"Alaana, I forbid you!" barked Kigiuna.

Alaana lifted the knife, holding the blunt end of the antler stock above Itoriksak's shin. She exchanged a look with her brother. She had never raised her hand to anyone, least of all her beloved brother.

"*I don't think I can,*" she said in the secret language.

"*Sila will give you strength to do what you must,*" replied Manatook.

It certainly didn't feel that way to Alaana. If Sila was waiting for a certain moment to come to her, this would have been a good one. But she felt completely alone. She couldn't bear the thought of injuring her brother, but she remembered the chilling scream of pain and fear that Itoriksak had uttered in the dream. It had sounded so real, so clear. She didn't want Itoriksak to die.

She recalled what Nunavik had told her, the terrible desperation in the walrus' voice and in his heart. If there is anything you can do to save your brother, the walrus had said, you must do it without hesitation.

Still she couldn't urge her hand to strike.

Itoriksak's soul-light seethed with emotion. Alaana saw many wondrous things in that light – her brother's pride at standing on the ice with the seal hunters, his hopes of a marriage to Agruta, his dreams of helming a family of his own. Alaana saw also Itoriksak's devotion to his family and his love for Alaana herself, and also the shadow that lay across his memories of dear Ava, lost to them in the spring. Itoriksak's soul was a complex and intensely beautiful thing.

287

There was nothing Alaana wouldn't do for her brother.

If she was to do this thing, she decided, she must look Itoriksak in the eye. Her brother's face had gone pale with fear, but he met Alaana's gaze.

"Get it over with," Itoriksak said bravely.

"I love you, brother," she said.

She brought the handle of the knife down as hard as she could. She knew she would only be able to attempt this once. It had to be a clean break.

She felt the shinbone snap below the butt of the knife. Itoriksak screamed in pain.

Alaana's heart almost stopped dead. It was exactly the same shriek as in the dream.

"I will bind his leg," Old Manatook said. "It will heal. Alaana will help me ease his pain." He took Itoriksak, who was whimpering and grunting, up in his arms.

Anaktuvik released his hold on Kigiuna. "It had to be done," he said.

Kigiuna fell to his knees. He'd never felt so humiliated and small. The way they had all ignored him and gone ahead with it as if he were irrelevant. Anaktuvik restraining him like a child. The other men looking on, now silently walking back to their positions. His son injured and in pain. And for what? All because of the shaman and his superstitions.

He watched as Old Manatook headed for the camp, carrying his son slung over his shoulder and with his daughter in tow.

"Wake up!"

Expecting Itiqtuq, Alaana was startled to see Kigiuna leaning over her. With the lamp all the way on the other side of the room, her father's expression was difficult to read in the gloomy *iglu*.

Kigiuna had been shaking her roughly, but stopped the

moment her eyes opened.

"You will come with us on the seal hunt today," he said flatly, his usual enthusiasm and good humor of the morning notably absent. "You'll take Itoriksak's place. You'll come every day until he is well again."

Without waiting for an answer, Kigiuna turned away. He slipped a second, heavy parka over the one he was already wearing.

"I go to Old Manatook's to see to my boy," he announced before crawling out the entrance hole and through the long windbreak to the outside.

Alaana threw off the sleeping furs and dressed herself. They had lived several days in this *iglu* and the interior walls had already melted and refrozen to a comfortable air-tight shell. It was relatively warm despite the incredible cold outside. But the house seemed so empty now, with Ava gone and Itoriksak temporarily staying at the shaman's *iglu*. Old Manatook had cared for Itoriksak throughout the night, soothing him with scented herbs and pain-dulling chants.

Alaana pushed off the sleeping counter, a high shelf of snow blocks blanketed with furs, and dropped to the floor. Her mother intercepted her immediately. Amauraq rubbed the sides of her face with her own cheeks and sent her to the table. "Have some tea," she said. "Eat something."

One of the advantages to the *iglu* was its low snow table, a much more comfortable place to eat than the numbingly cold floor. A soapstone lamp sat atop an old tent skin that covered the table. Pilarqaq had just taken a piece of frozen blubber from the blubber bag and was happily beating it with the pounder. Her hair, such as it was, had been pulled up into a tight knot with a special hair comb Kigiuna had made for her. The comb incorporated a series of blackbird feathers which helped to obscure the bare patches of her scalp. Her cheeks held an unusually rosy glow and Alaana still thought her the most beautiful woman she'd ever seen. She hummed a pleasant song as she worked.

"Eat as much as you can," said Maguan between bites of a delicious stew that his wife had prepared. "It's a long, cold wait out on the sea and nothing else to eat until we return."

Amauraq brought another bowl of stew and set it before Alaana.

"You must look out for her, Maguan. If she gets too cold, send her back." She paused for a look out the ice window. Kigiuna's hazy outline was visible through the slab of clear, fresh-water ice as he noisily cleared the accumulated drifts from the front of the house. Amauraq addressed Maguan, "Your father can be so stubborn. I'm counting on you to be sensible. Alaana is only twelve. I don't want her coming back with her ears or any of her toes frozen off."

She turned to Alaana, saying, "Have some more tea. Warm up. Eat."

Pilarqaq, satisfied that the blubber oil was liquefied, threw the dripping piece of blubber on the lamp. The light flared up. She was still singing her song.

"Someone's very happy this morning," observed Amauraq. Pilarqaq did not answer.

"That's a fine way to act," Amauraq continued, "with a broken leg in the family."

"Oh, I'm sorry, Mother," said Pilarqaq. "It's just that Maguan and I feel so blessed. The Moon Maid has smiled down on us."

"What?"

Pilarqaq's hand went absently toward her belly. "We are going to have a baby."

"A baby?" Amauraq asked loudly, "And how is it you didn't tell me?"

"I just did."

***

290

The winter camp was the largest camp of the year. All the Anatatook families gathered together for the communal hunts required to bring in winter seal. Set only a little way out on the smooth sea ice at the inlet of the bay, the snow houses were arranged in a rough semi-circle for each family grouping. The *iglus* varied in size and design according to the number of occupants, the smallest belonging to Old Manatook. Alaana glanced at the shaman's *iglu*, barely visible in the darkness, and wondered how Itoriksak was feeling. It was too dark to see much of anything. The half-Moon provided only a dim twilight that skipped across a hint of mist skirling up from the ice.

The dog teams howled for food as the hunting party left them behind. Alaana paused, for normally it would be her chore to see that the dogs were fed. But not this day.

Every able-bodied man in the camp went out to hunt seal. They walked in a long line, their heavy double parkas making them appear bulky and squat. Their mood was grim but determined. Seal-hunting was not pleasant or exciting work. They couldn't expect to get more than a few seal per outing, a chore that would see them spend the entire day exposed to the merciless cold.

Kigiuna and Maguan carried harpoons, long straight shafts of antler tipped with chipped flint blades. Alaana carried the *tatiriaq*, a large fox-skin bag that held the rest of the seal hunting equipment.

Maguan optimistically predicted that they could expect this outing to bring many seals. He thought it would be an especially lucky day because of Pilarqaq's happy announcement. Anaktuvik chided him for mentioning his wife on the hunt, which was unmanly talk and likely to bring bad luck.

Maguan took the criticism hard but his uncle dismissed it after all, saying that it was perhaps understandable given the extreme joy of the occasion.

The group arranged themselves along the line of the *aayuraq*.

The *aayuraq*, a break in the sea cover caused by the shifting pressures, left a ridge of jumbled ice that had been forced up. Beside the ridge was a thin depression where the exposed water had only recently frozen over, an ideal place for seal to make their breathing holes.

The men took their places at the holes they had marked out earlier. Maguan waited closest to the bay, Kigiuna and Alaana at the next hole out.

"You can never tell which hole they'll come up," Kigiuna explained as he bent to sweep away the drift that had gathered about the hole during the night. "But, working together," he made an expansive gesture across the wide berth of the bay, "we cover as many as we can."

Kigiuna peered into an opening the size of a bowhead's blowhole, then bent to sniff at it, proclaiming, "It's a good one." He shattered the thin seal of new ice with the butt of his harpoon. Using a long, curved shoot of bone he explored the size and shape of the hole under the ice, describing it to Alaana in detail.

He set the *kaiptaq*, a slender antler rod topped with a black button of musk ox horn, into the hole and explained how it would jiggle if the seal approached. "We won't be able to see the seal through the hole, but the *kaiptaq* will guide my thrust. You get only one chance and no seal again for a long time. Their heads are soft, but you have to strike hard and sure even so."

Kigiuna told Alaana to smooth the snow they had disturbed. "And tamp it down," he added. "That's important. The seal is smart. He'll judge the light as he comes up. If he thinks someone is waiting for him, he won't come. Then you're waiting all day and never see any meat."

After cutting a snowblock for them to sit on, Kigiuna fixed his harpoon rest in the snow beside him where he could reach it in an instant.

"Mind your toes," Kigiuna cautioned. "Rest your feet on the fur *tatiriaq* instead of the cold snow. Now, we wait."

The most important thing was to remain very still and not make a sound. The challenge being not to freeze. Her hands in their mittens deep in her sleeves, Alaana was thankful for the low wind. If not too much snow was blown in their faces, she thought she might be all right.

The silence was intense. Alaana felt miserable, the severe weather the least of her troubles. Her father had spoken so coldly to her, she could hardly stand it. Sitting and watching like a stone figure, Kigiuna wouldn't look at her. He acted as if he could not take his eye away from the tell-tale *kaiptaq* for even a moment.

Which was worse, Alaana wondered, the strained look on her father's face when he insisted Alaana go to study with the shaman, or this — the stony face that went with his insistence that Alaana work the ice instead? Her father was unhappy either way, and so was she.

Kigiuna kept moving his lower lip a little as if he wanted to speak but nothing came out. Maguan, sitting at the next hole, waved enthusiastically at them, but that only served to make things worse.

Eventually Kigiuna could put it off no longer. His voice came out of nowhere, dry and low. "You disobeyed me yesterday."

"I didn't want to," said Alaana.

"I forbade you to strike Itoriksak."

"I didn't want to."

"Tcha!" said Kigiuna. "You didn't want to do any of it."

"I didn't!"

"I know."

Kigiuna paused. He looked up from the jigger but his eyes, so deep in the hood, could barely be seen above clouded breath. "And yet you did what you thought was right. No matter what I said. No matter you had to hurt your own brother. That's a hard thing."

"I'm sorry for disobeying—"

"And well you should be. I'm still in charge of the family, not Old Manatook. If I ask you to walk off a cliff, you do it. If I tell you to jump in, you do it."

"Yes, Father."

"I was worried for your mother. I thought she would be upset at what happened, her darling boy hurt. I thought she would cry and cry. But she sees it differently. Everyone sees it differently. Your mother says you're a hero." Leaning forward so Alaana could see he was smiling a little, he added, "Of course, any man who listens to a woman makes himself ridiculous. I'm only telling you what she said."

Alaana didn't know what to say. She hadn't felt like a hero. She'd felt like a fox caught in a trap. "I can't let harm come to Itoriksak. Or anyone else. I have to protect them, if I can."

"I tried to protect Itoriksak," muttered Kigiuna. "But Itoriksak gets hurt either way. And who will protect you? It should be me, but I don't know how. I don't want harm to come to you. One does not need to believe in spirits to know the dangers of being the shaman. He's the first target in an enemy attack. I've watched them kill each other, I've seen them die. They have to be hard men. You're not like that, Alaana. At least that's what I would've said yesterday. But not today. I'm sorry for doubting you."

Kigiuna paused, breath slowly snaking away from his face.

"I don't want you to be a hard woman. I don't want that life for you, Alaana. You are very precious to me."

Alaana's eyes welled up. This was the opposite of what she had expected. It took all her effort to keep the tears back. She was absolutely not going to cry in front of her father right in the middle of the seal hunt. Besides, her eyeballs would freeze.

Her father looked around at the positions of the other hunters. Maguan waved again.

Kigiuna did not return the wave, raising his eyes instead to the starry sky. "I wish I knew," he said softly, "I wish I could see."

I wish I didn't have to see, thought Alaana. "Do you have to know? Do you have to see in order to believe?"

Kigiuna's smoldering gaze studied the snow and the ice and the stars. "Yes," he said. "I do."

Suddenly he held up the palm of his hand for silence. He had heard a slight something, a distant knock against the bottom of the ice. Now Alaana heard it too. A sharp claw scratch nicking the sheet.

"It's coming!" Kigiuna hissed. His harpoon was up and ready. He stood over the hole, knees bent, his entire body tensed and alert.

An odd sort of a grunt rumbled under the ice as the seal's head hit the undersurface. Kigiuna reacted as if it were a sound he'd never heard before. The seal cried out under the water, releasing a deep whoosh as the breath exploded from its lungs, but it wouldn't come near the hole to breathe.

Alaana realized what was happening. "It's not going to come up. It's not going to come near me. It's just like the dogs."

"What?"

She hesitated, not wanting her father to think her a cursed freak. "Old Manatook says I have the taint of Sila on me. The dogs can smell it, that's why they avoid me. I guess the seals are the same." She felt terrible. What else could go wrong? "I think if I don't go off the ice, none of us will get a seal today."

Kigiuna stared down at the hole. He didn't know if he believed what Alaana was saying, but he had no other reasonable explanation close at hand. The girl's tortured expression was enough. He shrugged his shoulders, saying, "Too cold anyway. I can manage. Go get some warm tea and check on your brother Itoriksak."

He watched his youngest child trudge away, the perfect picture of failure and dejection. Alaana stopped for a moment to visit with Maguan. They spoke animatedly, as if Maguan was relating some great new idea. Kigiuna was intrigued, watching Maguan sweep his arm around to illustrate the plan.

Alaana headed across the ice, going not toward the camp but taking a wider circular path that led eventually back toward Maguan.

Suddenly Maguan rose to his feet, the harpoon in his hand and poised, ready for the thrust.

"Here it comes. It's coming!" he announced. He felt no compulsion to remain silent. There was no fear of scaring the seal any more than it had been already. Alaana was driving it forward, right toward Maguan.

His indicator shot up, bobbing all the way out of the ice as the frightened seal struck it with its head.

"Stop!" shouted Old Manatook. Appearing practically out of nowhere, he yanked on the rear of Maguan's hood, sending him tumbling backward.

"Stop this foolishness immediately," said the old shaman. "This seal was not freely given. You will bring the Sea Mother's wrath down on us all."

Turning to his student, he said, "Alaana, you should know better than this by now. Let's go. We have important things to do."

CHAPTER 26

RETURN TO LOWERWORLD

"This is distinctly unwise."

"Oh Nunavik, you worry too much," said Alaana. She adjusted the brown mask of elder wood. It was too large for her face. The eyeholes didn't sit right and she could only glimpse the golden form of the ethereal walrus through the round central hole that was meant for a mouth. With her nose pressed up against the seasoned wood, she smelled its mix of sharply defined scents — the lightning, the soil, the tree bark.

"Old Manatook will be angry when he finds out," warned the Walrus. His yellowed tusks flicked disapprovingly.

"He's always angry anyway, the grumpy old polar bear."

"The greasy old fart," added Nunavik, unable to refrain. "But that's not the point."

Alaana remained indignant. "Old Manatook doesn't think I can do anything on my own. If he finds out about this, he'll learn something about me. This is my twelfth winter. I'm almost a woman now. I can take care of myself."

The Walrus snickered, sending his whiskers circling in a little arc around his mouth. "Can you? Can you really? Besides, that ridiculous *tunraq* is keeping the beat all wrong."

Weyahok did seem to be having a bit too much fun. The little lump of soapstone had produced a pair of sturdy legs and was happily bouncing up and down atop the drumhead.

Alaana gave him new instruction, saying, "Keep the beat steady and slow, like a dreaming heart."

"Not sleep now," said Weyahok. "Want play!"

"We'll play later," promised Alaana. "Now we do important shaman work, understand?"

"Shaman, shaman. Work, work."

"Right. So keep it steady and slow. And don't stop after I'm gone. I'll let you know when I want to come back. I'll whisper to you in the secret language. Then make five sharp raps. Got it?"

"He can't even count to five," snapped Nunavik. "This is extremely ill-advised. You should be getting some rest. You don't look well."

Alaana waved him off. "I'm fine," she said unconvincingly.

"Concentrate on your studies then. Instead of wasting your strength on flights of fancy."

"I have to check on the lake children, don't I?" said Alaana. "I promised Weeana."

"I'm speaking to a big lump of soapstone wearing a parka," snapped Nunavik. "You and Weyahok are exactly the same. There's no difference at all."

"Shaman, shaman," said Alaana. "Work, work."

"That's not funny. You should know, Alaana, I don't have a particularly strong manifestation in the Lowerworld. I'm a creature of the sea, I can't be of any help to you down there."

"I already told you. I don't need help."

The Walrus folded his flippers across his broad chest. "Well, be clear on this. I won't be held responsible for whatever happens, I just won't be."

Despite the continued nattering of the walrus, Alaana was eventually able to put aside her distractions, forget that her body was seated in the *karigi*, and visualize the hollow tree stump she had encountered once before. She peered into the hollow of the old stump. The way opened before her, and she dove down into it.

This time she found the tunnel far less frightening, and felt more in control. Maybe she was better off doing some things without the stern eye of her teacher looking over her shoulder. She passed through the unnamed ocean with its waters of pure joy and temptation, slid down the whirlpool, and was coughed up onto the floor of the cave.

She emerged into the same cavern she had visited on her first journey. She thought perhaps her *inuseq* was better able to travel paths already known to her. She saw the interior of the cave through the purplish tint of the spirit-vision. The floor was littered with a myriad of tiny crystals each aglow with their own little soul-light.

"And you left that silly thing beating the drum!" said Nunavik, his voice echoing from somewhere far above.

Alaana cocked an ear. The drumbeat was still there, off in the distance. "And he's doing a good job of it too."

"Have you no sense at all? You've no wits left to you, that is to say if you ever had possession of any to begin with." Nunavik's complaints came through at a much lower volume and less annoying pitch in the Lowerworld. Alaana could observe no sign of the glorious golden walrus aside from a faint glow surrounding the segment of ivory tusk in her hand. "No sense at all."

"I'm twelve winters now," said Alaana.

"And I'm twelve hundred. But do you listen?"

"Shhh," said Alaana, "Now, you listen. There's a strange voice here."

A melodic humming could be heard coming from the far end of the cavern. Alaana went to investigate, strictly avoiding the cracks in the floor. This time she intended to give the lurking *lumentin* a wide berth. The far side of the cave ended in a disappointingly solid rock face.

"If you've come to visit the lake," reminded Nunavik, "I believe you left it in the exact opposite direction. I suggest you stick to paths you've traveled before. That way you might not find yourself getting lost immediately."

Alaana pressed her spirit-hand against the wall of the cave. She could feel the vibrations from the other side. Several voices gently hummed beyond the wall, taking turns as if in polite conversation.

Alaana reached out. She ran her hand over the smooth rock, seeking out the very spirit of the cave. The soul within the rock was incredibly old, barely perceptible.

"*Brother Stone,*" whispered Alaana in the secret language, "*Long have you rested here, supporting the worlds above on your great broad shoulder. Would you grant a young traveler one small favor?*"

There came no answer. Alaana continued, "*Would you part this way for me?*"

"He's asleep," said Nunavik.

"Brother Walrus?" asked Alaana in a playful wheedle.

"That's Uncle Walrus to you," snapped Nunavik.

"How loud can you roar, I wonder? A fine well-built bull like yourself? Son of Big Bellow and all? Can't you wake him up?"

"Well, don't you think you're clever?" returned Nunavik. "You nearly outsmarted me that time. I'm sure I could rouse the cave spirit. If I wanted. Which I don't! Absolutely not. I'm not here to help get you into trouble."

"Hmmf," said Alaana.

"That's strange," said Nunavik, "I thought I heard Old Manatook just now."

With another grumble Alaana turned to walk away, but movement at the cave wall caught her eye. Soundlessly, the rock

300

separated as if it had been water, revealing an entrance to a deeper chamber.

"Did you do that?" she asked Nunavik.

"No. Did you?"

"I don't think so."

A deep voice, sounding rough and uncertain as if it had not spoken in ages said, "Enter."

Alaana stepped into the adjoining chamber, a small space no larger than her family's tent back at the camp. The walls of the cave sparkled with encrusted crystal. Jutting shards in emerald green met a heap of blue amethyst as it joined the floor. A strange, tongue-like formation of shimmering scarlet hung from the ceiling, and in the corner nested an intricate formation of delicate white gems. The clusters held odd, irregular shapes as they clung to the walls. Each contained a distinct and powerful spirit, making the chamber seem to Alaana as if full to bursting with colorful light.

"He has returned to us," said the blue. Its voice echoed in the small chamber as if commanded by one who was terribly wise and as old as the earth itself.

"I predicted it would be so," said the green.

"Returned to us after all this time." This came from the white.

"What is that he brings?" asked the green.

"Curious-looking thing," added the blue.

"Some type of fish." This came from the white.

Nunavik bristled. "Fish? Fish! Does a fish have luxurious tusks like these? Show me the fish that has a sexual organ such as this!"

Alaana cringed, glad no one could see the walrus or whatever he was trying to show.

"Silence," said the green.

"Let the great spirit speak," said the blue.

Alaana was puzzled. "Me? My name is Alaana. I've come from the people of the world above."

"He does not know," said the blue.

"I'm a girl," said Alaana, "Not a he."

"We must keep the secret," said the scarlet.

"As we keep all the secrets." This came from the white.

The crystals went immediately dark, leaving Alaana in complete silence.

She glanced around the gloomy, lifeless cave. "What secret? What did they see, and what did they call me? Great spirit?"

Nunavik said nothing more except, "I think it would be best for us to leave."

Alaana stepped forward, reaching out to the green cluster of crystals.

"Look there!" said Nunavik. "Fangs! Fangs! Remember I said keep away from anything with fangs."

A small black scorpion had crawled out of a crack between the crystals.

"Do scorpions have fangs?" asked Alaana. "I've never seen one before."

"Of course they do," squawked the Walrus. "Great big ones."

"No. I don't see any."

The scorpion raised its claws. Its tail quivered.

"Stop gawping and move!" said Nunavik. "We can settle that question another time. Back away quickly."

The wall slid closed as they passed, cutting them off from both scorpion and crystals alike.

"You're awfully quiet now, Uncle Walrus," said Alaana.

"And you're far too noisy, as usual."

"Why did they think I was a boy?"

"Who knows what they think? They probably don't expect a

girl to be travelling between the worlds, I'd guess."

Alaana made her way to the cave opening and out into the forest. Again she thrilled to the sight of the vast legion of trunks and roots, leaves and branches. The majesty and infinite variety took her breath away. This was really why she had longed to return here. The marvelous trees.

But she must not forget the lake. She set off in the direction she thought she remembered traveling before, but none of these trees looked familiar. She kept trying to find that certain one, the giant she remembered as the great-grandfather of them all. In short order she had to admit to Nunavik she was completely lost.

"This does not surprise me," said the Walrus.

"Do you know the way to the lake?"

Nunavik said, "I'm rather more interested in the way back to the *karigi*."

Alaana let out an exasperated sigh. "You were right. You're no help at all."

Some small thing struck the back of Alaana's head. When she turned around, another bounced off the front of her spirit-parka. She saw this one clearly. It was the top half of an acorn.

"Hmm-hum, play with us, spirit."

Alaana turned round again to find a trio of the little men of the woods leaning casually against the base of a tree.

"Ho-hum. Run and follow," said one as he dashed away behind the trunk. A moment later the smiling face of the *ieufuluuraq* peered expectantly around the opposite edge of the tree.

"Hum-hum. Play! Play!" said another. This one stood slightly taller than the rest, the top of his head on an even line with Alaana's knee. His large eyes sparkled gleefully under thick auburn brows and the fine tuft of fur atop his head bore a distinctly reddish tint. His parka was the same reddish color, belted at the waist with a little piece of twine. He motioned with a stubby arm for Alaana to

303

follow. His upper lip curled playfully. "Come, come."

She stepped forward.

"No," warned Nunavik . "You didn't come down here to play about with the lowerfolk. Don't dawdle. Twelve winters remember? What about the twelve winters?"

Alaana took another step forward but tripped over a loose root crossing her path. As she fell, the slender ivory tusk rolled from her hand onto the forest floor of cluttered leaves and branches.

The little man with the reddish fur snatched it up, giggling, and plunged through the underbrush. The creature was so short Alaana could only see the bushy tail pinned to the back of his jacket flapping upward as he went. She darted forward, just in time to see the tip of the tail as it vanished into a little hole in the ground.

"Nunavik! I can't follow."

"Of course you can," said Nunavik, his voice trailing off as the little man carried him further away.

Of course, Alaana thought. She shrank her spirit-form to fit the bolt hole. With a rising panic she plunged into the darkness. A narrow, low-ceilinged tunnel forced her to scamper forward on hands and knees. There was no natural light but the purplish haze of the spirit-vision saw her through. The tunnel opened up into a sizeable warren. The walls of this oblong chamber were supported by crude wooden pilings that marked three possible exit tunnels.

"Nunavik!"

Alaana thought she heard the walrus' distinctive "Ackk!" trailing back from the left-most opening.

Crawling awkwardly on hands and knees she was sure she'd never catch the nimble little creature she was after. Her nose passed close to the floor, littered with rodent pellets and half-gnawed bone fragments. The pungent odors of rank fur and raw earth filled the narrow tunnel.

The tunnel led to an underground dwelling. This area must have been directly below one of the trees as it had for its sturdy walls a pair of plunging tree roots. She found one of the *ieufuluuraq* women here cradling two of her furry young. The little mother was startled slightly at her sudden appearance, then waved cheerfully at her unexpected visitor. She wore a loose parka crudely trimmed with white fur at the belly and throat. She smiled, her face pleasantly round and feminine despite shaggy cheeks and pointed teeth.

Other children played at shields and spears using little branches taken from the wood. She called to them in a peculiar chattering language, interrupting their game. Alaana stumbled around them, crashing into a pile of empty nut-cases each large enough to use as a soup bowl. She crossed a hard-packed floor covered with small flat stones, and ran into the tunnel the mother had indicated.

Not far ahead she glimpsed the *ieufuluuraq* who had snatched Nunavik. The rascal seemed to be waiting at a crossroads but moved quickly when Alaana caught up. The tunnels were vast and confusing, winding their way back and around, twisting and turning and splitting frequently to rejoin the main network beneath the trees.

Alaana caught a flash of red fur as the little squirrel-man dashed up the hollow of a tree. She made quick pursuit, finding natural handholds along the rough surface of the bole. She climbed up the interior of the tree, sprouting long-fingered hands tipped with sharp claws to aid in the ascent.

She passed knot holes that offered breathtaking views of the forest from various heights. She wanted to stop and look but pushed on for fear of losing the red-furred little man who had taken Nunavik. Worse yet, she realized the beat from the *karigi* had lost its rhythm entirely. Weyahok had grown bored and begun tapping out a lazy, disorganized dance on the drumhead.

"Weyahok," she called. "Weyahok! Stay to the beat. The heartbeat of the dreamer. If you don't keep the way open for us, we won't be able to get back!"

"I'm lonely," said Weyahok. "Come and play."

"Play later. Shaman work first," said Alaana. "Shaman work."

Reluctantly the little *tunraq* took up the proper measure again, and Alaana resumed her climb through the inside of the tree.

The pursuit led her out through an empty knothole and onto a thick, jutting branch. Alaana's red-furred quarry turned and leered back at her. His face pulled into a blunt sort of a muzzle, now appearing much more squirrel than man. He scampered off the end of the branch and leapt across to a neighboring tree. Alaana followed, for it was only a short hop from branch to branch, a bushy tail having sprouted from her hindquarters for balance.

The branches were alive with playful parka-wearing squirrels. Darting along the thoroughfares crossing her path, they scurried up and down. Some swatted her with their soft, furry tails or gave her a playful poke in the belly as she went by.

Alaana kept her eye on the red squirrel as it leapt nimbly to a higher location. She climbed along the shaggy bark, digging into the soft wood with clawed hands and feet. Then she was flying along the branch with perfect balance, using the natural spring of the slender branchlets to bounce up and find a place on the next tier. She moved quickly, leaping from tree to tree, rolling along the springy foliage, falling backward and catching herself and then plunging onward, up and down and then back around. There was a sheer joy to racing and flying among the branches and she lost himself in the exhilarating feeling, Nunavik almost forgotten.

A bone-chilling shriek cut through the windless forest. Alaana nearly toppled from her high branch.

A sudden and total silence fell over the wood — no bird song, no scurrying of squirrels through the branches — as the entire world held its breath, waiting for some awful evil to pass.

The stillness lingered for only a moment. Then came another harsh, ugly screech. This sound, however, produced the opposite reaction than the stultifying effect of the first. It served as a call to action.

The squirrels moved with new purpose, coming at Alaana with violent malevolence. Two of the squirrels collided with her at the same instant, charging from different directions. They knocked her off the branch and sent her tumbling down through the leaves. She bounced off the branch below and, with a desperate grab, caught herself on another. Another inhuman shriek split the air and two squirrels crashed down onto the branch beside her. The branch snapped loudly, sending all three plummeting to the soft ground.

Alaana, momentarily stunned by the fall, opened her eyes to find a ring of the squirrel men surrounding her. She had not realized they possessed such sharp, slender teeth.

"Take her, Hmm-hum," said one, his eyes wide, his voice hoarse.

"We'll feed her to it, Har-umm."

"Bite her, Hhhhhmm."

Rows of spiked teeth sank into her legs and she felt their hot sting as intensely as if her spirit-body were flesh and bone. There were so many of them. She was trapped. Her only hope was Weyahok. Alaana listened for the distant beat of the drum. She could hear none.

"Weyahok! The five beats! Weyahok!" she said frantically, but the connection had been broken. There was no way back.

The little men shredded Alaana's pants with their raking teeth, and bit into her legs. Using tatters of the spirit-trousers they bound her hand and foot. Alaana decided to enlarge her *inuseq* back to its original size in order to better fight them off. Too late. She abandoned the attempt when she felt the tightening bonds threaten to cut off her hands and legs.

The *ieufuluuraq* dragged her along the forest floor by her feet, leaving the back of her head to bump and thump against every tree root and jutting stone.

Up ahead the woods loomed twisted and dark. Alaana felt a deluge of doubt and fear as they plunged forward, as if she had passed through one realm of emotion and into another. Everything was different on the other side. The air hung thickly, smelling of burnt ochre. The soul-lights of the trees blurred and obscured as the spirit-vision became warped and unreliable. This was a bad place, a place of fear and madness. But where was she?

The concept of direction lost all meaning. Was she spinning around? Twisting, turning, even the ground underfoot had grown liquid and strange. There was no up or down.

Even as the surroundings changed, the denizens of the forest warped into bizarre shapes. Trees melded with rock, sheltering empty hollows that were themselves vast expanses. Alaana, breathless, was dragged deeper into confusion.

At the center of this chaotic realm sat a sort of throne. The branches of the trees merged and fused together to create a barbed and twisted arbor, sprouting weirdly-shaped leaves. The perverted carcasses of small forest animals were draped among the brambles, their exposed innards forming part of the thorny arch of the bizarre bower. Alaana noted with sickening horror that the animals were still breathing despite having been turned inside out.

She found herself in the presence of a strange creature. The sight of it sent Alaana's senses reeling dizzily but she dared not look away. She could feel its will, nightmarish and undeniable, pulling her apart.

"Five beats," she said desperately. "Five beats." It was no

use. If Weyahok could hear her at all, her words must sound like gibberish on the other side.

The *ieufuluuraq* with the reddish pelt lay squealing and shivering before the hideous creature enshrined in the throne's madness. Nunavik's tusk was there, dropped carelessly onto the shifting morass of the corrupted forest floor. When Alaana grabbed the talisman, she could hear the walrus' distant screams. Alaana sobbed. It sounded as if her friend was being ripped apart.

A bird-headed and broad-winged demon prince shifted on the throne. Alaana sensed the power of this creature's mad will. The glimmering bird eyes turned their cold, cruel gaze upon her. From its mouth came that same inhuman shriek of anguish that had so disturbed the *ieufuluuraq*.

Alaana screamed as her own spirit-form stretched and contorted, bones twisting and snapping, remolding themselves under the influence of the demon's shifting madness.

"It doesn't belong here," said Alaana. Within this world of swirling insanity, only that one statement seemed to be still right and true. "It doesn't belong."

"Feathers and beaks," said Nunavik weakly.

Alaana found momentary strength in the old walrus' words. She was on the right track. The bird-thing did not belong. Trapped here, in an unfamiliar and skyless world, it had been twisted and driven insane. Lost and in pain, it had not the strength or knowledge to return.

Alaana struggled to her feet, Nunavik's tusk clasped tightly in her fist. The solution was at hand. The answer, she thought, was so often the same. Take the monster's pain away. There was only one way to go. They must simply travel up.

She realized what must have happened. Five of the seven spiritual worlds were aligned on a vertical axis. At the very bottom lay the festering Underworld, home to demons and evil spirits. The

Lowerworld came next, sitting directly below the world that the Anatatook called home. The Upperworld hovered directly above, and crowning them all was the cosmic realm of the Moon and stars.

With five worlds existing on the same axis, occasionally a wayward soul fell from one spirit realm to the next.

Alaana called out to the demon prince. The cruel bird eyes cast their incisive gaze upon her, but saw no threat in her outstretched hand, no harm in her open soul. The head cocked slightly, then bowed slowly forward toward its feathered chest.

She took the bird-thing's soul in her hand and, Nunavik in the other, readied herself to bring it home. She would save them both, if only she knew which direction was up. The thing's madness still swirled around her, tearing up the emptied bower in a whirlwind of shattered branches and spiked leaves. Alaana felt so disoriented and sick, with everything spinning in several directions at once. There was no way to be sure. She must take her best guess, going on instinct alone.

With a burst of energy, she took flight. The distorted image of the forest shifted and ran like melting wax. Branches became firm once more; broken and splintered though they may be, they had been restored to peace. The squirrel men, released from the spell of madness, gathered around their fallen friends. Alaana looked away from the sight of the mutilated bodies. Nothing could be done for them.

Her spirit soared through the canopy of the Lowerworld and through the rock of the cave ceiling. She felt a great sense of relief at leaving the madness behind, like shedding an old, rotten skin. But her exaltation at flying free was dulled by the extreme exertion, and the nagging suspicion that this was likely the final time she might ever do it. There was so little of Sila's fading gift still left to her.

Picking up speed, she sailed through layer after layer of bedrock and soil, through the ever-frost, and up into Nunatsiaq.

She did not pause as, breaking the ground cover, her *inuseq* blasted through some poor soul sitting on a flat rock, sharpening a spearhead.

"Sorry, Iggy," she whispered, having knocked a puzzled Iggianguaq onto his plump backside.

Alaana shot up into the sky. Her spirit flew past the peaks of the ice mountains and into the Upperworld, a world of blue skies and endless clouds. So wide open, so free.

The Upperworld was a strange land of air and clouds, which was no land at all. It was a place of winds foul and fair, all of which had voices and personalities of their own. She heard snippets of their conversation as the winds discussed the matters of the day. In the distance she saw the far pavilion of the Morning Dawn who resided in quiet contemplation among the Upper-people.

The bird-thing in her hand transformed as she rose higher and higher. The thorny head resolved into a round ball of downy feathers. The eyes, no longer menacing and wild, looked at her with surprise and gratitude. The little gull spirit cooed softly.

A flock of the Gull People materialized out of the misty skies all around Alaana. With a grateful sigh, she stopped rising. She had flown so much higher than ever before, and must soon go back down. But first she wanted to drink in this one, wondrous glance at the Upperworld and its strange denizens.

A pair of Gull People rapidly approached, soaring and gliding on the talkative winds. They had impressive wings, large and gray, stretching so far that the feathers at the tips blended into the very mist itself.

One lofty spirit presented herself to Alaana with a proud countenance that was distinctly female. The Gull's elegantly feathered head offered a flash of yellow beak as she squawked tentatively at Alaana. Alaana released the chick.

The Gull said, "Tiffivilliq, my baby, we've found you at last."

She took the little spirit snugly under her vast wing. "How did you fall child? Didn't we tell you to flap hard, flap hard? Oh, never mind — my poor baby chick, we were so worried."

Her mate, a huge gull spirit with expansive black-tipped wings and a luxuriously fanned tail regarded Alaana with a wise and gentle gaze.

"Thank you, young traveler, for your help."

Alaana wished she had time to answer, but already she began falling back down. The pull of Nunatsiaq was too strong to resist. A group of little sparrow spirits tried to help, flitting closely around, but they weren't strong enough to prop her up. Alaana thought of the sparrow shaman that Nunavik had mentioned, but couldn't recall her name. And then she found herself helplessly falling, with no chance to right herself.

"Weyahok!" she cried. "Now would be a good time for the five beats."

The five beats on the drum, just barely heard as they drifted up through the spirit of the air, called her back to the *karigi*.

Alaana opened her eyes. She found herself face down on the prayer mat.

Her entire body ached. Rolling over, the first thing she saw were Old Manatook's crusty old mukluks. The old shaman held the drum beater in his gnarly fist.

"Sun and Moon, girl," he said sternly. "What trouble have you gotten yourself into?"

Weyahok peered out from behind the drum, looking as guilty and foolish as was possible for a featureless gray lump of soapstone.

Alaana didn't care to answer. She was only concerned with the fate of her friend Nunavik.

The tusk fragment lay misshapen and dark in her hand. Alaana couldn't discern the light of the ethereal walrus within. She feared Nunavik was very much the worse for wear. His voice could only barely be heard, making a strange high-pitched squealing sound, "Nnneeeeeeeee."

"Uncle Walrus," she asked. "Are you all right?"

Old Manatook took the piece of tusk and peered at it. "Why is it you can not ever listen?" he said to Alaana.

"It's all my fault," she said uselessly. "He's dying, isn't he?"

Old Manatook cocked a bushy white eyebrow. "He's had worse over the years." He frowned, then added, "I think."

Alaana was beside herself but the old shaman comforted her, saying, "I trust he'll be all right. Give him some time to straighten himself out."

Old Manatook sniffed at her, scenting the Upperworld, a realm where Sila held great sway. There was no need to ask his student if she had encountered the great spirit there. If the girl had met her spirit guardian she would have returned exultant and full of energy, not half-dead and on the brink of collapse.

Alaana looked balefully up at her teacher. "I shouldn't have gone traveling alone."

Old Manatook nearly leapt at the chance to chastise the girl, but decided against it. Never mind, he told himself, she was called for a reason. And she had answered the call. "I'm glad you did," he said, though somewhat reluctantly. "It's good to see you acting on your own account at last, though I wish you'd promise not to do it again until I say you are ready. No more traveling alone! Or at all! You have to save your strength for the initiation."

"I promise," said Alaana, "But I did find the thing that was harming the Lowerworld, and I saved her. A little lost chick."

"You'll have to tell me all about it," said Old Manatook softly. "After you've had some rest."

Alaana glanced down at the tusk. "But the Walrus…"

"Give him time."

313

CHAPTER 27

TRAPPED

Makaartunghak and Yipyip strained with anticipation at the harness of Old Manatook's sled. Though it seemed ridiculous to think that the little black dog could possibly keep up with the magnificent huskie, Yipyip was already testing the traces. Old Manatook, sensing the dogs' eagerness to set out across the fresh ice, cinched the lines tight.

"How long will you be away?" Alaana asked her teacher.

"At least a full turning of the Moon," replied Old Manatook.

Alaana glanced up at the glowing crescent high in the black sky of mid-day. "Can't I come with you?"

Old Manatook's bushy white eyebrows twitched with surprise. He tried to conceal his smile by hoisting his bag of supplies atop the stanchion. "There are things I must do outside the Anatatook, pathways I must walk alone."

Acting on impulse Alaana grabbed his hand, turning him toward her. "Why can't you tell me?"

Old Manatook took a deep breath, running his fingertips along his curly white beard. "One day. For now you'll do better to have some rest. Spend time with your father, your family."

A few months ago Alaana would have been pleased by that idea, but she was different now. She had become much more interested in mastery of the Way. The world of the spirits, as dangerous and disturbing as it might be at times, seemed the only place she could truly belong. Her father and Maguan spent all their time out on the ice hunting seal in the dark with the other men. She felt so out of place in the winter camp. People looked at her strangely, her old friends didn't want her, her own family didn't know what to do with her.

"Look after Itoriksak," said Old Manatook. "And visit with Higilak. She knows all the stories and legends in the world and will tell you which ones are true. I don't like her to be all alone in winter when I'm gone."

"Then why do you go? Where do you go? Alone in the dark?"

"I'm not alone," said the shaman. He slapped Makaartunghak heartily on the back. "I will tell you everything one day. When you are ready to hear me."

Alaana was tired of secrets, tired of cryptic answers and half-truths, of blurred soul shapes and mysterious errands. "But…"

"That's enough," said Old Manatook. "Stay away from trouble. Have some rest. You're to face your initiation soon. There is much more for me to teach you before then, and we will have little time when I return."

Then why was he going, she wondered. It seemed all too much at times. She watched Old Manatook pull away on his sled. The old shaman was correct on one point. Alaana was very, very tired.

In the full dark of winter, even Alaana had trouble seeing anything. The spirit-vision provided little help. With all the animals deep in their burrows there were so very few souls to light her way. The vast spirit of the snow was stretched thin over the land, providing only a dull purple haze. The rocks lay all asleep, the water locked down in icy slumber. She might not have been able to find Miki except that she already knew where his family kept their trap line.

In the deep winter cold that made every breath a chore she could not remain outside for very long, and neither could Miki. But this was her only chance to get him alone. With all the grown men busy at the blowholes, Miki must tend his father's fox traps.

Miki's soul-light burned brightly against the bleak tundra. Alaana jogged ahead to catch up to him. It was a complicated light, flickering orange and red and yellow like fire at its core, cool blue at the edges. Miki had so many varied passions and cares. His light was different than when Alaana had last spoken to him two moons ago. Miki was changing.

"Miki," she said. "You shouldn't be out here alone. It's too cold."

"My father's too busy for the traps," he answered. "And you know how my mother loves fox fur."

He held up one of his catches, but Alaana couldn't see it in the darkness. Its soul-light had already gone.

"I have to talk to you," she said.

"I've a lot of work to do." He reached down into the trap and reset the trip line. After he removed his hand, he balanced a flat stone at the top.

"A lot of work," he said. "I don't have time for play anymore."

That's just it, Alaana thought. No more time for play. She remembered early spring and her friends sliding down the ice. That was the last time for them, the last really good time. And, mourning the death of her sister, she had missed it.

"Do you have time to talk?" she asked. "Just for a moment?"

Miki kicked a little snow over the stone trap, burying it underground. He poked a hole in the snow so that the next fox might smell the bait.

"I was scared for you," he said. "When your arm got stuck, the look of pain on your face, the way you screamed, I thought you were going to die."

"That was a long time ago," said Alaana. "You should forget about it. It was just a little stone spirit teaching me a lesson. Just a joke really. I made a mistake."

"A shaman can't make mistakes."

Alaana was silent. He was right.

"Don't you see?" Miki added. "You're the last person I'd have chosen to be the shaman."

"You didn't choose," said Alaana. "Sila did."

"You're too much like your father. You never do what you're told, you're always asking too many questions. Remember how red-faced Civiliaq used to get? When you tried to make him explain about the spirits?"

"I'm learning," Alaana said. "And it's not all bad, either. There's a woman in the Lowerworld married to a lake and little men who turn into squirrels. There's an entire world beneath our feet. And in the sky. I wish you could see."

Miki shook his head, closing his eyes. "I don't want to see."

"Miki," said Alaana, "I can fly!"

"Flying is dangerous," he returned. "Especially when you don't know what you're doing. The baby murres fall, straight out of the nest. And a crow snaps them up."

Miki bundled up the fox he'd caught and headed back toward the camp. Alaana watched him take a few steps then went after him.

"You don't think I can do it," she said. "You don't think I'm strong enough."

Miki said nothing. He looked away, and in the darkness Alaana could not see his face.

"I can do it," she insisted. "I'll show you. I'll make it. Won't

317

you be surprised?"

"I hope you do," said Miki. "I pray that you make it."

"And then?" asked Alaana. "When it comes time to marry?"

"I'll be with someone else," he said flatly. "Don't you see? The shamans aren't like the rest of us. Kuanak with his trembling hand and one half-dead eye, Civiliaq with his writhing snake tattoos, and that horrible Old Manatook. I can't bear the thought of you like that, hard and ruined from dealing with the spirits. But it's going to happen. Even lately, your sweet little smile is gone from your lips.

"The spirits are more frightening than anything. The wild wind, the fever demon, the great *turgats* — we can't see them but they're always up there, somewhere above us, and they don't care what suffering and pain they cause. I don't want to think about them. That's the shaman's duty. The shaman's burden, not mine. And, like it or not, your husband must share that life. I want no part of it."

She didn't know what to say. She wanted children and skins to sew and fish to cook in the pot. And more children. And a husband. She wanted Miki. "I love you," she said.

"I'm sorry, Alaana," he said. "I can never be married to the shaman. I don't want to watch my wife suffer and die. I couldn't. If I have to watch you corrupted and destroyed, it has to be from a distance."

Alaana watched him walk away.

CHAPTER 28

SPIRIT KAYAK

"Unseen forces are always at work."

Alaana stared at the speaker's back. He seemed but a tiny speck against a magnificent panorama — a vast expanse of white, untrodden snow blanketing the ice-bound waters. In the midst of winter's long night, with the ice field lit by starlight alone, she could not make out its full extent. The horizon was a journey of at least six sleeps by even the fastest sled, ending in the shadowy blues at the feet of the ice mountains in the distance.

"What we call reality is not certain," continued her teacher. "Nor is it solid. It is itself a shifting sea. Every state of being is a trance state, including the one that we consider to be ordinary reality. Did you know that?"

"You're not Old Manatook," said Alaana.

"No," said Civiliaq as he turned around. "Far from it. But that does not make my lesson any less true." He smiled his characteristic smile.

Alaana noticed the intricate designs that covered Civiliaq's arms and bare chest were drawn backwards, as figures most often appeared in the dreamlands. The magnificent tattoos blazed as if with an inner fire, lending them a scarlet glow that stippled the edges of his bare skin.

319

"Oh," said Alaana. "I'm dreaming."

Civiliaq bowed at the waist. "Again, that is not a reason to dismiss the lesson."

At that same instant, the scenery behind the dead shaman started to burn. The snow took on the color of sunset; the ice mountains caught fire, turning a blistering red. And a herd of huge beasts, which Alaana recognized as the long-dead *mamut*, could be seen crossing the horizon.

"Listen to me, little bird," said Civiliaq. "There are things Old Manatook isn't telling you. Remember what you saw at Uwelen? When he was revealed as a man with an empty face?"

"How could I forget?" said Alaana. When Old Manatook had dropped his guise of white bear he had, for a brief instant, worn a ghostly face. Alaana sensed the owner of that face to be a murderer, cast out from his band, who had beaten his wife almost to death, a terrible man who had been caught up for his sins and skinned alive.

Civiliaq tapped his black crow feather lightly against the side of his nose. "What if I said that is the true face of Old Manatook?"

"I wouldn't believe you. He was testing me. That was just a disguise."

"Was it? Testing you? I wonder why Old Manatook would have need of testing you. Is it because he is suspicious of you? Is it because he doesn't trust you?"

Civiliaq moved his hand before his face. In their passing his fingers left the shaman wearing the guise of Old Manatook, caught in an expression Alaana knew painfully well. It was a look of disdain.

Civiliaq waved the face away. His own clean-shaven, sturdy features smiled dismissively. "Have you yet seen his true soul-shape? I doubt it."

"It's true, Manatook keeps many secrets," said Alaana. "But he says he will tell me some day." She paused for a moment, before adding, "And I believe him."

"Ah, I see. He makes many promises. And in the meantime, he distrusts and misleads you."

Civiliaq sat down on a bench of glittering crystal that suddenly formed beneath his buttocks. He motioned for Alaana to join him. "I don't tell you this to make you feel badly, Alaana," he said, "only to illustrate my point."

Alaana didn't sit. Although it was good to see Civiliaq again, she found she trusted him only as much as she had before, which was not all that much. When she was younger she had often marveled at his tricks and haughty good humor. The shaman made little pebbles dance on the beach, or whipped up a wind so that the whirling snow made it seem as if he had momentarily disappeared. All the children loved his stunts. But now, seen through the eyes of her new experiences, Alaana recognized these as petty tricks that any shaman could perform, and probably shouldn't.

"You left me to die on Dog-Ear Ridge," said Alaana.

"I tried to help," insisted Civiliaq. "If you'd only done what I asked, but you didn't. I could no longer hold that shape. It was all I could do to take the demons away with me in the end."

Alaana sighed. She didn't think there had ever been any demons that day at all. She didn't know what to believe.

"Well, it appears you no longer trust me as well," said Civiliaq. "And that is a pity, since I've always been a good friend to you."

"You brought the fever demon among us in the first place," said Alaana hesitantly. "The thing that killed Avalaaqiaq."

Civiliaq scowled. "Not so. That was caused by Kuanak! Do you carry any grudge against him?"

Alaana shrugged.

"Listen to me," said Civiliaq, kindly, "Speaking of your poor lost sister, have you ever wondered as to the reason why you survived when she did not?"

321

"Tell me!"

Civiliaq motioned for Alaana to calm down. "I don't know all the answers, but I do know some things. It's not enough simply to tell. Some things I must show you. Come with me to find the truth."

Alaana balked. She knew where Civiliaq wanted to lead her, where the shaman must take her. Civiliaq's soul had been bound to the Underworld ever since he died at the hands of the fever demon. And Alaana was not sure she trusted Civiliaq enough to brave that dreaded realm.

The Walrus On The Ice would know what to do. Alaana longed to ask Nunavik for his advice but the *tunraq's* spirit was still incapacitated from their disastrous interaction with the bird-thing in the Lowerworld. My fault, thought Alaana. Again, my fault.

To Alaana's surprise the vision of Civiliaq vanished, though his voice spoke across the spirit of the air, "*To learn the secrets reserved for the dying and the dead, you must come to the Underworld. I am waiting there for you. Follow my instruction.*"

The red light suffusing the dream tundra suddenly extinguished, leaving Alaana alone in the murky dark. At her feet, a long white snake was circling. Nunavik's strict admonition against snakes and fanged creatures rang again in her ears. The snake sank downward through the snowy ground like a burning ember still circling and circling. Alaana peered into the tunnel left in its wake but all was darkness below. On second thought she was glad the belligerent walrus was not present to caution her against taking this chance. This was definitely not a good idea, but she was going to do it anyway. She must know the answers.

Alaana plunged into the tunnel. She was falling into death, and she found it surprisingly easy.

The route to the Underworld seemed composed entirely of pain. Invisible knives tore at her, shredding skin and stabbing at the joints of her arms and legs. She had to force herself to remember that she possessed neither skin nor body at the moment. This was, as far as she could tell, still a dream. How long would the pain last, she wondered desperately. How far is the journey to the Underworld? She had never visited that frightful realm before.

She suddenly feared that the tunnel would deposit her in a lake of fire.

"Put that out of your mind, this instant!" demanded Civiliaq. As Alaana struggled to comply, she hit the ground. She felt so weak she could hardly think straight, let alone stand up. She had landed on a plain of black volcanic rock, charred and crumbling beneath the palms of her hands. But no fire. A shadow image of the fiery pit crossed her mind. Had she just narrowly averted destruction? Civiliaq's warning had saved her life, she was certain of it.

Before her lay a bleak plain so totally unlike the world that she knew. The ground was sooty, without snow or ice, and there was no sky. It was completely disorienting, this plain of desolation which brought with it a heavy feeling of dread, of eternal hunger and woe. People milled about, or sat huddled up with their heads hanging down, their eyes and faces closed, looking weary and pathetic. Other unfortunates emerged from the dreary houses scattered around the plain. These dwellings were without windows or doors, and the souls of the dead simply passed through the walls. They were all slowly converging on Alaana.

"These are the noqumiut," said Civiliaq's disembodied voice, *"the dead who abide here. They are the souls of lazy hunters, they know only perpetual hunger."*

"What do they want with me?"

"You look ill Alaana, so sickly and pale. They take you for one of them. Get up. Show them that you are still alive."

"How can I? What must I do?"

Alaana forced herself to her feet. What could she do to prove she was alive? She began to sing the song Aolajut had offered to the first snipe of spring:

"First little bird of spring, we welcome you,
Pretty little bird of spring, bringing us the new year,
Blameless as the blue sky,
Good tidings you bring this year to us all."

In the darkness and oppression of the Underworld it was difficult to sing such a merry tune. Alaana could go no farther, but it had been enough. The forlorn dead turned away, disappointed and horrified by the spirit-girl. They had no wish to be reminded of songs, and happy times, and all they had lost.

Alaana was gripped by a sudden panic. "Is Avalaaqiaq here?"

"*No. She is at Agneriartarfik. The Land of Day. The village one can always return to, located high in the sky, where great herds of caribou roam and there is always plenty of good things to eat.*" Alaana was glad for that.

"*Now walk away from them. And don't go so close to the lumentin. Just get out into the open.*"

It was only at that moment Alaana noticed the herd of enormous black *lumentin* lumbering in the distance. These bloated creatures were much more grotesque than the emaciated things she had glimpsed from the other side through the cracks in the Lowerworld. There was no lack of food for them here. They barely resembled caribou, enormously fat, moving slowly on tiny legs, with large rheumy eyes and spiked antlers that gleamed like carved obsidian. Even at this distance they exuded an air of extreme danger and menace. What were they grazing on? Alaana couldn't see, but a chorus of horrific screams rang out whenever one of them lowered its head to the plain of low grass. Were those people?

"*You have to see the Man Who Keeps The Skins.*"

"But who is he?" asked Alaana. "How do I find him?" She wobbled on her legs, feeling disoriented and weak. Was she really in the Underworld or still asleep? She could hardly see the *lumentin*

324

now, her spirit-vision had dimmed so much. Was she dying?

"Step forward a few more paces."

"There is nothing here," said Alaana desperately.

"Spin around three times and then jump as high as you can."

Spin around? Alaana was reminded of the children's game of playing at shaman. She could no longer play that game, the motion caused such painful flashes of light and darkness. More than anything else, she just wanted to lay down and sleep. But that was one temptation she must not indulge. She knew that would be the worst thing she could do.

She began to spin. The dizziness was extreme, the disorientation total.

"Push up! Jump!"

Push up, push up. Which way was up?

"Just jump as high as you can."

Alaana jumped.

She found herself inside a strange room, curtained by hanging skins of various shapes and colors. The air of the smoke house was thick and heavy with soot, the floor littered with cracked bones and shredded skin. The Man stood in the center of the room working at a long, pale hide that hung from the thatched ceiling. Alaana had never seen a man so large and hairy, with teeth like a bear jutting forth from blackened lips. He wore a mottled patchwork of tattered and decaying skins, a peculiar garment that swayed and writhed independently of the movements of his body.

In one corner of the house his wife squatted, chewing on the skins. Her muffled grunts of satisfaction blended with odd sounds that came from the skin itself, shrieks and howls of torment. She paused to smile seductively at Alaana, if any display of such enormous teeth could be called seductive, gesturing for her to draw near. With blood and grease trickling down, she licked at her lips.

The Man's clawed hand raked the skin before him, oozing fat

and blood as he scraped it clean. Alaana thought perhaps he'd been too rough, having torn a hole in the hide. Looking closer she realized the round hole was a mouth. It was the skin of a human being. The lids flew open and the eyes rolled toward her, full of helpless misery.

"What do you want?" asked the Man. His voice rumbled through the smoke house, a terrifying combination of growl and cackle. His fiery gaze was full to brimming with pain and suffering.

"Ask for me by name," said Civiliaq.

"I want to see Civiliaq the shaman," said Alaana.

"And what will you barter?" demanded the Man.

"I don't know."

The Man took the skin of Alaana's cheek between two of his long filthy fingernails. The pinch brought tears to her eyes. The Man shook his shaggy head, finding her skin unacceptable for some reason, and let go. His merciless eyes searched Alaana up and down, inspecting her from top to bottom.

"You're a pathetic little specimen, aren't you?" he snarled. "And much too brash coming in here like this. I'm going to strip you to the bone."

Alaana shrank back in horror, but hadn't the strength to make a run for it.

The Man grunted and cocked his head to the side appraisingly. "Perhaps plumped and stuffed you might make a passable seat cushion for my wife's festering backside. I don't see — wait. What's that, and that?"

The Man ran the back of his clawed hand down along the air in front of Alaana. The motion caused a searing pain in the joints of her arms and legs, all the places that had hurt so much when she had passed down the tube to the Underworld.

"A fair trade," said the Man. "Come along."

Alaana stood gasping. Trade? What kind of trade?

The Man led her into a back room of the smoke house, an area partitioned off by thick black skins. As they passed, the wife reached out for Alaana but the Man cuffed her hand away. There were rows and rows of skins, rolled and tied with sinew and ranked along the walls. The Man dug roughly through the piles, carelessly tossing a few on the floor to be immediately trampled underfoot by his thick hairy legs. One of the bundles squealed pitifully as it was stomped.

"Here it is." The Man unrolled a thick black *lumentin* hide, crawling with ticks and lice. He carelessly stretched the lumpy skin across a table.

"This is the one. Be off and hurry up about it."

He pointed to the navel on the skin, and the tiny opening began to expand. The Man dug a long, cracked fingernail into the opening and stretched the navel until it was the size of Alaana's hand.

"Well, go on!" roared the Man Who Keeps The Skins.

Alaana took hold of the greasy skin with both hands and pulled the navel open. The danger was irrelevant. Any fate would be preferable to another moment under the Man's hateful eye. In she went.

Civiliaq's prison was a tiny cavern, barely large enough to contain the spirits of both the man and the girl. The chamber had no exit that Alaana could see, and certainly none that Civiliaq might use. The room was teeming with large black flies. Though they swarmed all over Civiliaq, they paid no attention to Alaana.

Alaana was now certain she had indeed traveled to the Underworld, for Civiliaq's appearance was entirely different from the dream-self he had projected earlier. His skin was blackened and burned, and continuously flaking off into the air around him. Again his impressive tattoos stood out in stark relief, this time white against the blackened skin of his chest and arms. Upon closer

327

inspection Alaana saw the tattoos writhed with tiny bottle-fly maggots. As the larvae traced the lines of his magical inscriptions Civiliaq twitched and shifted uncomfortably.

"Yes," he said, "Look closely little bird. See what happens when a shaman is brought low."

Most of his hair had been burned away. The blackened skin sagged lifelessly down from his face. Only the whites of his eyes and teeth, and the pink inner folds of his lower eyelids were visible against the dark. He was naked, except for the tattered rags that had been his pants.

"But how did this happen?"

"That's not your concern," snapped Civiliaq. His bitter expression softened quickly. "How do you think? Through weakness. Through ignorance. We must not let that happen to you."

Civiliaq jerked his head forward, snapping his jaws at a black fly crossing in front of his face. Alaana noticed his hands were held behind his back.

"Your arms are bound?" she asked.

"You won't be able to release them." Civiliaq turned his body so that Alaana could see. Behind his back his forearms were fused together, the bones twisted and melded like the vines on a tree.

"It doesn't matter," said Civiliaq. "I have what I need to accomplish our journey."

"Journey?"

Civiliaq snapped unsuccessfully at another fly. "What I know is this: You, my dear, are not a true shaman."

"I don't understand," said Alaana weakly. Feeling as if she could stand up no longer, she sat on the ground opposite the shaman.

"Your power comes from below the Underworld."

"Below? What lies below the Underworld?"

"I don't know. No one knows. But your power comes from the other side of the ocean, from the very center of the world."

"Is that what you saw? Up there on Dog-Ear Ridge? Is that what you saw when you looked at my *inua*?"

"Perhaps," said Civiliaq with a malicious shrug. "Feel it for yourself. Put your hand to the ground. You can feel it from here."

Alaana pressed her spirit-hands along the floor of the cavern. Civiliaq was right. She could feel a strength, her strength, calling out to her from far below. It was true. But as far as she knew, there was no world below the Underworld. There was nothing down there.

"Is it Sila, down there?" Alaana asked. "Is that why he hasn't come to me?"

"I can't say, but I doubt very much the wild wind blows all the way down there. We'll have to go and see."

"You keep saying that. But how?"

"I will—" Civiliaq stopped short. With a successful jerk of his head he managed to get a passing fly into his mouth. He chewed carefully for a moment then spit out the wings onto a considerable pile that lay beside him.

"Just so," he said. "I have a method of transport. I will lead you there. Then you will know the answers you seek."

The shaman's eyes rolled back, his blackened and crusted lips drew apart, and he began a power song. He used some other dialect of the secret language than that with which Alaana was familiar. It was a potent spell in any case, and she could sense shifting energies within the tiny cavern. Civiliaq chanted quickly and with great intensity, seeming rushed and desperate. As his intonations rose in pitch, all the tiny wings of the blackflies drew up off the floor. They skirled about the cavern, miraculously knitting themselves into sheets and planks which surrounded the two of them, creating an ethereal kayak.

Alaana watched the spirit-kayak take shape, afraid to touch its delicate surface and cause it to crumble in her hands. The floor of the kayak formed beneath them. It shifted uncertainly but seemed solid enough.

"Don't worry, little bird," said Civiliaq. "All will be made clear in a moment. In this way we make rock as to water and pass through. Nothing can hold us."

Alaana's side of the kayak began to tip downward and she saw that the shaman was true to his word. It settled into the stony floor of the cavern as if it were lakewater. There was a sense of great strain, the terrible sound of reality tearing apart. Suddenly the kayak broke into two separate parts and Alaana's half went speeding through the rock, bearing her down.

A panicked inner voice, speaking in the familiar sarcastic tones of Nunavik, warned her that this was one journey too many, one that would take her too far from the world she knew to ever return. It was already too late. Too weak, too tired, she had fallen for Civiliaq's trap.

With a sudden lurch, the kayak stopped. The fragile craft trembled and hissed and began to move backward, retracing the path it had traveled.

When her end of the boat re-entered the prison, Alaana saw the room had been transformed into a much larger cavern. She was met by a friendly, if dour, face.

Kuanak was there, grabbing her half of the kayak with both hands, pulling it back. Alaana had never beheld Wolf Head's spirit-form before. Despite the feral sharpening of teeth and nose, and the frill of coarse gray fur along the chin and mouth, she easily recognized the features of the long-lost Anatatook shaman. Above, toward the upper reaches of the cavern was Civiliaq's half of the boat. It was being pulled back down by three radiant spirit-wolves with brilliant white fur.

Civiliaq crashed to the ground. The spirit-kayak dissolved away, becoming bottle fly wings once more. The three large white wolves stood against him snarling and snapping. Alaana saw that Civiliaq's arms were unbound, his hands free, now resembling the blackened claws of the *lumentin*.

"You pathetic wretch!" fumed Kuanak. "Is this how you would buy your freedom? With the soul of this girl?"

Civiliaq stood up. Ignoring the frustrated yapping of the wolves, he stepped toward Kuanak, his hands balled into fists. "What does a man unjustly imprisoned care about fairness? About balance? There is no balance for me."

Kuanak leveled his long pole of narwhal tusk at Civiliaq. "You would sacrifice this child, when it was your own doubt and fear that put you here."

"And I suppose you had nothing to do with it? I could've beaten that demon, if you would've helped."

"You rushed ahead."

"You lagged behind! Manatook came flying to your aid when you were hurt, but the two of you were perfectly content to leave me behind, to leave me here to rot. This is your fault Kuanak. You didn't appreciate my abilities, you lured me into petty competitions. You brought that demon down on us. And Manatook rushed to your side, abandoning me."

Kuanak slowly shook his head. "Humility is a lesson slow in the learning, especially for you," he said. "If you continue to blame others for your own mistakes, you will be stuck here for a long time."

Wolf Head glanced upward and frowned, drawing Alaana's attention to the ceiling of the cavern. The rock face was descending rapidly as the cage shrank back to its previous dimensions. Alaana realized that in a few more moments it wouldn't be large enough to hold all three of them.

Civiliaq saw it too. He took a half step forward, his eyes locked on the power staff.

A tiny blue spark danced along the ivory surface of Kuanak's weapon. Civiliaq backed down. A twisted smile crossed his bitter lips. He knew he was beaten. "My own mistake, yes. A minor transgression, to which any man might succumb. I doubted myself. But I've learned my lesson, I tell you. I've had much time to think." Civiliaq lifted his chin and spoke confidently. "And I realize that I *am* good enough. I always was. I've put aside all doubt and fear. If I only had the chance to show you—"

"I have seen enough," said Kuanak.

"I'm sorry, little one," said Civiliaq. He glanced at Alaana and his downcast face, ruined and burned as it was, painfully demonstrated that he spoke the truth.

Kuanak looked sadly at Civiliaq. "I have little hope for you."

"Hope? I don't need your hope, Wolf Head. Nor your pity. I just need a second chance. Just one more chance."

Kuanak sighed. "I have abandoned you once, my brother. And with good reason, I abandon you again."

Kuanak called his wolves to his side. He turned to Alaana and said, "We have no more time here. I wish I could do more for you Alaana, but I too am constrained. The spirit of a dead shaman clings to the weak and unwary, and Civiliaq clings to you. I must use all my power now simply to keep him off of you. You must hurry back where you belong. Now, where is that damned bird?"

He cocked his head to listen, but apparently didn't hear the sound he sought. "No matter," he said. "There is more than one way to wake you up."

So saying, he touched the tip of his staff gently to Alaana's chest. The blue flame sparked through the spirit-parka and jolted her awake.

She opened her eyes. Itiqtuq lay beside her bed but the little amulet's screeching had already been silenced. The auk skull had been crushed, the eyes pulped, the little tuft of feathers scattered. Itiqtuq had been destroyed, crushed by Civiliaq's hand, she supposed.

She felt worse than ever. Pains in the head, an ache in the body, a weariness in her soul.

She took a moment to drink in the familiar surroundings of bed and home. But reassurance was not swift in coming. Had that been a true spirit journey or all just a dream? Such a question was irrelevant. Dreams were real. She had traveled and she had seen. The more important question was whether Civiliaq had been lying. The doomed shaman had become so malicious and twisted in his torment. The things he had said about Sila, her power and the center of the earth — had they all been merely parts of his ruse?

Alaana feared she might not soon find out. Again Civiliaq had laid accusations at Old Manatook's door. This was yet another dream she dared not reveal to the old shaman.

As she pulled her sleeping furs close Alaana noted with a small measure of satisfaction that the ghosts of Uwelen had been left behind. They had been taken as payment by the Man Who Keeps The Skins. A fair trade, the Man had said and Alaana heartily agreed. She might sleep a little more peacefully this night. She was so very tired.

CHAPTER 29

IN THE COLD AND DARK

"The break-up caught us on the ice," said Old Manatook. *"The sea swelled beneath our sled. With a tremendous crack the ice churned and broke apart."*

"Stranded on the ice like a wayward pup," commented Nunavik. The ethereal walrus sat beside Alaana in the tiny practice *iglu.* It had been ten sleeps since his terrible experience in the Lowerworld, and his voice had finally regained its natural sarcastic tone. He looked no worse for wear with the exception of a slightly lopsided indentation along one side of his gloriously golden head.

"Hardly a pup." Old Manatook was twenty paces away, his mindspeak message carried along the spirit of the air between the two practice *iglus. "But the situation was desperate."*

The unbroken darkness of winter was the perfect setting for such a tale. Old Manatook had already related how, many years ago, he had embarked on a dangerous trip across Crescent Bay to help a dying friend.

His friend Muraoq had come to him, saying his hunting partner had fallen terribly ill at their winter camp in Big Basin. Muraoq thought Patagona might be going to die. His legs and knees had swollen so badly he could not move.

It was the time of *sikuliqiruq* at the beginning of spring, when

334

the sea ice first begins to break up. Patagona's situation was dire. They didn't have enough time to trek all the way inland to the point where they could ford the Forked River, and still hope for any chance to save Patagona. They must risk the sea. The pair hitched up their dogs and set out by sled across the unsteady ice field covering the bay. Scudding along at top speed, they felt ice buckle and strain beneath the sled's runners. The flats were already broken up but the floes were large enough for the dogs to leap from piece to piece. It was a harrowing journey, with the ice sheets bobbing in the water at every advance of the team.

Halfway across the channel the floe tipped completely and the sled went over, dragging all the dogs down into the water. Muraoq and Old Manatook were left trapped on the bare ice, without sled or team, adrift at the mouth of the Forked River.

"Why not ask the river for help?" asked Alaana.

"That's no use," said Old Manatook.

"He did just that," said Nunavik. "As I recall, he went down on hands and knees, begging for his life, there on the ice."

"River spirits are aloof and distracted. They are not easily swayed."

"By the young and inexperienced," added Nunavik smartly.

"Hmmf. Yes, I was young once," huffed Old Manatook.

"If you can believe it," snickered Nunavik. "He didn't always smell this bad either."

"We drifted for two sleeps, without boat or team," continued Old Manatook, *"when things turned even worse. A hunting party of the Chukchee found us as we lay sleeping on the ice. They took hold of us, recognizing me as a shaman. They intended to keep me as a slave, bound hand and foot, until such time as I pledged my service to them. Failing that, they vowed to pry my secrets from me at the edge of a blade. As proof of their grim intentions, they drilled Muraoq through the head."*

"Why not ask the binds to release?" asked Alaana.

"The ropes had already been convinced otherwise."

335

"The Chukchee had a better shaman," said Nunavik dryly.

"In time, my chance came and I took it," continued Old Manatook. *"I ran from the enemy camp, but I could only get to the shore and no further. A hundred paces of fast-moving water separated me from the next island."*

"What did you do?" asked Alaana.

"The only thing he could do. He called me for help," said Nunavik.

Alaana thought she picked up a small sound coming across from the other practice *iglu*, something like a low growl.

"When I saw the pathetic state he was in," continued Walrus On The Ice, "I turned toward the sea and called my brethren. Hah! You should have seen it! They came. Indeed, they all came, so many, so many — as numerous as shells on the beach. They lined up in the water, all the fine bull walruses of Nunatsiaq, and Manatook simply walked across to the next island, his feet passing atop the flats of their heads."

"It didn't stop the Chukchee from coming after," said Old Manatook. *"I had bought some time to think while they manned their boats, but I was trapped again, and with the enemy bearing down fast."*

"So what did you do?" asked Alaana.

"Yes, what did you do?" chimed Nunavik.

Old Manatook's response was muffled. Alaana leaned forward intently, sifting through the strands of the air for any message on its way across. She shook her head. "I'm sorry teacher, I didn't hear that properly. My skill at receiving is not what it should be. Say again?"

"Not your fault," said Nunavik to Alaana. Then he projected loudly, "Heya! You crusty old man! We didn't hear that. Speak up!"

"I asked for help," said Old Manatook.

"Yes once again." The old walrus bobbed his golden, though slightly misshapen, head in a show of glee.

"*That's what helper spirits are for, isn't it?*" growled Old Manatook.

Nunavik was quick to take offense. "Helper spirit my big bulging backside! I taught you more than Balikqi ever did."

"Who's Balikqi?"

"*Don't be ridiculous,*" answered Old Manatook, ignoring Alaana's question. "*It was I taught you how to travel to the Moon and the Celestial world, and don't you forget it. An entire world which you didn't even know existed. Of the seven worlds, you only had six until you met me.*"

"My blood, the Moon didn't help you so very much stuck on that island, did he?" Nunavik turned toward Alaana, "It's a good thing I felt sorry for him. I couldn't help myself, he looked so pathetic…"

"*Pathetic? This comes from a piece of ivory tusk? I could've tossed you into the water, and still I might. You'd never be found again.*"

Nunavik grumbled loudly. "Maybe you should have thrown me away. But not surprisingly, you didn't. Perhaps you were too busy begging me to help you out of danger once again."

Alaana chuckled. "Tell me, Uncle Walrus, what did you do?"

"Sunk their boats. All but one, since I supposed our junior shaman might need a way to get home."

"*It's not much of a story beyond that,*" said Old Manatook. "*That left one boat and her crew still coming onto the island. They left their kinsmen floundering in the icy water. The blood feud was in their hearts. They wanted so much to kill me.*"

"Oh, but that's not the end," said Alaana. "What happened?"

"*Hmmf. I killed them all and took their boat. The first I killed with a spear throw. It was a spectacular throw. Three hundred paces.*"

"With a little help," snorted Nunavik. "His aim was off."

"*What's this?*"

"I guided that spear. You would've missed."

"*Nonsense! I never miss.*"

337

"Hah!" barked the Walrus. "Listen to that! Whatever happened to the essential humility of the shaman?"

"Humility is one thing. Accuracy is another. The first I killed, with no assistance from anyone at all, with a spear throw. The second I stabbed in the groin with his own knife, and the third I strangled to death. In that way I satisfied my own blood feud. I had not forgotten the drilling of my friend, Muraoq."

Deep in winter's long night, Alaana lay unable to sleep. Her father's constant tossing and turning on the platform was keeping the whole family awake.

Finally Kigiuna sat up on the bed.

Alaana peered over at him, but the wick on the soapstone lamp had burned down so low she couldn't see anything. In the gloom of the family *iglu* Kigiuna didn't seem to notice her.

"Wake up," he said. "Amauraq, wake up."

Amauraq sat up, slowly coming awake. "What's wrong?"

"Louse me."

Without a word she brought the fish-oil lamp closer to the sleeping platform. As the warm sphere of yellow light distinguished the two of them against the icy soot-grayed walls, Alaana watched her mother bending over her husband's scalp, going through his hair looking for the nits.

Kigiuna let out a long, low sigh and Alaana knew it was more than just a few biting lice that was bothering him.

"Alaana spends too much time with Old Manatook." Kigiuna spoke in a sad voice instead of his usual strong, imperious tone. "She should also learn how to sew the skins, how to cook. She should be spending time with you and Pilarqaq."

Alaana thought this suggestion sounded pretty good, but there was little hope for change.

"She is learning important things," whispered Amauraq.

"There are other things than skins and kettle pots."

"How do I know what she's learning?" asked Kigiuna loudly. Pilarqaq's snoring ceased abruptly, and Alaana realized the rest of the family must also be awake, though nobody dared to speak or sit up. "She's my daughter. How do I know what Old Manatook's filling her head with? She won't talk about it."

"She can't," whispered Amauraq.

"Can't."

They sat for a few moments in silence, with the exception of an occasional snap as Amauraq cracked the nits between her teeth.

"Trust Old Manatook," she said softly. "He's been our shaman as long as I can remember, and things have been well."

"I seem to remember there were times we went hungry," said Kigiuna. "People died for want of food. Men perished out on the ice. Sickness came among us. Have you forgotten?"

"No," she hissed, "I have not." Her tone was heavy with a note of painful loss, and Alaana knew who she was thinking about. Nearly a full year had gone by, and Ava was still very much in their thoughts. "But it's not good to speak of those things," she continued. "It's not Old Manatook's fault people break the taboos. The spirits are powerful and dangerous. They are things common people can't understand or control."

"I've not seen any of it," grumbled Kigiuna. "The wind is just the wind. The snow is just the snow."

"Only the shaman can see those things."

"Does he? He appeals to the spirits and *turgats*, yet it's my two strong hands that bring in the kill. It's the patience of the hunters, our courage out on the ice, our skill."

Maguan made a vague grunting noise meant to sound as if he were turning in his sleep. Alaana suspected her brother was offering some small measure of support for Kigiuna's position, from one hunter to another. Kigiuna was neither a shaman nor a man of any great importance, but his bravery, and his strength, could never be questioned.

Amauraq paused to dig a fingernail into the louse she'd just caught, cutting it in half. "You were there with the rest of us in front of the *karigi*. You saw them fight the demon."

"I saw them die. That was all I saw."

"They healed the people, they saved Alaana."

"But not Ava."

The mention of her sister's name brought down a wall of stony silence. It was not unusual for any of them to mention her by name, but only in reference to some happy moment of shared memory. They did not refer to her death. Alaana peeked out from her sleeping furs. Her mother's face had become a frozen mask.

"Quipagaa led my people through the pass," she said softly.

"Your grandfather? You were only a child then. You don't remember. That's nothing more than an old story."

"It is not." Amauraq spoke softly, but firmly.

Annoyed at her insolence, Kigiuna slapped her hand away from his scalp. "I said it is," he growled.

Having said her piece, Amauraq allowed her husband the final word. There really was no point in arguing the matter. The conversation lapsed as Amauraq's fingers worked their way along the long black hair that trailed down the back of Kigiuna's neck.

"I'm worried for Alaana," said Kigiuna. "She's not eating, not sleeping. Spending so much time with the old man. I don't like it."

Her father's words threatened to break Alaana's heart. The rift between her father and the shaman deeply worried her, and it was all the worse now she heard it from Kigiuna's own lips. Alaana's new responsibilities consumed so much of her time, she had been so distracted by the urgency of the training. She must find a way to make it clear to Kigiuna that her growing fondness for the shaman did not threaten her love for her real father.

Amauraq's sigh rustled through the *iglu*. "She was always different, wandering off alone all the time. Staring at the river or the mountains. Or the birds. It's a difficult thing she does, our little one. But I have no doubt." She cracked another nit with her teeth and spit out the pieces. "She's a very strong girl."

"She doesn't look well."

"Something better will come of it. Something important."

Kigiuna clicked his tongue dismissively, "How can you say that?"

"Because I believe it is true," said Amauraq.

"She isn't happy," said Kigiuna flatly. "She hasn't been happy since this whole thing started. She doesn't smile anymore."

Alaana hadn't realized she'd been acting that way at all. She had been laughing just that morning in the practice *iglu* with Nunavik.

"Something great will come of it," said Amauraq again. "I know it's true."

Kigiuna lay back down. "Enough talking. Time for sleep."

Higilak could not sleep, the platform had grown so cold beside her.

She sat up, pulling the furs close. Whenever Manatook went away, the *iglu* was always so chilly and bleak. Her life seemed held in abeyance until his return. The relentless, aching feeling in her heart only made matters worse. And then she realized with a start, her husband had not gone away.

"Manatook?"

Squinting into the darkness, she could see the outline of her husband's back as he kneeled working at some task on the floor of the *natiq*. She thought she could smell magic in the room.

"Husband?"

"You should sleep," said Old Manatook.

341

"It's cold in this empty bed."

He reached over and, with a tap of his finger, sparked the wick of the lamp to life. The seal-oil flared warmly.

"That's not what I had in mind," she said. "What are you doing there?"

"I worry for Alaana," said Old Manatook. "I'm making an amulet to help her. Owl feather and eagle feather."

"The Walker In The Wind."

"Yes."

"Sila," she mused. "Such a restless and uncertain spirit, as the stories tell it."

Old Manatook stood, hanging the leather thong of the amulet onto a peg set into the snow wall of the *iglu*.

"Sila did not come to her when we were at Uwelen," he said flatly. "Alaana quieted the dead with her own power but that power has not been replenished. As it fades, her strength goes too."

Higilak sighed softly. "It does not go well with her."

"She's growing weaker every day. Her light grows dim and her life is slipping away with it. If Sila has forsaken the girl, she will die."

"What can be done?" Higilak asked, holding the furs open so that her husband could crawl inside.

"Not enough time," worried Old Manatook. "Never enough time. When spring comes, it will be too late. I must hold the initiation as soon as the light comes again, and no later. And it shall be a true initiation. The girl's life must be at stake in order to see if Sila is committed to her. There's no other way. If she can not bring Sila to aid her, then Alaana will die."

Higilak pulled her husband close as he settled beneath the furs. Their shoulders touched, their legs intertwined. She nestled her face into the sweep of his long neck. A welcome warmth flowed from him, but his body was so tense.

"Is she ready?"

"I don't know," he replied in words laden with frustration.

Higilak drew a deep breath. Manatook cared for Alaana as if she were a daughter. And that was a rare bond indeed, especially for her husband. The couple had never had children of their own. Higilak dearly loved all the children of the Anatatook, had held each of them on her lap at one time or another, made their faces light up with stories of myth and wonder. She helped to educate and teach them, imparting to them truths their real parents couldn't or wouldn't dare reveal. As they were each different, she loved them all, Alaana but one among them. But Manatook had no time for children. It had always been Civiliaq who entertained and enlightened the young. Manatook's time was reserved for more serious matters.

It was ironic that Manatook, a man who could hold back a raging snowstorm, who could drive demons to ground, and who brought babies down from the sky when barren women were in need, could not persuade the Moon Maid to provide one for himself. He knew Higilak's suffering on the matter, how she longed for a strong, dutiful son for her husband or, perhaps better yet, a daughter to lighten their hearts. But he had made the matter clear. Such a thing was not possible for them, though heaven and earth themselves be moved.

And if he believed it impossible, it could not happen.

"I don't know if she's ready," continued Old Manatook, "but she's going to have to be tested. Making an amulet to help her. That's all I can do. I can't summon her guardian spirit for her."

Higilak had never heard her husband speak in such a helpless tone. She knew he had the wisdom to accept defeat when there was no hope for success, such as his inability to provide them a child. Circumstance had never shaken his confidence this way before. The depth of his concern for Alaana had thrown him completely off

343

balance.

"Why doesn't Sila ever come when she calls?" asked Old Manatook. "Is it because she's a girl? Then why did Sila call her in the first place? Something is wrong and I don't know what it is, and I don't know what to do."

Higilak knew what advice her husband would give himself in this situation. "Do what you must. Just believe."

"Hmmph," said Old Manatook. "And then there's Kigiuna. I know what's in his heart. I can't say that I blame him. If Alaana dies, Kigiuna will want blood."

Higilak drew back from her husband's embrace. She needed to see what was in his eyes, but he wouldn't return her gaze.

Old Manatook was fixated on the opposite wall of the *iglu*. "If Alaana dies, I will have to kill Kigiuna or he will kill me."

"If he attacks you, you must put him down. Without you, the people will have no shaman…" She paused, holding back from saying what she truly meant. The people would suffer without him, but she would die. She could not go on without her husband, of that she was certain. But she knew Manatook wouldn't be swayed by such a minor detail as leaving a widow, his primary concern would always be for the Anatatook. "No shaman at all, and then where will they be? You must defend yourself against Kigiuna. It's his life against all of ours."

"Hmmff. Not so." Old Manatook raised his face so that she could see clearly what was in his heart. Not hesitation. Not weakness. "It's not that simple. During the test, I am as much a part of the initiation as the girl. I am not separate. As her sponsor and teacher my feelings directly impact the result. If Alaana senses that I am brooding Kigiuna's destruction, there will be no hope for success. Therefore I must resolve that I shall not kill Kigiuna if it comes to it. He shall kill me."

Higilak looked away. She could not stand his resolute stare.

As always her husband, the shaman, meant exactly what he said.

He would not turn away from Alaana, would not endanger the girl even if it should mean his own life. Higilak smiled thinly. She would be foolish to expect a father to do any less.

As if by its own accord, the lamp winked out.

There would be no sleep for either of them now. After a moment, she slipped back into his embrace. They held each other. In the cold and dark they held each other and waited for a dawn that would not come for many sleeps.

CHAPTER 30

INITIATION

"How many... how many sleeps?" Alaana forced the words from her parched throat.

"Seven," replied Nunavik.

Alaana pushed the air out in a dry chuckle. "That's all? No sly comment about how stupid I must be to have lost count?"

"No," said the Walrus On The Ice.

"Seven," said Alaana. She lifted the beater from the head of the drum, but didn't have strength enough to do more than that. Her fingers felt numb against the handle. Truth be told, she could feel little at all.

"I'll do that for you," said Nunavik softly. The drum rang out in the close confines of the tiny snow house, sounding a slow, dolorous beat. Alaana sat on the floor. Naked, she leaned forward, her arms tucked into armpits, her legs hugged together, curling herself around whatever body heat remained. Her clothes had been taken away along with everything else. Anything that recalled her home or her family, or the Anatatook themselves, had been removed. She possessed only amulet and drum.

Her eyes drifted closed. She wanted very much to sink down into sleep.

Alaana had been asleep seven nights ago, snug in her furs,

when the call for this initiation had come. She hadn't slept well for many days, going in and out of dreams, with nightmares more frequent than ever before. Kigiuna, too, was always restless beside her.

On that night Old Manatook's blurry *inuseq* had manifested in the air near the *iglu's* domed ceiling. *"It's time,"* the old shaman had said. She slipped her parka over her head and dressed as quietly as possible, not wishing to wake her family. Then she crept outside into the cold pre-dawn gloom.

Old Manatook carried her to a small ceremonial sled just large enough for one passenger. By tradition, she was not allowed to walk or stand upright until the initiation was complete. The Anatatook camp lay quiet and all still asleep. A brilliant stripe of orange streaked a snowy horizon of dark gray, heralding the first dawn of spring. There were no crowds assembled to see her off, no shouts of encouragement or wishes of good fortune, and no dog team to pull the sled. Old Manatook took up the traces himself.

Alaana lay on the sled, facing back toward the camp. As Old Manatook readied himself to pull away, Kigiuna came bolting out of the *iglu*.

"It is time," said Old Manatook firmly. No less a statement than a warning.

Alaana saw the pained expression that crossed her father's face, a mixture of revulsion and concern. It was the same kind of worry she had seen only once before, when Ava was sick with the fever. Alaana wanted to console her father — to tell him this was not a call to danger or death but just a chore to be done, a step on her path — but she was prohibited from speaking.

"Look after my daughter," said Kigiuna. "Take care that nothing happens to her."

Old Manatook, irritated by both the interference and the sublime threat, said nothing more. Alaana lay motionless as the sled moved away.

"Wake up! Wake up!" said Itiqtuq, bringing Alaana's thoughts back to the present.

Having sprouted tiny threadbare wings on either side of the skull, the little *tunraq* flitted about her face, eyes agog. Alaana responded with a grunt to indicate she hadn't quite been sleeping.

"Concentrate," urged Nunavik. "You must make Sila come. Can you say the words? If you sing, the shivering will go away."

Alaana hadn't realized she'd been shivering. She coughed softly. She was too thirsty to sing, too dry to chant any more. She stared at a crust of snow Old Manatook's boots had roughed from the surface of the floor when he had carried her inside. She imagined reaching for it, putting the cool snow into her mouth.

"You must not drink but what he brings you," said Nunavik sternly.

"I know." It had been two days since Old Manatook had brought the few sips of water and the scrap of meat that had been her only nourishment since the beginning of this ordeal. Two days. And it would soon be daylight again. A faint haze had replaced the circlet of starry sky in the little *iglu*'s vent hole, marking the few moments that the sun would peek above the horizon. Maybe Old Manatook would come again today. Maybe there would be a cool drink or some scrap of food. Alaana could only think of food in a disinterested, abstract way. She no longer felt hungry; all competing sensations were dwarfed by the incredible thirst. In the same way she no longer felt the cold. In fact it seemed to be getting warmer...

The beat of the drum trailed away. Alaana's mind sank to a lower level, a place below the reality of the *iglu*, a vast emptiness with no beginning and no end. She could find no familiar sign by which to find her way home. There was only the burning thirst, an all-consuming fever. A hand reaching out for her, long slender fingers, sharp, curving nails. Was that her mother's voice calling softly to her, there and then gone, lost beneath the ever louder thumping of her own heartbeat? Surely Amauraq had never sung such a strange, melancholy lullaby. No. It was her!. An unmistakable stink of helplessness and despair. Alaana recoiled from the sight of that hideous face, the leering hag who had killed so many including Kuanak and Civiliaq and her poor dear sister, the demon who had heralded the start of this incredible journey. But the fever demon had been defeated, driven down into the ice by Old Manatook, far away, so far from this place. Was it reaching out to her from that distance, or from somewhere deep within? Was there some lingering taint of the fever still lurking inside her soul?

Her head hurt, her throat burned, her eyes were sealed shut.

"There are no barriers," Old Manatook had told her once. "All realities are one. There is no separation between vision and reality, no inside and no outside."

The withered old hag, the Red Ke'le, looked just the same as she had during the time of the fever. Her eyes, small and black, regarded Alaana as intently as a hungry owl studies its prey. She flicked her lips with the tip of a rotten gray tongue. As the demon reached for her, Alaana felt the pull of eternity in her grasp.

"Aneenaq?" said Alaana, the name a painful rasp.

The clawed hand recoiled. Yes, she was also Aneenaq, a little girl lost and alone, and left to die. Old Manatook had driven her down, had beaten her into the ice, but he had not helped her. He had not released her from her suffering and torment. From her hunger. She had sought to be a twisted mother to the children she had snatched from the Anatatook, just as she had longed to be a beloved child to her own. Old Manatook had bested her, but he had not released her, as Alaana would have done. As she would do. "I promise," she rasped. If ever there was the chance again, she would help Aneenaq's restless spirit find peace.

Alaana's eyes opened. Dawn had indeed come again. The faint light from the vent hole illuminated the interior of the snow house as a dull white blur broken only by the golden glow of the Walrus.

"Beneath the... blue sky," she said to Nunavik. "I remember the words. I remember."

She looked to the Walrus for some sign of encouragement but there was none. The golden glow did not belong to the walrus at all. The golden figure resolved itself into a much smaller form, nestled within the rounded contours of a fur-lined parka. It was Avalaaqiaq.

Alaana felt pulled in two directions at once. One part suffered again the terrible crushing pain and loss; the other basked in the joy of seeing her sister once more. All the pleasant memories she carried with her. The crooked smile, the hair flopping over her eyes, the tickling laugh.

She thought what a relief it would be to join her sister among the murmuring voices, to laugh and play, even if it meant suffering the everlasting chill of death itself.

"Of all the foolish, misguided notions..." grumbled Old Manatook. "Go away!"

Sitting cross-legged in his own tiny snow house a hundred paces from the one that housed Alaana, Manatook monitored his student's progress. Unseen, listening but unheard, felt but not known, he smoothed the ripples forming in Alaana's mind. The girl's approach was all wrong. It was as if she had forgotten everything she had been taught. Still concerned with her family, still plying for aid and comfort they could not give, when she should be directing her efforts at Sila.

Old Manatook raged partly at himself. He was no good teacher for young children. This was folly on a grand scale. Either the girl did not listen, or her teacher was a fool. Helplessness tugged at his soul. In truth, there was little left he could do. Alaana was dying.

At least he had drawn the ghost girl's attention. "I said go away! Leave her be!"

"I won't," said Ava. "She's my sister. She needs me!"

"She needs to be rid of you," said Old Manatook. "If she called out to you, she was mistaken. Now go away."

"I won't leave her to die alone," said Ava. The child's lips pursed with resolve.

"She needn't die at all. And she most certainly is not alone, as you can very well see."

Their eyes met. Ava's cheeks quivered as her face flooded with emotion.

"Why didn't you come for me?" she asked. "I was so frightened in that cave. It was so hot and I couldn't breathe. The other children, they couldn't play or speak to me. They could only cry and moan. They were already dead. And that terrible old woman, she tried to smother me. When she hugged me it felt like knives cutting me up. I kept calling out for help, for Civiliaq and for you but you didn't come."

"I came, Nautchiaquraq," he said, using the first name Ava had been given at birth, when Manatook had delivered her into the world. The name meant 'Little Flower'. "I came."

Ava remembered how Old Manatook had arrived at last, dripping demon blood from his hands and teeth. How he had swung open the gates. And the other children of the Anatatook, those who had come after Ava, were released and sent back to their families and their lives. And when she had turned to leave, she could not go with them. The way was barred for her. She was left with the rest of the dead children. She had become one of them.

The memory was a bitter one, bringing ghost tears to sting at Ava's eyes.

"Do you want the same for your sister?" Manatook asked. "Now leave her be, Little Flower On The Tundra. It's not her time to die."

The old shaman's words were enough to push the bewildered spirit away.

Manatook turned his attention back to his charge. He could only meddle so much. Alaana was supposed to be alone, exposed to the rigors of the elements, depending entirely on her own helper spirits. But the training period had been so short for this one. Was the girl ready? Of course, that was the question this test was meant to answer.

It was an excruciating ordeal, one that would either change Alaana forever or destroy her, and it was almost as difficult for him to stand by and watch. But this was the Way, naked existence without the distractions of family and community, with all worldly concerns stripped away, her *inua* laid bare to the spirits. Thirst and hunger and pain should be driving her to reach out, to seek deliverance by way of Sila instead of dredging through the past.

Old Manatook felt the grip of Quixaaragon's talons at his shoulder.

"She must not die!" said the creature.

"Don't you think I know that?"

Manatook glared menacingly at the thing perched on his shoulder. The helper spirit looked remarkably solid for a creature made of white smoke. Its head, crowned with a ring of short, elegant horns, swayed on a long slender neck with slow, sinewy movements in time with the beat of its wings.

"Pay attention!" snapped the familiar, "The girl's determination is wavering."

"And so is my own," admitted Old Manatook. "Sila is an unreliable guardian spirit. I have known no other who could claim him. So fickle and unpredictable. The wild wind ranges far, what if he is too distant to hear the call?"

"There is no sense in questioning the will of the spirits." Quixaaragon jabbed a pointed beak at the shaman.

"Do you know? Will Sila answer?" spat Old Manatook. The little dragon irritated him. It spoke with such authority, as if it saw a bigger picture than he was able to appreciate. He was tired of stumbling about in a snowblind haze. He had resolved to do whatever he could to help the girl, but none of this had been his own decision. The situation had been forced upon him every step of the way by powers that would not bother to explain themselves to one as insignificant as a crusty old shaman.

The dragon ruffled its downy wings. "How could it be Sila's will to spark Alaana to greatness and then just let her die? I remind you. Doubt is not allowed."

"I have no doubts," snapped Old Manatook. "My way is clear. To help my people whenever and however I can. I know my abilities and my own weaknesses. Whatever the spirits want from me, I will do. Whatever kind of sacrifice they demand this day, I will make. But what about the girl? If she should fail the test I will know the reason why if I have to wring the answers from your scrawny neck."

Old Manatook felt a twinge of satisfaction as the *tunraq's* beak snapped shut.

"Time is running out," said Quixaaragon. "There are still doubts in Alaana's mind. They must be purged."

"I know," replied Old Manatook.

Suddenly Quixaaragon barked at him, "Go outside. Hurry! Someone comes."

There for just a moment, a golden flash, and then pulled away.

"Ava, don't go!"

But her sister's face was already fading, drawn backward by a multitude of hands and arms into the mists of the other side. For a moment Alaana glimpsed some of the faces beyond the shifting mass of fog that obscured the distant lands.

A man leaned forward. His face was not so different from her father's, but for the plumpness of middle age and the raw red scars cut across the forehead.

It was the ancestor she had glimpsed through the skylight once before — Ulruk, who had been her father's father. Alaana met the specter's eyes full on; they glimmered with reflections of the past, echoes of the strife and struggle of a life well-lived.

"I don't trust Manatook," her grandfather said. "I never did."

He went on, "When I was attacked by a brown bear, Manatook tended my wounds, he bound my mangled arm. But something struck me wrong about the shaman as he worked over me. The smell of the bear was on him too. And it shouldn't have been.

"When I lost my arm I blamed Manatook. My wife said it was my own fault, that if I had not doubted him, he might have been able to save that arm. But listen. He came to us from outside. He wasn't Anatatook; neither was his wife. His clothes didn't fit him right. He was taller than the Anatatook men, and had the full beard and bushy eyebrows of a *kabloona*.

"He didn't smell right," said Ulruk. "I could tell. In those days I could smell when a storm was rolling in, long before the sky got dark, and I knew when a bull walrus would strike even before the creature knew it himself. You can't trust him. He's an outsider."

Alaana recalled the way Old Manatook had protected her, how he had saved her life at Uwelen and many times since. The way Old Manatook's attitude toward her had softened, the bonds they had formed, the feelings of parental respect and love.

"I don't believe that," said Alaana. "I think, Grandfather, that you are mistaken."

Ulruk's image was replaced by that of his son, Kigiuna. Time had no meaning in the white room. Memory seeped into reality once more. "Take care of my daughter," Kigiuna had warned, as Old Manatook pulled Alaana away on the sled.

"Concentrate!" said Nunavik. "Use the chant."

But Alaana could not concentrate. The echo of Kigiuna's disapproval had disturbed her too much.

"This is foolishness," said Old Manatook, blocking Kigiuna's advance. "You can not be here!"

Kigiuna pressed forward. "It's been seven sleeps. I'm worried about my daughter."

"And well you should be," said Manatook, "but it's not your place to interfere."

Kigiuna's blazing scowl spoke volumes. He was beyond angry. He was afraid, and Old Manatook knew Kigiuna did not scare easily. A frightened man was a dangerous one.

The old shaman wasn't intimidated by Kigiuna. He could rebuff any attempt at violence easily enough. But this turmoil was too dangerous. Alaana's little *iglu* lay only a few paces away. She might hear their voices, and if she sensed their discord, all would be lost.

Kigiuna stood only a finger's breadth from the shaman, glowering up into his eyes. "I am taking her home."

Old Manatook spoke calmly, "This does not help. She will sense your fear, your anger. Your actions are endangering her."

"I have no more use for talk," said Kigiuna, drawing a long hunting knife from a sheath strung at his waist. "Stand aside."

Old Manatook eyed the weapon. It was a sharpened flat of caribou antler. The glimmer of the reindeer's spirit that lingered

355

deep within the blade was amenable to his influence. If he asked it, the knife would collapse into a dull lump all the way down to the hilt, melting as a piece of tallow in the heart of the lamp. But such a strategy would gain him nothing. Kigiuna would not be stopped by a petty show of magic.

Instead he said, "Alaana and I share the same fate. I promise you Kigiuna, I will not return from this place alone. We pass this ordeal together, or not at all."

"That's not good enough. I'll tell you once more. Stand aside."

"You must not interfere. Our goal is the same. The only way to help Alaana is to see her through this trial. And I am the only one who can accomplish that. You must go away, or ruin her completely."

"I won't leave her. She's my daughter, old man. Mine!"

Lightning flashed in Old Manatook's eyes. "She is your daughter Kigiuna, but I am her father also."

Kigiuna showed no inclination to back off. A burning concern for Alaana had propelled him across the stark snowy wastes in the dead of night. He would not give up. There seemed little else Manatook could say or do to earn his trust. Perhaps only one thing.

Old Manatook tore open the front of his parka, ripping the faded caribou hide down to his waist. He stepped forward, pressing the bare skin of his chest against the point of Kigiuna's blade. "Kill me then, and have done with it!"

CHAPTER 31

BIRTH

"He's trying to kill me," Alaana said weakly. "Old Manatook's trying to kill me!" Even now she could feel the old shaman's looming presence, his fingers digging into the ether between them, his mind pressing itself close. "My father knows it. My father…"

"You know that's not true," said Nunavik.

"He's an outsider," said Alaana.

"It doesn't matter. He's proven himself," insisted Nunavik. "He's only done right for the people, and for you. You've come to know Manatook better than anyone. Trust your feelings."

Alaana didn't know what to think, or to feel. There had been a time when Old Manatook had seemed distant and frightening, but that was in the past. Wasn't it? Alaana was surprised at how easily those suspicious feelings came rushing back despite the warmth that had developed between them.

The golden walrus appeared before Alaana in the empty white room. "You've begun to appreciate what life is like for him, the constant danger and the weight of his responsibility. The sacrifices he must make. You know he has the good of the people at heart always. He protects them from harm, cures them when they transgress, begs their food from the *turgats*. Even now he is protecting you. That is what you feel. He hasn't left your side.

Now return to the chant. Beneath the blue sky, beneath the white cloud..."

But Alaana would not give voice to the chant; she couldn't.

Nunavik groaned. "Sit still, child! Stare straight ahead. Only in this way will you receive the wisdom and guidance of the ancestors."

"Weyahok?" said Alaana. She envisioned the smooth lump of gray soapstone floating before her in the white room.

"Stone will help," said Weyahok. "Help."

"Ackkkk! I said the ancients, not that wretched, stupid little thing. This is serious business."

"Weyahok?" said Alaana.

"Manatook good," replied the little soapstone *tunraq*. "Manatook good."

"Fine," said Nunavik. "Now that settles that. There's no more time, Alaana. Appeal to Sila now. Concentrate. Use the talisman he gave you."

The talisman of Sila. Eagle feather bound to owl feather. Both birds of the air, both tokens of keen spirit and purity. The feather of the snowy owl represented death and the eagle stood for clarity. Alaana could see nothing in the empty *iglu*, only blinding white. Her hands had gone numb, perhaps they had disappeared entirely. She didn't remember if she was still holding the talisman. It didn't matter. She summoned an image of the talisman with her mind.

"Beneath the blue sky,
Beneath the white cloud..."

Nunavik squawked, "Don't just repeat the words, use them! Send the prayer questing outward, expanding in all directions. Seek your guardian. Beg his assistance. Now is the time. This is the last chance."

But Alaana still couldn't concentrate. Besides the physical

discomforts of empty stomach and raging thirst, she felt the nearness of Kigiuna. Her father's disapproval for the endeavor had never felt so strong or so palpably real.

But there was more than just her father. Standing behind him was Amauraq, firm in her belief in Alaana's calling. Alaana had always appreciated her mother's unfailing faith in her cause, and found tremendous strength in it. Her mother spoke of destiny. And standing behind Amauraq was her father, Quipagaa, struck blind and lost in darkness. But then, touched by the eagle, again he could see. He could fly with the eagle. He could fly. And so could Alaana.

Alaana felt Quipagaa's passion, basked in his joy. She was soaring beside Quipagaa, in the tail winds of the eagle.

"You are different from me," said Quipagaa, "You have no need of wings. You don't ride the wind, you are the wind." Her grandfather's toothless grin beamed, spittle trickling out of his mouth to be lost in the passing wind. He had freed the people from the pass and he had risen above, leaving his withered old frame behind, flying free. Below him the ocean and the mountains, above him only sky.

"The secret to flying is simple," said Quipagaa, "It's the same as the secret to everything else. It's simply this: you mustn't be afraid."

"I'm not afraid," said Alaana softly.

The silence gave way to a fleeting wail of wind.

"Sila?"

There was no answer.

"Do not doubt," said Nunavik. "Sila is the way forward. The only Way for you."

But Alaana couldn't help questioning the intentions of the wind. Maybe fickle Sila had chosen the wrong one? Alaana didn't feel special. She was just an ordinary girl. And how could a girl hope to be shaman? Some mistake may have been made, or perhaps Sila had already finished with her and wasn't coming back.

"Faith," said Nunavik. "Without that a shaman is nothing. He would fade into the eternal night, drawn away by the spirits, never to return."

The walrus' tone was ominous as he added, "We can't have that happen to you, Alaana. I couldn't bear it."

Faith in someone she had encountered only once, deep in the delirium of fever, and never again.

"Do not give up!"

Alaana flinched. Was that the strident voice of Nunavik, or Amauraq, or Quipagaa? Or had it been Old Manatook, shouting in her mind? There were quite a lot of people, Alaana realized, with a hand in this game.

Nunavik, for all his snide comments, bent toward her with as serious a look on his big round face as Alaana had ever seen. "I can't invoke Sila for you, Alaana. You must do that. The chant..."

"I can't remember the chant..." said Alaana hopelessly. "I'm not the one."

The great walrus spirit bellowed long and loud. "Listen. You are very special Alaana, though you don't believe it yourself. Your *inua* is laid bare to me, just as I see the souls of others. Perhaps the trouble comes from your inability to see your own. Let me be a mirror to you."

Alaana felt a tug on her soul. She had not the strength to resist.

"Use the gift Sila has given you, use the spirit-vision. See yourself."

The world shifted into the weird iridescences of the spirit-vision as Nunavik invoked for her the *allaruk*. A blissful sense of unity with all things filled Alaana's mind once again. This was her greatest treasure, the memory of that one moment of clarity she had experienced at the hands of Sila. Oh, why had she ever been shown that? If she could take it away—

She wouldn't. She would never let go that profound revelation which had transformed her mind, heart and soul into a new being, reborn in a moment of pure understanding.

Nunavik showed Alaana the wonder of her own beautiful soul. Her *inua* held the most righteous, blue-white light, she had ever seen. Layer upon layer, it was completely serene and yet simmering with potential power.

"Of the many shamans I have known, your *angakua* is the purest I have ever seen," said Nunavik. "Your honesty I have witnessed for myself. No shaman can achieve great things unless he is totally honest. Humility you also have in abundance. This is important if you are to keep from being corrupted by the power at your disposal. And you have compassion for all things. Honesty, humility, compassion. These are the same qualities, in fact, which make Old Manatook such a good shaman."

Alaana, struck speechless, gasped at the sight.

"Now beg Sila for help," said Nunavik.

"The chant..."

"Yes, that is the proper way to beg their assistance. The only way."

"Beneath the blue sky," said Alaana. "Beneath the white cloud…"

Nunavik was desperate to help.

He had grown very fond of this girl; he did not want to lose her. In his many, many years he had lost too much. Not this.

But what could be done? Alaana was repeating the chant, but only weakly. She still did not realize the need for Sila's aid, not with the depth necessary to form the bond.

Failure was imminent, the smell of death drawing near.

Alaana's breathing had become shallow and irregular.

The girl was a puzzle. Her soul-light was so pure and strong. But there were two sides to every connection, and Nunavik knew very little of Sila. The Walker In The Wind was so different from the walrus' own guardian spirit. His beloved spirit—

That was the answer.

"Alaana," said Nunavik, "have I ever told you of my own guardian spirit? Set aside the chant for now. Listen.

"Qityabnaqtuq, the golden starfish. A lesser *turgat* to be sure, but he has always been a good and faithful friend to me. He can be distant at times, as he sleeps down below at the bottom of the sea. He stays out of the way of greater spirits, or at least the louder and more pretentious ones.

"Qityabnaqtuq has the gift of foresight, Alaana. He is here with us — he is never far from me. Look upon the things he has to show."

Nunavik felt a warm glow infusing his spirit, the sense of peace that told of the nearness of the golden starfish. A series of images flashed before his eyes and he made sure that Alaana witnessed them as well. They saw Maguan, beaten and bloodied, flung on the snowy ground. He was nearly dead. Tugtutsiak lying unconscious, his soul stolen away by a ruthless demon. The people looked down at their helpless leader, their spirits broken. A child, lost in the shadow world, calling out for her mother. The Anatatook camp completely destroyed by an unnatural, raging storm.

Alaana sat up straight, her eyes wide with shock. "These things must not happen!"

"These things will happen," replied Nunavik. "They are certain. Qityabnaqtuq does not jest. Only one question remains. Will you be able to help when they do?"

"I have already decided that!" said Alaana. "I love them. I

will do all that I can for them. Always."

"But how?" asked Nunavik. "How are you going to help them? Don't you realize you can't do it alone? When the winds of fate howl, when the big hand reaches down for them, only with Sila's help may you avert the storm.

"Put aside your resentment, girl!" said Nunavik. "Your old, normal life is long gone! You walk the path Sila has chosen for you. There is no turning back. Raise your voice! The great spirits are so far above us, they don't hear us when we whisper. They only hear us when we beg! This is the Way!"

"Great Sila," Alaana's voice rang out, strong yet humble, "Help me to help them!"

"Yes! That's more like it," said the Walrus. "Call to him."

Alaana spoke passionately:

"Beneath the blue sky,
Beneath the white cloud,
Keeper of the echo in the high mountains,
Keeper of the winds across the wide sea,
Master of the wild wind,
Come to me."

"More!" said Nunavik.

"Please," said Alaana. "I beg you! Come to me!"

Kigiuna tightened his grip on the knife in his hand, its tip just above Old Manatook's heart. The knife was solid, lethal. The leather grip felt hot, as if it might scorch the palm of his hand. "It's a trick," he said. "It's all a trick!"

"Kill me then, and be done with it!" said Old Manatook. He pressed his flesh forward, into the blade. A stream of blood was let, trickling in a thin crimson line down the middle of his chest. Beneath the break in the skin, Kigiuna thought he saw a patch of white fur.

363

Kigiuna jerked the knife back. In all his life he had never killed another man. Unlike Old Manatook, who he knew to be a cold-hearted killer. He didn't know if he could do it. "I don't want you! I want her!"

Kigiuna tried to go around the old fool, who stood barring the way to the tiny *iglu* that held his daughter. Old Manatook wouldn't let him pass.

"I can't let you do that," said the shaman in deep, even tones. "You'll kill her."

Kigiuna stepped back, confused. "You offer to let me finish you right here and now, just as easy as that, and yet you still insist on keeping me from going to Alaana? You've finally gone crazy, old man. Don't you know I'll simply kill you and then take her away?"

Old Manatook smiled. Of all things, he smiled. "You may kill me, but even dead I shall not let you disturb her."

That smile enraged Kigiuna. This was no game. His daughter lay dying in the tiny *iglu*. He was certain of it.

"I don't believe you," said Kigiuna. "And I'm not afraid of ghosts."

"You will be."

Kigiuna stepped forward, knife at the ready. Again the old man offered no resistance other than standing in the way. But this time it didn't matter. Alaana's safety was the only thing that mattered. Kigiuna knew that if he killed the shaman the Anatatook men would take revenge on him. They would exile him or kill him themselves. But he didn't care so long as Alaana would be safe.

"So be it!" he raged, driving the blade toward the shaman's heart.

His murderous advance was pushed back by a sudden gust of wind. Kigiuna was thrown to the frozen ground.

The knife, yanked from his hand, flew away across the tundra. From all around he felt side winds pulling in toward the center, sucking the air away from his lungs. A hundred paces ahead a gigantic funnel rose up. A column of spinning air extending halfway up into the night sky. Kigiuna felt a surge of horror as the towering whirlwind spun and turned directly toward them.

"It's a trick!" he spat. The words whipped away from his mouth, stolen by the wind.

"This is no trick," replied the shaman, his eyes aflame.

"Then what is it?"

The whirling mass drew nearer, picking up loose snow and gravel, filling their ears with a tremendous buzzing sound as if a thousand swarms of flies rode on the eddying wind.

"A blessing," said Old Manatook. "A blessing that will flay the skin from your bones!"

The approaching column had reached one of the little *iglus* on the plain. The whirling blast of wind and snow pinched in the middle to form a narrow waist at the center, the upper half rising to mix with the clouds, the lower settling to churn the tundra below. And at the center of the spinning tumult rose Alaana, limp and naked, hovering in the air.

"Alaana!" cried Kigiuna, "Alaana!" Again his words were stolen by the wind. Old Manatook threw himself atop Kigiuna, driving him to the ground. The storm was raging out of control but Kigiuna saw no flash of fear or doubt on the old man's stony features. The whirlwind pelted them with snow and hailstones, hurling rocks and chunks of ice at them. Kigiuna tried to push Old Manatook away, but the shaman was determined to protect them both with the flat of his own back. Kigiuna twisted under the old man's arm, straining to see what had become of his daughter.

"Alaana!"

Old Manatook held firm, saying, "She's safe. Sila has come to her at last."

***

Sila came.

A surge of unexpected strength filled Alaana and her exhaustion drained away. The force came from outside and deep within at the same time. Her body flew upward on a raging torrent of wind and snow, and Alaana felt Sila fold down over her as a protective blanket. All-encompassing, a soothing balm to her hurt, a warming touch to her frostbitten skin, a light to her eyes. Sila lifted Alaana as if she were an inconsequential bit of fluff, which of course she was in the shadow of his magnificent presence. Though she was lifted up, she felt herself paradoxically to be sinking, sinking into the softness, the warmth, the grace of her guardian spirit who offered endless comfort and protection.

"My dear little one," said the voice of the wind, "I do regret all that you have suffered, and also the greater portion which you yet will suffer. But there is tragedy in every life. And joy. And you will know both of these in great measure."

The vast soothing balm that was her protector calmed Alaana's mind, as the intense cold took all feeling from her body. The world spun below her in a dizzying circle. Even if she had wanted to reply, she could not speak.

Sila, as the voice that is all voices, said, "Together we will see it through. There is a great wrong that must be righted. Know this: I will walk with you. The road will be difficult. I can not come whenever you may call. But when it is darkest, look for me. I shall not leave you until your work is done."

Alaana absorbed the great spirit's message as if from a distance. The newfound strength departed, leaving her tired and weak. All the air had gone from her lungs and she was unable to draw in another breath. She was extinguished as the tiny flame of the lamp when the great north wind blows. Surely there would be no journey for her, there could be nothing more. Only the embrace of sweet oblivion.

"Here is my secret," said the Walker In The Wind, "I need you just as much as you need me."

Alaana fell to the ground.

"Alaana!" Kigiuna screamed.

The thunder parted, the whirlwind cut in half before his eyes and dissolved away. The wind had torn and carried off all the ice around the space where the tiny *iglu* had stood. The snow house had been scoured completely away, leaving only a patch of bare earth in midwinter, scarring the white landscape with a crude circle of brown.

Kigiuna and Old Manatook rushed toward Alaana. She lay face down in the center of the circle. Old Manatook reached her first, moving with an unearthly swiftness.

As Kigiuna watched Old Manatook turn Alaana over, he knew his worst fears had been realized. His daughter was dead. The shaman cradled Alaana in his arms.

"You old fool!" roared Kigiuna in a red rage. "You witless old fool!"

Old Manatook shook Kigiuna off. He planted one hand flat in the middle of Kigiuna's chest, holding him back like a dog. His expression was determined and thoughtful. A definite glimmer of hope shone in the shaman's eyes. Kigiuna had no choice but to keep back.

Old Manatook straightened Alaana's body as it lay, arranging the girl's arms flat against her sides. He brushed the windswept hair from Alaana's pale, lifeless cheek.

Placing one hand on either side of her face, Old Manatook bent over the child.

Though it cost him a small portion of his own soul, Old Manatook reawakened his student with the breath of life. As he kindled Alaana's *inua* back to life, their spirits mingled for an instant.

He felt her power rise again, and he tasted it carefully. Something strange. Something wrong.

Alaana's eyes fluttered open, her lungs gasped the cool air.

The strength and luster of Alaana's rekindled *angakua* was redolent with light and energy, stronger than ever before.

"Sila is powerful," said Alaana softly.

"Yes," said Manatook. "Sila is powerful." In this fragile state it would not be wise to tell her otherwise. Let her confidence, so hard won this day, not be shattered. But there would come a reckoning for the trick that had been played on them this day.

Old Manatook whispered in the girl's ear, "You are now as my daughter. But that does not diminish the other. Now you have two fathers."

Kigiuna swept Alaana up in a cathartic embrace. This lasted for some time, the man muttering quietly to his daughter, offering desperate promises, protestations of love and whatever else. Manatook paid no attention; he was weak and shaken to the core.

When Kigiuna finished, he turned to face the shaman. He tried to frame some words of thanks, not knowing quite how to proceed, but Old Manatook cut him off. "You should return ahead of us to the camp," he said. "Ready the people. Tell them their new shaman returns to them today."

Old Manatook draped the coat around Alaana's naked shoulders.

"This was sewn for you by my wife, Higilak." It was a ceremonial parka, fashioned from an albino caribou hide. Alaana gratefully felt its warmth surround her.

"It's inlaid with polar bear teeth for strength and caribou ears for luck," said Old Manatook. "If you concentrate you'll notice a tiny portion of Higilak's spirit imparted to the skin, such care did she take in sewing this for you. I have put your things in the pocket."

Alaana's hand felt the familiar contours of an auk skull, a small lump of soapstone and a portion of walrus tusk.

"They're gone," she said. "Where have they gone?"

"Who?" asked Old Manatook.

"Nunavik. Weyahok. Even Itiqtuq. They're all gone."

"Don't worry yourself over them," said Old Manatook. "In many ways spirit helpers are just like mortals. They like to go visiting too. You can never be certain where they've taken themselves."

"What if they don't come back?"

"Then we shall have to work just a little bit harder," said Old Manatook. "One step you have ascended, one goal attained. There is much more for you to learn. This was just another step on your journey; it may take the rest of your life to understand what you have experienced in this one brief moment."

"Nivliqtiriarit! Cry out with joy! Our new shaman has come!"

Old Manatook timed their arrival perfectly. The first streak of orange came pouring over the horizon as they topped the rise, bringing with it the golden haze of the dawn. With the sparkling dawn breaking at their backs, Alaana appeared resplendent in her new white parka. "Timing is everything," whispered Old Manatook, "and a little sunlight on the snow never hurt either."

Alaana was met by all of the Anatatook, assembled at the edge of the settlement to await her arrival. She had never seen so many warm, joyous faces. Everyone was cheering. Cheering for her. She felt happier than she had ever been.

She felt flush with power. She finally understood her place among them. Having at last gained the approval of Sila, there was nothing she couldn't achieve.

Almost nothing. Mikisork smiled at her, a tear in his eye, and then he lost himself in the crowd, having stepped behind the others.

Maguan hugged her close. "I knew you would make it," he said into Alaana's ear. Alaana realized her elder brother was as proud and happy as she had once been to see Maguan land his first seal.

Over her brother's shoulder, Alaana caught sight of Kigiuna. Her father wasn't basking in the adulation of the crowd. His eyes didn't have the glint of a man pleased with the status that having a shaman in the family would bring. His face still held a far-away look, burdened with a host of unspoken worries and cares.

Old Manatook left her in the embrace of her eldest brother. The old shaman felt weak and badly in need of rest. He was not needed here. This celebration was for Alaana.

Higilak broke away from the crowd and rushed immediately to her husband's side. Seeing his unsteady condition, she propped herself under one of his arms to help him to their *iglu*. He leaned only the slightest bit on her; she could never hold his weight.

"There was never any doubt," she said. "I knew you'd bring her through."

"Hmmph. She has come through," replied her husband, "but not in the way I expected. Always with her there are mysteries heaped upon mysteries. Why should her initiation be any different?"

"It doesn't matter," she said. "When Kigiuna went out after you I feared the worst. I knew he meant to kill you."

Old Manatook snickered. "Hah. He tried."

"But you said you weren't going to stop him."

"I didn't. His eyes were opened by the spirits themselves. He will be a great help to his daughter from this day on, I think."

"You made everything right," she said, squeezing his arm.

"I had less to do with it than you imagine."

"So you say. You are as humble as ever, my beloved husband.

I'm just happy you and Alaana have both returned, alive and well."

"I can't stay long," said Manatook softly.

Higilak sighed. "It doesn't matter. You're here with us now."

CHAPTER 32

ANOTHER BIRTH

Old Manatook drew in a deep, cool breath. The feeling was nothing short of pure invigoration.

"Alaana was right," he said. "There is nothing better than a draught of cold winter air. A long journey before me. A strong heart beating within my chest. Whatever lies ahead, I am ready for it."

He stood in the shadow of a great white berg, a half day's travel from the shore, an old man with a lined face, tall and wiry, dressed in a faded parka and furry polar bear trousers. He glanced back at the distant winter camp where all the Anatatook families had joined together to work the sea for seals.

"They can do without me for a while. After all, they have a fresh new shaman in Alaana."

"A bit too fresh," said Quixaaragon. The helper spirit sat perched atop a ledge in the ice cliff.

"Hmmmf. The seal are still plenty enough to keep the men busy. The raiders are far to the south. Whatever lays ahead, she can handle it. She's different now. I see new strength of purpose in her since the initiation."

"An odd sort of initiation. Sila came?"

"Something came," said Old Manatook grimly. "But it was

not Sila. Not the Walker In The Wind. Of that I am sure."

"Then what?"

"I don't know. Something pretending to be Sila."

"Pretending?" Quixaaragon searched the old shaman's eyes. "And you won't tell her?"

"How can I? Reveal to her that her call had not been answered? Shatter her confidence and leave her helpless. Without confidence she can do nothing."

"But misplaced confidence?"

"Can work just as well. For now. There's nothing else I can do. Take Sila away from her and replace it with what?"

Quixaaragon fluttered its leathern wings.

Old Manatook leaned closer. "You know?"

"No," replied the white dragon.

"You were there, watching from round the corner. What did you see?"

"I saw nothing," said Quixaaragon. "I felt something. A spark. An echo."

"There's more to it than that," growled Old Manatook. "Have it out!"

Quixaaragon snickered, flicking the tip of a wing as if to remind the old shaman that threats, implied or otherwise, were singularly useless against a dream made of white smoke. "I felt a connection, that's all. Very faint. A connection to the one who dreamt me."

"And who is that?"

"I don't remember. It was so long ago."

"Sun and Moon! Doesn't seem like something you'd be likely to forget."

"Perhaps I never knew."

"Don't be coy with me, little spirit!" said Old Manatook. He thrust his hand into the space where the bird-like head, crowned with a ring of small horns, stared placidly back at him. His fingers grappled only empty air.

Old Manatook turned away. He regarded in turn the trail he'd taken from the Anatatook winter camp and the open tundra that lay before him. "I can't replace her faith in Sila with nothing. That's for certain. One day she'll find out. Then we'll know."

"Someday," said Quixaaragon, who had reappeared in the niche in the cliff.

Old Manatook sniffed carefully at the night air, finding the way before him clear of the scent of any potential adversary. "There is too little time left. I must go."

"You'll make faster travel if you go without the sled and dogs," suggested Quixaaragon.

"You're right about that."

Old Manatook unhitched his pair of dogs from the traces. He carefully dismantled the small sled, bundling the whalebone runners in the sealskin cover and tucking them all safely under a small ledge in the icy cliff face. Makaartunghak sniffed at the area, then paused to mark the spot with a spray of his urine.

"Go," Old Manatook said to the dogs. "Go back to camp. Wait for me."

Makaartunghak, reluctant to comply, continued trotting back and forth at the base of the cliff.

Old Manatook launched a booted foot at the gigantic huskie. "Go, I said! Go."

Yipyip circled the big dog, nipping at his hindquarters. Makaartunghak, sufficiently annoyed, lurched after the little black dog as she led him back along the icy shoreline.

"Will you watch over her?" asked Old Manatook.

"I'll be here."

"So little time," he said again. "I've wasted too much time here already. You don't know how badly this skin itches after a

374

while."

Old Manatook whispered a brief appeal to Tornarssuk to fill him with strength and for speed on his journey. *"Great Bear, help me on my way."*

"Perhaps Alaana could help you and your people in their Great Work," suggested Quixaaragon.

"No. The bears of the mountain take care of our own troubles. Alaana stays here. She has no part in it."

Quixaaragon squawked slightly. "Don't be so sure."

"Have you anything else to say on that matter? Or only more hints and vague insinuations?"

Quixaaragon twisted its head gamely to the side, saying nothing more, and then faded from sight.

Old Manatook sneered at the place the dragon had been, and then turned north. He sniffed again. A strong wind sweeping down from the polar pack carried a fleeting message for his nose, a narrow whisper of fast-moving air. He smelled trouble.

Old Manatook circled the cliff of ice, heading around to the north. A series of rocky bergs lay spread out ahead, gray-blue in the dim wintry light. He paced along, following first his nose and then a series of tracks in the snow. The thick pads of the polar bear had evidently passed this way, and not long ago. He came to a place where the tracks were cut through by the passage of a pair of sleds.

Old Manatook quickened his pace, now hearing the calls of the Chukchee hunters. They said, *"Takkotakko! Takkotakko!"* and *"Nanook!"* which identified their prey as a white bear.

Peering around a massive chunk of ice Old Manatook came upon the scene of the hunt. The bear, a sizeable male, was already cornered, harried by the darting attacks of the sled dogs. Cut off from escape to water, it was backed up against a towering rock face. The dogs worried the bear as it tried to climb the rock. Set off-balance by their furious attacks and a constant need to spin around to protect its rear, the bear couldn't escape up the rocks.

Even through the icy mist, Old Manatook's keen eyes counted eight dogs and three men. The bear barked back at the dogs and swatted at them, held at bay as the men readied spear and bow. These hunters were not Anatatook, whom Old Manatook had forbidden to hunt the white bear. They didn't know him. These strangers wouldn't listen to an old man calling off their hunt even if he was a shaman of the Anatatook. So there was nothing else to do but reveal himself.

And enter the fray.

The old shaman dropped his cloak of human skin. For the first time he noticed the small puncture Kigiuna's knife had made in the front. Free of his disguise of being a man, he stood tall. Rearing on his hind legs he stretched furry paws to the star-studded sky with a satisfied growl.

He stepped forward, a gigantic figure cutting through the mist.

The nearest Chukchee hunter cried out in terror as Old Manatook loomed suddenly beside him, coming as if from nowhere, a tower of white emerging from a flurry of snow.

Old Manatook let loose a deep bone-rattling challenge. At full height he stood head and shoulders above the human hunter. His unexpected and ferocious roar had a chilling effect on the men.

To the hunters any bear close at hand was a dangerous bear. But now the game had changed. One bear cornered was prey. Two on the loose were white death.

One of the dogs leapt at Old Manatook. With a swing of a massive paw, he struck the huskie behind the shoulder, heard a snap as its spine broke in two. It went hurling toward one of the hunters, a missile of dead meat that collided with its master and toppled him into the snow.

The hunter nearest Old Manatook screamed again but,

standing his ground, launched a panic attack with his spear. Old Manatook knocked the shaft to the side and took a swipe at the man. His huge raking claws left the front of the hunter's parka shredded crosswise, a row of shallow cuts etched across his chest. That was enough. The man broke and ran for the sleds.

Routed, the others followed after him, calling off their dogs.

Someone fired a parting shot and an arrow hit Old Manatook in the thigh. The long spruce shaft bounced away but the tip, a barbed arrowhead of caribou antler, made its mark. The wound was nothing more than a nuisance. The barb had only skinned his thigh and drawn a small stream of thick, red blood.

The rescued bear arched his muzzle toward his savior. Old Manatook recognized him easily by a crescent-shaped scar above his right eye and the tawny color of the fur at the sides of his long neck. His name was Bakklah.

Still, a formal greeting was in order. The two bears circled each other in a slow spiral, ears laid back. After a few eager sniffs their heads drew together until the tips of their black noses nearly touched. Old Manatook gave his friend a sociable slap on the shoulder that knocked him back a step.

"*Bakklah,*" said Old Manatook, speaking now in the secret language of the shamans, a method of speech formed by mind rather than lips and tongue. "*I'm glad to see you again. It's very lucky I came along when I did.*"

The other bear bowed his head deeply, settling almost to the snowy ground. It was the only proper way to show respect for his shaman.

Bakklah tilted his head at Old Manatook's wound, coming closer for a look and a sniff.

"*I'll live,*" said Old Manatook. Bakklah nodded, then swiveled his head back in the direction from which Old Manatook had come. The huge bear whimpered slightly.

"Yes, I have been gone a long time," said Old Manatook. *"I had something important to do."*

Bakklah turned his head back again, pointing his muzzle in the direction of the north, to the stronghold of the bears of the ice mountain.

"No, not more important that the Great Work," said Old Manatook. *"Just more urgent."*

The other bear became agitated. He swung his massive body around and around, growling softly. With great effort, he was able to form one single word in a language forbidden to him. *"Come."*

"Hmmf," replied Old Manatook. *"I know, I know. I've done what I had to do. Now I can leave them for a while, and not have to worry. Not too much, anyway. Let's go."*

With rapid loping strides the two melted into the tundra, white disappearing into white.

Alaana crinkled her nose at the pipe Aquppak brandished in front of her face. The bitter scent of tobacco intruded on the crisp air of the spring morning.

"It was a gift from Putuguk," Aquppak said. "Given with a promise — when the freeze-up comes again I'll go out on the ice. This winter I'll be a man."

The pipe was a slender taper of walrus tusk, expertly crafted. Alaana recognized the delicately carved piece as the handiwork of her father.

"Let's try it," suggested Aquppak.

Chuckling at her friend's wide-eyed enthusiasm, Alaana touched her finger to the dried brown leaf inside the bowl and politely asked it to spark to life.

Aquppak took a long puff on the pipe stem, and burst into a fit of coughing that nearly toppled him from his seat. Still choking out puffs of smoke, he righted himself and held the pipe out for her.

"Alaana! Alaana!"

A pair of men came rushing toward them. Maguan was in front, his friend Avilik close behind.

"Is Old Manatook here?" asked Maguan, gasping for breath.

"No," replied Alaana, "He's gone on a journey to the north."

"Ugh," said Maguan. "Then you'd better come."

"What's wrong?"

"It's my wife Tahkeena," said Avilik. "She's giving birth. And there's trouble. We need the shaman."

"Hurry," said Avilik as he drew aside the entrance flap to his tent. "Go in."

Alaana hesitated. The smell of blood was strong. She didn't know anything about childbirth, except that men weren't allowed to be near a woman in labor. In the three moons since her initiation, Old Manatook had taught her nothing of such things. But there was no one else.

A terrified groan came from inside. Avilik's face sagged gravely. Maguan ventured a smile at Alaana and nodded his head encouragingly. "Go ahead, sister."

Alaana stepped in.

Tahkeena crouched in the center of the tent, squatting above a hole cut into the bare ground. Suuyuk, the midwife, stood behind Tahkeena, helping to press the baby out. As not even the midwife was allowed to touch a woman in labor, Suuyuk applied her leverage through a sling of skins wound around Tahkeena's waist just above the mound of her belly.

"It doesn't come out," said Suuyuk.

"Well, I…" mumbled Alaana.

"Come on," said Suuyuk. Alaana stepped closer.

Tahkeena glanced at her hopefully. Her brow was plastered with sweat, her hair was in wild disarray, her face blotched with tears. Her cheeks were flushed from the strain, and Alaana saw red flecks in the white of her eyes.

"I…" said Alaana.

Tahkeena screamed. But what began as a sound of pain stretched into a deep groan of intense effort. Suuyuk tugged on the seal thong, but gained no obvious benefit.

Alaana swallowed hard. She couldn't let them see her hesitation. "I'll do what I can," she said.

"You can help?" panted Tahkeena, her eyes half-closed with exhaustion.

"I can help."

But what to do? She knew nothing of this. She was perilously in need of help herself. Help. That was it.

"Sila," said Alaana.

Suuyuk shot her a wary glance. Alaana lapsed into the secret language of the shamans, saying, *"Beneath the blue sky, beneath the white cloud; Keeper of the echo in the high mountains, keeper of the winds across the wide sea…"*

Tahkeena was heartened by this approach. Her groans took on a new determination, but Alaana felt no better. No connection was established, no response returned. She wasn't surprised. In the three moons since her initiation, she had seen nothing of Sila again.

"Be strong," she said to Tahkeena, catching her eye.

She reached into her pocket, circling her hand around the walrus tusk amulet. She was certain Nunavik would know what to do. Surely the Walrus On The Ice had seen birth and death more times than anyone could count. Alaana called out to the *tunraq*, using again the secret language. Again there was no answer and again this was no surprise. Her helper spirits were gone.

But she still needed help. Tahkeena groaned once more. She was becoming weak and exhausted. The hole in the floor was filling up with water and blood.

If only Old Manatook were here.

"Manatook? If you can hear me, father—" She stopped abruptly. She realized she'd been using common language. Suuyuk peered warily at her from behind the enormous pregnant belly. The old woman smirked and glanced at Alaana with ire in her one good eye, her suspicions confirmed. She saw Alaana for what she truly was — an inexperienced and useless child who had no place in the birthing tent.

The midwife clucked her disappointment, then reached down and placed her hand between Tahkeena's legs. "Still it does not come," she said. "It's stuck. I fear for the baby."

"Mind your tongue, Suuyuk," said Alaana. "The baby will be fine. I am certain of it."

Tahkeena's groans became louder and more frantic. Reassuring words were not enough. If only Alaana could find a more direct way to help.

"Manatook," she hissed again, this time in anger. Why must he spend so much time away?

Suddenly Alaana had a new idea, and she thought it was a good one.

"Kuanak!" she called out. No use.

The labor pains worsened. Suuyuk wiped the sweat from Tahkeena's brow with a bloody hand, leaving a streak of red across her forehead.

"Nalungiaq?" said Alaana. She watched the expectant mother closely, but again each pain seemed worse than the last.

"Kukkook?" She struggled to recall the name of anyone else who had died recently. There was something Old Manatook had told her. If an unused name-soul was attracted to the baby, it might ease the passage.

Tahkeena screamed even louder than before. A gush of fresh blood plopped down between her legs.

"Avalaaqiaq," said Alaana.

A change came over Tahkeena almost immediately. She gasped as if the baby had somehow shifted inside her. She groaned again but this time the sound had a much lower register, evoking a sense of renewed determination.

"Avalaaqiaq!" said Alaana. "Yes, Avalaaqiaq!"

Suuyuk probed the space between the legs again and came away with a reassuring nod. Tahkeena pushed a few more times and the baby came down into the recess in the ground, the afterbirth following immediately. Suuyuk snatched up a soft piece of bird-skin and wiped the newborn clean. "It's a girl, a beautiful girl."

The baby was put directly into the *amaut*, the big pouch on the back of her mother's coat.

"*Naaklingnaqtuq*," the new mother said, declaring that the baby was lovable. "My husband will be very happy. He wanted a girl. Our little Avalaaqiaq."

Alaana took a deep breath. Nearly a year had passed since the death of her sister. Her name-soul must have been waiting all that time, following the Anatatook from place to place. Alaana had acted just in time. If not reassigned within a year, her sister's name might have turned into an *agiuqtuq*, a revengeful spirit causing sickness and death. She had done well today.

Alaana ventured a little closer for a peek at the baby's face. Avalaaqiaq, she thought, welcome. She wondered if the baby, like her dear sister, would have the marvelous laugh and the crooked smile.

Suuyuk cut the square flap of hide beneath the afterbirth and bundled it up so that it might be properly buried.

"Thank you, *angatkok*," she said.

EPILOGUE

Alaana walked alone, the Anatatook winter camp at her back. It had been three sleeps since Old Manatook had gone off to the north on the latest of his mysterious errands. She had no idea how long the shaman would be away, nor the purpose for his journey.

But she had her own errand to perform, and for this she had waited until her teacher was far away. She wished she didn't have to risk going to the Underworld alone, but it wouldn't do to bring Old Manatook. Not this time. As she had feared, Nunavik and her other helper spirits had indeed disappeared. Had Sila chased them away? Alaana might have believed such a thing of Weyahok and Itiqtuq, but not Nunavik. Much more likely the walrus had gone looking for something, and Alaana believed that one day he would return.

And so, she was alone.

When she reached the face of the ice cliff, far from even the best-sighted among the Anatatook men, she took off her parka and trousers. She lay the garments atop the crust of snow. Spring had come once again and the sun rode halfway up the blue sky, offering its mysterious light and warmth.

Naked, she drew a long, deep breath of the frosty air. She took it all in — the sunlight bursting across the tundra, the big blue sky, the chill that stung at her bare skin, the frigid air in her lungs. She was ready for anything.

This journey, she had determined, must be undertaken with neither weapons nor spiritual garb. No protective amulets, no ceremonial blade. She kept only the talisman of Sila, a solitary eagle feather linked to an owl feather, strung about her neck. And in her hand the black raven feather which had once belonged to Civiliaq. His terrible fate still bothered her. She had once admired Civiliaq, before desperation had corrupted his soul. Civiliaq had done his best to save Avalaaqiaq, even at the cost of his own life. True, his arrogant feud with Kuanak had caused the fever demon to come among the Anatatook in the first place, but he had journeyed below with the others to make things right.

Alaana had listened to Old Manatook tell the story, especially the part where Civiliaq had confronted the demon by himself only to be undone by his own doubts. Although he had subsequently tried to manipulate Alaana and damn her to a fate even more terrible than his own, Alaana could only sympathize with the desperate actions of a tortured man. She had witnessed firsthand the disgraced shaman's horrific torment in the Underworld. And when he had asked his brother Kuanak for a second chance, Wolf Head had turned away. But now, Alaana realized, she and Civiliaq were also brother and sister.

Old Manatook had condemned him to his prison by not killing the fever demon in the first place. Alaana had decided that another encounter with the demon was a risky measure, but well worth the danger. She would not leave her brother to suffer.

Alaana sat cross-legged on her folded parka. Even with the warming sunlight, it was cold. And the gnawing fear, welling up from inside, sharpened the chill. There was nothing she feared more than that horrible hag. It had preyed on her when she was sick and helpless. And it had killed her sister. It was time for a reckoning.

Old Manatook had avoided teaching Alaana how to journey

to the Underworld, but she had already received that lesson courtesy of Civiliaq. Such a journey did not require drum or song. She slowed her breathing; she set her heart to the dreamer's beat. She cleared her mind. The only thing she required was the serpent. She visualized the snake, the white snake spinning around in the snow, creating the vortex. Slow the breathing, slow the heartbeat. Put aside the fear.

She was alone, but she believed she could do this. She must.

The snake spun round and round. Alaana watched it form a circle about the size of a cooking pot. She saw the snow fall away into the void as it bore through ice and dirt and down into the everfrost below. The roaring tunnel beckoned; she had only to fall into it.

Alaana leapt. The plunge was drastic and breathtaking. She anticipated the searing pain as before, the sensation of a gullet lined with knives cutting away at her soul. But that didn't happen this time. And she realized the cuts she had suffered before were caused by doubts. She had no doubts about this. She had a clear goal and a pure motive.

Her *inuseq* landed with a thump on the floor of a wide, dark cave. The impact was softened by a bed of tiny crystals in blue and green. Alaana sat up. Naked, alone, with no protection against the many dangers she must face. Only one solitary black raven feather which, in this reality, manifested as a slender spike of obsidian.

The spirit-vision showed the cave in deep purple tones. The room was filled floor to ceiling with intricate webs and tendrils, each as sharp as a carefully honed blade. As Alaana brushed past them the webs chimed notes of guilt and shame, speaking with the baleful voice of missed opportunities. Alaana passed through the poisonous strands as if they were smoke. They could not affect someone who harbored no bitterness, no regrets. None at all.

The weaver of the web crouched on its haunches in the

385

corner, filling the cave with the hissing sounds of its heavy breathing. Its many rheumy eyes swiveled in her direction. A score of shaggy limbs tensed as it lifted its trembling bulk from the floor.

Alaana had never seen anything as sad or pathetic. Its anguished thoughts, which radiated from the creature in a bilious cloud, were too much to bear. Alaana wished she could soothe its suffering but there was nothing she could do. But just as she could not heal such a pitiful creature, it could not do any harm to her. It slunk back toward the corner.

The next chamber held a pack of snarling *itgitlit*. The misshapen dogs advanced toward her, their human hands slapping the floor of the cavern with an odd sound as they ran. Beneath their furry hoods and peaked ears their faces looked at her with sadness and confusion.

Alaana wondered whether the *itgitlit* had originally been dogs or men, and how they could have been brought so low. But even in the Underworld dogs had an aversion to her and the pack halted their charge. Heads hanging low, they drew back and moved silently out of her way. A few showed their teeth and snarled impotently but instead of tearing her to pieces, they parted to let her pass.

The next cave was the one where the battle had taken place. Below this floor of ice, the fever demon had been imprisoned by Old Manatook's thundering blows. She kneeled before the patch of rough ice.

Thoughts of the demon made her heart skip a beat. Its leering smile, that hideous mouth whose dry, cracked lips gave way to a gullet of raw flesh and writhing maggots. The sickening ichor that it had force-fed her as mother's milk. Alaana gagged, remembering its sour, corrupted taste.

She was breathing heavily, her heart beating too fast. She was afraid.

The contours of the cave shifted and changed. A black, oily

mass gathered in the shadows. The roiling, bubbling monster slithered toward her.

All was lost.

The black cloud surged forward, seething malevolence. Alaana had no place to turn.

Suddenly a snarling, snapping whirlwind cut through the murk, slashing and hacking, throwing globs of the oily spume in every direction. A creature of demonic fury burst through. It was Yipyip.

The soul of the little coal-black dog appeared no larger in the Underworld than in the physical world but its might in spirit was undeniable. It attacked the oily froth with an intense ferocity, nipping at it from every direction until the monster turned away from its intended target. Yipyip pressed her attack further still, driving the creature from the cavern. Alaana gasped with relief. She silently thanked the little dog for chasing away her own dark thoughts and fear, the greatest monsters of all.

Now is the time, thought Alaana. The last chance. There must be no hesitation.

She held the slender spar of obsidian over the cavern floor and drove it down. In this reality the raven feather was not quite the savage dagger that Civiliaq had once wielded. It was a thin, frail spike almost crumbling in her grip. But in Alaana's hands she knew it would be enough. She stabbed the slender dagger into the ground at precisely the spot where Manatook had bested the fever demon. The point of the dagger created only the tiniest pinhole in the surface of the ice.

A great tearing sound shook the cavern. The ground ripped asunder, and a gout of noxious black smoke came bubbling up from the chasm. Alaana did not shrink back from it.

The smoke thickened and coalesced into a vague, towering form. The mass of smoldering vapor had no face or distinguishing features, but it let out a sound much like a gratified sigh.

"You should not have come here," the demon said. "You should not have released me. You will die for that mistake, little shaman."

Alaana stood to face it. "No mistake."

"You'll say otherwise after I've crunched your eyeballs and licked the marrow from your bones."

"Perhaps," said Alaana modestly. She, like her father Old Manatook, was willing to sacrifice herself to save another. There was great power in that strategy, Alaana thought. The gesture, if genuine, could be completely disarming to an opponent possessing even the slightest whisper of conscience. She was counting on it.

"I'm not afraid of you, Mother," she said.

"Mother?"

In the blink of an eye the cloud of black smoke transformed into a giant woman. More than twice as tall as Alaana, she stood naked except for plumes of thick gray smoke which seethed from her charred and blackened skin. Her hairless head tilted down toward Alaana, the eyes as hot as open flame. She ran heavy, steaming hands across an exaggerated bosom and down curvaceous hips. "Why did you call me that? Why did you set me free?"

"Why do you think?"

The demon's surprised look was replaced by an expression of twisted glee. Blackened lips curled upwards at the ends, peeling back from a row of wickedly pointed teeth.

"It doesn't matter," she said. "Such a pretty girl. Let me wrap my arms around you. In my burning embrace you will come to love me. I will make you love me if I have to cut you to ribbons to do it." She spread her arms wide, dripping with melted fat and strings of gristle.

Alaana smiled. As foul as she was, a living nightmare, she was beautiful too. She was vengeance personified. She was pure retribution.

"But I do love you already," Alaana said.

Startled again, the demon halted her advance. She reduced in size and shape to that of an ordinary young woman. She wore fine black hair, carefully drawn back from the oval of her face with a slender strap of sinew. Her nose was slightly too large and round to be considered beautiful, her lips full and pleasant. Her eyes were small and held a willful radiance and a subtle vulnerability.

"Are you sincere?"

"You see that I am," she said, "Aneenaq."

The woman made a startled sob.

"Yes, I know you," Alaana said. "I know how you've been wronged. I understand."

"No you don't. You can't."

"Yes, I do. The stones out on the tundra have long memories, and they speak to me. They bore witness to your suffering, abandoned by your own mother so that your brother might live. The cliffs near Dog-Ear Ridge remember you. You went there often as a young girl to gather fresh eggs and listen to the song of the murres at roost. I know your pain, Aneenaq, and I love you even if no one else does."

The woman let out a soft moaning sound.

"How I suffered," she said. "Left to starve in the cold. My own mother..."

"There's more to it than that. The land takes but it also gives. Your sacrifice was not for nothing. Your brother survived."

Aneenaq's brow wrinkled. In all the years of rage and suffering she had never looked at it that way.

"I bring news of the murres," said Alaana. "It's springtime once again."

"Springtime?"

"They roost again on the cliffs by the sea, singing their song."

Aneenaq, a little girl of nine or ten winters, looked up at Alaana with tearful eyes. Alaana thought her beautiful, though she was still black around the mouth from the starvation. "Oh, how I want to hear it."

"Then go to the cliffs and listen. And then if you pass beyond the divide perhaps you'll see your mother again. She waits for you on the other side. Maybe you can still find her."

"She murdered my sisters!"

"Your sisters were spared from the death of starvation. The cruel death that you suffered. She killed them because she loved them."

The little girl shook her head. "No."

"Don't doubt my words," said Alaana. "There are stones at that place that still remember the splash of your mother's tears."

"She left me there alone, she killed me."

"That was long ago. They're all on the other side now. Your brother is there, though you may not recognize him at first. He died a very old man. Perhaps you would like to meet his children."

"Children?"

"Yes," said Alaana, "I believe they will call you Aunt Anee."

The little girl sobbed again. And then she was gone.

Alaana had never felt so invigorated and at peace.

The ground cracked open at her feet. The withered ice fell away, as broken as the spell that had bound Civiliaq below. Alaana breathed a sigh of relief as she watched the ghost of the shaman claw his way out of the hole.

"Remarkable," said the spirit of the dead shaman. "This I did not ever expect."

Civiliaq gazed with amazement at his hands, which had been restored from the clawed husks that had served him during his imprisonment. He clasped them together, testing their strength.

"I thank you," he said to Alaana. "It's good to see my little bird has truly taken wing. I owe you a considerable debt."

"Then pay me back now," said Alaana. "Promise you won't seek revenge against Old Manatook or the others."

"Revenge?" said Civiliaq. He appeared to be taking a deep breath, though surely ghosts had no need of air. "Already forgotten."

A frown crossed his handsome features, and he grunted softly. "I am pulled away. I must go, and so should you."

His booted feet lifted from the ground and as he gazed up at the ceiling of the cavern he smiled. "I go where the dead shamans go. Perhaps we shall meet again one day, Alaana. Perhaps."

"Wait!" cried Alaana. "You saw something. When you looked at my *inua* that time on Dog-Ear Ridge. You know something!"

Having passed halfway to the ceiling Civiliaq halted his assent. His face strained with the effort.

"I must take my place in the sky. We'll meet again. I am certain of it."

Alaana spoke quickly, the words pouring out in a torrent. "You know something about my spirit guardian. You said my power comes from beneath the Underworld. Why won't you tell me the answer?"

A gentle smile from Civiliaq. He shook his head. No.

"You can't tell me, or you won't?"

"It's not time. One day you'll know."

"Wait!" shouted Alaana.

"You had best get back," said Civiliaq at last. "Your people need you."

THE ADVENTURE CONTINUES IN:

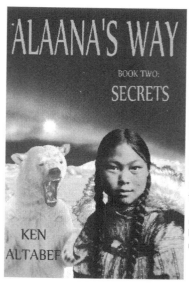

SOME SECRETS REFUSE TO STAY DEAD...

Alaana, an inexperienced young shaman of the Anatatook people, must face arctic werewolves, bloodthirsty raiders, soul-stealing demons, and the vengeful ghost of a massive polar bear as she uncovers dark secrets left behind by her teacher Old Manatook.

As she struggles to win the respect of the village headman she journeys among the polar bears of the Ice Mountain, to the terrifying Underworld, the bottom of the sea, and even to the Moon itself.

Seeking answers to the riddle of her mysterious power, she must choose between the love of two very different men.

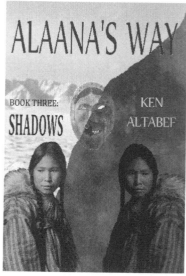

THE HIDDEN WORLD...

Alaana, now a successful shaman for her Anatatook people, must journey throughout the spirit lands in search of her daughter's lost soul. She is accompanied by her deadly tupilaq a reanimated seal that lives only for revenge.

An ancient Sorcerer, accidentally freed from captivity by the Anatatook shaman, launches a plan to reshape the world, threatening them all. As this legendary villain's secrets unfold, Alaana's husband is torn between the real world and a horrific shadow land in his own effort to rescue their daughter before time runs out.

With Alaana wounded and under attack, and the entire Anatatook people in disarray and danger, the shaman's husband may be their only hope.